NO TIME LIKE THE FUTURE . . .

One of the technologies I see in our future that is presently indistinguishable from magic is the ability to travel in time. If a present-day scientist were confronted with a real time machine, he would certainly say that the machine had to be run by the rules of magic. His argument would go like this: Science is based on logic. Anything that produces logical paradoxes is not science. Time machines produce logical paradoxes. Therefore, if time machines exist, they must use magic, not science.

Yet, two of the most respected and tested theories of physics, both the Einstein Special Theory of Relativity and the Einstein General Theory of Relativity, allow time to be manipulated. Although we are presently far from being able to control the energies and masses that will be required to make a time machine suitable for human use, these theories give us the physical principles behind time travel.

How do we make a time machine?

What most people don't realize is that one type of time machine already exists. Various versions of these machines can be found in university and government laboratories. They are used every day by the scientists there . . .

BAEN BOOKS BY ROBERT L. FORWARD

Rocheworld

Return to Rocheworld
(with Julie Forward Fuller)

Ocean Under the Ice
(with Martha Dodson Forward)

Marooned on Eden
(with Martha Dodson Forward)

Rescued From Paradise
(with Julie Forward Fuller)

Indistinguishable From Magic

INDISTINGUISHABLE FROM MAGIC

SPECULATIONS AND VISIONS OF THE FUTURE

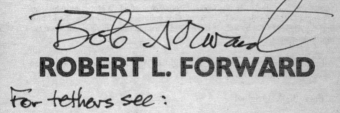

ROBERT L. FORWARD

For tethers see:

Pages 69-89, especially
Pages 72-74 which is a
"Vision" of HASTOL.

BAEN

INDISTINGUISHABLE FROM MAGIC

This is a work of fiction All the characters and events portrayed in this book are fictional and any resemblance to real people or incidents is purely coincidental.

Copyright © 1995 by Robert L. Forward

A Baen Books Original

Baen Publishing Enterprises
P.O. Box 1403
Riverdale, NY 10471

ISBN: 0-671-87686-4

Cover art by David Mattingly

First printing, September 1995

Distributed by Simon & Schuster
1230 Avenue of the Americas
New York, NY 10020

Typeset by Windhaven Press, Auburn, NH
Printed in the United States of America

ACKNOWLEDGEMENTS

My thanks to Larry Niven, Jerry Pournelle, and Ben Bova, who first encouraged me to write down some of these "crazy" ideas and to Arthur C. Clarke, Philip Chapman, John Cramer, Edwin Dodson, Freeman Dyson, Dani Eder, Rod Hyde, Keith Lofstrom, David K. Lynch, Hans Moravec, Charles Sheffield, and Frank Tipler, who helped in a number of technical areas.

I also want to acknowledge the long term support of Dr. George F. Smith, Senior Vice President and Director of the Hughes Aircraft Company Research Laboratories, who, during my 31 years at Hughes Research Labs, allowed me to spend part of my time poking at the cracks in the boundaries of scientific knowledge in an attempt to break through. It is hoped that this book will widen those cracks so we can begin to develop some of those technologies that we can glimpse on the other side that are presently indistinguishable from magic.

CLARKE'S THIRD LAW

"Any sufficiently advanced technology is indistinguishable from magic."

—Arthur C. Clarke
Profiles of the Future

CONTENTS

✧ INTRODUCTION

Each day we see on television or read in the papers about some new advance in technology. In most cases we take the news in stride, for we have heard of similar things. But for our ancestors of only a few generations ago, these new technological achievements would have been indistinguishable from magic.

It *is* magic—future magic—and we live with and use it daily. Direct broadcast satellites instantaneously bring us pictures of events from anywhere on the globe like the magic crystal ball of the Wicked Witch of the West; powerful laser beams destroy the missiles of our foes like a bolt of lightning from the hand of Zeus; air-cushion boats magically levitate and walk over the surface of the water; genetically tailored microorganisms produce insulin, eat oil spills, and leach copper ores like miniature golems animated by our biological magic; the magic spectacles of radar let us see beyond what the unaided eye can see. The wonders that take place every day of our lives would have amazed our parents thirty years ago, bewildered our grandparents of sixty years ago, and would have raised cries of "black magic!" a century ago.

The now-prosaic microwave oven is an excellent

example of future magic. If you want to cook a large beef roast with heat, it takes four hours. It doesn't matter if the heat comes from wood, coal, oil, electricity, nuclear energy, evaporating black holes, sunlight, or cow dung—it takes four hours to cook a roast with heat. An ancient cook brought from the caves a million years past and taken to a kitchen a thousand years in the future, might not understand the source of the heat in a "black hole" oven, but after a few minutes of watching it cook a beef roast he would be able to prepare an urus roast that would be done to perfection. Yet show him your microwave oven cooking a roast in a half hour and he would be bewildered by its magic. The technology that produced the microwave oven did not develop a new source of heat, it developed "magic" heat—heat that is generated *inside* the meat, not applied to the outside, so the roast gets done in the "magical" time of thirty minutes instead of six hours.

A number of years ago the famous science-fiction author Arthur C. Clarke propounded what is now known as Clarke's Third Law: "Any sufficiently advanced technology is indistinguishable from magic." It used to be that technology evolved slowly, and generations could go by with almost no change in the way things were done. Every decade or so, however, something new would be added to the existing base of technology. A blacksmith would find that a blade would take on a different temper if it were quenched in oil instead of water. A sea captain would find that his crew didn't come down with scurvy if he took along a few barrels of limes. A doctor noticed that he never saw a milkmaid among his smallpox patients.

In those days, the words "sufficiently advanced" meant hundreds of years in the future. For back then there was time enough between those new advances in technology to allow people to accept them and absorb them into "the way things are done." But even then, there was a resistance to change. It took the Royal Navy over a century to make limes part of the normal diet of a seagoing "limey"; and Edward Jenner's 1798 introduction of the concept of vaccination is regarded as magic by the ignorant even today—"How can you possibly make someone well by making them sick?"

Events move much faster these days. There are more scientists, doctors, and engineers active now. The rate at which they produce new technology has been accelerated by the prior technological inventions of the printing press, radio, television, and now the communication satellites and data links that spread the information about each new technological advance rapidly around the globe, making it almost instantly available to other researchers. The power of each researcher is also magnified a thousand fold by the electronic slaves they created—the computers. These range from the handheld pocket wonders of the engineers to the giant electronic genies that serve a hundred masters at one time.

Nowadays, the distance in time where future science fades into future magic is only decades away. The best example is spaceflight. Who in 1929, in the bleakest days of the depression, would have thought that in four decades there would be a man walking on the moon?

Here we are today, living among and using those magical wonders that were so impossible that our parents and grandparents couldn't even imagine them. What will be the magic in our future? It is hard to predict, because if we can tell exactly how it can be done and when it will be done, then it is no longer future magic, but future technology.

There are, however, some magical things coming in our future that can now be glimpsed, although dimly. Aided by existing theories, we can guess at these magical wonders, but we are very uncertain of how we will attain the technologies that will be needed to turn them from wishful thinking into hard reality. Whether they will come true is not known. The theory on which some possible future concept is based may be wrong and it could never come to pass. The theory may be correct, but the technology needed to achieve the goal may require a material that just doesn't exist. It may be that the theory is correct, and the technology is possible, but we decide that the effort involved is more than it is worth. Or, it may be we will be too busy exploring other realms of future technology that we think are more important.

In the following pages are some of the magical things that I can see through the uncertain curtain of the future. Things that are theoretically possible, but so far from our present technical capabilities that they seem almost magical. In the next pages, through the differing media of fiction and non-fiction, we will visit that black magic marvel of gravitation, the black hole; travel through time and space in time machines and space warps; float through the air without wings, defying gravity; climb into space on a magic beanstalk; fly through the solar system on antimatter rockets; and then sail off to the stars on beams of light.

There is magic in our future. How and when it will come we can only guess. But come it will—and sooner than you think.

Recommended Reading

For those who would like to read a little more on some of the technical topics discussed in this book, I have selected a few references for further reading out of the many books and scientific papers that I used as background material in preparing the manuscript. You will find these listed under *Recommended Reading* at the end of each of the science speculation chapters. The book and magazine references can be found in any good library, but the scientific journal references will require that you arrange a visit a nearby university library. Most university libraries allow the public to visit the library during certain hours, although they usually do not let the public check out books. Most have, however, extensive (and comparatively cheap) copying facilities.

Arthur C. Clarke's speculations about the future and his three laws can be found in: Arthur C. Clarke, *Profiles of the Future: An Inquiry into the Limits of the Possible*, pp. 29 and 36 (Holt, Rinehart and Winston, New York, 1984).

Many of the scientific concepts discussed in detail in the various chapters of this book were briefly touched upon in a speech I gave to a group of science fiction writers in 1974. The notes for that speech can be found in my science "fact" article: "Far Out Physics" published in the August 1975 issue of *Analog Science Fiction/Science Fact*, Volume 95, Number 8, pages 147-166. The speculative concepts in that article, along with similar concepts from a number of articles that I had written for the magazines *Omni, Science Digest, Science 80, Galaxy*, and *Analog Science Fiction/Science Fact*, were turned into a popular science book, *Future Magic*, which is now out of date and out of print. This book, *Indistinguishable From Magic*, containing a combination of science fact and science fiction, is intended as a replacement for *Future Magic*.

✧ ANTIMATTER

Antimatter is our first example of a new technology which, despite being almost indistinguishable from magic, is nevertheless real. Once found only on the starship *Enterprise*, antimatter is now being made daily at laboratories around the world. Despite the proclivity of antimatter to mutually annihilate with anything it contacts, antimatter has been made, stopped, captured, and kept for months at a time in "bottles" made of electric and magnetic fields. Soon, bottles filled with antimatter will be transported around the world to be used by physicists for basic research into the fundamental mysteries of nature, by doctors for finding and treating cancer tumors, and by engineers for a multitude of practical applications, such as isotopic imaging, nuclear transmutation, and, one of these days, space propulsion.

What is this almost magical stuff called antimatter?

Our world is made of normal matter. The matter is in the form of atoms. The atoms have a heavy nucleus at the center made up of particles called protons and neutrons. Surrounding the nucleus of each atom is a cloud of electrons. Everything we normally experience is made up of these three stable particles: protons, neutrons, and electrons. Each of these three particles consists of a bundle of raw energy, wrapped up by nature into a compact, stable ball that we call matter. We don't really know why the proton and neutron weigh about the same, and yet are 1840 times heavier than the electron. We don't really know why the electrical charge on the electron is *exactly* equal and opposite in sign to the electrical charge on the proton. We don't really know why all the other characteristics of each particle are the way they are. That is still a mystery. It is as if each of the different particles had some special kind of quantum-mechanical "glue" to hold it together. The type of glue defines the amount of energy that can be bundled up into that particular kind of particle, and the various properties, such as mass, spin, and charge, that the resulting bundle should have.

For a long time after the electron and proton were discovered in the atom, scientists were puzzled at the asymmetry of nature. Why did the carrier of the positive electric charge, the proton, weigh so much more than the carrier of the negative electric charge, the electron? Then, in the mid-1900s, the scientists solved the puzzle by finding that each particle had a "mirror" twin. The mirror particle for the electron was the positron, a particle that had exactly the same mass as the electron, but the sign of its electric charge was reversed. Like the electron, the positron acted as if it were spinning like a top, generating a detectable magnetic field. Since the positron had a positive charge while the electron had a negative charge, the magnetic fields were oppositely directed to the spin axis in the two particles. Thus the positron is the mirror image of the electron as seen in a "magic" mirror that reverses the charge on the mirror particle as well as reversing right and left handedness as does a normal mirror. [See Figure 1].

The mirror particle for the proton is called the antiproton. It has the same mass as the proton, but its charge and magnetic moment are reversed. There is also a mirror twin for the neutron called the antineutron. Since both the neutron and antineutron have no charge, it is hard to tell them apart. The neutron spins about its axis, however, and even though it is electrically neutral, it does have a magnetic field. The mirror neutron also has a magnetic field, but its spin is in the opposite direction to the magnetic field direction.

Since normal matter is made up of atoms built from electrons, protons, and neutrons, then it should be possible to make antimatter out of atoms built up from positrons, antiprotons, and antineutrons. Antimatter would be just like normal matter but with the charges reversed. For example, normal hydrogen is made of a single electron orbiting a proton, while antihydrogen would be made of a positron orbiting an antiproton.

There is an important difference between the two forms of matter. Whereas a particle made of normal matter is a bundle of energy held together with

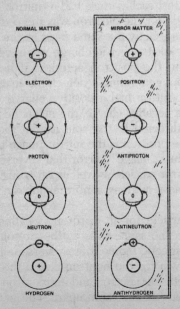

Fig. 1
An imaginary "magic" mirror shows the differences between normal matter and antimatter.

quantum-mechanical "glue," the mirror particle is a similar bundle of energy held together with "antiglue." Each "glue" turns out to be a solvent for the other! Thus, when an antiparticle meets a normal particle, the two glues dissolve each other, and the energy contained in the two particles is released in a micro-explosion. The mass of both particles is *completely* converted into energy. The amount of energy that is released is given by the famous Einstein equation $E=mc^2$ (one of the few equations you will ever find in a newspaper). This complete conversion of mass to energy makes antimatter a highly efficient, compact, light-weight, almost magical source of energy. One milligram of antimatter combined with one milligram of normal matter produces the same energy as twenty tons of the most energetic chemical fuel in use today, liquid oxygen and liquid hydrogen.

According to the known laws of physics, particles and antiparticles should always be created in equal and opposite pairs. If matter and antimatter are always created in equal amounts, then half the universe should be made of antimatter. There should be antimatter galaxies containing antimatter stars illuminating antimatter planets populated with antimatter beings. If such antimatter galaxies existed, they would have large, tenuous clouds of antihydrogen gas surrounding them, just as our galaxy sits inside its own cloud of normal hydrogen gas. If there were regions where the normal matter galaxies and the antimatter galaxies lie near each other, their hydrogen clouds would overlap. In this overlapping region, the antihydrogen positrons would annihilate with the hydrogen electrons, releasing two gamma rays with exactly 511 million volts of energy. Astronomers using gamma-ray detectors flown on spacecraft such as the High Energy Astronomical Observatory have looked carefully for these characteristic gamma rays which indicate that matter is annihilating with antimatter. Once in a while, they detect some of these gamma rays, but every source found can be identified with a known neutron star or supernova, which occasionally produce small numbers of antielectrons. No source has been found which indicates that large amounts of antimatter exist anywhere in the universe. This mystery of the missing antimatter is one of the major unsolved problems of physics. Whatever the reason, the experimental fact is that only regular matter seems to occur in nature. If we want antimatter, we will have to make it.

Antimatter is now being made with the aid of huge "atom smashers." These machines use combinations of electric, magnetic, and radio fields to push against the electric charge on an electron or proton to accelerate them up to velocities close to that of light. The unit of energy that is used in particle accelerators is called the electron-volt or eV. If a metal plate has a positive voltage of one volt (a regular flashlight battery produces 1.5 volts), then an electron will be attracted to that plate. Just before the electron reaches the plate, it will have an energy of one electron-volt (1 eV).

Your television set produces about 20,000 volts inside (that is why there is a notice telling you not to open the back of the set). The electrons in the TV tube therefore reach 20 keV (20 kilo-electron-volts), and have enough energy when they strike the back of the screen to make the phosphor glow. A million volt machine can accelerate electrons (or protons) up to energies of 1 MeV (1 million electron-volts or 1 mega-electron-volt). At 1 MeV, an electron is moving at 94% the speed of light, while the heavier proton is only moving at 1/20th the speed of light. (The proton is 1840 times heavier than the electron so it doesn't have to move as fast to have the same energy as the electron.)

To get energies greater than a few million electron volts with just an electric field is difficult, because high voltages have a tendency to leak off into the air or emit corona discharge from sharp points even in a good vacuum. Once an electron or proton beam has been set moving using electric fields, however, it is possible to send radio waves traveling along in the same direction as the beam of particles. If the radio waves are properly tuned, the charged particles can gain energy from the moving radio waves just as a surfboard gains energy from a water wave. By this technique, energies of thousands of millions of volts, or giga-electron-volts (GeV) have been reached.

The basic method of making antiprotons is to start by accelerating normal matter protons to high energies in a proton accelerator. [See Figure 2.]

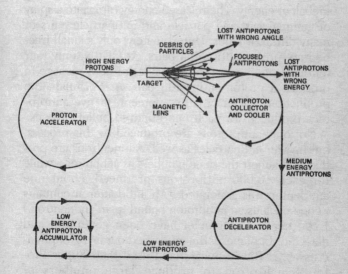

Fig. 2—The present method for making and capturing antiprotons.

Scientists at the European antimatter factory at CERN in Switzerland accelerate their protons until their kinetic energy is 26 GeV. At the US antimatter factory at Fermilab in the USA, the proton accelerator is operated at 120 GeV. The amount of energy bound up into the mass of a proton is 0.938 GeV. Thus, any proton with a kinetic energy greater than 1 GeV has more energy in its motion than it has in its internal mass. A proton with a total energy of 120 GeV has within itself enough energy to make 120 protons, or 60 proton-antiproton pairs.

The high-energy "bullet" protons are then slammed into a target made of a thick tungsten or copper wire. In the wire, the bullet protons collide head-on into one of the metal nuclei. The kinetic energy of the bullet proton is released at a single point in space as a tiny fireball of energy. The released energy turns into a spray of gamma rays, and particle and antiparticle pairs of many different kinds. Unfortunately, only a small fraction are proton-antiproton pairs. At CERN, only four tenths of one percent of the bullet protons manage to produce a proton-antiproton pair. At Fermilab, the production efficiency is five percent, or five antiprotons produced for each one hundred bullet protons.

Not only antiprotons are produced by this process, but heavier antiparticles as well. Antineutrons are produced in almost the same numbers as antiprotons, while for each 10,000 antiprotons produced, about one antideuteron is generated. (An antideuteron contains in one nucleus an antiproton bound to an antineutron.) Even heavier antinuclei have been generated and detected. In one experiment carried out in 1978, physicists at CERN in Switzerland used their Super Proton Synchrotron to produce large numbers of antideuterons, 99 antitritium nuclei and 94 antihelium-3 nuclei. (Antitritium has one antiproton and two antineutrons, while antihelium-3 has two antiprotons and one antineutron.) These heavier antiparticles were sensed by sending them into a detector where they, unfortunately, were immediately annihilated. It would be another decade before methods were developed so that antimatter particles could be kept after they had been generated. So far, this has only been done with antiprotons.

It isn't easy to capture the antiprotons. They come out of the target in a broad spray at a wide range of angles and a wide spread in energy. But, with the aid of a lens made of magnetic fields and a magnetic particle selector, the negatively charged antiprotons can be separated from the remainder of the debris consisting of particles which have a different charge and mass than the antiproton. The antiprotons that are collected are then directed into a magnetic ring where they are accumulated. The best capture efficiency anyone has been able to accomplish to date is only one percent. Ninety-nine percent of the antiprotons that are generated are lost.

The antiproton collector ring also contains methods to "cool" the captured antiprotons. When the antiprotons are first made, they have a wide spread of energies and velocities. Some antiprotons are moving faster, and some slower, than the average velocity. Particle physicists then use various techniques to get all the antiprotons to travel at the same speed in the collector ring. The antiprotons still have lots of kinetic energy because of their high average speed, but their "temperature" is low because the variations in the energy are small. They are "cooler" than before.

Once the antiprotons have been captured and cooled in the collecting ring, most of the hard work has been done. The vacuum level in the collecting rings is so low that the antiprotons can be stored in the rings for days at a time. Scientists can then add more high-energy antiprotons at any time and increase the number being stored. A typical antiproton collector ring holds as many as a trillion antiprotons at any one time. This many antiprotons has a mass of about two trillionths of a gram. This may not sound like much antimatter, but if the two trillionths of a gram of antimatter were annihilated with an equal amount of matter, the total energy released would be about three hundred joules of energy, enough to light a 100-watt bulb for three seconds—enough energy to *see*.

Now that the antiprotons have been collected and cooled, they are sent to an antiproton decelerator, which is really nothing more than the proton accelerator run backwards. The slowed antiprotons are then captured and stored in a ring machine called a low energy antiproton accumulator. Once the engineers have all the machines tuned up correctly, the efficiency of cooling, transferring, decelerating, and storing the antiprotons at low energy is quite high—more than ninety percent. But considering the terrible losses during the initial processes of making and capturing antiprotons, the overall losses are quite high.

The collection efficiency at Fermilab is presently about 0.04% (only one antiproton is captured for every 2,500 antiprotons that are made). If we add in the five percent production efficiency of the target, that means that only one antiproton is captured for every 50,000 bullet protons sent into the target. In terms of energy, the efficiency is even worse. One antiproton, when annihilated with a proton, will produce about 2 GeV of energy. But, to get that one antiproton required 50,000 bullet protons, each with 120 GeV of energy—for a particle energy efficiency of one part in three million. Then, since the proton accelerator that makes the bullet protons is only five percent efficient at converting wall-plug energy into proton energy, the overall energy efficiency is only one part in sixty million. As a result, antimatter is presently a very expensive synthetic fuel—

about ten trillion dollars per milligram—or two cents per million antiprotons. Fortunately, there are ways to improve this efficiency. Besides, there are some things, that only antiprotons can do, that make them worth even this exorbitant cost.

When first introduced to the concept of antimatter, one of the questions incredulous people have is: "How do you 'hold' onto this 'stuff' that disappears in a burst of energy the instant it touches normal matter?"

The scientists at CERN in Switzerland and Fermilab in the USA have demonstrated one solution to this problem. Their "bottle" is an evacuated tube bent into a ring. As the beam of antiprotons goes around inside the ring at high speed, it is directed and focused by magnetic fields to keep it from hitting the walls of the tube. Antiprotons have been kept for weeks in such a ring. The rings can also slow down the antiprotons so they can be put into a trap that is more portable than a ring.

The trap presently being used to hold antiproton is the Penning trap. [See Figure 3.] It has side walls made of a carefully machined metal ring about five centimeters (two inches) in diameter. The inside surface has a hyperbolic shape. Above and below the hole in the ring are two domed metal end caps, also with hyperbolic shapes. This trap is placed in a vacuum chamber inside the bore of a superconducting magnet in a large thermos jug containing liquid helium. The magnetic field from the superconducting magnet runs along the axis of the trap from one end cap to the other. There is a small hole in one end cap to allow the antiprotons to enter the trapping region in the center.

To capture an antiproton once it has been inserted into the trap, the end caps are given a negative charge and the ring a positive charge. The negative charge on the caps repels the negatively charged antiproton, keeping it from going in the axial direction. The antiproton will attempt to move radially outward toward the positively charged ring electrode, but the magnetic field will keep it moving in a circle. If the magnetic field is strong enough, and the trap is cold enough, the antiproton will never get to the ring, and it will be permanently trapped in a tiny circular orbit.

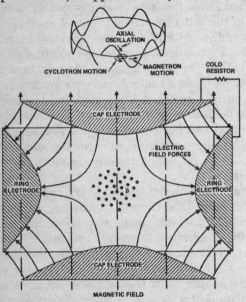

Fig. 3—Penning trap for antiprotons.

Since 1986, the TRAP collaboration, led by Gerald Gabrielse of Harvard University, has used Penning traps at CERN to capture antiprotons. In order to improve the antiproton capture efficiency, they modified the design of the traps by using a multiplicity of elongated cylindrical electrodes and flat end windows instead of hyperbolically shaped electrodes. The multiple electrodes allow them to make a trap inside a trap. The inner trap is designed to hold a cloud of electrons, while the outer trap is designed to hold antiprotons, which have the same negative electric charge as the electrons, but are 1840 times more massive. CERN's low-energy antiproton accumulator ring provides the antiprotons, sending them in short intense bunches through an evacuated pipe to the trap, which is positioned at the end of the pipe. The antiproton bunches are only a quarter of a microsecond long and contain one hundred million antiprotons each.

When the bunched antiprotons first hit the aluminum entrance window of the trap, their speed is so high they pass right by the protons in the aluminum nuclei without having time to annihilate. But as they penetrate the entrance window and continue to encounter atoms, their negative charge repels the electrons belonging to those atoms and knocks some of the electrons out of their orbits. For each electron that an antiproton removes from an atom, the antiproton loses a little energy and slows down. The total speed lost by the antiproton in traversing the entrance window depends on the window's thickness, which is critical to the success of the trap. If the window is too thick, all of the antiprotons will be stopped in the window and annihilate. On the other hand, if the window is too thin, the antiprotons will enter the trap with too much energy and will escape out the other side. If the window's thickness is chosen correctly, about ten thousand of the one hundred million antiprotons that entered the window will exit the window with a velocity that is low enough that the antiprotons will be turned around by the three thousand volt negative potential of the exit window at the other end of the trap. The reflected antiprotons then head back down the twelve centimeter long trap toward the entrance window by which they entered the trap. The entrance window has a small positive voltage on it that allows the antiprotons to enter the trap at low energy. Just before the quarter-microsecond pulse of antiprotons returns from the other end of the trap some third of a microsecond later, the trap is "slammed shut" by applying three thousand volts to the entrance window in less than a fiftieth of a microsecond. The antiprotons are now trapped.

The TRAP collaboration has used a Penning trap to hold about a hundred thousand antiprotons for two months *without losing any*. If a single one of the trapped antiprotons had collided with a left-over air molecule, or had touched the trap walls, it would have instantly annihilated and produced a large number of high energy particles and gamma rays, which would have been easily detected. One of these Penning traps could easily hold up to a trillion antiprotons. The traps are very small in size, and, when powered by nine-volt batteries, can be transported from site to site, or even across continents and oceans. (They do require large thermos-like containers full of liquid helium to keep them cold, so they are more pickup-truck portable than hand portable.)

Some of the most exciting and near-term uses for antimatter will be in medicine. The numbers of antiprotons that are being produced in one day's production at the present facilities are more than adequate not only for research, but for treatment and cure of hundreds of cancer patients. Ted Kalogeropoulus, a physicist at Syracuse University and his colleague Levi Gray, have found that a small number of antiprotons can be used to create density images of the interior of an object—including human bodies. They have used computers to conduct simulated experiments which have led them to believe that this new form of imaging will have several significant advantages over current methods of taking pictures of the inside of the human body, such as CAT scans, which use X-rays.

Their antiproton imaging technique should give better pictures than CAT scans, with one hundred times less radiation dose to the patient. With antimatter, the same beam that images a tumor could also zap it. By increasing the number of antiprotons beamed at some particular point, doctors could deposit enough energy right into the tumor to destroy it.

The number of antiprotons needed is not large. A million antiprotons will produce a high quality picture of a single plane through the body, and a billion antiprotons will produce a high quality three-dimensional image of a large volume such as the head or chest area. More antiprotons would be needed to kill the tumors, depending upon the size. A trap containing one day's antiproton production from CERN or Fermilab would be sufficient to image a thousand patients, or treat many dozens of cancer tumors.

The next step in developing an antimatter technology is to make and store antimatter in the form of antihydrogen atoms and molecules. Conceptually, this is easy. You merely combine antiprotons and positrons to form antihydrogen. Being of opposite charge, they will automatically attract each other. Unfortunately, like a comet being attracted to the Sun, as the positron is attracted toward the antiproton, it gains so much speed during its infall that most of the time the positron just zooms around the antiproton and flies back out again, avoiding capture. What is needed is a third particle nearby to steal away a little of the kinetic energy of the incoming positron so it becomes captured in an orbit around the antiproton, creating an antihydrogen atom.

In July 1992, the Second Antihydrogen Workshop was held in Munich, Germany. It was attended by over one hundred scientists. In one of the papers presented at the meeting, one of the scientists estimated that about thirty antihydrogen atoms had already been produced as an accidental byproduct of an experiment at Fermilab, but had gone undetected at the time. It is interesting to note that there were more scientists at this meeting on antihydrogen that there had been antihydrogen atoms made to date!

Most of the papers discussed ongoing experiments to be the first to make antihydrogen at low energies where it could be trapped and studied. Most of the approaches involve first trapping a large number of positrons, which are relatively easy to make and trap, then putting an antiproton in the same trap. It is expected that the antiproton will capture one positron to form antihydrogen, while the other positrons will act as the "third body" to take away the excess energy. It is not easy, however, to design a trap that will hold heavy negatively charged antiprotons and light positively charged positrons at the same time.

Others at the conference described their techniques for holding onto the antihydrogen atoms once they are made. Since an antihydrogen atom has no net charge, it cannot be stored in the Penning traps used to hold positrons and antiprotons. One proposed technique uses a trap made of ultraviolet laser beams. The other trap techniques take advantage of the fact that an antihydrogen atom is slightly magnetic and can be captured in a trap made of opposing magnetic field coils with a magnetic field minimum at the center. This same type of trap can also hold antihydrogen molecules and antihydrogen ice. Scientists already have demonstrated magnetic field traps that can levitate and hold balls of liquid and frozen normal hydrogen, so the traps should work equally well with antihydrogen.

Electric fields can also be used to store and manipulate antimatter. If a ball of antihydrogen ice has a slight excess electric charge, electric fields can be used to move it around. A weak beam of ultraviolet light can be used to drive positrons off the antihydrogen ice ball to keep it charged. Experimenters at the Jet Propulsion Laboratory have been experimenting with such traps for use in zero gravity laboratories on Spacelab and the Space Station. They have already used such traps to stably levitate balls of water ice in one Earth gravity. Since antihydrogen ice has a much lower density than water ice, the same apparatus should be able to levitate a similar sized ball of antihydrogen against thirteen gravities.

Thus, experiments are underway that are expected to result in the production, cooling, and trapping of small amounts of antihydrogen. But once made, can it be kept? Will the residual air left in the trap annihilate with the antihydrogen ice ball, heating it up and causing a catastrophic chain reaction? Will antihydrogen atoms evaporate from the ice ball, travel to the walls of the trap and annihilate, starting a chain reaction?

The experiment involving the trapping of a hundred thousand antiprotons for two months with *no* annihilations occurring, showed that a trap kept at liquid helium temperatures has a vacuum good enough to store antimatter for months at a time without *any* loss. Experiments on the evaporation rate of normal hydrogen ice versus temperature, indicate that if the antihydrogen ice ball in the trap is kept below two degrees above absolute zero, only a few antihydrogen molecules a day would evaporate from the surface. Even if these escaped the trap fields and annihilated on the walls of the trap, calculations show that the energy released would not be enough to cause a heat chain reaction to start. Thus, once we have made and trapped antimatter, we can be confident that we can keep it for long periods of time until it is used. One exciting future use for antimatter is in space propulsion. Not for powering the space warp drives on the starship *Enterprise*, but for powering more pragmatic engines called antimatter rockets.

To travel you must move. To move you must have energy. To get energy you must convert mass. Every time you burn a tankful of gasoline to take you and your automobile further down the highway, mass has disappeared. In the process of burning gasoline, some of the mass of the gasoline has been converted into energy. With chemical fuels, like gasoline and rocket fuels, the amount of mass that gets converted is parts in a thousand million. With fission energy, using uranium or plutonium as fuels, the amount of mass converted becomes parts in a thousand. With fission fuels like hydrogen and deuterium, the mass conversion ratio reaches almost one percent. Yet all of these fuels are eclipsed by antimatter, for when antimatter meets normal matter *all* of the mass in both the antimatter and the normal matter gets converted into energy. Since normal matter is easy to come by, one could say that antimatter is a magical fuel that is two hundred percent efficient!

You may have heard that mixing antimatter with normal matter produces gamma rays. The first antimatter that was produced was the positron, the mirror particle to the electron. When positrons are mixed with electrons they *do* produce all of their energy as gamma rays, which are very difficult to cope with. When antiprotons are mixed with normal protons, however, the resulting energy does *not* come out as gamma rays. Instead, the proton and its mirror twin turn into a collection of particles called pions. On the average there will be three charged pions and two neutral pions. The neutral pions almost instantly produce gamma rays. These gamma rays can be stopped by a shield to produce heat to run the auxiliary systems.

The other sixty percent of the energy released, however, is in the form of highly energetic charged pions. The charged pions have a short life, but since they are traveling at 94% of the speed of light they cover a distance of twenty-one meters (sixty feet) during their lifetime, which is more than enough to extract the kinetic energy from them. [See Figure 4.] After they decay, they turn into other charged particles called muons. The muons will travel nearly two kilometers (over a mile) before they decay, turning into positrons and electrons. The charged particles can be used to heat normal matter, like water or hydrogen, to produce a hot plasma. The hot plasma can be ejected out a rocket nozzle to provide thrust or used to power electric generators.

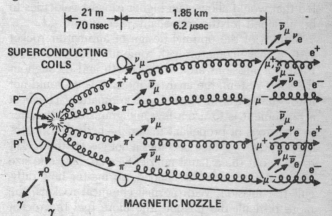

Fig. 4—Rocket thrust from proton-antiproton annihilation.

An even simpler first-generation antimatter rocket engine consists of a cylinder of tungsten about thirty centimeters (one foot) in length and diameter, weighing about a third of a ton. Antiprotons are injected into a cavity in the center of the cylinder, where they annihilate with the hydrogen gas kept there. Most of the gamma rays and charged pions that emerge from the annihilation process are stopped in the tungsten block, depositing their energy in the tungsten and heating it up.

There are holes running through the cylinder, through which pass the ordinary hydrogen gas. The hydrogen enters the tungsten heat exchanger cold, and emerges at high temperatures, in the process keeping the tungsten from melting. This hot hydrogen gas is then expelled from a nozzle to create thrust. The speed of the emerging hydrogen is two or three times the speed obtainable from chemical rocket fuels. These antimatter rocket engines are limited in their performance by the melting point of tungsten. Reaction chambers made of magnetic fields are now being studied that would allow even higher exhaust velocities to be obtained for the propellant. [See Figure 4.]

Studies of the optimal design of antimatter rocket systems have come up with some unexpected results. First, for missions around the Earth and throughout the solar system, the analyses indicate you should not use equal parts of matter and antimatter. The best arrangement is to use a few milligrams of antimatter to heat tons of propellant material—hydrogen, methane, or water—which becomes a hot gas for the rocket to spew out the exhaust nozzle. Second, only one size of antimatter rocket is needed, no matter how difficult the mission. With normal chemical rockets, the more difficult the mission, the more fuel the rocket must carry, and the larger the rocket becomes, especially the propellant tanks. This is not true for optimized antimatter rocket missions. Going up to low Earth orbit, orbiting the Moon, making a round trip journey to the surface of Mars, or traveling to the stars, can all be done with the same sized vehicle!

The optimum antimatter vehicle contains a fuel tank that holds an amount of propellant that has only four times the "dry" (or empty) mass of the vehicle. (Most chemical rockets carry twenty to sixty times their dry mass in fuel.) If the mission is easy, the vehicle will carry only a few milligrams of antimatter and use it to heat the propellant to a hot gas, which is expelled out the nozzle to provide thrust to the vehicle. If the mission is difficult, the vehicle will take along more antimatter, but the same amount of propellant, and use the antimatter to heat the propellant until it is a blazing hot plasma that has a much higher exhaust velocity. Even for a mission to the stars, the amount of antimatter needed is measured in kilograms, not tons.

Still, since the present production rate is one trillionth of a gram a day, while space propulsion needs many milligrams per mission and grams per year, it will be decades before antimatter becomes a product that is bought and sold like gasoline or diesel fuel. There are many, many, many difficult problems left to solve in the production, capture, cooling, storage, transport, and use of this extremely potent, extremely expensive, nearly magic source of raw energy. But as one skeptic after another takes a look at the problems that have been overcome and the problems still left to be solved, it begins to look as if there are no "showstoppers." There is no physical reason why antimatter, in some form, cannot be made and stored in enough quantity to produce the kilowatts and megawatts of prime power and propulsion power needed for rapid space travel.

The production efficiency of the present machines is abysmally low. Fortunately, the low efficiency is not due to any fundamental limitation, and can be improved by orders of magnitude. The reason for the low efficiencies of the present machines is that all of the antimatter production facilities built to date have been built under limited budgets. Production efficiency has been sacrificed to such considerations as speed, cost, science requirements, and national pride.

In a study I carried out for the Air Force Rocket Propulsion Laboratory, I showed that if an antiproton factory were designed properly by engineers, instead of by scientists with limited budgets and in a hurry to win a Nobel prize, the present energy efficiency (electrical energy in compared to antimatter annihilation energy out) could be raised from a part in sixty million to a part in ten thousand or 0.01%, while at the same time, the cost of building the factory could be substantially lowered compared to the cost of the high precision scientific machines. From these studies, I estimated the cost of the antimatter at ten million dollars per milligram. This may sound like a lot, but at ten million dollars per milligram, antimatter is already cost effective for space propulsion and power. At the present subsidized price of a Space Shuttle launch, it costs about five million dollars to put a ton of anything into low Earth orbit. Since a milligram of antimatter produces the same amount of energy as twenty tons of the most energetic chemical fuel available, then a milligram of antimatter costing ten million dollars would be a more cost effective fuel in space than twenty tons of chemical fuel costing ten times as much.

Antimatter is no longer science fiction. It is real, and is being made daily for scientific purposes. Within a few years, traps containing antiprotons will be transported around the world for research and medical purposes. Before the century is out, antihydrogen, and perhaps other antiatoms, will be made and kept in storage. As the 21st century progresses, new applications will be found for antimatter. Its price will come down as production starts.

Antimatter at the present cost of ten trillion dollars per milligram has already been proven cost effective for scientific experiments to win Nobel prizes. Antimatter at a hundred million dollars per milligram would definitely be cost effective for unmanned probe missions to the rings of Saturn and manned missions to Mars. When the cost of antimatter starts to drop below ten million dollars per milligram, then many new applications come to the fore, for now antimatter is cheaper in energy delivered to orbit than any chemical fuel, and possibly even cheaper than nuclear fuel.

Where will we get the energy to run these magic matter factories? Some of the prototype factories will be built on Earth, but for large scale production we certainly don't want to power these machines by burning fossil fuels on Earth. There is plenty of energy in space. At the distance of the Earth from the Sun, the Sun delivers over a kilowatt of energy for each square meter of collector, or a gigawatt (1,000,000,000 watts) per square kilometer. A collector array of one hundred kilometers on a side would provide a power input of ten terawatts (10,000,000,000,000 watts), enough to run a number of antimatter factories at full power, producing a gram of antimatter a day.

We know how to make antimatter. We know how to store antimatter. With a fully developed antimatter technology, the solar system and the nearby stars can be ours. There is no question about the feasibility of the technology, it is only a matter of scaling and cost. The question is not: "Can we do it?" It is: "Do we *want* to do it?"

Recommended Reading

B. W. Augenstein, et al., editors, *Antiproton Science and Technology* (World Scientific, 1988).

David B. Cline, *Low Energy Antimatter* (World Scientific, 1986).

John Eades, editor, *Proceedings of the Antihydrogen Workshop*, Hyperfine Interactions, Vol. 76, pp. 1–402 (1993).

Robert L. Forward, "Antimatter Revealed," *Omni*, Vol. 2, No. 2, pp. 44–48 (1979).

Robert L. Forward, "Antiproton Annihilation Propulsion," *Journal of Propulsion and Power*, Vol. 1, pp. 370–374 (1985).

Robert L. Forward and Joel Davis, *Mirror Matter: Pioneering Antimatter Physics* (John Wiley & Sons, 1988).

Gerald Gabrielse, "Extremely Cold Antiprotons," *Scientific American*, pp. 74–85 (December 1992).

✧ TURN LEFT AT THE MOON

In the previous chapter, "Antimatter," I summarized what we know about the science and technology of antimatter. Most of that material was condensed from a non-fiction book, Mirror Matter: Pioneering Antimatter Physics, which I coauthored with science writer Joel Davis. Instead of making the book completely non-fiction, however, we included a running science fiction story, with a portion of the story appearing as a lead-in to each technical section. Each portion of the story had to cover, in a brief fictional manner, what would be discussed in more detail in the following technical portion. Even with this limitation, I found it possible to put together a short narrative that had a reasonably coherent story line, while still covering all the important aspects of the potential impact of antimatter on future science, technology, medicine, and commerce.

The story, as written, does gloss over the radiation hazards of antimatter. Antimatter annihilation does not produce neutrons, as does both nuclear fission and nuclear fusion. As a result, antimatter fuel does not generate secondary radioactivity in the machines that use it, or produce lots of radioactive waste that needs to be disposed of. Nevertheless, it does generate copious amounts of hard gamma rays during the annihilation process, which are only exponentially absorbed by a *radiation shield. As a result, some small amount of radiation is always going to leak through even the best shielding. In these days of zero risk environmental regulations, I am afraid that it is unlikely that antimatter will be used for any purposes other than scientific research and medical imaging and treatment, even if we could find a way to get the cost way down below ten million dollars a milligram, which is what would be needed to make some of the applications discussed in the story economically feasible. I was working on the technical background to my novel* Martian Rainbow *at the time this was written, so you will find a lot of Mars detail in this short story, as well as a number of antimatter powered vehicles in the novel.*

This version of "Turn Left at the Moon" is the draft that I turned over to my co-author. The version to be found in Mirror Matter *is a shorter, jointly authored version.*

———

Johnny took yet another look at the blinking mauve polka dot clock with the bright green numbers on the upper part of his screen. The clock said 1740 Friday 25 Sept 2035. He still had another twenty minutes to go on the homework tutor before he could quit for the day.

"The berker thing must be broken," muttered Johnny as he changed the colors on the clock to red stripes with electric blue numbers. The tutor was getting annoyed with his slow response to the last question and had started adding beeps to augment the flashing question mark.

"If $6x+3=27$, what is x?"

Johnny mumbled briefly to himself, typed 4, and stuck his tongue out at the screen as it replied with a blinking red "EXCELLENT!" He sighed and started paying attention to the tutor so he would be through his homework before Mom and Dad got home from work. But it was hard to concentrate knowing that Gramma Ginny was probably dying.

It wasn't long before the afternoon lesson was over and the colorful clock chimed the hour as Johnny heard the high-pitched whistle on Mom's Supertrain far off down the valley. Johnny turned off the tutor before it could turn itself off and ran to the picture window that looked down from their home in Les Houches in the French Alps to the deep valley below. Johnny could now see Dad's wheeltrain from Switzerland way off to the right. It was late tonight and Mom would beat Dad to the station for the second time this week.

The Supertrain from Italy slowed from its two-hundred kilometer per hour speed by pumping its kinetic energy back through the linear motor built into its super-conducting levitracks and came to a halt. The trees prevented Johnny from seeing much, even through Dad's binoculars, but soon he saw a tiny figure walking to their Nissan electric, parked at one end of the parking lot where his parents knew it could be seen from Johnny's window. The figure waved upward once, then turned and waited for the wheeltrain from Geneva to arrive.

Mom had first met Dad right there in that very station in a large crowd of holiday skiers. She, a materials engineer from the USA and he a physicist from the nearby CERN nuclear research center in Switzerland. By the end of the two weeks they had spent skiing together, they decided to spend the rest of their lives in the Alps. Mom easily found a job with the European Space Agency at the rocket fabrication and test facility in nearby Turin in Italy, and they had lived in Les Houches ever since Johnny had been born—fifteen years ago.

Dad's train finally arrived. Shortly thereafter the family's high powered superconducting electric car started its zooming ascent up the mountain. The Nissan disappeared into the foliage and Johnny had time to worry about Gramma Ginny again. She was feeling real sick and he might never see her again. The thought made him feel sad. He cheered up as he caught a glimpse of the car coming around one of the hairpin turns on the road up to their home. Soon Mom and Dad were in the house.

Later, they were all sitting around the dining room table, having dinner.

"Today was a big day at CERN," said Dad. "We had over two hundred scientists, including a dozen Nobel Prize winners, come in for a special triple anniversary meeting. It's been fifty years since Carlo Rubbia and Simon van der Meer were awarded the Nobel Prize for using antiprotons colliding with protons to discover the W and Z particles. They held the ceremony in the center of the old Low Energy Antiproton Ring, which has just been declared a Historical Monument."

"That will keep the accelerator engineers from cannibalizing it for the parts," said Mom.

"There were two other anniversaries celebrated at the same time," continued Dad. "The eightieth anniversary of the discovery of the antiproton at Berkeley in 1955, and the one-hundred and second anniversary of the discovery of the first antiparticle, the positron, back in 1933 at Caltech."

"Those kind of meetings are fun, but time consuming," said Mom. "What about your research on the anticarbon fusion cycle?"

"The antimatter engineers at the heavy ion collider factories have been finding us enough antihelium nuclei in the output from the colliders to keep our experiment supplied, but we still haven't been able to replicate the Sun's carbon cycle by fusing three antihelium nuclei into anticarbon."

"Wasn't that the whole point?" asked Mom. "If the

cycle doesn't work with antimatter the same as it does with matter, then maybe that explains why we can't observe antimatter anywhere in the universe."

"That may be the reason," said Dad, "or it could be that we are just not doing the experiment right. The fusion machine that we are using does a fine job of fusing normal matter helium into carbon, but it could be that the few residual molecules of air that are unavoidably left in the vacuum chamber are helping the reaction somehow. Then, when we try the same experiment with antihelium, the few residual molecules are of no help to the antimatter version of the reaction, since they are normal matter instead of antimatter. We'll have to try lots of variations before we can say anything definite. Six months to a year is my guess. In fact, we'll be shut down for the next three months while the engineers rebuild the fusion machine with an antiproton beam 'vacuum scrubber' to annihilate those residual air molecules and get a better vacuum." Dad took a sip of wine. "How did things go at the ESA test facility?"

"I got almost nothing done," said Mom. "I kept worrying about Mother. I had my technicians run a few of the new high temperature plasma rocket nozzles through the antiproton flaw detection facility, but I couldn't get myself to call up the data to analyze the results. Instead, I spent the day rearranging my computer files."

"I'm sure Mother Ginger is going to be all right," said Dad. "Staying under pressure twenty-four hours a day for weeks at a time is bound to do things to your ear."

"Mother has been an underwater environmentalist for nearly thirty years. This is the first time ear problems have made her so dizzy she can't even swim, much less walk. I think it's something more serious."

Johnny remained quiet. He liked Gramma Ginny a

lot. One time he had visited her and Granpa John at their underwater house in the little village, 'Atlantis Too,' on the ocean floor off California. They flew out in a helicopter to the small landing pad above the underwater community. The landing pad was just a minor speck on the otherwise clear ocean horizon view from Santa Barbara. The offshore oil drilling rigs that used to clutter the horizon were now all underwater. They went down to Atlantis Too in a slow elevator that changed the pressure as they descended to the large underwater village below. Granpa John had taken him out to see the underwater oil drilling rigs and showed Johnny the new antimatter drill bit he was testing.

"It holds a little container of frozen antimatter that has enough energy to drill through a kilometer of hard rock," Granpa John had said. "It doesn't vaporize a large hole like a 'Star Trek' disintegrator ray, but instead there are six antimatter beams that punch six tiny holes in the rock and fracture it so the rock drill has no problem grinding it up. The combination goes through hard rock like a hot knife through butter." Later, in Gramma Ginny's kitchen, Johnny had heated up a knife on the electric stove and tried it. A hot knife sure made a mess out of a quarter-kilo of butter.

Granpa John had also showed him the compact power plant that generated all the electricity needed to run the oil rigs and energize the underwater homes of the workers. A small antimatter powered submarine was hovering over the plant when Granpa John drove by the plant in his electric submersible. "They are bringing the monthly supply of antimatter to run the power plant," said Granpa John. "Expensive fuel, antimatter, but at least there are no ashes left to haul away."

Gramma Ginny had also taken him on trips through kelp beds and down into deep canyons. She would use the arms of the manipulators on the submersible to snip off pieces of kelp or pick up oysters and put them in a basket. "I'll have to check these for pollution," said Gramma Ginny. "My last batch from this area showed signs of oil pollution, although there are no drilling rigs anywhere near."

They went down into a deep canyon. It made Johnny's stomach feel funny as the submersible flew over the edge of the underwater cliff and zoomed down into the blackness below.

"Aha!" said Gramma Ginny as she stopped their descent and flew the submersible back up the cliff. There in the searchlights of the submersible were black blobs of tarry stuff oozing out of a crack in the side of the cliff and slowly rising upward through the water. "An oil seep," she said. "I'll have to send a crew over to seal it up."

The telephone beeped in the kitchen and woke Johnny from his daydream. He returned to his dinner while Mom went to the telephone. Fortunately, Mom and Dad had been too busy talking to each other to notice that he had let his food get cold. What little Johnny could hear of the telephone conversation was bewildering.

"Mother! How are you?"

"Oh dear! That's terrible news."

"Oh wonderful! That's good news."

"Oh really!?! That's terrific news."

"Yes! We'd love to. I'll call you right back."

As Mom came out of the kitchen, Dad said, "Your mother must be feeling better if she made the telephone call herself."

"She just went in this morning for an antiproton CAT scan on her head," said Mom. "There was nothing wrong with her ear, but they found a small brain tumor that was pressing on her ear and causing her vertigo."

"A brain tumor!" said Dad. "That sounds serious."

It sounded *terribly* serious to Johnny.

"That's what I thought too," said Mom. "But it was so small, that they just turned up the current in the antiproton beam and cauterized it right there. She was able to walk out of the hospital by herself. The first thing Father had her do was give me a call. Mother said that she had had a lot of time to think while she was lying in bed these past weeks. She had made a decision that once she felt better, she was going to take the time to do some things that she had been postponing for far too long. She has decided to take a vacation tour to Mars!"

"Wow!" said Johnny. "I've always wanted to go to Mars."

"Well you can," said Mom. "She has invited us along. Granpa John has to stay and work on a new oil field, so she's taking us along for company."

Four days later Mom, Dad, and Johnny were passing over the North Pole in a Boeing HT-303 Hyperplane flown by All World Express. It was an antimatter augmented hypersonic airplane that flew from Paris to California in three hours. As they came into the Palmdale Interplanetary Spaceport, they could see the large dry lake at Edwards Air Force Base to the north.

"That's where the first Space Shuttle landed," said Johnny, who had been reading through his history files in preparation for the trip.

"See that long line in the desert to the left of the dry lake bed?" said Dad. "That's what's left of the first antiproton factory. It used a long superconducting linear accelerator that goes for twenty kilometers across the desert. Thirty years ago they used that machine to make enough antimatter to run the first antimatter powered rocket. We have much better machines now, that are a lot smaller and much more efficient."

Johnny took his gaze from the window, pulled his portable computer out of his shirt pocket, and started reading about the Palmdale Spaceport. There was a rumbling noise as the landing gear dropped down from the sleek underside of the California Comet.

Gramma Ginny and Granpa John met them at the Palmdale Spaceport and they spent the next day resting, packing for the long trip, and getting checked out by the Spaceport medical staff. So far, Mars had been kept free of almost all of the communicable diseases except the common cold, and the Mars authorities wanted to keep it that way. There was some concern over Gramma Ginny's recent tumor operation, and whether she might have a reoccurrence of the problem during the trip. In that unlikely event, she would just repeat the treatment. The lightweight antimatter CAT machine was a standard piece of medical equipment onboard the Mars Longliner since there was plenty of antimatter available from the fuel tanks to operate it.

The time finally came to leave for Mars. Two hours before the flight they all took their space-sickness pills. Fortunately, space medical research had finally found a solution to that problem. They said goodby to Granpa John, boarded the transfer bus, and were taken out across the large field to the long runway that stretched across the desert. At the end of the runway, ready for its flight into space, was a McDonnell-Douglas AS-3 Spaceclimber, the antimatter augmented aerospace plane that was to take them to the o'neil at L-4. There they would board the Mars Longliner for their trip to Mars.

Johnny looked out the window of the bus as they approached the sleek craft. It had the general shape of a pointed paper airplane, but a fancy one with twin tails. The surface was covered with grey-white insulating material that protected the spaceplane on reentry. The spaceplane was actually smaller than the hypersonic aircraft that they had used to travel from home to the Palmdale Spaceport. As they got closer, Johnny noticed that there were no wheels, and he could see right under the spaceplane to the other side. The plane was floating in the air a half-meter off the ground. The Spaceclimber used superconducting levitation landing gear that consisted of upside-down bowls of superconducting material built into the frame of the spaceplane, behind the heat insulation skin. Built into the runway were the superconducting magnetic field motors that held up the spaceplane by pushing on the superconducting bowls.

The sixty passengers were carefully tucked into their seats according to size and weight. Johnny and Gramma Ginny were put in the front row, and Johnny got one of the windows. The engines were started at low level and the Spaceclimber started its long glide down the runway, the superconducting motors in the runway saving on fuel by catapulting them up to speed and into the air. As the markings on the ground turned into a blur, the engines burst into a roar and Johnny was pressed into the back of his seat as they took off into the sky.

"One kilometer," said the Captain. "Two . . . Three . . . Four . . ." Insulating shields slid over the windows as the acceleration grew stronger. The Spaceclimber shook slightly as it broke through the sound barrier. "Six . . . Eight . . . Ten . . . Rockets on." The sound of the engines changed as they switched from an airbreathing mode to a rocket mode. "Fifteen . . . Twenty . . . Twenty-five. Antimatter augmentation on." The muffled roar of the engines increased as milligrams of antimatter were added to double, then triple the thrust from the rockets. The rockets stopped abruptly and they were left in free fall. The window shields slid back and the Captain turned the Spaceclimber upside down so everyone could look out the top ports at the curve of the Earth below. The sky had turned from blue to black.

"We'll be at L-4 in about twelve hours," said the

Captain. "In about one hour we'll be passing through geostationary orbit altitude. We'll pass close to the big glasser that supplies energy for the West Coast communities in North and South America. You shouldn't have any trouble seeing it. The solar cell array is thirty kilometers wide by three hundred kilometers long and produces ten million megawatts of power. That's ten thousand gigawatts, or two thousand old-time Earth power plants. It's also ten terawatts—ten times the total world output of power fifty years ago. This is just one of four glassers. The others supply power to the East Coast of the Americas, Europe, and Russia, while a fifth one is under construction over Asia."

The Captain turned the Spaceclimber so they could see the glasser through the top viewports. "If you look closely in the narrow gap at the center of the solar cell array, you can see a round disk a few kilometers in diameter that sends multiple beams of microwaves to the various power receiving stations in the oceans or at isolated locations in the mountains or deserts. Fortunately, the new underground superconducting power line technology has made it possible to locate the receiving sites far from any populated areas.

"If you have very good eyes, you also might be able to spot the antimatter factories in the gap between the two halves of the solar cell array. If the Earth doesn't need the full power output from the glasser, then what's left over is used for making antimatter. Antimatter thus becomes an economical way of storing, in a compact form, the solar energy that would otherwise be lost forever. Some of the antimatter is shipped to Earth, but most of it stays in space where it's used for powering space vehicles."

Johnny watched intently as they glided past the huge sunlit structure. Dad had left his seat and had floated over to hang above Gramma Ginny and look out Johnny's window.

"I can see the microwave disk real easy," said Johnny. "Are those four little dots the antimatter factories?"

"The two that look like doughnuts are the antimatter factories," said Dad. "The smaller spheres are for processing of materials from the moon and asteroids."

The Spaceclimber passed through geostationary orbital altitude and continued its climb through space. Meals were served and Johnny had fun playing with his food in free-fall. The Captain had the ship positioned so that the Moon could be seen by looking forward out of the upper viewing ports, while the Earth could be seen looking backward out the ports. As the Spaceclimber traveled, the Earth stayed in the same place in the viewports and got smaller, while the Moon stayed the same size and rose up in the viewport frame until it was nearly overhead. As they approached Dyson City at L-4, the Captain rotated the ship and fired the engines to bring them to a halt at the docking port of the o'neil.

Dyson City had the shape of a huge rotating wheel. There was a basic framework of open girders about two hundred meters in diameter rotating about once per minute to produce just enough gravity to give a sense of "up" and "down." Two opposite quarters of the wheel had been filled in with a curved pressure hull that was fifteen meters in diameter. To Johnny, Dyson City looked like a doughnut with two big bites taken out of it. They landed at the center hub of the wheel and took an elevator down to the A sector. As the elevator descended, they all floated to the bottom of the elevator and began standing on their feet once again.

They disembarked on the upper deck of the A section. Four meters above them was a large curved window that looked inward to the hub and beyond to the curved window of the C sector. Johnny looked up and saw people there. They were upside down, standing on their ceiling, and looking downward at them.

A large mirror to one side of the o'neil reflected the sunlight into the windows and down through the lightshafts to the farms on the decks below. They had a day before they would board the Mars Longliner, so they began to explore Dyson City. Dad headed for the C sector to visit the Russian cosmic ray scientists, Gramma Ginny went to the lower decks of the A sector to visit the hydroponic gardens, and Johnny followed along with Mom as she visited the construction work going on in the B sector. Although all the sectors were open to everyone, the A sector had primarily been built by the Americans and held the various experimental facilities that they were interested in, while the C sector had been constructed by the Russians. The European Space Agency was expanding Dyson City into the B sector. Because Mom was an engineer for ESA, she got to visit a control center where they could look out a window where construction workers in hard suits with powerful propulsion units and strong manipulators were assembling the various components into a new section.

As they entered the control room, they saw the workers bringing up some titanium alloy plates that were to undergo one last inspection before being welded into place to form the bottom pressure hull and "bedrock" of the huge curved structure. A two by three meter plate was floated in front of the scanner and a beam of antiprotons was swept back and forth over the five centimeter thick plate. Inside the control deck, Johnny and his mother watched the image build up on the screen. In ten seconds the scan was done. To Johnny it looked like a dull grey rectangle. Mom's eyes were keener.

"There is something in the lower left corner," said Mom at the same moment that the computer drew a red oval in the lower left corner of the grey rectangle.

The operator rotated and expanded the image and used the contrast controls to bring out the flaw. She started to push the "reject" key, for one certainly does not want to use flawed titanium plates in the construction of Dyson City. If it failed, the results could be catastrophic.

"It doesn't look too bad," said Mom. "I don't see any evidence of a void."

"Just a collection of line dislocations," said the operator. "They probably can be annealed out." She shifted her hand and pushed the "rework" button instead. The plate was prominently tagged and moved by the spacesuited outside construction workers to a separate facility. There, a separate team of workers moved their heavy duty antiproton beamer into position and turned it on. Within moments, a nanogram of antimatter heated up that local region deep inside the titanium plate without heating it up anywhere else, and the dislocation flaws in the plate were annealed away. The annealed plate would not be used for its original purpose in the main pressure hull. However, it would still find a use in Dyson City. It was retagged and moved into a special storage orbit. Meanwhile, another plate was brought over by a space construction tug and its interior imaged. This plate was fine. The construction workers moved it into position ready for welding. Dyson City continued to expand.

Everyone went to bed early that night as they adjusted their sleep schedules to space time. Activity in Dyson City went on continuously since most of the observatories and experimental laboratories were on twenty-four hour shifts, but those not on shift work lived according to Greenwich Mean Time, which made it easy for Johnny and his Mom and Dad, since they only had to shift one hour from French time. The next "morning" they were taken out on a Dyson City shuttlecraft to the Rockwell IT-2 Longliner operated by Mars Tours Unlimited. The Longliner was aptly named, as it was a half-kilometer in length. The main body was a long girder in the shape of a triangular truss structure that connected the three main components. At the front of the Longliner was the control center and the passenger compartment. Near the center of the truss beam were the propellant tanks containing the liquid methane that was going to be heated by the antimatter and expelled to provide thrust. At the rear of the Longliner were the liquid drop radiators, the radiation shield, and the antimatter rocket engine.

Since the antimatter engines were off, the shuttlecraft took them near the rear of the Longliner to let the passengers see the marvel that had opened up the solar system to tourism. The scotty for the Longliner was traveling out to the ship with the passengers, so he gave them a detailed description of his pride and joy.

"The antimatter rocket engine is not much bigger than some of the chemical rocket engines used on the big boosters back in the 1990s," said the scotty. "It's three meters in diameter inside the annihilation chamber, while the bell of the nozzle expands out to ten meters to get the maximum thrust out of the hot exhaust gases. In each second of operation, the engine uses three milligrams of antimatter to heat fourteen hundred grams of propellant. The power level is five-hundred gigawatts, about fifteen times the power level of the early Saturn Five moon rockets."

The shuttlecraft moved on to the other side of a thick metal disk about three meters in diameter. It was fifteen centimeters thick at the center and tapered down to a few centimeters at the rim. Right in back of the metal disk was a large rectangle about as big as a kitchen refrigerator.

"The big metal disk is the radiation shield, while the rectangular box on the other side is the antimatter storage container," continued the scotty. "Antihydrogen pellets weighing about ten micrograms each are extracted from the electrostatic storage container and sent through a vacuum line that runs through the shield. The antimatter pellets are injected into the center of the reaction chamber of the engine where the anti-hydrogen annihilates with the hydrogen and carbon molecules in the methane. The reaction products are gamma rays and charged particles called pions. Most of the gamma rays are stopped in the walls of the reaction chamber where they are used to preheat the propellant. Some of the gamma rays get out of the engine, so that's why we need the shadow shield to protect the passenger compartment up front. The charged pions are trapped by the strong magnetic field bottle that's generated by the high temperature super-conductor loops you see wrapped around the pressure chamber and nozzle. They also help keep the hot propellant from getting too close to the walls and melt-ing it. All the materials used in the making of the engine are especially chosen low mass isotopes that do not produce long-lived radioactive byproducts if they are fissioned by an escaping gamma ray or pion. Within a day after the engine is turned off it's safe to work on."

They next came to three long narrow troughs that stuck out for thirty meters to each side of the narrow truss backbone of the ship. Further along the truss were a thirty-meter-long array of tiny spray nozzles.

"Those are the 'squirters' and 'catchers' for the liq-uid drop radiators," said the scotty. "When the anti-matter engine is on and we need to get rid of waste heat, the liquid drop radiators are turned on. Red hot drops of liquid metal come streaming out of the squirter nozzles and stream outward into space to cool off. The cooled droplets are then caught by the collector, the cool liquid metal is piped down to the engine components to cool them off, then the hot liquid is returned to the squirters again. Although you will never see them in operation from the passenger compartment except through the rear monitor video cameras, they give the Longliner an impressive glowing triangular tail as it journeys through space. Looks just like a flaming arrow."

They next passed the large propellant storage tanks at the center of the Longliner. There were three of them, each a squat cylinder fifteen meters in diameter and three meters thick, stacked along the truss of the Longliner like beads on a stick.

"These are the propellant tanks. They hold the reaction mass that's heated by the antimatter in the reaction chamber of the rocket engine," said the scotty. "Theoretically, you can use anything you want for propellant in an antimatter rocket. It all gets turned into a blazing hot plasma of ions and electrons by the annihilation pions. Both liquid hydrogen and water have been used successfully in antimatter engines, but we prefer methane since it has four hydrogens for each carbon atom, so it's almost as good as pure hydrogen, but it's much more dense than liquid hydrogen, so the size of the tanks are reasonable. These tanks hold eight hundred tons of methane, or four times the 'dry' weight of the Longliner. If we were taking the tour to Saturn's rings instead of to Mars, we would still only load on eight hundred tons of propellant, the only difference is that we would take more antimatter to heat the same amount of propellant hotter. The reason for three tanks is safety. If one of the tanks is penetrated by a meteorite and we lose propellant, we can make do with the contents of the other two tanks. We just use a little more antimatter and heat the propellant hotter, thus getting the same amount of total thrust out of less propellant. The propellant also provides a little more radiation shielding."

The scotty kept up the chatter as the shuttlecraft moved slowly along the length of the Longliner, where they boarded the passenger compartment. Johnny and Gramma Ginny shared an outer stateroom with a heavy porthole, while Mom and Dad had an inner cabin. Everyone spent most of the time on the upper deck with the large viewing windows and the video monitors for the remote cameras that let them look aft, and the long distance cameras that were coupled to powerful telescopes that gave them close-up views of distant objects.

The captain of the Mars Longliner met them in the lounge on the upper deck and described the details of the trip.

"We'll first take a short hop over to the Moon to pick up more passengers and some supplies for the Mars base. Then, we'll turn left at the Moon and head straight for Mars. In the old days, with limited rocket power, it was necessary to take a long roundabout elliptical orbit from one planet to another. You had to 'lead' the target planet by almost a half-orbit. With the increased rocket power that antimatter gives us, we just aim for the target planet and drive straight to it. Mars is fairly close at this time of year, so we'll only have to travel about one astronomical unit—the distance between the Earth and the Sun.

"To keep you passengers comfortable, we'll travel at constant acceleration for half the journey, go into free fall for a few minutes while I flip the liner 180 degrees, then decelerate until we are in Martian orbit. On this journey, we'll be traveling at one-sixth Earth gravity, which is about one lunar gravity, or one-half Martian gravity. The total travel time will be seven days. I hope you enjoy your journey."

They had the obligatory "lifeboat" drill, but instead of putting on lifejackets and reporting to their lifeboat stations, they each went back to their stateroom, packed a little emergency bag with necessities, then waited. After about five minutes, the individual room viewers were turned on by an emergency override signal, and the captain's face appeared.

"This is a test. Solar Storm Alert! Everyone bring your emergency bag and report to the Solar Storm Shelter. Repeat. This is a test of the Solar Storm Alert system. Everyone report to the Solar Storm Shelter."

Johnny and Gramma Ginny took their emergency bags, and following everyone else, they headed for the center of the ship where they were ushered through a revolving airlock by the stewards into a small cylindrical room packed ten high with nested banks of chairs. Once Johnny was in his chair, he could see nothing but Gramma Ginny to his left, a strange man to his right, and the captain on the tiny viewscreen in front of him. The viewscreen was nestled under the seat of someone else stacked just above him. The captain started to speak.

"That was excellent time—twelve minutes. We'll have a good deal more warning than that for a solar storm, so when you hear the Solar Storm Alert, go to your cabins, get your emergency bags and report to the storm shelter. The shielding in this room is sufficient to protect you from the radiation of even the worst solar storm. You will notice that this room has revolving airlocks at the four entrances. This is also our shelter in the extremely unlikely event that we start to lose cabin pressure. When the Loss of Pressure announcement is made, do not go to your staterooms for the emergency bag, but report immediately to the shelter. A steward with an airmask will be there to direct you through the airlock. Above all, do not panic; even a large hole will require more than ten minutes to lower the ship's air pressure by half. Now I will turn you over to the Head Steward."

The face of the head steward appeared on the screen. "A solar storm can last up to a week," she said. "Today we are going to pretend we have a four day storm.

During a storm, no one is allowed to go to their cabins for anything. During a bad storm, one minute outside the shelter will give you a radiation dose that will make you sick. Five minutes is enough to kill you. When you enter the shelter you must bring everything you need in your emergency bag or do without. As you notice, there is nothing to do in this room but sit. There is a large reading library available through your individual consoles, provided you remembered to bring your reading glasses."

Johnny heard Gramma Ginny groan as she searched through her emergency bag for the nonexistent glasses.

"There are four toilets and four showers in the cylindrical bulkhead at center of the room," continued the head steward. "We have plenty of soap, water, and even toothpaste, but did you remember your favorite razor and toothbrush?" Johnny heard mutterings from around him.

"It's now the end of day one, and time for a refreshing shower and a change of underwear," said the head steward. More groans.

"It's the start of day two, we'll be serving a cold but nourishing breakfast, and it's time to take the morning medicine your doctor has recommended." Johnny heard a word he wasn't supposed to hear.

"I think the lesson is clear," said the head steward, with an amused smile. "When you repack your emergency bags back to your staterooms, please make sure that they contain everything you could possibly need if you had to spend the rest of the trip in the shelter. Good day."

It wasn't long before the Longliner was in a high orbit above the Moon. The captain had left them in a gravity gradient stabilized mode that kept the viewing ports at the front of the ship constantly facing the lunar surface. The ship was so long that the slight amount of gravity gradient was enough to drift them forward so that they were touching the windows.

Dad was especially interested in the stop at the Moon since his CERN European Nuclear Research Organization was building its next particle accelerator ring on the moon. The sizes of the machines needed to win the next Nobel Prize were now so large that they could no longer be fitted into the continent of Europe. This ring was designed to circle entirely around the Moon, hopping from mountain top to mountain top where possible, and from tower to tower when it had to pass over the lunar plains. The new machine was called the LUPEC, for LUnar Positron-Electron Collider. A beam of electrons was going to circle around the Moon in one direction while a beam of antielectrons or positrons was going to circle around the Moon in the opposite direction. At six different mountain tops spaced around the Moon, the two high energy streams were designed to pass through each other to produce particle-antiparticle collisions approaching one thousand tera-electron-volts of energy or one peta-electron-volt. The LUPEC was actually going to be cheaper to build than the previous, much smaller, machines built on Earth. There was no need to dig an underground tunnel to provide a shield for the stray synchrotron radiation from the high speed electrons and positrons, or to install a vacuum pipe to keep out the air.

At one point, the circular orbit of their spacecraft nearly matched the track of the ring on the lunar surface below, and Dad pointed out the mountain-top sites and the towers under construction as they passed over them. Over on the lunar backside the LUPEC passed near a large installation, mostly underground.

"That's the first large antimatter factory that was built off the Earth," said Dad. "The Russians constructed it here on the lunar backside in 2020, powering it with large nuclear reactors instead of solar cells. It was designed to produce about ten kilograms of antimatter a year. It's still in use, but we have much more powerful and efficient antimatter factories now at the glassers around Earth."

Johnny watched the lunar scenery roll by until he fell asleep floating in free fall. Dad strapped him into a chair in the lounge and let him sleep. He was finally awakened by the klaxon announcing the starting of the engines for their journey to Mars. The noise of the horn woke Johnny up.

"Are we there yet?"

The weeklong journey to Mars was uneventful, with no meteor strikes, no solar storms, and no space pirates. On the second day they passed close enough to an incoming comet that they could observe it with one of their telescope-equipped cameras. The ship's scotty was controlling the camera and commenting.

"It hasn't developed much of a tail yet," the scotty said, "and probably won't, since it's an old comet and doesn't get too close to the sun. Those comets are where we get the methane and other hydrocarbons that we use for propellant in our antimatter ships. Underneath the dark carbon-dust surface is a dirty snowball of frozen methane, water, carbon dioxide, and ammonia. We save the nitrogen in the ammonia for fertilizer, and convert the rest into hydrocarbons and water."

The turnaround came early on the fourth day. The captain had them go to their staterooms and strap in for the maneuver. Mom had given Johnny a space-sickness pill at breakfast, but he had fooled around with it, rolling it across the table in the low gravity, and had lost it. When turnaround came, Johnny's breakfast turned around too and came up all over the stateroom. Fortunately Gramma Ginny caught most of it in midair with a towel before the ship acceleration returned and plastered it to the floor and bedding.

Later on in the fourth day the captain made an

unexpected announcement. "If you come to the main viewing lounge, you may be able to see one of the fastest objects in the solar system. There is an Interplanetary Express overnight delivery rocket from Earth to Mars catching up to us. It has just made turnover and is pointing its nozzle in our general direction. Since we have also made turnover so the front of our ship is pointing at Earth, you should be able to see the express rocket easily from the front view windows."

Everyone crowded into the lounge and looked out at the bright star moving visibly toward them. The ship's scotty had the telecamera on it too, but you could see little on the screen but the glare of the antimatter powered exhaust.

"The engineers on Mars had an electrical fire in the control room for the main antimatter power plant at Tharsis Base," said the scotty. "The express rocket is bringing in a new control computer. Those little rockets are engineering marvels that put my engines to shame. They accelerate at ten gravities and reach more than one percent of the speed of light at the half-way point to Mars. Then they flip over and decelerate at ten gravities—getting to Mars in just under twenty-two hours. A true interplanetary overnight express. It's a wonder to me that the engines can survive under the heat, stress, radiation, and acceleration they are under."

"That's one of *my* rocket engines," said Mom quietly but proudly to the scotty. "Our plant builds the engines for Interplanetary Express, and I safety-scan all the engines before they go out."

On the seventh day Johnny woke up early.

"Are we there yet?"

"Almost," said Gramma Ginny. "I can see Mars down at the bottom of our viewport. Hurry and get dressed and we can go out and watch them dock at Phobos. Better take another space-sickness pill." She handed him a pill and a sipper of water from their washstand, and waited until she saw him swallow the pill.

Right after breakfast the klaxon sounded and the main antimatter engines were turned off. The Longliner had matched orbits with Phobos and the landing crew at Hall Station were bringing out a flexible passageway to connect the ship to the tiny moon. They had a half-day on Phobos before they went down to the surface of Mars, and a tour-guide took them on a tour to some nearby sites around Hall Station.

"As you saw when you docked, Phobos is not round and varies from twenty to twenty-seven kilometers in diameter. The reason that it's not round is that the gravity field is too weak to pull the planetoid into a spherical shape. In fact, the gravity is so low, you can almost jump off this planetoid. So you will all be roped together in groups of twenty with two experienced guides at each end."

They all soon learned the slow bounding kangaroo hop that enabled them to move along the dusty surface. Johnny was near the middle of his group and often found himself floating along many meters from the surface. They visited the automated comet and asteroid observatory that searched for new comets and asteroids that were in orbits that might take them into the inner reaches of the solar system where they could be harvested of their metals and volatiles. The longest journey was to the center of Stickney crater, where a team of geologists were using an antimatter drill to map the trapped ice and other volatiles under the surface. The comet head which had made the ten kilometer wide crater in the twenty kilometer wide moon had brought with it a lot of water ice.

They spent the "night" in their staterooms aboard the Longliner and early the next day boarded the Mars aerospace plane that was to take them to the surface of the planet. It was a McDonnell-Douglas AS-3M

Marsclimber, a Mars version of the Spaceclimber that had taken them off the Earth to L-4. They drifted away from Hall Station using chemical rockets, and as soon as they were a safe distance away from the planetoid, the antimatter augmented rocket engines burst forth a flaming plasma jet and the Marsclimber fell out of orbit and dropped toward the surface below. Johnny again had a window seat, but just as things were getting interesting, the insulation shields slid over the viewing ports and they had to watch the rest of their fiery descent through the thin Martian atmosphere on the video.

Since this was a tour group, the captain of the Marsclimber halted their descent when they reached low Martian orbit. He opened the viewing ports, rolled the Marsclimber until the upper view windows were facing the surface, and gave them a guided tour of the planet through the next few orbits. It was winter in the southern half of Mars and the South Pole icecap was fully developed.

The aerospace plane then reignited its antimatter augmented rocket engines, dropped out of low orbit and spiraled downward once again. The extra large air intakes began to suck in the tenuous Martian atmosphere and the engines switched to airbreathing mode. But since the Martian air was mostly carbon dioxide and wouldn't burn, the antimatter had to supply all the energy to heat the air for thrust.

The aerospace plane sailed in over Solis Planum and landed at the long runway at Tharsis Base in the shadow of Pavonis Mons. Although Mars had an atmosphere, it was only one percent that of Earth. As far as the human body was concerned, it was a vacuum. A crawler came out to the plane, mated with their airlock, and took the tour group to the Penelope Hotel in the sprawling town of Boston outside Tharsis Base.

"It sure feels good to get some weight back on after

all those days at low gravity," said Dad. "Thirty-eight percent Earth gravity is just right, you feel light, but your feet stay on the ground." Johnny didn't really like it. He much preferred bounding around in low gravity like he had seven league boots on.

For the next two weeks the tour guides kept them busy visiting one site after another. An antimatter powered Mars Hopper rocket zoomed them in one large leap to the top of Pavonis Mons, then over to Olympus Mons, each twenty-seven kilometers high, then back to Tharsis Base. An antimatter powered crawler took them on an overnight, overland journey to the chaotic terrain that formed the western end of the Valles Marineris.

"It sure looks like underground water subsidence to me," said Gramma Ginny. "But where has all the water gone?"

They next boarded a Mars Airglider. Although the atmosphere is very thin on Mars, an airplane can fly if it has a large enough wingspan. Fortunately, the fuel it carried weighed almost nothing at all, since the energy source for the airplane was the same as most of the vehicles on Mars—antimatter. The Mars Airglider took them slowly down the Valles Marineris, often flying a kilometer or so below the cliff edges of the three-kilometer-deep fissure in the skin of Mars. The deep canyon went on for thousands of miles and they stopped for the night at "Chasma Corners," where the main chasm branched out into two smaller valleys.

The next day they took the northern route along Capri Chasma for a thousand kilometers, then headed north across Chryse Planitia to visit the Mutch Memorial. Viking Lander 1 was still there, surrounded by a low fence that encircled the site at ten meters distance. The ancient lander was covered with red dust and beginning to look like the boulders that it squatted among.

The next hop was a long one, as they flew directly north and finally landed just after midnight in full sunlight at Camp Boring at the entrance to Chasma Boreale. The winds off the pole were too tricky to risk the Mars Airglider, so after some rest, they traveled in a heated antimatter snowmobile that took them up Chasma Boreale to see the layered cliffs of ice and dust that rose up hundreds of meters on each side. Johnny wished that he could go out and make a Martian snowball, but he knew the mixture of water ice and frozen carbon dioxide would be too cold to touch, much less pack into a snowball.

Their last stop was the lowest spot on Mars, the bottom of the Hellas Basin. This region was four kilometers below "sea level" on Mars and the air was much thicker. This was also the site for the other major spaceport on Mars. The two weeks on Mars went all too fast for Johnny.

"Do we have to go so soon?" he asked.

"Perhaps you'll come here some day again by yourself," said Dad. "Haven't you always said that you wanted to be the pilot of an aerospace plane? Perhaps your first command will be a Marsclimber instead of an Earth Spaceclimber. Have to get good grades in school though . . ." he added.

Johnny made a disgusted face. Dad was always jerking him about his schoolwork. He could do better though, he had to admit.

The vertical ascent on the Marsclimber went much faster than their leisurely descent had, and they were back at Phobos in a few hours. During their two weeks on the surface of Mars, the Longliner had gone back to Earth and was now back with a new load of passengers. This time Johnny and Gramma Ginny took the inner cabin and let Mom and Dad have the viewport. They were two days out from Mars when the big moment of the year, and perhaps the decade, rolled around. It was time for the launch of the first interstellar probe to Alpha Centauri. Mom knew all about it, since it was one of her rocket engines that was going to send the robot probe on its way.

"It was one of those coincidences that occurs only rarely on a production line, even a precision production line such as we have for rocket engine assembly," Mom was telling the captain at dinner. "I had heard rumors about Number 33 even before it came to me for inspection. Every part for every pump, actuator, and subassembly had exactly the right tolerance, no more, no less. Every subassembly performed at the top of its range. The assemblers began to talk about Number 33 and take special care when they were working on some part of it. By the time it got to me for final flaw inspection I could find no flaws *anywhere*. Then, in the final test stand checks, Number 33 set a record for efficiency and thrust that has not been exceeded to date. We knew we had a special engine and we decided not to deliver it to International Express, but keep it for a special time. That time is now."

"Do you mean the engine on that interstellar rocket is the same type that's used for the overnight express rockets?" asked the captain in amazement.

"The interstellar rocket is going to accelerate at ten gravities, just like the overnight express rocket. Since they are antimatter rockets, the mass ratio will be the same for the interstellar rocket as for the overnight express, four tons of propellant for a one ton vehicle. The major difference is that instead of having to go at ten gravities for one day, the interstellar rocket is going to have to keep up the ten gravity acceleration for eighteen days," said Mom. "Eighteen days at ten gravities multiplies out to half the speed of light. We think Number 33 can hang together for eighteen days."

"Amazing!" said the captain.

"There are a few differences, of course," said Mom. "The fuel tanks will hold liquid hydrogen instead of liquid methane to improve the exhaust velocity, and instead of carrying three hundred grams of antimatter, the interstellar rocket will be starting out with three hundred kilograms. The combustion chamber will be running at a higher temperature since we'll be using a higher ratio of antimatter to propellant, but the superconducting coils around Number 33 have already demonstrated a stronger magnetic bottle than any other rocket, and the cooling systems were also the best we have ever seen. I'm sure Number 33 can do it."

The ship's scotty had found the coordinates for the launch point of the interstellar rocket and had the longest focus telescope pointed in that direction. The rocket was at a safe distance from L-5, not far from Feynman City, where most of the advanced space engineering took place. The scotty had half the video monitors showing the countdown as broadcast by an Earth television station, while the other monitors showed the view through the ship's long focus telescope, which was watching the dark region near the tiny speck of light that was Feynman City. The countdown was down to five minutes. The video link from Earth was showing the long sleek lines of the interstellar vehicle. The words "Centauri Express" were written on the body, while the engine proudly showed the number "33."

"Of course, the launch has already occurred," said the scotty. "Since it takes the television signals more than six minutes to get to us here out near Mars."

After about five minutes of waiting, there was a gasp from everyone as the monitors showing the view through the ship's telescope lit up in a brilliant glow and a bright streak started moving visibly across the screen. Two seconds later, on the screens carrying the television relay from Earth, the proud 33 disappeared in a puff of ash, the liquid droplet radiators turned into bright red triangular feathers, and the Earth broadcaster announced in a loud voice, "We have ignition!"

Some of the people near Johnny seemed bothered by the delay, but Johnny knew all about the one second time delay from lunar orbit to the Earth and back out again.

Johnny looked proudly over at his Mom and found her face full of concern, her hands tightly clenched. She seemed to be muttering something.

"Go! Go! Go!" she was whispering. After a long minute she seemed to relax. She leaned over and whispered to Dad. "If it was going to blow, it would have done it by now. Number 33 is on its way."

"There it goes!" announced the scotty, as the bright streak faded into a tiny white light.

"There it goes," whispered Mom to herself, "and part of me is going with it."

"There it goes," whispered Dad to himself, "from a white streak in a bubble chamber to a white streak through interstellar space in just a hundred years."

"There it goes," whispered Johnny to himself, "and I'm gonna be captain of the first ship to follow it."

✧ BEANSTALKS

The concept of a stairway to heaven is a recurring theme throughout mythology. From the Far East came tales of magicians who could toss the end of a rope into the air, where it would stay, hanging from seemingly nothing. In the ancient children's story, "Jack and the Beanstalk," a beanstalk grows up into the clouds and Jack climbs up the beanstalk to find adventure and riches in the clouds. In the Old Testament we have two examples. In the Book of Genesis, Chapter 11, Verse 4, early mankind used bricks mortared with bitumen in an attempt to build themselves a tower with its top in the heavens. Then later in Chapter 28, Verse 12, Jacob dreamed that there was a ladder set up on the Earth, the top of it reached to heaven, and the angels of God were ascending and descending on it.

Today, we know that one sure way to get to the heavens is to use rocket power. In fact, rockets have been so successful that other methods to reach the heavens have been nearly forgotten. How about those other ancient techniques? Can we build a tower or magic beanstalk and climb up to the stars? Or can we hang a rope ladder onto the nearest star and lower the ladder down to the ground?

Although it may be hard to believe, it may not be too long from now that instead of leaving Earth using rockets, we will emulate Jack and climb up a magic beanstalk to find our own adventure and riches in space.

Or, instead of a beanstalk based on magic, perhaps we can build a modern version of the Tower of Babel.

Is it possible to build a tower up into space? Aerospace engineer Dani Eder has carried out feasibility studies to see if very high towers could be built as platforms to lift telescopes up out of the atmosphere, or as an aid in launching rockets into space. It turns out that under reasonable engineering limits such as cost and adequate safety margins, steel towers could be built up to six kilometers high and aluminum ones to almost ten kilometers high. For comparison, Mount Everest is about nine kilometers above sea level (but on a very broad base). A tower built using presently available graphite-epoxy composite materials could reach a height of fifty kilometers, the altitude that officially designates the boundary of space. But it seems like the limits of the compressive strength of materials will prevent us from ever raising a tower up to the 400 kilometer altitude that the Space Shuttle flies at.

How about a modern version of the Hindu rope trick? Out at the very special distance of 36,000 kilometers from the surface of the Earth (about six Earth radii), there now exist dozens of satellites in geostationary orbit. Here the rotation of the satellite in its orbit is 24 hours, exactly equal to the rotation of the Earth below. Thus, as you stand on the Earth and look up into the sky, the geostationary satellites stay fixed in one position above you while the stars slowly rotate from east to west.

Suppose some friendly giant in a geosynchronous satellite were to let down a long cable—36,000 kilometers long. If the cable were strong enough to hold its own weight, then the cable could reach down to the surface of the Earth. It would be a Skyhook, a magic beanstalk in reverse. Given adequate supplies stashed along the way, a lightweight spacesuit, and enough time, a person would be able to emulate Jack and climb up into space (resting along the way occasionally to enjoy the scenery) instead of having to use a rocket.

One of the first persons to think of the concept of a cable hanging down from geostationary orbit was a Soviet engineer and popular science writer named Yuri Artsutanov. In 1957 a fellow graduate of the Leningrad Technological Institute told him about a tiny whisker of material that was so strong that it could support a 400 kilometer length of itself in the Earth's gravity field. Artsutanov realized that a hanging cable that long would have part of its length far away from the Earth where the gravity field is weaker. Consequently the length could be even longer. Also, if the cable were tapered it could be made even longer still. He worked out the relatively simple equations, but he never published them in an engineering journal where they could be found. Instead, he published the idea as a popular article in the Sunday supplement section of *Komsomolskaya Pravda* (Young Communist Pravda) in 1960.

A Skyhook would be built from the middle out, starting with a cable-making machine at a Central Station in geostationary orbit. For balance, the machine would extrude two cables, one upward and one downward. The cables would be thin at first, then, when the length of the cable hanging down became longer, the thickness of the cable would have to be increased to provide enough strength to support the increasing weight below. The thickness of the upward-growing cable would also have to increase as the cable became longer, but for a different reason. Instead of the Earth gravity pulling on the cable, the pull is due to the centrifugal force from the once per day rotation about the Earth.

If the extrusion rates of the two cables are carefully controlled, then the net pull on the Central Station in geostationary orbit would be zero, and the cable laying machine would remain in geostationary orbit. Eventually, the lower end of the cable would reach the ground (or the top of some convenient near-equatorial mountain) 36,000 kilometers below. At that time, the outgoing cable would be 110,000 kilometers long. The outgoing cable has to be longer than the Earth-reaching cable because of the way the gravity forces and centrifugal forces vary with distance.

If everything was done smoothly and slowly, there would be no horizontal motion of the cables. In fact, the gravity and the centrifugal forces combine to produce a force that helps to maintain the cable exactly vertical. The bottom end of the long cable could now be anchored to the ground so it doesn't blow about in the winds, and a large counterweight (a small asteroid) would be attached to the outer tip. The counterweight, like a stone in a giant sling, would keep the cable under moderate tension to help keep it straight.

A nearly magical material would be needed to construct a Skyhook for the Earth. What is needed is a material that is both strong and light. The best would be a Skyhook made from a tapered fiber of perfect diamond crystal. Unfortunately, making tapered diamond fiber will require the use of a fabrication technology that is presently indistinguishable from magic, and we will have to wait a while for that. In the meantime, crystalline graphite fiber is the best candidate material. Theoretically it is twenty times stronger than conventional steel and four times less dense, making it potentially eighty times better than steel for Skyhook cables. It is because of this high strength-to-weight ratio that you find graphite fibers used in tennis rackets, fishing rods, golf clubs, and other sports equipment. Weaving large cables of graphite fibers with strengths near that of the present tiny whiskers is the major technical hurdle that must be overcome if terrestrial Skyhooks are to became a reality. In the coming years we can expect the strength of the graphite cables to improve until they are adequate for terrestrial Skyhooks. Interestingly enough, they are already more than strong enough for constructing Skyhooks on the Moon and Mars.

Actual measurement of tiny graphite whiskers shows a tensile strength of over two million newtons per square centimeter or three million pounds per square inch. With that strength, a one square centimeter cable of crystalline graphite could lift 210 tons in the gravity field of the Earth. A one centimeter cross-section crystalline graphite cable weighs about 220 kilograms per kilometer of length, so with a 210 ton lifting capability, a graphite cable could support almost a 1000 kilometer length of itself in the gravity field of the Earth. By building the cable with a taper to it, it can be made even longer. Fortunately, the gravity field of the Earth decreases with altitude, so that less taper is needed at the higher altitudes. With a taper of ten-to-one, a graphite cable could be built to go all the way out to synchronous orbit, some 36,000 kilometers above the Earth's surface—and beyond.

The first cable to be lowered down would have a total mass of about 6000 tons. It would have a diameter of about one millimeter at the Earth's surface and would be able to lift only one or two tons. The initial cable, however, could be used in a boot-strap operation to lift more cable up from Earth until it was strengthened a hundred times. Once the Skyhook is in place, then it could be climbed like the proverbial magic beanstalk. For smaller diameter cables, special electrically powered cars would be built to climb up on the outside. If the Skyhook design used a number of cables arranged in a hollow structure, the electrified tracks could be built inside the structure. As each car climbs the beanstalk from the Earth's surface into geostationary orbit, it would consume an appreciable amount of electrical energy. The cost of the electricity, two dollars per kilogram, would be much less, however, than the present cost of using rockets, which is five thousand dollars per kilogram.

As the cable cars climb up the Skyhook, they are always positioned above their anchor point on the Earth below, but like a stone in a sling, they have a higher absolute velocity through space than the anchor point. An object dropped from a cable car during the first few kilometers of travel would fall nearly straight down to the surface below. As the car climbs higher, the point of impact would move toward the east, since the object would leave the cable car at a higher horizontal velocity than the more slowly moving anchor point on the surface of the Earth below. At the 25,000 kilometer point on the cable, an object dropped from the car would have so much horizontal velocity that it would sail over the horizon of the Earth and go into a highly elliptical orbit. At altitudes higher than 25,000 kilometers, objects dropped out of a cable car would go into orbits that became more circular, and closer to a 24 hour period, as the cable car approached 36,000 kilometers.

The turnover point for the cable cars would be the Central Station at 36,000 kilometers up. Here the gravity and centrifugal forces balance. If you drop something out of the cable car (or step out yourself), there will be no motion relative to the cable car. At this point the cable car is traveling horizontally at geostationary orbit velocity. Communication satellite payloads brought up on the cable cars would be simply floated out to become synchronous satellites.

Cars continuing beyond the Central Station would be pulled along the cable by the ever-increasing centrifugal force, like a skater at the end of a "crack-the-whip" chain. The cable cars would have to brake to keep from flying out too fast. If the braking were done by an electric motor, the braking energy could be turned into electricity instead of heat and used to raise the next cable car on its way up.

On reaching the ballast stone, the cable car would be 150,000 kilometers from the center of the Earth and moving with a horizontal velocity of eleven kilometers a second. If the cable car were to let go of the cable at just the right time, the car (now turned spacecraft) would be able to coast slowly to Saturn on a minimum energy orbit or travel rapidly to all the other planets nearer than Saturn.

By reversing the process, returning payloads can be brought back to Earth without the use of heat shields, braking rockets, or atmospheric braking. Also, a Skyhook is a conservative system. If electric motors are used to lift payloads up the elevator and brake payloads going down the elevator, and the mass flow is the same in both directions, incoming traffic would provide all the energy needed to power outgoing traffic.

An Earth Skyhook would be an engineering marvel. The job of building the 36,000 kilometer section down to the Earth would be equivalent in difficulty to building a suspension bridge completely around the Earth. In order to lift appreciable loads, say 100 tons at a time, the Skyhook would have to weigh about 600,000 tons. Fortunately, the carbon needed for the graphite fibers can be found in special kinds of asteroids called carbonaceous chondrites. After the carbon was extracted from the asteroid, the remaining slag could be used as the counterweight.

The construction job would be staggering in scope. To build the 36,000 kilometer Earthgoing section of the Skyhook in five years would require an average construction rate of cable and track of 20 kilometers a day. After the Skyhook was built, the cable cars would have to travel at more than 6,000 kilometers per hour (ten times faster than a jet airplane) in order to make the trip up to the Central Station in less than six hours.

Some kind of magnetic levitation design for the track and cars would be needed, for no rubbing or rolling contact can be tolerated at those speeds.

For protection against space debris, the Skyhook would probably be constructed of many interconnected cables in a large open structure. Thus, orbiting debris smaller than a meter in size would cut only one cable at a time and the slack would be taken up by the others until repairs could be made. Even if cut completely through, the Skyhooks would be quite safe, since the entire structure is in orbit. If a large object like an out-of-control airplane or satellite accidentally cut the cable, the portion below the cut would fall to the ground, but the portion above would stay almost in the same place, rising only slightly because of the reduced load. After things had quieted down, a new starter cable could be dropped down from the cut-off end, and contact reestablished with the Earth's surface.

Mars is the best planet in the solar system for a Skyhook, having both a shallow gravity well and a high rotation rate. Since the 24.5 hour rotation rate for Mars is nearly the same as that of Earth, while its gravity field is only thirty-eight percent that of Earth, a Mars Skyhook using graphite would have to mass only forty times what it could lift. Mars also has a twenty-kilometer high mountain on the equator, Mons Pavonis, that can be used as an anchor point, and a small moon, Deimos, that is available at almost just the right orbit to act as the counterweight. As Arthur C. Clarke showed in his novel, *The Fountains of Paradise*, the problem of a possible collision between the Martian Skyhook and the moon Phobos can be avoided by deliberately exciting the first vibrational bending mode of the Skyhook so that the cable "twangs" to one side just as Phobos passes by. Similar techniques could be used on Earth to avoid the thousand or so larger satellites that orbit the globe.

The first precursors of these Skyhooks have already flown in space. Although the Space Shuttle is a remarkable vehicle that can haul large payloads into orbit, it has one major problem. The volume of space that the Space Shuttle can reach is limited to the small region just outside the atmosphere of Earth. The Shuttle cannot fly up to higher orbits. In fact, nearly all satellites launched by the Shuttle have to have a booster rocket to put them into their final orbits.

It turns out that there is a way for the Space Shuttle to put spacecraft into their proper orbits without using rockets. The Shuttle can use a long cable or tether to "fly" the spacecraft into another orbit. But what makes the spacecraft on the end of the tether "fly" to different altitudes is not the pressure of air, but the tides of gravity.

Because of the way that gravity and centrifugal forces work at orbital altitudes, it is just as easy to send a tether up to a higher altitude as down. The Shuttle, in its orbit about the Earth, has the pull of the Earth's gravity exactly canceled by the centrifugal force due to its orbital motion. It is in free-fall. If the Shuttle sends a spacecraft down on the end of a tether, the spacecraft will experience a stronger gravity pull, but its motion will be that of the Shuttle, so the centrifugal force is smaller than the gravity force and the spacecraft is pulled downward. If the Shuttle sends a spacecraft up on the end of a tether, the Earth gravity pull will be weaker, but the spacecraft, moving at the same speed as the Shuttle, experiences a centrifugal force that is stronger than the gravity, so the spacecraft flies outward.

The first test of a space tether was attempted in July 1992 using the Space Shuttle. Unfortunately the test had to be aborted early because a too-long bolt jammed the reel for the tether line. In the planned Tethered Satellite System (TSS) experiment, a conducting tether 2.5 millimeters (a tenth of an inch) in diameter and twenty kilometers (twelve miles) long was to deploy an Italian research spacecraft upward from the Shuttle. The spacecraft was to be made electrically positive, so as to collect electrons from the ionosphere and pass them down the conductive tether to the Shuttle, which would put the electrons back into the ionospheric plasma with the help of an electron emitter. The motion of the conducting cable through the magnetic field of the Earth was expected to generate up to five thousand volts of electrical potential between the two ends of the tether, and produce up to five kilowatts of electrical power. (The electrical energy, of course, would come from a decrease in the kinetic energy of the Shuttle, causing a decrease in its orbital altitude.) The next TSS experiment on the Space Shuttle is scheduled for 1996. It will involve a repeat of the electrodynamic experiment using a twenty kilometer upward-going tether. This will be followed a year or so later by a 120 kilometer downward-going tether trolling an aerodynamic experiment through the upper atmosphere of Earth.

The first successful tether experiment was carried out in March 1993 by a group led by Jim Harrison and Chris Rupp of NASA Marshall Space Flight Center in Alabama. The tether hardware was manufactured by Joe Carroll of Tether Applications of California, a one-person small business. Carroll wound the tether on its spool in the loft of his home, showing that you don't need to be a giant aerospace corporation to make workable space hardware. The tether was a twenty kilometer long braided polyethylene string, that was three-quarters of a millimeter in diameter and massed seven kilograms. The SEDS (Small Expendable Deployment System) tether experiment piggybacked on a U.S. Air Force Delta II rocket that launched a Navstar Global Positioning Satellite from Cape

Canaveral. After the satellite had been released from the booster stage and the primary mission had been accomplished, the SEDS package was activated an orbit later, and the SEDS payload deployed over Guam. As the payload drifted away from the Delta booster, it pulled the tether off the spool though a tension controller. The constant pull of the tether applied a deceleration force to the payload that slowed it down and caused it to fall below the booster. By the time the full twenty kilometers of tether had been pulled out one orbit later, the payload had been slowed enough that it could no longer stay in orbit, and it fell into the atmosphere at the preplanned reentry point over Baja California. This experiment showed that something as simple, cheap, and as benign as a ball of string can replace a retro-rocket for precisely deorbiting payloads from space.

In the next SEDS experiment, carried out in March 1994, the tether remained fastened to the Delta booster stage, and the payload hung down below the Delta as they both orbited the Earth. The objective of this experiment was to collect data on tether lifetime due to meteoroids cutting the tether. The 20-kilometer tether was at the seven kilometer point after 4 days, but was not cut again during the 55-day mission.

The lifetime of tethers in space is limited by space debris. Recent measurements of crater number versus size on aluminum panels which had spent six years in space, indicate that most space debris is still caused by micrometeorites and not manmade space debris. Using this recent information on space debris, the lifetime of the TSS electrodynamic single-strand tether with its diameter of 2.5 millimeters and length of twenty kilometers would be predicted to be six months. For the follow-on aerodynamic experiment tether with a smaller diameter and a length of 120 kilometers, the predicted lifetime is only a half a month. Longer tethers would have even shorter lifetimes unless their diameter (and consequently their mass) were increased.

The lifetime problem has been overcome with the design by the aerospace engineer, Rob Hoyt, of a failsafe multistrand tether that increases the single strand lifetime by factors of a hundred or more with no increase in mass. The lifetimes of this multistrand tether are so long, and the degradation is so graceful and failsafe, even in the highly unlikely event of multiple cuts in close proximity, it looks like these multistrand tether designs will never need repair during their operational lifetime. With this tether design available, transorbital, lunar, and interplanetary propulsion scenarios can be contemplated without undue concern for manmade space debris or natural meteorites.

As the NASA engineers fly more of these space tether systems without incident, then perhaps some of the more risky tether experiments can be attempted. A payload can be sent upwards a number of hundreds of kilometers from the shuttle on the end of the tether. Normally a satellite at this altitude will be moving slowly, but the Space Shuttle will be pulling it along with a velocity appropriate to the Shuttle's much lower orbit. Since the upwards deployed satellite is moving faster than normal, if it is released from the end of the tether it will fly up into a higher elliptical orbit. The peak of this orbit could be high enough to catch onto a tether hanging down from a space station in geostationary orbit. Longer tethers could even launch a payload into an Earth escape trajectory.

Simple tethers may also be useful in planetary exploration. In one proposed approach, a surface sampling payload is sent out ahead of a spacecraft in low orbit around one of the airless bodies of the solar system, like the Moon, Mercury, the asteroids, or one of the smaller moons of the outer planets. The main spacecraft would then pull on the tether, slowing the payload down so it is shifted into an elliptical orbit that intersects the surface of the planet ahead of it. The payload would then drop like a well-walked wet fly and touch down for five to ten seconds on the surface of the planetoid. As the main spacecraft passed by, it would pull up the payload containing surface analyses and the valuable core sample extracted during its brief sojourn on the surface.

There is another version of the Skyhook, which I call the Rotavator. It uses a cable that is much shorter than the geostationary orbit Skyhook. The Rotavator rotates as it orbits about the Earth, the ends of the cable touching down near the surface. This concept was the brainchild of Yuri Artsutanov, the same person who also first thought of the Skyhook. In 1969 Artsutanov published the idea of synchronously rotating cables as a popular article in the magazine *Znanije-Sila* (Knowledge is Force). The magazine illustrator's title drawing for the article shows a huge wheel rolling over the surface of a small Earth—an apt illustration of the concept, since the rotating cable acts like a pair of spokes rotating inside an invisible wheel. It was Hans Moravec, however, who published the first technical paper on the concept.

The Moravec design for a Rotavator uses a cable that is 8500 kilometers long. This is two-thirds the diameter of the Earth, but only one-quarter the length of a 36,000 kilometer geostationary Skyhook. The central portion of the cable would be put into an orbit that is 4250 kilometers high within a period of 183 minutes. The cable would be set to spinning at one revolution every 122 minutes. Three times each orbit, once every 61 minutes, one of the ends of the cable would touch down into the upper portions of the Earth's atmosphere. These entry points would be the three ports of embarkation from the Rotavator Transportation

System. Because of the large dimensions of the bodies involved, the ends of the cable would seem to come down into the upper atmosphere nearly vertically, with almost no horizontal motion. The cable, although made of one of the stiffest materials known, would still have some stretch to it. This means that a coupling vehicle at the end of the cable could use jets and aerodynamic forces to "fly" the elevator car at the end of the cable to a rendezvous point. This could allow the elevator car to arrive ahead of its nominal touchdown time and delay its return to orbit. There would be almost a full minute available for dropping off and picking up cargo and passengers.

A 8500 kilometer long Rotavator made out of crystalline graphite and designed to touch down three times per orbit would have a taper of about twelve to one. To be able to lift a 100 ton cargo into space it would have to have a total mass of about 7500 tons. At touchdown the end of the cable would approach and leave the Earth with an acceleration of 1.4 Earth gravities. Counting the one Earth gravity field of the Earth itself, there will be a total acceleration at liftoff of only 2.4 Earth gravities, less than that experienced by the Space Shuttle astronauts.

A future scenario for a Rotavator Transportation System would probably work like this: You check in at any one of the major hypersonic airports around the world, clear Earth customs, and board a small capsule six meters in diameter and twenty meters long. The capsule will look like a section cut out of a modern widebodied jet aircraft. There are seats for about thirty passengers, with cargo space below. There is a diminutive cockpit/control center in a bubble topside, containing an alert capsule crew. The crew checks on the sealing of the capsule as it is carried away on the bed of a truck to the corner of the field, where automatic rollers move the capsule onto the flatbed spine of a hyperlift cargo airplane. Fairings slide out to merge the body of the capsule into the midsection of the plane. Now aerodynamically restored, the aircraft taxis down the field and takes off. It reaches altitude over the nearby ocean and accelerates to Mach 3. The capsule crew has little to do except monitor the radar displays while the crew of the hyperlift plane takes it higher in altitude and speed, heading southward for a rendezvous in space and time with the Rotavator. The rate of climb of the aircraft slows as the atmosphere becomes thinner. The plane passes through the fifty kilometer altitude that used to mark the difference between a pilot and an astronaut, but there is no pause as it climbs higher on its powerful oxygen-augmented jets.

There is crackling conversation between the aircraft crew, the capsule crew, and the tether grapple crew still hundreds of kilometers overhead, diving downward on the rapidly dropping grapple-craft at the end of the Rotavator cable. The aircraft crew unlatches the capsule and dives down and away, leaving the wingless egg to soar on through the nearly empty upper atmosphere in a long arcing trajectory that will end in a parachute recovery if something goes wrong. The capsule sails upwards toward the rendezvous point with its crew busy. Looking out the sides through the heavily tinted windows, you can see attitude control jets flash as the crew keeps the capsule in proper position and orientation for the pickup. You then look up through the ceiling ports to see a similar flaring of jets from the grapple-craft streaking vertically downward, trailing a long thin thread. The grapple-craft comes to a hovering stop a little way above the capsule, then slowly drifts downward.

Carefully, taking their time, the grapple-crew attaches the four grapple hooks to the lifting lugs at the top of the capsule. The capsule crew confirms attachment, then the grapple-craft adds its jets to those of the capsule to match speed with the cable. The free fall environment of the dropping capsule is slowly replaced with an upward acceleration. In ten seconds, the acceleration reaches 2.4 gravities, and you are glad that you are strapped into the comfortable seat beneath you. Having started at 80 kilometers altitude, in five minutes the capsule reaches 260 kilometers altitude and a velocity of 1.2 kilometers per second. The acceleration slowly drops as you continue your ride into outer space, traveling on the whip end of a fine thread. After thirty minutes the capsule is at the high point in its giant swing through space and you look down on the blue-white globe 8500 kilometers below. There is a warning klaxon and an announcement from the capsule pilot. You strap in securely, there is a multiple click as the grapples release, then you and the capsule are in free fall, heading for the Moon with a velocity of nine kilometers per second. You settle down with a good book. It will be twelve hours before you get there.

After two books, two meals, and a nap (disturbed by the unfamiliarity of free fall), the capsule arrives in the vicinity of the Moon. Here it is again met by a grapple-craft crew on the Lunar Rotavator and is lowered almost to the lunar surface. There the capsule is handed over to a jet-tug that takes you to Copernicus Base. You are home once again, in familiar surroundings, and glad to get away from the oppressive gravity, air, and crowds of Earth.

A Rotavator on the Moon would have an enormous advantage over rockets for providing resupply and crew rotation needed for space industrialization. A Lunar Rotavator could be made with presently available materials, like the superfiber Kevlar. With a density of only 1.44 times that of water and a tensile strength of 280,000 newtons per square centimeter (400,000 psi), it has about five times the strength-to-weight of steel.

Kevlar is presently being used in large quantities for bullet-proof clothing, radial tires, and parachutes. A 130 ton Kevlar Rotavator around the Moon would be able to lift and deposit ten tons every twenty minutes. Rotavators could also be used on any of the other moons in the solar system. Jupiter's Ganymede and Saturn's Titan are larger than the Earth's Luna, but a Kevlar Rotavator with a taper of six to one would suffice for these bodies.

A variant of the Rotavator concept is the Bolo satellite. The Bolo is a more modest version that is shorter in length, but rotates faster. It has been studied in detail by the former scientist-astronaut Philip Chapman as a possible near-term addition to a more general space transportation system. His basic design is a rotating cable with relatively large end-mass stations. Some versions have a central station at the center of mass of the system.

In the Chapman design for a Bolo Space Transportation System, one Bolo would be in low Earth orbit and the other would be in geostationary orbit. A payload would be launched from the Earth using either a rocket, the Space Shuttle, or some new hypervelocity single-stage-to-orbit vehicle. The payload would go into a low energy arcing trajectory that would rendezvous with the lower tip of the Bolo in low Earth orbit. The payload is attached to the Bolo and the launch vehicle returns to Earth. The payload is released from the Bolo at the highest point of its swing. This puts it into a transfer ellipse orbit with the apogee near geostationary orbit. At the top of the transfer orbit the payload would rendezvous with the second Bolo, whose center of mass is in geostationary orbit. If the payload is going on to the Moon or elsewhere, it waits until the direction is right and is slung by the Bolo into an escape orbit. If its destination is geostationary orbit, it is hauled up the cable of the Bolo to the Central Station and floated off to join the rest of the satellites ringing the Earth at 36,000 kilometers altitude. While awaiting the next payload, the angular momentum and energy of the Bolos would be replenished by means of on-board, high-efficiency solar powered thrusters.

A big advantage of the Bolo Space Transportation System is that the payload would not have to be launched with the normal full orbital velocity of almost eight kilometers a second that is needed to get into low Earth orbit. Instead, the payload only needs to reach six kilometers a second. This relatively small change in required launch velocity capability translates into a fifty percent increase in payload mass delivered to a Bolo rendezvous compared to insertion into low Earth orbit. More importantly, the reduced velocity requirement greatly increases the feasibility of constructing a single-stage-to-orbit (SSTO) aerospace plane than can take off from a normal runway and deliver payloads into space.

At maximum throughput, this system is capable of transferring over 4000 payloads of twenty-five tons each or 100,000 tons to geostationary orbit each year. This is thirty times the mass of the Bolos in the system. For a while, as we built space stations and solar power satellites, the mass flow outward will be greater than the mass flow inward. The energy and momentum in the payloads comes from the Bolos and it will be necessary to haul up propellant to keep the Bolos spinning and orbiting at the proper altitudes. To minimize the amount of propellant needed, it would be desirable for the mass flow down through the Bolo system to equal the mass flow up.

To supply energy to a Bolo system, a new breed of wildcatter might spring into being. It might be profitable for some entrepreneur to haul back an iron-nickel asteroid and sell chunks of it to the Bolo Space Transportation System operators—not for raw materials to build things, but as a source of energy to power the Bolos. Blocks of asteroid would be sent swinging down the Bolo system as payloads came swinging up. A simple drag brake, made from asteroidal material, might be sufficient to reduce the terrestrial impact velocity below the speed of sound and the asteroidal material would pile up into a mountain of nickel-iron ore that could be sold for scrap (by the same entrepreneur) after all the valuable gravitational potential energy had been extracted from it.

Similar spinning Bolo cables in solar orbits between the planets could act as transfer points or "momentum banks" to cut the travel time between the planets in the solar system. Instead of heading off on a low velocity trajectory toward a distant planet that may be in a bad position on the other side of the Sun at that time of year, the capsules would head at high speed for the nearest momentum transfer Bolo. As they approach the spinning cable, they would chose the point along the spinning thread that matches their approach velocity. Once attached, the capsule would then move along the cable, climbing up or down in the centrifugal field, until the capsule reached the point on the Bolo that had the velocity needed for the next leg in the journey. There would be a short waiting period until the direction was correct, then with a command to the attachment hooks, the capsule would be freed from the Bolo to go flying off into space toward its distant objective. As long as more mass is dropped inward down the gravity well of the Sun than is going out, no energy source would be needed to operate this interplanetary space transportation system once it was set into motion.

Hanging a cable down from the sky using the tensile strength of materials is just one way of making a magic beanstalk. There is another way. Like Jack's magic beanstalk, this beanstalk grows from the ground up, but unlike a Tower or a Skyhook, it does not depend upon either the compressive or tensile strength of materials. I call it the Space Fountain, for it holds objects up in space in the same way that a water fountain supports a ball bobbing at the top of its vertical jet of water.

The Space Fountain concept originated in early 1980 in the etheric depths of a computer net. Some scientists who usually work in artificial intelligence, Marvin Minsky of MIT, and John McCarthy and Hans Moravec of Stanford were speculating back and forth over the net about variations on the Skyhook concept with some scientists at Lawrence Livermore National Laboratory who usually work on laser fusion, Roderick Hyde and Lowell Wood. One of the ideas was a method of supporting the upper ends of a Skyhook at altitudes that were much less than geostationary orbit altitudes. This would be done with a stream of pellets that would be shot from a space platform hovering motionless up at 2000 kilometers altitude to another platform partway around the Earth. The pellets would be deflected by that platform to the next platform until the polygonal pellet stream made its way around the Earth back to the original station. The deflection of the pellets at each station would be sufficient to support that station in the gravity field of the Earth at that altitude. Since the stations would be only 2000 kilometers from the surface of the Earth instead of 36,000 kilometers, it would be more feasible to find materials strong enough to hang Skyhooks from the stations down to the surface of the Earth. There was still some concern expressed by the computernet debaters whether a strong enough material could be found to make a cable even 2000 kilometers long.

I joined the discussion on the net at about that time and suggested that instead of a dynamic compression hexagonal pellet stream held together with Skyhooks under tension, a pellet stream be shot straight up from the surface of the Earth to support a pellet deflector station at the upper end that would reflect the pellet stream back down to the surface again. There was initially some skepticism by the others on the net that the idea would work, because of the Earth's atmosphere at the lower altitudes and the Coriolis forces due to the rotation of the Earth. Further hard work and detailed engineering calculations by Rod Hyde showed, however, that the concept was valid. Hyde has now worked out all the engineering design details for a Space Fountain right down to the design of the transistors to switch the currents in the projectile accelerators and decelerators.

In the Hyde design for a Space Fountain, a stream of projectiles is shot up the bore of a hollow tower. As the projectiles travel along the tower they are slowed down by electromagnetic drag devices that extract energy from the upgoing stream and turn it into electricity. As the projectiles are braked, they exert a lifting force on the tower which supports the weight of the tower. When the projectiles reach the top of the tower, they are turned around by a large bending magnet. In the turnaround process they exert an upward force on the station at the top of the tower, keeping it levitated above the launch point. [See Figure 5.]

As the projectiles travel back down the tower they are accelerated by electromagnetic drivers that use the electrical energy extracted from the upgoing stream of projectiles. The push exerted by the tower drivers also acts to support the weight of the tower. The projectiles reach the bottom of the tower with almost the same velocity that they had when they were launched. The stream of high speed projectiles is then bent through 90 degrees by a bending magnet so that it is traveling horizontally to the surface in an underground tunnel. The projectile stream is then turned in a large circle by more bending magnets and energy is added by electromagnetic drivers to bring the projectiles back up to the original launch velocity. The beam of projectiles is then bent one more time by 90 degrees to send it back up the tower again to repeat the cycle. Thus, the Space Fountain acts as a continuous mass driver with captive projectiles. The various parts of the external structure are stressed by the transfer of momentum from the pellet stream. Together, the stressed structure and flowing projectile stream form a rigid, stable structure that is not limited in height by the strength of materials.

Since the projectiles are slowed down or sped up just enough to balance the gravitational force on the tower at every point, there is no requirement anywhere for ultrastrong materials. In the lower parts of the tower there will have to be an airtight pipe supported between the Deflector Stations to keep out the atmosphere so that the drag on the projectiles is negligible. But after the first one hundred kilometers the only structure that would be needed is a minimal framework to hold communication and power lines, and the guide tracks for the elevator cars.

To first order, no energy is needed to support the Space Fountain. When the projectiles return to the base of the tower, they have essentially the same speed and energy as they started with. Their momentum has been changed, but not their energy. As a result, the input power required to support the Space Fountain is determined by the inefficiency in the electromagnetic motors and air drag on the projectiles.

One of the major advantages to the Space Fountain concept is that it can be built slowly from the ground up. The driver loop and the bending magnets in the

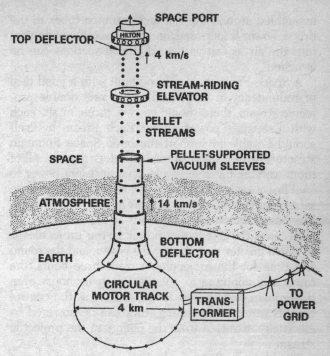

Fig. 5—Space Fountain

Base Station are constructed first, then the Top Station with its turnaround magnets is constructed right above it. The system is loaded with projectiles and tested out at full power with the Top Station sitting safely just above the Earth's surface. Once these major components have been thoroughly tested out, then the power is increased, and the projectile velocity rises until the Top Station starts to lift off the ground. More projectiles are added and the Top Station rises up a few hundred meters, pulling up out of the ground a section of vacuum pipe and the first Deflector Station with it. The next Deflector Station and section of pipe are assembled around the exit and entrance tubes to the driver, power is increased, and the Space Fountain rises into the air as fast as the additional sections can be attached.

A Space Fountain should be built with a good deal of redundancy in it. Instead of just one double projectile stream, there should be two, three, or six, each with a separate power supply. Each stream by itself should be able to support the basic Space Fountain structure with a small amount of safety margin. All of them working together would have sufficient power to haul heavy loads up into space while providing adequate safety margin for minor failures and other problems like heavy transverse wind loads at the surface.

Because the circulating power in the projectiles is so much greater than the driving power, and the round trip time for the projectiles is over three hours, the tower will continue to operate for many hours even if the main drive power failed, as long as the control circuits were still operating (they can be powered by electricity extracted from the energy in the projectile stream).

The elevators that would take payloads up the Space Fountain could conceivably ride up tracks on the tower structure using electrical power supplied by the tower, treating the Space Fountain solely as a mechanical structure. A more attractive option would be to design the tower structure, the Deflector Stations, and the elevator cars so that the cars can interact directly with the projectile streams themselves rather than coupling to the tower structure at all. In this manner, both the momentum needed to hold the elevator car up in Earth gravity and the energy needed to raise it to a higher level will come directly from the projectile stream.

One straightforward design, which I used in my science fiction novel *Starquake*, had a Space Fountain with six separate pairs of projectile streams in a hexagonal pattern. Each Deflector Station was hexagonal with two triangular cutouts to let the triangularly shaped upgoing and downgoing elevators pass through. Each elevator rode on three pairs of projectile streams, dragging on the upgoing streams and pushing on the downgoing streams. Their couplers were strong enough that they could decouple from one or more projectile streams and ride on the rest. By doing this sequentially, they could pass over the stream couplers to the Deflector Stations.

What is most amazing about the design studies that Rod Hyde has done for the Space Fountain is that none of the design parameters requires the use of exotic materials. As Rod Hyde likes to point out, this is a Skyhook that we can build now. Yes, the structure is immense in mass and length compared to anything that we build now. Yes, it will take years to power it up and push it into the sky. Yes, it will take a city-worth of power to keep it running. But the payoff is enormous. The Space Fountain can carry a payload at any one time that is two percent of its total mass. If that payload moves at a reasonable speed of one kilometer per second once it gets out in vacuum, it can make the 30,000 kilometer trip up the Space Fountain in eight hours. At that rate, the amount of mass transmitted into space by just one Space Fountain is six million tons per year, just for the cost of the electrical power to run it. This is indeed a magic beanstalk that could open up space for exploration, industrialization, and finally colonization.

A Space Fountain does not have to go straight up. The projectiles from the Base Station could be sent off at an angle in a large partial orbital arc that intersects the ground some distance away. A second Base Station could then receive the stream of projectiles, turn them around and send them back to the first Base Station, completing the loop. This concept has been studied in detail by Paul Birch and Keith Lofstrom. The Keith Lofstrom design is called a Launch Loop. It has a long straight section on top that is used to launch payloads into low Earth orbit. The projectiles used in the Launch Loop are bars of iron. The ends of the bars are interleaved like tongue and groove boards into a continuous ribbon of iron moving at twelve kilometers a second. Surrounding the two high-speed projectile streams is a non-moving hollow double-track system that shields the moving projectile stream from the atmosphere. The track contains sensors, cables, control electronics, permanent magnets, electromagnets, and parachutes in case of catastrophic system failure. The track supports itself by hanging one centimeter below the ribbon of iron using the attractive forces from permanent magnets augmented by active electromagnetic control forces to maintain the spacing. The track is also designed to support vehicles that ride on the outside of the stationary track using electromagnetic levitation, while extracting kinetic energy by coupling magnetically to the high speed iron ribbon inside the track. The ribbon of iron bars is launched from the West Turnaround Terminal by a mass driver at about a fifteen degree angle to the surface. The ribbon climbs to about 120 kilometers altitude where it is deflected by the West Deflector Station into a trajectory that follows the Earth's surface below.

The path of the iron ribbon is that of the orbit of a satellite at 120 kilometers altitude modified slightly by the weight of the track that it must support. The twelve kilometer per second "orbital speed" of the iron ribbon is much greater than the true orbital speed of eight kilometers per second at this altitude, so the ribbon has a tendency to fly outward. This net upwards force on the ribbon means it can support a weight of over a kilogram per meter of length of non-moving track while remaining parallel to the Earth's surface. This "straight" portion of the Launch Loop continues on for 2000 kilometers to the East Deflector Station, where the ribbon is deflected downward to the East Turnaround Terminal. There the ribbon of iron bars is turned around, brought up to speed with the mass driver and launched on the return path. The vehicles are hauled up on 120 kilometer long elevator cables to the West Deflector Station and placed on the acceleration track. They are launched from there to the east in order to utilize the rotation of the Earth to aid in reaching the desired terminal velocity. The vehicles slip-couple to the rapidly moving iron ribbon with magnetic fields and accelerate at three Earth gravities. Depending upon their desired final destination, the vehicles can be launched with any velocity up to Earth escape velocity of eleven kilometers per second. The Launch Loop can be used for landing by simply reversing the process, with the kinetic energy of the returning vehicle being put back into the iron ribbon instead of being dissipated as heat. The excess energy can be used to launch another vehicle or turned back into electricity by using the electromagnetic mass drivers as electromagnetic brakes. A single Launch Loop could easily launch a five ton vehicle to escape velocity every hour with an input of 200 megawatts of electrical power. At five cents per electrical kilowatt-hour, that amounts to two dollars per kilogram for launching payloads into space.

An ultimate extension of the Launch Loop concept would be an orbital ring of projectiles. Like many beanstalk concepts, the idea was independently invented by a lot of people, but the person who has done most of the hard engineering studies is Paul Birch. In the Paul Birch design of an Orbital Ring system, a ring of massive projectiles is placed in a low Earth orbit. Riding on this ring, supported electromagnetically, are Ring Stations that stay in one place above some designated point on Earth. Hanging down from these Ring Stations are Skyhooks made from cables with high tensile strength to mass ratio.

Paul Birch has found that since the Ring Stations can be used to deflect the projectiles in the Orbital Ring sideways as well as vertically, it is possible to deliberately cause the Orbital Ring to precess around the Earth instead of staying fixed in inertial space while the Earth rotates beneath it. By making the precession rate large enough, the Orbital Ring can be made to precess at the once per day rotation rate of the Earth. The orbit is now "geostationary" without having to be either at the normal geostationary altitude or even in the equatorial plane. This means that using the Orbital Ring concept, a Ring Station can be positioned above any point on Earth that is desired, and anywhere on the globe can be served by a Skyhook instead of just the poles and the equator. A network of Orbital Ring systems crossing, for example, at the poles, could cover the whole planet with an array of Skyhooks and geostationary Ring Stations. Once a payload has climbed up the Skyhook and reached the Orbital Ring, it can then accelerate horizontally by coupling to the moving projectiles in the Orbital Ring. If there were Orbital Rings around each moon and planet, then transport around the solar system would be fast, easy, and inexpensive.

Tethers, Skyhooks, Rotavators, Bolos, Orbital Rings, Launch Loops, and Space Fountains are definitely forms of space transportation that are almost indistinguishable from magic. Yet soon we will see the first experiments with tethers hanging both upward and downward from the Space Shuttle. If those experiments are successful, then the NASA engineers will become more comfortable with these strange new rocketless forms of space propulsion. They will start to pay attention to their own studies, which show the great benefits to be obtained from the use of long tethers for inexpensively hauling large quantities of mass into and around in space.

Newer materials with higher strength to weight ratios are already coming out of the organic and inorganic materials laboratories, driven by the trend toward composite materials in aircraft, automobiles, and sports equipment. These newer materials will make Tethers, Rotavators, and Bolos technically feasible and perhaps even commercially viable now that good engineering solutions have been found for the space debris problem.

Even the projectile stream concepts might come to fruition within the foreseeable future. The first closed loop projectile systems would be used for energy storage. They would be completely underground and used to provide load leveling in an electrical power grid. Next will come long underground kinetic energy power transmission lines, then perhaps a completely enclosed, nonelectric replacement for the overhead line or third rail in subways and electric train systems. We will then be ready to consider Launch Loops, Orbital Rings, and Space Fountains.

One use for the Space Fountain concept will be in constructing tall antenna masts for news events and military operations. Perhaps after a few years of experience with the Fountain Masts, the braver camera crews might be willing to ride up on the Top Station for better overhead shots. Once experience has been gained with smaller Fountain Masts, larger Fountain Towers, perhaps ten to twenty kilometers high, might prove to be commercially viable for radio and television broadcasting in the Plains states and the steppes of Asia. Fountain Towers might also prove to be an economical alternative to communication satellites for point-to-point television and FM radio communication between the various islands of some of the smaller nations in the Pacific Ocean.

The real test of confidence in the Fountain Tower concept will be when buildings many kilometers in height are constructed using Fountain Towers as support beams to hold up the building. There would naturally be multiple redundancy in the number of Fountain Beams in each corner of the building. Each Fountain Beam would have an independent control power supply and there would be enough inertia in the flowing streams of projectiles to stay up for hours even in the event of a main power failure. Finally the Fountain Towers would rise higher and higher until they went into space. We would then have a true Space Fountain, reaching upward into the heavens.

The arched fountain structures can start small. The first ones may be demonstrations for Congress. Fountain Bridges made using subsonic cables inside steel tubing will arc across the Potomac, following the path of George Washington's silver dollar. With the development of superconducting magnets and accelerators, projectile-supported Fountain Bridges can be made across the Channel, the Sahara, the Alps, the Bering Strait, and the waters that separate the Third World islands in the Pacific. Finally the Fountain Bridges will arc so high they will reach into space and become Space Bridges.

There the Space Fountains and the Space Bridges will connect to a system of Orbital Rings running from pole to pole and around the equator in a globe-encircling interlinked network. Built and maintained by the larger nations, the EarthLink net would allow rapid transportation anywhere on Earth and easy access to the solar system. For access to space, all a Third World nation would have to do is build its own Space Bridge or Space Fountain. One end would be firmly embedded in its own soil while the other would be attached to the EarthLink that unites all the nations of the world into one. Once off the Earth, the vehicles of each nation could then couple to the high speed projectiles inside the EarthLink rings to withdraw enough of the energy to send the vehicle on its way into Earth orbit, or on to the Moon and the planets. The projectile stream inside EarthLink would slow slightly as some of its energy is lost, taken away by the disappearing vehicle, but it will gain it back again when the vehicle returns with its massive cargo and passengers, and its equally important, but massless, cargo of knowledge.

Recommended Reading

Ivan Bekey, "Tethers Open New Space Options," *Astronautics & Aeronautics*, Vol. 21, pp. 32 ff (April 1983).

Ivan Bekey and P.A. Penzo, "Tether Propulsion," *Aerospace America*, Vol. 24, pp. 40–43 (July 1986).

Paul Birch, "Orbital Ring Systems and Jacob's Ladders," *Journal of British Interplanetary Society*, I, Vol. 35, pp. 475 ff (1982); II, Vol. 36, pp. 115 ff; III, pp. 231 ff (1983).

Arthur C. Clarke, "The Space Elevator: 'Thought Experiment' or Key to the Universe?," *Advanced Earth Oriented Applied Space Technology*, Vol. 1, pp. 39 ff (Pergamon Press, London, 1981).

Robert L. Forward and Hans P. Moravec, "High Wire Act," *Omni*, Vol. 3, No. 10, pp. 44–47 (July 1981).

Roderick A. Hyde, "Earthbreak: Earth-To-Space Transportation," *Defense Science 2003+*, Vol. 4, #4, pp. 78–92 (August/September 1985).

Hans Moravec, "A Non-Synchronous Orbital Skyhook," *Journal of the Astronautical Sciences*, Vol. 25, #4, pp. 307–322 (October–December 1977).

✧ RACE TO THE POLE

The previous science speculation chapter, "Beanstalks," discussed various possible mechanical technologies, such as towers, beanstalks, and skyhooks, to place things in the sky without having them in orbit around the Earth. There is another technique for hanging things in the sky, and I have the patent on it—U.S. Patent 5,183,225 "Statite: Spacecraft That Utilizes Light Pressure and Method of Use," filed 9 January 1989, issued 2 February 1993. The unique concept described in the patent is to attach a television broadcast or weather surveillance spacecraft to a large highly reflective lightsail, and place the spacecraft over the polar regions of the Earth with the sail tilted so the light pressure from the sunlight reflecting off the lightsail is exactly equal and opposite to the gravity pull of the Earth. With the gravity pull nullified, the spacecraft will just hover over the polar region, while the Earth spins around underneath it. Since the spacecraft is not in orbit around the Earth, it is technically not a satellite, so I coined the generic term "statite" or "-stat" to describe any sort of non-orbiting spacecraft (such as a "weatherstat" or "videostat" or "datastat").

To a person standing on the Earth, the statite will be seen to rotate around the pole once a 24-hour day. If the statite is stationed close to the pole, the circle it makes is small, and more people in that hemisphere can observe the spacecraft for the whole day without it dipping below the horizon. The angle between the Sun and the sail becomes smaller the closer the statite gets to the pole, however, decreasing the light pressure force, so the hovering altitude of the spacecraft increases. In the wintertime, when the North Pole is always on the shadowed side of the Earth, it is easy to have the spacecraft hover directly over the North Pole as a polesitter. It is harder to do in the summertime, when the North Pole is in constant sunshine, but a detailed analysis that takes into account not only the gravitational attraction of the Earth, but the gravitational attraction of the Sun, and the centrifugal force due to the once per year rotation of the spacecraft around the Sun, shows that it is possible to have the spacecraft hover over the sunlit North Pole, provided it is more than 250 Earth radii away.

I originally had the idea for the polesitter back in 1979 when I was working for the Hughes Aircraft Company. But when I worked out the equations and put numbers into them, I found that even for lightsails with very low mass-to-area ratios, the minimum altitude at which the sail would hover was thirty to one hundred Earth radii, many times the six Earth radii altitude of the communication satellites in geosynchronous orbit. The round trip communications time delay from the ground up to the spacecraft and back again was many seconds, obviously much too long for the polesitter to be used as a communications satellite, one of the primary business lines of Hughes, so I dropped the idea. The polesitter concept was revived in 1986 as a possible method of providing continuous surveillance of the polar regions as an early warning system for ballistic missile defense. The concept was kept secret for a few years while the Hughes Defense Systems people tried to interest the Department of Defense in the concept. But with the end of the Cold War in 1989, the *idea was declassified. Hughes didn't want to patent it, since they felt that geosynchronous satellites were adequate. I, however, didn't want to make the same mistake that Arthur Clarke did, when he didn't obtain a patent on his geosynchronous orbit communication satellite idea, so I obtained the rights when I left Hughes in 1987 and filed the patent. So far, I haven't made any money. But with the increased use of direct broadcast television spacecraft, weather surveillance spacecraft, and data link spacecraft, all of which are not bothered by a few seconds time delay, plus the increased crowding of the satellites along the geosynchronous orbital arc, I hope that before the seventeen-year life of the patent runs out on 2 February 2010, that the fictional story that follows becomes reality, and I can collect some royalties. A science fact article describing the statite concept, "Polesitters," was published in* Analog Science Fiction/Science Fact, *Volume 110, No. 13, pages 88-94 in the December 1990 issue. This is the first time this fiction story, based on the science fact article, has seen print.*

———

The race to the South Pole was on!!!

The video news reporters had a field day making comparisons of this modern-day race in 2011 with the first race to the South Pole between Amundsen and Scott exactly one hundred years earlier. This time, however, it was Andy Hawke against "Scotty" MacPherson. But instead of risking their lives by pulling their sleds to the pole across the barren ice of Antarctica, they were risking their fortunes by sailing their videostats to the pole across the barren vacuum of space.

Andy was more experienced and better financed. His first *Polestat* had already claimed the prime position over the North Pole a little over a year ago. Dubbed the *Hovering Hawke* by the press, it was a powerful multichannel broadcast satellite hung under a kilometers-wide square light sail. It hovered stationary in space over the North Pole by balancing out the combined gravity forces of the Earth and Sun with light pressure from the Sun. Now the enormous revenues from the sale of broadcasting services to Canada, Alaska, Russia, northern China, northern Europe, and the Scandinavian countries were financing Andy's entry into the race for the South Pole.

Scotty was a young impetuous "Johnny-Come-Lately" from Australia whose entry was still on the ground. The only "race" going on was the racing stream of promises and public pronouncements coming from his constantly moving mouth. Still the race made news and Scotty had no trouble finding video cameras to talk into.

"Now, in this room you can see the ultrathin film being laid between the front and back support webs," said Scotty into the video camera, an eager gleam showing up in his light blue eyes. The cam'er moved his camera's point-of-view away from the animated face under the mop of red-brown hair and zoomed through the thick glass window into the large airless room. Hanging from the tall ceiling at one end was a complex apparatus shuttling spools of fine wire back and forth, weaving a ten-meter-wide web of wires that arched down to join a similar web coming down from a duplicate weaving apparatus at the other end of the room.

Just where the two wide webs joined together was a glowing furnace. From the furnace misted a fine spray of molten aluminum onto a long, rapidly rotating metal cylinder. The liquid aluminum instantly froze into a ultrathin metal film which was pulled off the bottom of the metal cylinder and sandwiched between the two wire webs. The wire and film sandwich was welded into a single wide belt by electrical current passing between two highly polished rollers, and then the belt was wound up into a long roll.

"The aluminum film is so thin you can see through it," said Scotty. "That's why we have to make it in a vacuum chamber. If air ever got to it, the oxygen would disintegrate it." He held up a small glass container containing a section of wire mesh with a shiny thin film of metal stretched over it. He put the container up to his eye and the video camera looked through the film at the dim image of his eye on the other side.

"Doesn't that defeat the purpose of the film?" asked the video reporter conducting the interview. "The way I understand it, the force needed to levitate your *Heliostat* is supposed to come from the sunlight bouncing off the film. If it's transparent, you won't get any lift."

"But the thinner you make the film, the lighter it is, so the easier it is for the sunlight to lift it," replied Scotty. "When you go through the numbers, it turns out the optimum thickness is when about forty percent of the light goes through the film and sixty percent reflects off." He stopped and pointed into the room. "That roll you see being made is the twelfth and last one. As soon as it's installed in its vacuum canister and attached to the spacecraft, we'll be ready to launch." He turned away from the camera and started to walk off. "Now, let me show you the spacecraft itself."

Scotty led the video reporter and the cam'er through a corridor into a large hangar-like building. In the center of the room was a tall cylindrical structure. Surrounding the central cylinder were eleven canisters, with space for a twelfth.

"The *Heliostat* has twelve long blades like a helicopter," said Scotty. "There are six blades on the top that will rotate in one direction and six on the bottom that will go in the other direction. We shoot the whole thing straight up in the air using a rocket, and once it gets to the proper position, we unfurl the light-reflecting blades like unrolling a window shade. The whole process takes only a few hours, even though the blades are twenty kilometers long."

The reporter interrupted. "Then the sunlight reflecting off the blades provides an upward light pressure force that counteracts the downward gravity force of the Earth, just like the *Polestat* Andy Hawke has over the North Pole."

Scotty looked slightly annoyed at the mention of Andy and his *Polestat*. "It isn't just the Earth gravity," reminded Scotty. "There is also the gravity force of the Sun and the centrifugal force of the motion around the Sun. The control problem of keeping the *Heliostat* balanced over the pole is very tricky, especially during the summer season of that hemisphere when the polar axis is over on the sunlit side of the Earth. That's why 'pole-sitters' have to be placed so far away from the Earth. If they get any closer than 250 Earth radii, they become unstable during the summer." Scotty then took them up on a lift to view the top of the towering spacecraft.

"This is the transmitting end that will point at the Earth," said Scotty. "Around the circumference are the rolled up 'petals' of the big transmitting dish. It's over a hundred meters in diameter. In the center you can see the microwave feed horns. If you look carefully, you will notice that each one is shaped like the continent they are going to serve, except they are reversed, right to left. After the microwaves bounce off the dish they produce a beam that just fits the continent, with no microwave energy wasted heating up the oceans around them."

"That one must be for the lower part of South

America," said the reporter, looking at the monitor while the cameraman zoomed in on each of the feed horns in turn. "But it stops about halfway through Brazil."

"My *Heliostat* is designed to serve those that are not well served by the geostationary satellites that hang over the equator," replied Scotty. "Anybody south of the Tropic of Capricorn has problems getting good reception from those equatorial satellites unless they live on the top of a mountain. Either something is in the way, or the path through the atmosphere is so long that by the time the microwaves fight their way through the air and clouds, they are so attenuated you have to buy a big expensive dish to get a decent signal. With my *Heliostat* hanging over the South Pole, you just point a small dish at the South Pole and sit back and enjoy any one of the dozen programs available from 'Mac-Vision, Limited' broadcast services."

"*If* you get there first," reminded the reporter. "Don't forget there's a race on."

Scotty didn't like being reminded of the race. The polar explorer Robert Scott had prepared poorly for his rushed dash to the South Pole. When he got there, he found that Roald Amundsen had beat him by a month. Discouraged and exhausted, Scott had died on his way back, trapped in a blizzard only eleven miles from his base camp. Scotty too was rushed, and had stretched the resources of his company to the limits to get his *Heliostat* built.

"I *will* get there first," said Scotty confidently. "I'm so sure of it, that none of the millions of receiving dishes I've sold has a clock drive on it. If you get the 'pole position' in this race, your ground receiver dishes can be fixed. The broadcast station that gets there second has to be placed off the polar axis, where it will rotate once a day around the pole. The receiving dishes then have to rotate once a day to track it. If Andy Hawke is so confident he's going to be the first one to the South Pole, then why do his dishes have 24-hour clock drives?"

"You seem to be taking an awful risk," said the reporter. "Andy's *Polestat* spacecraft is already launched and on its way."

"That square-rigged klunker that Andy uses is heavy and slow," said Scotty. "It takes forever to deploy . . . and needs humans around to take care of hangups. He may have launched already, but he had to start with the help of the manned station in GEO. It will take him forever to fly that thing from GEO down to the South Pole. When he arrives, he will find my *Heliostat* already there."

Suddenly a loud klaxon blurted out a warning. Scotty frowned and started running back across the hangar toward the corridor leading to the winding room they had just left.

"What's happened!" panted the reporter as he and the cam'er caught up with him.

"The winding mechanism must have jammed in the middle of a roll," said Scotty as he ran through the corridor.

When they got to the winding room, the workers had gotten things under control. The weaving machines that manufactured the wire mesh webbing were now motionless and the spray of metal from the still glowing furnace had been turned off, but the floor of the room was stacked high with a slowly slumping pile of silvery metal ribbon. The cam'er panned his video camera over the mess as the video news reporter unctuously intoned what he was sure would be heard and seen all over the world on the evening news that day.

"And so the challenge of the brave Aussie engineer-entrepreneur to the mighty American conglomerate of Andrew Hawke looks like it has suffered a serious setback. A setback that is almost sure to cost 'Scotty' MacPherson first place in the 'Race to the Pole.'"

❖ ❖ ❖

"How long will it take us to get the blade room back into running order, Jane?" Scotty asked one of the engineers sitting around the conference table.

"Fortunately the web weavers weren't damaged," replied Jane. "However, one of the welder rollers developed scratches when a loose wire wound up around it, and it needs to be repolished. It's being flown to Germany right now—in your private jet."

"Germany!" said Scotty, eyes turning icy blue under a fierce frown. "Why isn't it being polished here?"

Jane, sure of herself, stared back at Scotty unafraid. "The tolerances on those rollers are beyond any conceivable manufacturing standard. They are a matched set, and the scratched roller is going to be repolished on the same machine that originally made them—by the same man. Let's hope the machine hasn't changed significantly in the past nine months."

"How many days?" said Scotty with a resigned tone.

"Minimum of three," said Jane. "The setup alone takes over six hours—and I insisted that the machinist work standard hours and get plenty of sleep. We can't afford another mistake."

"Three days!" said Scotty. "There goes the last of our margin." He sat there shaking his head, his brain whirling with alternative plans. Suddenly he brightened. "If we get everything else ready to go, then put on the last blade canister while the *Heliostat* is sitting on the launch pad, then we can still win! It only takes fourteen hours for our pop-up rocket to put the *Heliostat* in place, and Andrew's *Polestat* has four more days of flying before it gets there."

"I'm afraid I have additional bad news," said a quiet voice from the back of the room.

"What now, Chin-Lee?" said Scotty, lips pursed.

The skinny young man pushed his glasses up on his

nose and his prominent Adam's apple bobbed as he swallowed twice in order to delay having to speak.

"I have been monitoring the trajectory of the sail of our competitor. There is something unusual happening. The actual trajectory is consistently ahead of my predictions. The only way I can make my computer model make sense is to assume that the total mass of the spacecraft plus sail is constantly becoming less with time. I don't understand it."

"I'm afraid I do!" said Scotty, face now very grim. "Andy's engineers just filed a patent for a new type of plastic-backed metal film. After about a week in space, with the Sun's ultraviolet shining on it, the heavy plastic backing evaporates, leaving just the light-weight film. I didn't think he would have the new technology ready for this flight, but evidently he did. What's his projected arrival time at the pole?"

"Thirty-two hours," said Chin-Lee, almost apologetically.

"Less than three days . . . that does it," said Scotty, dejectedly. "Andy is going to get the stationary position above the South Pole and we're going to have to stand off a few degrees and rotate around the pole."

There was a polite cough from Scotty's left. It came from the company Treasurer, William Baker.

"What is it, William?" said Scotty.

"May I remind you that the nearly two million receiver units that you have already sold do not have provisions for rotation," said William.

"A simple polar mount and a 24-hour clock is all that's needed," said Scotty. "How much could that possibly cost? A few dollars at most."

"Thirteen dollars and seventy-two cents," replied William, looking at a small piece of paper. "Then there is the not so minor matter of installation, all over the outback in Australia and New Zealand, the savannas of South Africa and the mountains and jungles of

Madagascar and South America. It's going to take over one hundred million dollars."

"But everything I've got is invested in the *Heliostat!*" said Scotty, alarmed. "I don't have an extra hundred million!"

"I know," said William, grimly. "But unless the hundred million is found, the receiver dishes will be worthless—and so will the *Heliostat*—and so will MacVision, Limited."

Scotty's face fell, and those around the boardroom table became pensive as bankruptcy for MacVision, Ltd., and redundancy for them all became almost palpable in its imminence. The minutes ticked on as Scotty's eyes stared blankly at the grain in the table in front of him. His body started to slump forward. William, concerned, reached over to grab his shoulder. Scotty shrugged him off.

"Go away," he said. "I'm thinking."

Suddenly he straightened up. "We'll fly with ten blades instead of twelve!" he said. "It'll cost us seventeen percent in lifting power, but that's only ten percent in hovering altitude." He looked around the table.

"Jane, tell the guys in Germany to forget the roller. We're going without it." He started to turn away, then turned back. "And remind them to send my plane back.

"Chin-Lee, I want constant updates on the position of Andy's *Polestat* and the estimated time of arrival over the South Pole.

"Rod, strip blade nine from the *Heliostat* to balance missing blade twelve. Then get the *Heliostat* out to the launch pad. We'll launch whenever you're ready. Keep the same launch trajectory—head from Woomera to the South Pole axis, then go straight up along the polar axis to 275 Earth radii and deploy the blades."

He stood up. "Everybody get a move on. This is a race!"

❖   ❖   ❖

Later, after a successful launch, there was a telephone call for Scotty in the launch control room as he monitored the trajectory of his rocket.

"Back off!" said the grim ruddy face of Andrew Hawke over the videophone.

"Not on your life!" said Scotty. "I'm on the pole and I'm going to stay there."

"You fool!" yelled Andy. "You're going to cause a collision and both our systems will come falling out of the sky."

"I'm not budging," said Scotty, grimly. "My rocket is right on the polar axis and if your klunky square-rig is in the way it's going to get a hole torn in it."

"Sir!" said Rod from a nearby console. Scotty turned to look.

"It's from a camera in the nose cone of the rocket," said Rod, pointing at his screen. The image showed a large square sail directly above. It grew noticeably. Scotty blinked involuntarily as the enlarging image of the sail filled half the screen. When his eyes reopened the sail was gone.

"Did we hit?" asked Scotty.

The answer came from the videophone.

"No," said Andy Hawke. "Fortunately for you, your rocket passed a few hundred meters in front of the leading edge of my sail. If it had been otherwise, I would be on my phone to my lawyers instead of talking to you."

Andy looked away for a moment, then returned to the videophone with a broad smile on his face. "My engineers inform me that my *Polestat* is now positioned directly over the South Pole. We initiated broadcast over all our channels instantly upon arrival. We are on the air and you aren't." He paused, then added in a gloating tone. "You've lost, Mr. MacPherson. Move your whirligig aside." The videophone went blank.

Scotty sat there in a daze, trying to think of what

he could do next to save his company from bankruptcy—but no ideas came. Rod's voice came drifting over from the nearby console. "Apogee reached . . . Deploy blades . . . Deploy antenna . . . Commence broadcasting . . ." The twelve seconds for the round trip delay time seemed to pass interminably. "Signals received!" said Rod cheerfully. "Loud and clear!" A weak cheer went up in the control room. Scotty cocked his head, then turned to look at Rod.

"Loud and clear?" he repeated. "With two missing blades the *Heliostat* stable position has to be above Andy's *Polestat* position. That huge metal sail should be blocking our signals."

"I believe I have the answer, Mr. MacPherson," said Chin-Lee. Scotty rushed to Chin-Lee's console. On his screen was the image of the South Polar sky as seen from a powerful telescope on the roof of the control center. Superimposed on the familiar southern constellations were two new stars, one above the other—and one of them was *his* star. They were very close together, but definitely separated one from the other.

"Although the *Polestat* of Mr. Hawke will block our signals over most of the Antarctic continent," said Chin-Lee, "it is not big enough to block the broadcast signals from our *Heliostat* to us here in Australia or the other continental regions in the Southern Hemisphere of Earth."

Fortunately, the two spacecraft used different frequency bands. Scotty would let Andy have the few customers in the frozen wasteland of Antarctica. They *both* could have a position over the pole.

There was a buzzing from the videophone and he went to answer it. It was Andrew Hawke again.

"My engineers inform me that the race to the pole had two winners," said Andy. "In fact, a large number of broadcast statites could be put over the South Pole without interfering with each other."

"Yes, I guess we both won, Andy," said Scotty, trying to be conciliatory.

"Not quite," said Andy, superciliously. "My *Polestat* is, in fact, closer than your wounded windmill, thus providing stronger signals and better service. I'm sure everyone will acknowledge that I won the race to the South Pole." He smiled smugly, then continued in a condescending tone. "I really must thank you for showing my engineers what should have been obvious. Service is already getting saturated in the Northern Polar regions. I was going to launch a large replacement *Polestat* for my North Pole station, but now I will just put up another *Polestat* underneath, and still collect revenue from the old one."

"Not if I put a *Heliostat* there first," replied Scotty.

"You stay away from my North Pole!" shouted Andy over the videophone.

"Care to race?" challenged Scotty as he blanked the screen on Andy's livid face.

✧ STARSHIPS

It was only a few centuries ago that the human race realized those bright lights in the night sky were suns, like our Sun. We then realized that those other suns probably had worlds orbiting around them, some possibly like our world. Since that time, one of the dreams of the human race has been to visit those other worlds in ships that travel between the stars. But as we began to realize the immensity of the distances that separate our star from the other stars, we began to despair of ever building a starship using the puny technology that the human race controls.

Science fiction writers, in an attempt to get their storybook heroes to the stars before the readers got bored, evoked starships with faster-than-light drives, space warps, and other forms of future technology that were indistinguishable from magic. At the same time, the general public evoked fantasy starships in the form of flying saucers flown *to* the Earth *from* other stars. These starships were propelled by antigravity or magnetism, and were piloted by benevolent little green men who would save the world from its folly.

If little green men can cross the great gulf, can we?

Yes. It is difficult to go to the stars, but it is not impossible. The stars are far away, and the speed of light limits us to a slow crawl along the starlanes. To travel to the stars will take years of time, gigawatts of power, kilograms of energy, and billions (if not trillions) of dollars. Yet it can be done—if we wish to.

And if we decide to go, what kind of starships can we build?

It turns out there are many types of starships possible, each using a different technology. There are some starships that we can build now. For these technologies we know the basic physical principles and have demonstrated the ability to achieve the desired reactions on a laboratory scale. All that is needed for the design, engineering, and construction of the starship is the application of large amounts of money, material, and manpower. There are also some promising starship designs that use future technology that is barely distinguishable from magic. Here we know the basic physical principles, but we have not yet controlled the future technology in the laboratory. Once we have turned that future technology from magic into reality, we can then proceed with starship designs based on those technologies.

It is not easy to comprehend the distances involved in interstellar travel. Of the billions of people living today on this globe, many have never travelled more than 40 kilometers from their place of birth. Of these billions, a few dozen have traveled to the Moon, which at a distance of almost 400,000 kilometers, is ten thousand times 40 kilometers away. Our interplanetary space probes have even gone past Neptune, ten thousand times further out at 4,000,000,000 (4 billion) kilometers. However, the nearest star at 40,000,000,000,000 (40 trillion) kilometers is ten thousand times further than that.

The spacing between stars is so large that there is no standard unit of measurement that gives any sense of the immensity of those distances. Even in terms of the distance between the Earth and the Sun, one astronomical unit or AU, the nearest star is 270,000 AU away. To cut interstellar distances down to size, we use the unit of distance which has the name of a unit of time in it, the lightyear.

A lightyear is the distance that light, traveling at 300,000 kilometers per second or 186,000 miles per second, travels in one year (which is 365.2422 days, 8766 hours, 525,949 minutes, or 31,556,926 seconds), thus, one lightyear equals 9,460,530,000,000 (9.5 trillion) kilometers. It takes light 1.3 seconds to reach the moon, 8.3 minutes to reach the Sun, 4.2 hours to reach Neptune, and 4.3 years to reach the nearest star system.

The nearest star system is called Alpha Centauri. Also known as "Rigil Kent," it is the brightest star in the southern constellation, Centarus, and the third brightest star in the sky after Sirius and Canopus. Alpha Centauri is not a single star, but a collection of three stars. The nearest of those stars is a small red dwarf called Proxima Centauri. The other two stars are a tenth of a lightyear further away and are called Alpha Centauri A and B. Alpha Centauri A is similar to our Sun, while B is slightly redder. These two stars orbit each other every eighty years, while Proxima circles the pair within a period of millions of years.

To carry out a one-way robotic probe mission to this nearest star system in the lifetime of the humans that launched the probe will require a minimum speed of ten percent of the speed of light. At that speed, it will take 43 years to get to Proxima Centauri and 4.3 years for the radio information to get back to Earth to tell us what the probe found as it zoomed through the three star system at a sizable fraction of light speed.

Much further away in the heavens are some single star systems with stars that are also similar to our Sun. These are felt to be our best candidates for finding an Earth-like planet. They are Epsilon Eridani at eleven lightyears and Tau Ceti at twelve lightyears. To reach these stars in a reasonable time will require starship velocities of thirty percent of the speed of light. At this velocity it will take nearly forty years for the starship to get there, plus another eleven or twelve years for the information to return to Earth.

Yet, although we need to exceed ten percent of light speed to get to *any* star in a reasonable time, if we can attain a cruise velocity of thirty percent of the speed of light, then there are seventeen star systems with twenty-five visible stars and hundreds of planets within twelve lightyears. This many stars and planets that are reachable with starships limited to less than thirty percent of the speed of light should keep us busy exploring while our future engineers are working on even faster starship designs.

No matter how fast we can make a starship go, we must resign ourselves to the fact that interstellar travel will always take a long time. Even if we had a starship that traveled at the speed of light, it would take over 4.3 years to travel to the nearest star system, then another 4.3 years before a message (or the starship) returns. We don't have speed-of-light starships yet, and won't for a long time. Although time will pass quickly for the crews on relativistic starships, decades and centuries will pass before the stay-at-homes learn what the explorers have found.

Why should we bother going to the stars if it is so difficult? There is one reason that should be obvious to us all. It is built into our genes. We cannot resist it. But it is so selfish, so *animal* . . . that we often try to ignore it.

We must go to the stars to spawn.

For the survival of the human race it is necessary that the human race leave the Earth. Homo sapiens has survived quite nicely on the Earth for tens of thousands and perhaps millions of years. So did the dinosaurs. But the dinosaurs are now extinct. If the human race is to survive, some small portion of it must leave this big blue egg and travel somewhere else to start a new branch of the human race.

For a while, we can escape the death of the Earth from ice ages, meteorite strikes, or other catastrophes by having some of our population in space stations, or by colonizing the other planets around our Sun. But to escape the ultimate death of the Sun, it will be necessary for the human race to establish viable colonies on planets that are around other, younger suns.

Another major reason for interstellar travel would be to find other intelligent lifeforms. Some argue that if the lifeforms on planets around other stars were intelligent, we could communicate with them by radio signals. Not all intelligent lifeforms will have radio, however. It is easy to dream up alien civilizations which are intelligent, have information and technology which would be of value to us, and yet, because of their environment, they can not and will not have radio technology. For example, life could evolve on an ocean-covered world in the form of intelligent whale-like or octopus-like creatures. These beings could be highly advanced in music, mathematics, philosophy, hydrodynamics, acoustics, and biology, but they would have no technology based on fire or electricity.

If there are beings with radio out there, and *if* they are willing to transmit gigawatts of radio power instead of just listening like we are, and *if* we listen in the right direction at the right time at the right frequency with the right bandwidth and the right detection scheme, then a radio search for intelligent extraterrestrials will make a significant contribution to our knowledge. However, interstellar exploration with automated probes, although still decades in the future, is more certain to produce a contribution of equivalent value. In my opinion, interstellar exploration with automated probes is complementary to a program to search for extraterrestrial radio signals, rather than competitive with it.

As Arthur Clarke said in his book, *The Promise of Space*:

"This proxy exploration of the Universe is certainly one way in which it would be possible to gain knowledge of star systems which lack garrulous, radio-equipped inhabitants."

Also, a lifeform does not have to be intelligent to be important. All life on Earth is made of the same stuff: carbon, hydrogen, oxygen, nitrogen, and trace elements organized into specific chemical compounds such as amino acids, sugars, proteins, enzymes, and other standard building blocks of life-as-we-know-it. The discovery of a different form of life will be extremely important.

A different form of life could have a drastically different chemistry, such as compounds based on the element silicon instead of carbon. This would be useful on planets where temperatures are too high for carbon-based lifeforms.

A different form of life might use a different kind of replicating mechanism, such as a tri-string form of DNA that uses two-out-of-three voting when making the new tri-string to block the effects of mutation. This would probably involve three sexes for procreation and would be useful on planets with high radiation environments.

A different form of life might have almost the same biology as Earth life, except one or two of the amino acids used in the DNA genetic code would be different. Or it might be that the compounds are almost exactly the same as those used in Earth lifeforms except that all the compounds are left-handed. (All the organic compounds produced by living organisms on Earth rotate the polarization of light passing through them to the right.)

It could be that the life found on other planets is *exactly* like ours in chemical structure, indicating a common origin. (This would *not* mean the alien animals would look anything like Earth animals. A mosquito, sequoia, human, octopus, whale, and duck-billed platypus are quite different in form, yet we all use the same genetic code.) Our search would then turn to find that common origin. The common origin could be due to the inexorable laws of biology, which only allows one type of life to form. The common origin could be due to a version of the panspermia theory, where life travels between stars as spores pushed by light pressure. Or the common origin could even be due to the "garbage" theory, that life on Earth formed from picnic garbage left by long-ago alien visitors to our barren planet. Once we have found a different form of life, our biologists and medical researchers will have their understanding of "life" stretched. They will then, probably, see new ways to understand, control, maintain, and repair our form of life.

The first travelers to the stars will be our robotic probes. They will be small and won't require all the amenities like food, air, and water that humans seem to find necessary. The power levels to send the first squadron of robotic probes out to the stars are within the present reach of the human race. If we wanted to, we could have the first interstellar probe on the way to the nearest star system early in the next millennium.

The design of the first interstellar probe is the critical driving item in any program for interstellar exploration. The rigors and length of a journey involving high accelerations with high energy density engines, the years of bombardment against interstellar matter at high velocities, and the decades of operation with no means for repair, or even diagnostic help from Earth, means that advanced designs for a self-diagnostic, self-repairing probe must be developed. Ultimately, the computer in the interstellar probe will have to exhibit semi-intelligent behavior when presented with new and unforeseen circumstances.

The requirement of multiple planetary exploration at each stellar system will limit the number and weight of the lander probes available and will put a premium on long range sensor capabilities to gather the same data from orbit. Yet, despite these needs for sensor performance, the energy requirements for achieving flight velocities of a few tenths of the speed of light are so large that the weight of the interstellar probe should be kept to a minimum.

What is desired in an interstellar probe is a large physical size (to give the transmitting and receiving apertures desired), and high power (for active sounders and data transmission), all combined with light weight. The design of an interstellar robot probe is a challenge, but an important one. For the mass of the interstellar probe determines the size and power of the propulsion system.

The most advanced form of flight-tested propulsion system we have today is electric propulsion. In this type of propulsion system, some source of energy is used to produce electricity and the electricity is used to expel the reaction mass at high speed to provide thrust. In most electric propulsion systems, the electrical energy is obtained from solar cells that convert sunlight into electricity. Unfortunately for interstellar missions, the light from the Sun rapidly becomes weaker as the spacecraft leaves the solar system, so that solar electric propulsion will not get us to the stars.

One possible method for overcoming the problem of the spreading of sunlight with distance is to consider laser electric propulsion. In this propulsion system, the incoherent sunlight is turned into coherent beams of laser light by using the sunlight to pump the laser. The laser energy is then used to illuminate specially designed solar cells that are optimized to absorb that particular color of laser light with high efficiency.

The size of the collector arrays could then be made smaller, resulting in a compact, lightweight, efficient energy power conversion system.

Comparative studies were carried out by engineers of the NASA Jet Propulsion Laboratory on the various forms of electric propulsion that might be used for extrasolar space missions to be launched around the year 2000. These studies indicated that a nuclear fission reactor was a better choice than a laser beam collector for the energy source for an electric propulsion system. A nuclear electric propulsion system would be capable of reaching an escape velocity of 150 kilometers per second or 1/2000th of the speed of light in twelve years, after using up all the fuel in the nuclear reactor. Such a spacecraft would be useful for exploring extrasolar space to search for trans-Plutonian planets and nearby "brown dwarf" stars. However, as the JPL engineers pointed out, at this speed it would take the nuclear fission powered electric propulsion system 10,000 years to reach the nearer stars. Long before it got there, it probably would be passed by a vehicle using a faster propulsion system. Thus, although fission reactors are a presently available source of controlled nuclear energy, because of the large masses needed in the fission reactor and the heat-to-electricity converters, nuclear fission powered electric propulsion systems do not seem to be an adequate form of interstellar propulsion.

A very old design for a nuclear powered interstellar vehicle is one that is propelled by nuclear bombs. Called the "Orion" spacecraft, it was invented in the late fifties at the Los Alamos National Laboratory by an inventor of the hydrogen bomb, Stanislaw Ulam. The original goal of the Orion Project was to send manned spacecraft to Mars and Venus by 1968. Because nuclear fuel is so much more powerful than chemical fuel, an Orion mission to Mars would have cost only a small fraction of the Apollo project, which only took us to the moon.

The Orion vehicle works by ejecting a small nuclear bomb out the rear where the bomblet explodes. The hot plasma from the nuclear explosion strikes a "pusher plate," which absorbs the impulse from the explosion and transfers it through large "shock absorbers" to the main spacecraft. Although it seems amazing that anything could survive a few dozen meters away from a nuclear explosion, a properly designed pusher plate with an ablative surface can stand not one, but many thousands of such nuclear explosions.

Freeman Dyson took these well-engineered ideas for an interplanetary spacecraft and extrapolated them to an interstellar spacecraft. The ship would necessarily be large, with a payload of some 20,000 metric tons (enough to support a small town of many hundred crew members). The total mass would be 400,000 tons, including a fuel supply of 300,000 nuclear bombs weighing about one ton each. (This is approximately the world's supply of nuclear bombs. What an excellent way of disposing of them!) The bombs would be exploded once every three seconds, accelerating the spacecraft at one Earth gravity for ten days to reach a velocity of 1/30th of the speed of light. At this speed, the Orion spacecraft would reach Alpha Centauri in 140 years. To give this ship a deceleration capability at the target star, it would need to be redesigned to have two stages. Although the Orion spacecraft has minimal performance for a starship, it is one form of interstellar transport that could have been built and sent on its way in the last decade.

In addition to nuclear bomb propelled starships, we can envision future nuclear technology which could make possible new kinds of nuclear powered starships. This future technology is called controlled fusion. Although our scientists are sure of the basic physical laws behind controlled fusion, our technologists have yet to demonstrate it in the laboratory. This is one form of future technology that is almost certain to turn from magic into reality within a few decades, since the Department of Energy is spending a large portion of its budget on a number of techniques for achieving a controlled fusion reaction on a scale suitable for use in power plants.

One technique, called magnetic containment fusion, involves the use of magnetic "bottles" to confine a high temperature plasma of deuterium (a hydrogen atom with an extra neutron in the nucleus) and tritium (a hydrogen atom with two extra neutrons in the nucleus) until the two forms of heavy hydrogen fuse together to make a helium nucleus and a high energy neutron.

Another technique, called inertial implosion fusion, attempts to compress tiny pellets of deuterium and tritium by hitting the pellet from all sides with either laser beams, electron beams, ion beams, or beams of high-speed shot. In inertial fusion, the energy and pressure from the incoming beams is supposed to compress the fusion fuel in the pellet, heat it up, and get it to fuse into helium before it has time to expand. It is the "inertia" of the fuel, pellet, and beams that keeps it contained long enough for the reaction to take place.

Once we have achieved controlled fusion in the laboratory, then we can start designing a starship based on those types of fusion techniques that turn out to be feasible. If we achieve controlled fusion by compression and heating of a plasma in a magnetic bottle, then perhaps all we need to do to convert the fusion reactor into a starship rocket engine is to allow the magnetic bottle to "leak" a little bit, and the hot plasma exhaust will produce thrust.

If we achieve controlled fusion by implosion of micropellets with beams of laser light, electrons, ions, or high speed shot, then the same technique can be used to implode the pellets in the throat of a rocket nozzle made of magnetic fields, which will turn the isotropically exploding plasma into directed thrust. Scientists at Lawrence Livermore National Laboratory have already anticipated the success of their laser-imploded fusion program. They have used their fusion plasma computer codes to design a magnetic nozzle for a laser fusion powered rocket for travel in the solar system.

The deuterium-tritium reaction presently being used in both the magnetic containment and inertial implosion fusion research projects involves the use of tritium. Since tritium is a radioactive material with a lifetime of twelve years, any interstellar rocket system using this reaction must have a method of generating the tritium on board. This can be done by capturing the high energy neutrons emitted by the fusion reaction in a blanket of lithium. The neutron causes the lithium to fission into a helium atom and a tritium atom, which can be extracted and used to make more fusion pellets. The weight and efficiency of this auxiliary system, while not serious for an interplanetary spacecraft, can limit the final velocity achievable by a starship.

Alternatively, research on magnetic containment and implosion fusion techniques could produce the higher pressures, temperatures, and densities needed to achieve fusion with other fuel mixtures that don't involve radioactive tritium. These reactors would fuse together fuels such as deuterium and helium-three (a helium nucleus that is missing a neutron), deuterium and deuterium, and protons with protons.

Thus, given some future advances in nuclear technology, we can already envision some propulsion technologies that will get a starship to the stars, although they only travel at one to three percent of the speed of light. At three percent of the speed of light, it would take over 300 years to get to the interesting star systems like Tau Ceti and Epsilon Eridani. These slow travel times for nuclear powered starships are longer than the present lifetime of a human being, so it looks like the travelers on our slow nuclear starships will have to be long-lasting robots rather than ephemeral humans, unless we can come up with some new type of biological technology that will allow a human crew to live longer than our presently allotted three-score-and-ten-year lifetimes. Biologists are presently studying the aging process in cells and multicellular organisms. They are finding that our cells seem to be programmed to stop replicating after a given number of cycles. If they can find the right genetic switch, perhaps they can turn off the aging process and allow us to live the centuries that will be necessary to explore the stars using slow nuclear rockets. With death dead, our only enemies would be accidents and boredom.

Other biologists are studying the process of suspended animation, by either freezing or hibernation. Sperm cells have been kept frozen for decades and are viable enough to produce thoroughbreds and beef cattle when thawed. Even fish and small mammals have been frozen and rethawed. Larger animals, such as people, will be significantly more difficult to freeze because of the need for rapid cooling and thawing to prevent the formation of damaging ice crystals. However, some future technological breakthrough that would now be considered indistinguishable from magic may make possible crews of "corpsicles" who experience the thrilling adventure of exploring one stellar system after another, without having to endure the boring drive through the dark between those adventures.

Scientists studying hibernating animals have found the hormone that initiates hibernation and have used the drug to induce hibernation in other animals. Whether this drug will induce hibernation in humans without causing serious side effects is unknown. Also, it is unknown whether hibernation actually increases lifespan, or just makes living possible when there is insufficient food. Still, there is enough biological research on suspended animation that one of these days we may use that method of keeping a crew alive long enough to carry out century-long exploration missions.

Even if these particular biological technologies do not turn into a real suspended animation capability, there is another method to carry out a slowship mission; let the people die, but allow their children to carry on. A slowship journey to the stars will send a colony of people off in a generation starship. Although only the first generation would be true volunteers, with enough thought and planning we could turn the slow moving starship into a truly acceptable worldship, with all the amenities and few of the problems of living on Earth.

Living on a worldship would be like living in a space colony, except that the colony would have some sort of fusion rocket to push it up to speed and bring it to a halt again at each target star. At each stop, it would refuel its tanks with hydrogen and helium isotopes from a gaseous giant planet like Jupiter. After a few decades of experience in space stations around the Earth, we may have enough confidence in the environmental support systems for a worldship that we could risk sending a colony on an interstellar mission.

The important thing to realize is that our present technology can take us to the stars. To be sure, our first robotic interstellar probes will be slow, consume a lot of power and money, and will return small amounts of data. If we find an interesting planetary system, it will take even more power, and more money, plus biological breakthroughs and crew dedication to take the slowships to the stars. It would be no different in principle than the Mayflower or the ships that colonized the Dutch East Indies. But, no matter how difficult, interstellar travel by slow starships can be done with reasonable extensions of present technology.

There is, however, a fundamental problem with any interstellar mission that travels at speeds less than ten percent the speed of light. For even as a worldship is launched onto its centuries-long journey, propulsion engineers back on Earth will be dreaming about more advanced propulsion systems that can make starships that travel faster than the ship that is leaving. Within twenty or thirty years, those advanced propulsion systems will no longer be a future technology that is indistinguishable from magic, but future reality. After another ten to twenty years, a faster starship will zip past the lumbering worldship, explore the new star system first, then set up a welcoming party for the worldship colonists as they are picked up and brought in by a second wave of fast starships.

Thus, until we run out of ideas for new propulsion systems, it seems to me that no interstellar mission should be launched if it takes more than one hundred years. Instead, the money for the mission should be spent on research to build a faster propulsion system or to find a new propulsion energy source.

In our near future is a magical propulsion energy source that is a thousand times more powerful than nuclear energy. This future source of energy that is nearly indistinguishable from magic is antimatter. As discussed in the chapter "Antimatter," this nearly magical type of matter represents a highly concentrated form of energy with the ability to release "200%" of its mass as energy. When a particle of antimatter, such as an antiproton, is put near a particle of normal matter, such as a proton, the two attract each other and almost instantly annihilate to completely convert all of the mass of both particles into energy. A spacecraft which uses antimatter as its source of propulsion energy could "drive" anywhere in the solar system with mission times ranging from weeks to a few months. A starship using antimatter could travel to the nearest stars in a human lifetime.

Although an antimatter rocket is the ultimate in rockets, it is not necessary to use the rocket principle to build a starship. A rocket consists of a payload, some structure, an energy source, some reaction mass (in most rockets the reaction mass and energy source are combined together into the "fuel"), and an engine that combines the energy with the reaction mass and expels it to provide thrust to the spacecraft. Because a standard rocket has to carry its fuel along with it, its performance is significantly limited. For missions where the final vehicle velocity V is much greater than the exhaust velocity v, the amount of fuel needed rises exponentially as the ratio V/v. Thus, as a practical matter, the final velocity of a rocket is limited to about two or three times the exhaust velocity.

It is possible to conceive of space vehicle designs that do not use the rocket principle and thereby avoid the exponential mass growth implicit in the design of a standard rocket. These are excellent candidates for starships. One example, and a favorite of science fiction writers, is the interstellar ramjet invented in 1960 by Robert Bussard.

The interstellar ramjet starship consists of a payload, a fusion reactor engine, and a large scoop. The interstellar ramjet carries no fuel because it uses the scoop to collect the hydrogen atoms that are known to exist in space. The hydrogen atoms are used as fuel in the fusion reactor, where the fusion energy is released and the energy fed back in some manner into the reaction products (usually helium atoms) which provides the thrust for the vehicle.

Bussard originally estimated that a 1,000 ton vehicle would require a scoop with a frontal intake diameter of about one hundred kilometers to achieve a one Earth gravity acceleration through interstellar space with a density of 1000 hydrogen atoms per cubic centimeter. The speed needed for the ramjet to start working is extremely low, so that conventional chemical rockets would suffice to get it started. As the vehicle increases its speed so that it approaches the speed of light, the interstellar fuel flow appears to increase in density due to its relativistic contraction in the space-time reference frame of the vehicle. As a result, the faster the interstellar ramjet goes, the more fuel it collects, so the faster it *can* go.

If an interstellar ramjet could ever be built, it would have many advantages over other possible starships. Since it never runs out of fuel like fuel-carrying rockets, and never runs away from its source of power like a beamed-power propulsion system, it can accelerate indefinitely. It is the only known starship design that can reach the ultrarelativistic velocities where ship-time becomes orders of magnitude longer than Earth-time. This would allow human crews to travel throughout the galaxy or even between galaxies in a single human lifetime.

A lot of invention and research is needed, however, before the future technology of a Bussard interstellar ramjet becomes distinguishable from magic. We must first achieve controlled fusion. The fusion reactor must not only be light-weight and long-lived, it must be able to fuse protons, not the easier-to-ignite mixture of deuterium and tritium. The reactor must be able to fuse the incoming protons without slowing them down, or the frictional loss of bringing the fuel to a halt, fusing it, and reaccelerating the reaction products will put an undesirable upper limit on the maximum velocity attainable. All of this needed technology is still indistinguishable from magic.

Other versions of the interstellar ramjet concept do

not require that the starship carry a fusion reactor. In these concepts, the ramjet scoop is used to scoop up the hydrogen in space. Instead of fusing the hydrogen into helium atoms, however, the hydrogen is heated either by antimatter carried on board, or by antimatter beams or laser beams sent from the solar system.

The major difficulty with any ramjet starship is the design of the scoop, which must be ultra-large and ultra-light. If the interstellar hydrogen were ionized, then a large, super-strong magnet might be sufficient to scoop up the charged protons. Although some stars have clouds of ionized hydrogen near them, most of the hydrogen near the solar system is neutral. Schemes that use laser beams or electron beams to ionize the hydrogen ahead of the ship have been proposed, but they are not light in weight nor low in power consumption.

The present scientific consensus for the composition of the local interstellar medium is that the solar system is embedded not far from the edge of a warm (10,000 degree) mostly neutral gas cloud with a radius of a few tens of lightyears and a relatively low density of 0.1 atoms per cubic centimeter. This is 10,000 times less dense than the 1000 atoms per cubic centimeter that would be preferred for an interstellar ramjet. That means that a scoop for an interstellar ramjet, instead of being 100 kilometers in diameter, would have to be 10,000 kilometers across to scoop up the same amount of fuel per second.

It gets even worse as we travel further from the Sun, for this warm cloud we are in is surrounded by a larger hot (million degree) ionized plasma with a density of only 0.001 ions per cubic centimeter that extends some 150 lightyears or more in all directions observed. This ubiquitous low density hot gas "bubble" is most likely the result of past supernova events.

Thus, for now, in regions near the solar system, the

interstellar ramjet remains in the category of magic. The concept of picking up your fuel along the way as you journey through "empty" space is too valuable to be discarded lightly, however, and I hope that future scientists and engineers will keep working away on the remaining problems until this vision of a future technology, which is presently indistinguishable from magic, turns into a real starship.

There is a another whole class of spacecraft that do not have to carry along any energy source or reaction mass, or even an engine. These spacecraft consist only of payload and structure. They work by beamed power propulsion. In a beamed power propulsion system, the heavy parts of a rocket (the reaction mass, the energy source, and the engine) are all kept at home in the solar system. Here, around the Sun, there is an unlimited amount of energy and reaction mass readily available. In addition, the engine can be maintained and even upgraded as the mission proceeds. Three examples of such beamed power propulsion systems have been published in the engineering literature. All of these versions can be built with "reasonable" extrapolations of present day technology. The examples are pellet-stream-pushed, microwave-beam-pushed, and laser-beam-pushed vehicles.

In the pellet-pushed-probe concept proposed by Clifford Singer, small pellets are used to push a starship. The pellets would be launched by a very long linear electromagnetic mass driver that would stretch across the planetary orbits of the solar system and be accurately aimed at the target star. The accelerator would be powered by energy sources using nuclear or solar power. The high-speed pellets would be intercepted by the starship and reflected back in the opposite direction, resulting in an increase in velocity of the starship.

The absolute pointing accuracy of the mass launcher

is not a serious limitation. A series of correction stations to adjust the trajectory of each pellet could be located downrange from the launcher along the pellet stream. Each station, for example, would be three times farther downrange and would produce one-third as much velocity adjustment. The coarser adjustments could be made electromagnetically or electrostatically, and the finest adjustments could be made remotely by light pressure from a laser or by interaction with a plasma gun or neutral atom stream. The starship would detect the incoming pellet stream and adjust its position to stay in the stream. One readily feasible method for accomplishing the interception of the high-speed pellets at the vehicle is to vaporize them into a plasma with a pulse of photons or particles. The high-speed ionized plasma would then be reflected from a magnetic field on the starship in a manner somewhat analogous to the expulsion of plasma from a magnetic "nozzle" in a pulsed fusion rocket system.

Extensions of the pellet stream concept include changing the pellet composition and velocity so that the pellets are made of antimatter or fusion fuel that is captured at a low relative velocity, then used in an engine for acceleration and deceleration. Deceleration could also be accomplished by rebounding the pellets from an expendable unmanned lead ship to decelerate the manned vessel at the target system. Of course, once the "interstellar highway" has been traversed once, then a pellet-stream launcher can be constructed at the other end for relatively easy two-way travel.

Another form of beamed power propulsion uses beams of microwaves to drive the starship. Microwave energy has the great advantage that it can be made and transmitted at extremely high efficiencies, although it is difficult to make narrow beams that extend over long distances. Because of the short transmission range, the starship being pushed by the microwave beam must accelerate at a high rate to reach the high velocities needed for interstellar travel before the starship gets too far from the transmitting system. The accelerations required are larger than a human being can stand, so microwave pushed starships seem to be limited to use by robotic probes. There is one design that looks quite promising. I call it Starwisp, because of its extremely small mass.

Starwisp is a light-weight, high-speed interstellar flyby probe pushed by beamed microwaves. [See Figure 6.] The basic structure of the Starwisp robotic starship is a wire mesh sail with microcircuits at the intersection of the wires. The microwave energy to power the starship is generated by a solar powered station orbiting Earth. The microwaves are formed into a beam by a large fresnel-zone-plate lens made of sparse metal mesh rings and empty rings. Such a lens has very low total mass and is easy to construct.

The microwaves in the beam have a wavelength that is much larger than the openings in the wire mesh of the Starwisp starship, so the very lightweight perforated wire mesh looks like a solid sheet of metal to the microwave beam. When the microwave beam strikes the wire mesh, the beam is reflected back in the opposite direction. During the reflection process, the microwave energy gives a push to the wire mesh sail. The amount of push is not large, but if the sail is light and the power in the microwave beam is high, the resultant acceleration of the starship can reach hundreds of times Earth gravity. The high acceleration of the starship by the microwave beam allows Starwisp to reach a coast velocity near that of light while the starship is still close to the transmitting lens in the solar system.

Prior to the arrival of Starwisp at the target star, the microwave transmitter back in the solar system is turned on again and floods the star system with

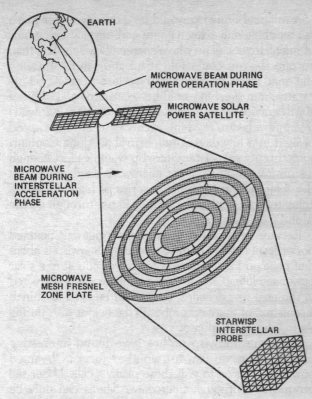

Fig. 6—Starwisp: a microwave-pushed interstellar probe.

microwave energy. Using the wires in the mesh as microwave antennas, the microcircuits on Starwisp collect enough energy to power their optical detectors and logic circuits to form images of the planets in the system. The phase of the incoming microwaves is sensed at each point of the mesh and the phase information is used by the microcircuits to form the mesh into a retrodirective phased array microwave antenna that beams a signal back to Earth.

A minimal Starwisp would be a one kilometer mesh sail weighing only sixteen grams and carrying four grams of microcircuits. (The whole spacecraft weighs less than an ounce—you could fold it up and send it through the mail for the cost of first class postage.) This twenty gram starship would be accelerated at 115 times Earth gravity by a ten gigawatt (10,000,000,000 watt) microwave beam, reaching twenty percent of the speed of light in a few days. Upon arrival at Alpha Centauri some twenty years later, Starwisp would collect enough microwave power from the microwave flood beam from the solar system to return a series of high resolution color television pictures during its fly-through of the Alpha Centauri system.

Because of its small mass, the ten gigawatt beamed power level needed to drive a minimal Starwisp is about that planned for the microwave power output of a solar power satellite. Thus, if power satellites are constructed in the next few decades, they could be used to launch a squadron of Starwisp probes to the nearer stars during their "checkout" phase.

Once the Starwisp probes have found interesting planets, then we can use another form of beamed power propulsion to visit those planets, called laser sail propulsion. Although microwave beams can only be used to "push" a robotic spacecraft away from the solar system, if we go to laser wavelengths, then it is possible to design a beamed power propulsion system that can use laser beams from the solar system to push a starship to the nearer stars, and then push the starship and its crew back home again.

Laser sail propulsion is the one method for achieving star travel with human crews that is closest to reality. It will be some time before our engineering capabilities in space will be up to building the laser system needed, but there is no new physics involved, just a large scale engineering extrapolation of known technologies. In laser sail propulsion, light from a powerful laser is bounced off a large reflective sail surrounding the payload. The light pressure from the laser light pushes the sail and payload, providing the needed thrust. The laser sail starship is about as far from a rocket as is possible. The starship consists of nothing but the payload and the lightweight sail structure. The rocket engine of our starship is the laser, powered by an energy source such as the Sun. The reaction mass is the laser light itself.

The sails that the laser craft would use would be advanced versions of the Sun-pushed light sails that have been designed by the NASA Jet Propulsion Laboratory for comet missions and fast trips to the asteroid belt. The lasers would be advanced versions of the high power laser arrays that were studied, built, and tested for the Space Defense Initiative Office of the Department of Defense. The basic physical principles of the lasers and sail are known; all that is left to do is the engineering.

For interplanetary operation and interstellar flight, the lasers would be in near-Earth space and powered by sunlight collected by large reflectors, sending their beams out to push the sails of the interplanetary fleet with the light pressure from their powerful beams. For pushing an interstellar starship, the lasers might work better if they were in orbit around Mercury. There is more sunlight there and the gravity attraction of Mercury would keep them from being "blown" away by the back reaction from their light beams. The lasers would use the abundant sunlight at Mercury's orbit to produce coherent laser light, which would then be combined into a single coherent beam and sent out to a transmitter lens floating between Saturn and Uranus.

The transmitter lens would be a fresnel-zone-plate lens with dimensions tuned to the laser frequency and consisting of wide rings of one-micrometer-thick plastic film alternating with empty rings. The transmitter lens would not be in orbit, but would either be freely falling (very slowly at that distance from the Sun), or "levitated" in place by rockets or by the momentum push from a portion of the laser light passing through it. The lens would be 1000 kilometers in diameter (as big as Texas) and mass about 560,000 tons. A lens this size can send a beam of laser light over forty lightyears before the beam starts to spread.

The first interstellar mission that could be performed with this laser and lens system would be a one-way flyby robotic probe mission to the nearest star system. The robotic probe would have a total mass of one metric ton, about one-third each of payload, support structure, and thin aluminum film reflecting panels. The sail portion of the probe would have a diameter of four kilometers.

The probe would be pushed at an acceleration of three percent of Earth gravity by an array of solar-pumped lasers with a total power of 65,000 megawatts or 65 gigawatts. While this is a great deal of laser power, it is well within our future capabilities. Power levels of this magnitude are generated by the Space Shuttle rocket engines during liftoff, and one of the ways to make a high power laser is to put mirrors across the exhaust of a high power rocket. If the acceleration is maintained for three years, the interstellar probe will reach the velocity of eleven percent of the speed of light at a distance of only one-sixth of a lightyear. At this distance it is still within range of the transmitter lens and all of the laser power is still focused on the sail. The laser is then turned off (or used to launch another robotic probe) and the robotic starship coasts to its target, flying through the Alpha Centauri system forty years after launch.

When I first invented the concept of laser-pushed

lightsails back in 1962, I thought it was obvious that since all the laser can do is push the lightsail, it would not be possible to use a solar system laser to stop the lightsail at the target system. The idea seemed to be limited to fly-by precursor robotic probe missions. It wasn't until twenty years later, while trying to find a new way of traveling to the stars for a novel I was writing, I realized that if the lightsail were separated into two parts, then one part could be used as a mirror to reflect the laser light back toward the solar system. That retrodirected light could then be used to decelerate the other portion of the lightsail. When I worked out the equations and put numbers into it, I found that not only was it a good science fiction idea, but it would really work. The concept has since been published as a scientific paper in the Journal of Spacecraft and Rockets, and one of the references to prior work in the scientific paper is my novel, *The Flight of the Dragonfly*, later reissued by Baen Books in a much expanded version as *Rocheworld*.

If the reports from the unmanned probes are favorable, then the next phase would be to send a human crew on an interstellar exploration journey. More than just the nearest star system will ultimately need to be explored, so I designed the laser lightsail starship to allow a roundtrip exploration capability out to twelve lightyears, so Tau Ceti or Epsilon Eridani can be visited within a human lifetime. I assumed the diameter of the lightsail at launch to be 1000 kilometers in diameter, the same size as the transmitting lens. The total weight would be 80,000 tons, including 3,000 tons for the crew, their habitat, their supplies, and their exploration vehicles. The lightsail would be built with three stages. There would be a disc-shaped inner "return stage" portion, 100 kilometers in diameter, that would carry the payload and crew, and return them to Earth. This would be surrounded by a ring-shaped "accelerator stage" portion, 320 kilometers in diameter with a 100 kilometer diameter hole. Together, these two sails constitute the "rendezvous stage" that would stop at the target star. This in turn would be surrounded by the "decelerator stage," 1000 kilometers in diameter with a 320 kilometer diameter hole. [See Figure 7.]

All three portions of the lightsail would be accelerated together at thirty percent of Earth gravity by 43,000 terawatts of laser power. At this acceleration, the lightsail would reach a velocity of half the speed of light in 1.6 years. The expedition would reach Epsilon Eridani in twenty years Earth time and seventeen years crew time, and it would be time to stop.

At a half-lightyear from the target star, the 320 kilometer rendezvous stage would be detached from the center of the lightsail and turned to face the large ring-shaped decelerator stage that remains. The laser light coming from the solar system would reflect from the decelerator stage acting as a retro-directive mirror. The reflected light would decelerate the smaller rendezvous sail and bring it to a halt at Epsilon Eridani.

After the crew explored the system for a few years (using their rendezvous stage lightsail as a solar sail), it would be time to bring them back. To do this, the 100 kilometer diameter return stage would separated out from the center of the 320 kilometer ring-shaped accelerator stage. The laser light from the solar system would hit the accelerator stage and be reflected back on the return stage. The laser light would then accelerate the return stage and its payload back toward the solar system. As the return stage approached the solar system twenty Earth-years later, it would be brought to a halt by a final burst of laser power. The members of the crew would have been away 51 years (including five years of exploring), have aged 46 years, and would be ready to retire and write their memoirs.

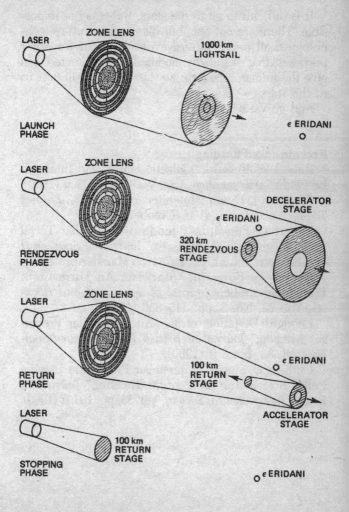

Fig. 7—Roundtrip interstellar travel by laser-pushed lightsails.

✧ ✧ ✧

It is difficult to go to the stars. But it is not impossible. There are not one, but many, many future technologies, all under intensive development for other purposes, that, if suitably modified and redirected, can give the human race a magic starship that will take us to the stars.

And go we will.

Recommended Reading

Robert W. Bussard, "Galactic Matter and Interstellar Flight," *Astronautica Acta*, Vol. 6, pp. 179 ff (1960).

Freeman J. Dyson, "Interstellar Transport," *Physics Today*, Vol. 21, pp. 41 ff (October 1968).

Robert L. Forward, "Roundtrip Interstellar Travel Using Laser-Pushed Lightsails," *Journal of Spacecraft and Rockets*, Vol. 21, pp. 187–195 (March–April 1984).

Robert L. Forward, "Starwisp: An Ultra-Light Interstellar Probe," *Journal of Spacecraft and Rockets*, Vol. 22, No. 3, pp. 345–350 (1985).

Leonard D. Jaffee, et al., "An Interstellar Precursor Mission," *Journal of British Interplanetary Society*, Vol. 33, pp. 3 ff (1980).

Clifford E. Singer, "Interstellar Propulsion Using a Pellet Stream for Momentum Transfer," *Journal of British Interplanetary Society*, Vol. 33, pp. 107 ff (1980).

✧ FADING INTO BLACKNESS

The previous science speculation chapter, "Starships," discussed a number of possible techniques for building a starship that is literally capable of traveling between the stars. In the many years that I have thought about the problems of interstellar flight, most of my effort has been on finding technical solutions to the propulsion problem. But there is another major factor in the feasibility of interstellar flight that has nothing to do with technology—it is economics—specifically the exponential growth implicit in interest rates compounded over many decades of time. The exponential growth of debt at compound interest is just as deadly to a mission as the exponential growth of mass ratio in a rocket.

Nearly all the ideas for interstellar flight involve the construction of some expensive high power propulsion system that drives the space vehicle to the speeds necessary to accomplish the mission. The vehicle and its propulsion system must be built and paid for at the start of the mission, while the payoff in knowledge does not come about until decades or centuries later. With luck, the payoff will be knowledge with such an astronomically high value that it will produce a net return on the up-front investment that is greater than if the money had been invested in a savings account at an interest rate greater than *inflation. Realistically, however, the probability of a large payoff is low. Even governments cannot ignore the "laws" of capitalism for long, or they will fall by the wayside—as witness the USSR and other communist governments.*

What is needed is an interstellar flight concept that is both technologically feasible and financially feasible—in that it either does not involve a high up-front cost, or produces a reliable and adequate return for the investor during the mission, with the promise of a much higher payoff if the mission is successful.

The best candidate is my "Starwisp" concept. It is a beamed power propulsion and power system that requires the construction of a large and expensive sunlight-to-microwave power station in space, and a large and expensive beaming dish. The vehicle itself is small, and although probably expensive per gram, its total cost would be insignificant compared to the beaming dish, which in turn would be insignificant compared to the microwave power station. Unlike an antimatter engine, or an interstellar ramjet engine, or a laser or pellet beaming device that must be operated for years during the mission, the microwave power station in the Starwisp system is only used for propulsion and power for a few weeks at the beginning and the end of the mission. In addition, while the other engines have no use other than as an interstellar propulsion system, Starwisp's microwave generator can be used as a power station during most of the mission, generating enough income to pay the investors back their initial investment plus a modest profit, while holding out the hope for a "killing" if the mission is successful.

In the following story, "Fading Into Blackness" I describe a possible scenario that would send Starwisp on its way into interstellar space without violating the "laws" of either physics or economics. The story was first published in the July 1988 issue of Analog Science Fiction/Science Fact, *Volume 108, Number 7, pages 60-69.*

"You are absolutely crazy!" James exploded. He hunched forward to sit perched on the edge of the plush sofa, his voice echoing in the cavernous office of his boss.

Michael Lord, media magnate, was leaning far back in his chair behind his desk, grinning like a student who has just thought of a great prank to pull. In back of him was a huge flatscreen showing a sunlit view of the whole Earth. The living image came directly from one of the dozen geostationary direct broadcast television stations that Michael Lord owned. Despite his annoyance, James's gaze was drawn once again to that brown and blue globe covered with clouds of wispy white. A fragile globe that was home to billions of humans.

This particular picture came from Station North America One that hovered over Canada, one of Michael Lord's first customers. It was near noon in Canada, so that particular full sunlight view of the Earth was being broadcast during every station break over every station around the globe. For the station breaks, the living image of the Earth was surrounded by the words, "LORD WORLD BROADCAST NETWORK LIMITED," the always varying, never-the-same logo of the Michael Lord empire.

Michael Lord had made his billions by finding a way around the International Telecommunication Treaty that controlled access to the geostationary orbit. He had realized that if he built broadcast stations that used a large solar sail to get constant thrust from sunlight, then the stations could be placed in artificial orbits that were many hundreds of kilometers north or south of the equatorial geostationary orbit, yet still only rotated around the Earth once a day. Since they were not in a natural orbit controlled solely by the Earth's gravity, his lawyers had successfully argued that his "stations" were not "satellites," and therefore were not regulated by the treaty.

James lowered his glance from the screen to find Michael Lord still grinning at him. "I *won't* let you do it! You can fire me if you want—I'm sure I can find lots of jobs at a million per year—but I won't let you throw away a hundred billion on this crazy scheme . . . this 'wisp' of glittering nothing."

"You just earned yourself a lifetime pension at a million per, Jamey," said Michael Lord, who had heard all this many times before from his old college roommate and fanatically faithful right-hand man. "But I hope you'll stay on at two million per in addition to make sure it's done right."

"*Sure* I can make sure—with your money I can make sure of anything. But to spend your entire net worth on this will-o'-the-wisp doesn't make sense to me. It won't get to Alpha Centauri for twenty years, long after we both are doddering old wrecks, if not dead. Then all it will do is send back pictures, which won't arrive back here for another four years or so. I also don't see why you are going to interrogate it on the trip out. All you'll get will be pictures of nothing."

"Exactly."

James did his job—as no one else could—nearly perfectly. One billion of Michael Lord's money went into design studies.

First was the design for the large solar power satellite, ten times larger than any that had ever been designed before. It would generate the fifty thousand megawatts of microwave power that would be needed to accelerate the interstellar probe up to twenty percent of the speed of light.

Second was the design for the radar dish that was to focus the microwaves into a far-reaching beam. It was ultralarge, four times larger than the diameter of the Earth, and ultralight, made out of a thin disk of fine wire mesh. The wire mesh disk was to be shaped into a nearly perfect parabola by centrifugal acceleration from a slow rotation of the disk combined with a linear acceleration from a million electric ion thrusters spaced around the periphery of the disk.

Finally, there was the interstellar probe itself, a wisp of ultrafine wire woven into a hexagonal mesh that was a kilometer in diameter, yet had a total mass of only sixteen grams. At each six-wire intersection of the mesh was a microcircuit, so tiny that all one hundred billion of the microcircuits had a total mass of only four grams. Its name was to be—"Starwisp."

"Fascinating," said Michael Lord, staring at the thin shred of black veil floating in the center of the large glass globe that James had placed on his desk. "It's so light it just floats there."

"Actually, it's levitated," said James. "There's a small battery-powered microwave generator built into the base of the globe. It produces a beam of microwaves directed upward. The microwaves bounce off the wire mesh with enough force to lift it against gravity."

"Open the globe and let me feel the mesh," said Michael Lord.

"I'm afraid I can't do that," said James. "In the first place, the wires are so fine that the mesh would tear at the slightest touch. Second, the globe is evacuated. The minute any air got to the mesh, it would be eaten away and all you'd have left would be a drifting cloud of microcircuit dust."

"Fascinating," said Michael Lord again. He had found the power control to the microwave generator in the base, and was pushing the miniature model of the

Starwisp probe up to the top of the globe, then letting it fall. He stopped for a second and looked up at James.

"Let's proceed with the next phase."

"If you insist," said James reluctantly, and started the long walk across the office. At the door he stopped and turned to look back at his boss. Michael Lord's gaze was again on the globe, watching the nearly invisible wisp as it rose and fell inside.

While James waited politely for Michael Lord to look in his direction, his attention was drawn once again to the constantly changing view of the living Earth on the flatscreen. This view was from Station South Pacific Two. On one side of the Earth he could see Hawaii, where they were. On the other side he could see the huge monsoon that was savaging the lower part of India. The news being broadcast that very minute over Michael Lord's worldwide news network was showing terrible scenes of havoc and human suffering. Like many others who had seen pictures of Earth from space, James was struck yet again by the thought of all mankind being just space travelers, wandering through the galaxy in a fragile blue globular spacecraft.

"Yet still we squabble," he thought.

James shook his head and lowered his glance from the image of the Earth and continued waiting. Michael Lord finally stopped playing with the microwave controls and looked up.

"I *still* think you are absolutely crazy!" James said vehemently, and slammed out the door.

It took five years and a good deal of Mr. Lord's money to start construction of the solar power satellite. But, even James had to admit it was a good investment. New scientific advances in methods for the direct conversion of sunlight to microwaves gave the solar power satellite an energy conversion efficiency of seventy-five percent. That was many times the efficiency of solar cells and twice that of ground-based power plants. The advent of room temperature superconducting power transmission lines had allowed the microwave receiving stations on the ground to be placed in uninhabitable deserts, oceans, and frozen wastelands far from the cities that needed the power. The customer list for the first five thousand megawatt section was oversubscribed even before it was completed, but Michael Lord insisted on reserving the first month of output for preliminary tests on a tenth-scale prototype Starwisp.

James sat back in the sofa, holding the remote control for the flatscreen on the wall. Michael Lord came out from behind his desk and joined him. The living Earth on the screen now came from Station South Africa One. James pushed the button on the remote control and the picture of the Earth was replaced by a picture of Powersat Alpha, the flagship of Lord Powersat Limited.

"Nothing much to show you here," said James. "I'm sure you have been monitoring construction progress yourself."

"I notice the microwave transmitter array in the center is no longer pointing at Earth," said Michael Lord.

"The engineers wanted to get maximum efficiency for this test," said James. "So they rotated the antenna array so that it points to the microwave dish in its high orbit over the South Pole. Once Powersat Alpha is up to full power the transmitting array will stay pointed at Earth. Using standard phased array techniques, it can feed power beams to a dozen Earth stations, while at the same time it's sending a beam out to the interstellar probe." He pushed a button on the control. All that could be seen on the screen were a few stars and a thin ellipse of pinkish-blue lights.

"This is the microwave dish that will turn the broad microwave beam from Powersat Alpha into a narrow beam. This tenth-scale model can form a beam that will reach halfway to Mars. The full scale model will form a beam that can reach Jupiter. You can't see the mesh, but you can see the exhaust from the ring of xenon ion engines around the rim."

James referred to a sheet of paper, then pushed the button for another channel. The long vertical ellipse of glowing electric rocket engines was replaced by a smaller horizontal oval of rocket lights.

"This is the flat mesh mirror that collects the microwave beam from Powersat Alpha and directs it down the axis of the beaming dish. The beaming dish stays pointed in the direction the probe is supposed to go, while the flat mirror wobbles slightly once a day to track Powersat Alpha below as it rotates around the Earth.

"It's a shame that the mesh structures are too fine to see," said Michael Lord. "Fortunately the electric rockets give us their outline. I presume you are not going to even bother trying to show me the scale-model Starwisp."

"Since I knew you would be interested, I had the engineers take out some video equipment and give it a try. They were actually pretty successful. By aligning things so the camera is on one side of the sail and the Sun on the other, they were able to get enough forward-scattered light to see the mesh. It's the same technique that they used during the Voyager flybys to take a picture of the rings around Jupiter." James gave the button another push and a bright oval of light appeared on the screen.

"There's 'Lord's Folly'," said James. "All two hundred milligrams of it. It's sitting out about half-way between the Earth and Moon, lined up between the beaming dish and Mars."

Michael Lord winced. "I thought 'Starwisp Prototype 0.1' was its name."

"That's its official name," said James. "But it's much too long for daily use. Since you didn't make up a name, I did . . ." He paused, "I *still* think you are absolutely crazy!"

Michael Lord smiled determinedly. "Let's see what . . . 'Lord's Folly' can do!" he said.

James took out a beeper-type communicator and held it up. "The microwave beam will be triggered at Powersat Alpha as soon as this signal gets transmitted through the earthcomm links," said James, "but it will take about a second for the beam to make it out to the beaming dish above the south pole, then almost another second before the microwaves reach the sail." He pushed the button and they both watched the illuminated oval on the screen as James counted.

"One-thousand one. One-thousand . . . There it goes! My God, Mickey, it's really working!!"

The glowing oval of mesh billowed slightly, then started moving off, slowly at first, then faster and faster as the constant ten gravity acceleration built up its velocity. The camera swiveled to follow it. The oval shrank, changed into a circle, then faded into blackness.

"Let's see the pictures it's sending back," said Michael Lord.

James looked down at the remote control and selected another channel. A high resolution picture of the Moon showed up on the left hand side of the screen. It was moving noticeably toward the edge of the screen as the prototype Starwisp accelerated in a direction to one side of it.

"At this distance from the transmitter there is more than enough microwave power impinging on the sail to power the microcircuits," said James. "The real test will be when the distance between them is lightyears, not Earth radii."

"Any engineer can calculate that," said Michael Lord, "and even *you* will have to admit that with the full-sized dish directing the microwave beam, that there will be plenty of microwave power flooding the Alpha Centauri star system to power the mesh circuits. What I was really worried about was the ability of all those billions of microcircuits to work together as an image processing computer. *Look* at that picture!"

"I've got to admit it's high quality," said James. "Better than the video cameras on your broadcast stations. In full color too."

"With a billion microcircuits, each with a photosensitive detector looking in a different direction and sensitive to a different color, you have everything you need to make a picture. It's just a matter of each microcircuit working with its neighbors to unscramble the billions of bits of data to make an image."

"We'll find out how well it performs tomorrow, when the sail approaches Mars," said James. "The engineers will lower the microwave power in the beam until it's as weak as it would be if it had to travel from the solar system to Alpha Centauri. The probe will only have one watt of power reaching it. And with that one watt the probe has to power a billion microcircuits with a billion photodetectors, and carry out a billion billion calculations for each picture."

"I'm looking forward to seeing Mars up close," said Michael Lord. "What time does . . . 'Lord's Folly' get to Mars?"

James chewed his lower lip as he consulted a schedule. For once Mickey might be right and he was wrong. "Lord's F— Starwisp Prototype 0.1 arrives within imaging distance of Mars tomorrow morning at 0920," he said. "It will be traveling at almost two percent of the speed of light. At that speed, it'll shoot past the orbit of Mars in just a few minutes."

"I certainly don't want to miss it," said Michael Lord. "I'll see you promptly at nine-fifteen and we can watch it together."

"I'll be here," said James. "And I'll bring a written apology along with my letter of resignation." He put the remote control for the flatscreen on the table in front of the sofa and left the office.

"And I'll file them the same place I filed all your other letters of resignation, Jamey," said Michael Lord to the closed door. He walked over to the table in front of the sofa and picked up the remote control. He pushed the button for one of the higher numbered channels that was used for calibration of the probe's imaging system. This channel used the photons coming from the backside of the probe that had managed to penetrate through the back of the thin microcircuits to reach the photodetectors from behind. It formed an image of objects in the direction that the probe had come from. It wasn't as good as the image from the front side, but it was still better than a standard high resolution video camera.

As Michael Lord switched on the channel, a picture of the Earth as seen from the probe appeared on the screen. The Earth was three-quarters full and flanked by the Moon, also three-quarters full. He watched for a few minutes as they shrank slowly on the screen. He smiled with satisfaction, then switched the flatscreen back to its normal full Earth living picture from one of his broadcast stations. It was from Station South Africa One, and if it was nearly midday in South Africa, it must be time for him to go to bed. He yawned and went through the door behind his office to his apartment.

The images of Mars were fantastic, even after the engineers had lowered the microwave power shining on the minuscule spacecraft to less than a tenth of a watt. There was now no question the technology worked. A large enough microwave dish could send a beam that could push a lightweight spacecraft to speeds approaching the speed of light. The same microwave dish could supply power to that same spacecraft over interstellar distances. And that same microwave dish could also receive return signals from the spacecraft many years later that contained real-time, high-resolution, color television pictures of the planets in that new star system as the high-speed sail sped through it. Now all that it was necessary to do was to spend the money to build it.

Fortunately, James was up to the task. Nearly eighty billion more went into the completion of the fifty gigawatt solar power satellite, but it started generating a net cash flow before it was completed. Another fifteen billion went into the full scale beaming dish, in a far orbit that took it high over the South Pole, guided by its electric ion rockets as the engineers tuned the millions of components so they would work as a whole. Then, finally, a kilometer wide sheet of thick plastic was unrolled far out in space in the southern skies of Earth. Printed on the plastic was Starwisp. First were the multitude of ultrathin wires that formed the body of Starwisp. At each intersection of six wires were the multitude of multilayered microcircuits that formed the brain of Starwisp. In each microcircuit were the multitude of photodetectors that formed the retina of Starwisp.

After baking for two days in the intense ultraviolet glare of the light from the Sun, the plastic backing decomposed. Starwisp now floated in space, naively looking at the light sources around it, and waiting for the first of the microwaves from Earth that would fling it outward to the stars.

❖ ❖ ❖

"It's taken five years and 122 billion," said James. "Instead of holding a majority interest in your properties, you are a minor stockholder. I hope you're satisfied."

"Of course I'm satisfied, Jamey" said Michael Lord. "I've always been satisfied with everything you have ever done for me. Haven't you arranged it so that I am still CEO of Lord Broadcasting Network Limited, even if I don't own it?"

James frowned in annoyance and begrudging acknowledgement.

"Besides," continued Michael Lord. "What is the use of making money if you don't spend it? I certainly can't take it with me."

"The one who dies with the most toys wins?" said James. "I never thought you were that type, Mickey. But you certainly have bought the most expensive toy ever made."

"Some toys are purely for fun," said Michael Lord, "Others are designed to educate . . ." He drew a deep breath. "It's time to launch Starwisp on its way. Push the button."

"That's your job," said James bruskly, handing him the special beeper with a single button.

Michael Lord shrugged and pushed the button.

Ten full minutes dragged on as the microwave beam shot out from Powersat Alpha around the Earth, flashed southward to the deflector mirror, bounced off the beaming dish, and shot across interplanetary space to Starwisp waiting patiently in the southern skies. Starwisp billowed slightly as the leading portion of the microwave beam struck it, then straightened out and started accelerating toward Alpha Centauri. Five minutes later, the billowing was seen on the flatscreen in Michael Lord's office on Earth as well as billions of video screens around the globe.

Starwisp accelerated at more than one hundred times Earth gravity, and was beyond the range of the monitor cameras within a few minutes. The news broadcasters, having nothing on their screens, switched to interviews of people around the world.

"Mr. Lord is daft, spending all his money like that. I certainly would have saved a little fer me kids and me old age."

"With millions of hungry people starving in Bangladesh and Ethiopia, it is criminal to throw away money on an egotistical whim!"

"*Eh bien* . . . I do not see the good of this."

"Dinkum nonsense!"

At the closing of the broadcast, Michael Lord had the living Earth logo for his network changed to an image of the Earth taken from the rapidly receding Starwisp. Even at the maximum magnification the mesh imaging system was able to supply, the Earth was noticeably smaller than the image the audience had been used to.

Starwisp continued to accelerate for ten hours under the powerful push of the microwave beam. By the time it had reached the limit of the beam, it had passed the orbit of Jupiter and was on its way out of the solar system at twenty percent of the speed of light. Some twenty-five years later, the human race would see pictures of new planets from its front side imaging system. Now, its back side imaging system was sending pictures of a familiar planet—Earth.

As the hours passed, the image of the Earth shrank on the screen. The hourly reminders of the shrinking blue-white globe during the day brought home to the human race the smallness of its triumphs, the pettiness of its squabbles, the frailness of its home. Soon many found themselves staring closely at their television screens, searching through the fluctuating pixels for the tiny dots that were the Earth-Moon system.

After just two days, Starwisp had passed out of the solar system, leaving Neptune and Pluto behind on its twenty year journey to the nearest stars. Even when the Sun started to appear at one side of the magnified image—the Sun itself was nothing but another star in the sky, lost among the multitudes of other stars.

Day by day, the world watched the Earth fading into blackness . . .

And grew up.

✧ ANTIGRAVITY

From birth to death, gravity pervades our life. Our every step, day-in to day-out, is a struggle against this relentless force. It cuts our baby knees when we fall. It pulls on our limbs so that our every motion is burdened by its enervating presence. It sucks our bodies into the mud, preventing us from soaring into the skies like the birds.

Will there ever be some future technology that will enable us to control gravity—some technology that today is indistinguishable from magic? Can we somehow find a way to "turn off" or "nullify" the gravity field of the Earth? Could we possibly arrange for a mass to push us gently away into the skies instead of hugging us firmly to its crushing bosom?

The answers are: Yes . . . Maybe . . . Someday.

But to control some force in nature, you need to know something about it. You need a theory of how it works, and the more detailed the theory, the better your chances of control. What do we know about gravity? What are the theories? How can we use those theories to nullify gravity?

The first Theory of Gravity, usually attributed to Ug the caveman, was simple:

"Things fall down."

This theory served Ug quite well in its time. Ug used his theory to make gravity his servant rather than his master. Instead of having to walk right up to a saber-toothed tiger to bash it in the head with a sharp rock (and getting all scratched in the process), Ug climbed a tree, and wisely using his theory of gravity, dropped his sharp rock down on the head of the saber-toothed tiger. This was the first use of gravity as a tool for the betterment of the human race.

It wasn't too much later that Ug found a way to use his new theory to nullify the effect of gravity. One day, while sitting high up on a slippery-elm branch waiting for a saber-tooth tiger to walk beneath him, he tossed his favorite sharp rock back and forth from one palm to another. His newly-developed and still-awkward opposed thumb missed a toss and the rock bounced away.

Not wanting to lose his favorite tool, Ug jumped after it. After his jump, Ug noticed a strange thing. The rock no longer fell down. Instead, it just hung there in the rapidly rushing air just an arm length away. By his jump from the branch Ug had made one gigantic leap for mankind toward the conquest of gravity. As he reached out and plucked the floating rock from midair, he thought about all the admiration he would receive around the cave fire that night as he explained the secret of nullifying gravity.

"Just jump," he would tell them . . . At that point the uprushing ground terminated his thought processes.

Ug would be amazed to know that even today we use his simple yet effective technique to nullify gravity. Each flight of the Space Shuttle utilizes his marvelous invention to make multiton communication satellites float weightless so mere men and women can push them around like leaden pillows. To nullify gravity, all the astronauts have to do is to use the Space Shuttle rockets to "jump" high enough that they can go into free-fall.

Unlike Ug, however, whose career as an astronaut ended in a second, the Space Shuttle astronauts can fall forever. That is because while the astronauts are falling vertically ten meters, their orbital velocity takes them horizontally eight kilometers. At this new point, the surface of the Earth below is now ten meters further away than it was before, so the astronauts can fall another ten meters without getting any closer to the dangerous ground. Thus, by using the Ug Theory of Gravity and constantly falling as they move, our astronauts can nullify the effects of Earth gravity.

The Ug Theory of Gravity served the human race well until sailing ships were invented. Then reports began to trickle in from the sailors that the world was round and that there were people living on large island continents on the "other side" of the Earth. Amazingly enough, even though they were obviously upside-down, they didn't have to hang onto trees or handles set into the ground, but instead walked around on their feet in just the same way that people did on the topside of the Earth. It was finally realized that the Ug Theory of Gravity, despite all its advantages, was not the correct theory of gravity and a new theory would have to be found.

Finally, in 1687, Isaac Newton discovered a better theory of gravity. The Newton Theory of Gravity is somewhat more complicated than the Ug Theory of Gravity, but the basic idea is quite simple:

"A mass attracts all other masses."

There is more to the Newton Theory of Gravity than that, but it consists mostly of details that are used for making accurate mathematical predictions.

Using his theory of gravity, Newton was able to predict the motions of the Moon and the planets in the sky to high accuracy. To carry out the calculations he had to invent a new form of mathematics, called "calculus," that revolutionized both science and engineering.

The first use of this new gravitational technology was to predict the future motions of the Moon through the starry background of the sky. Navigators on ships far at sea could measure the position of the Moon in the sky, compare it with the predictions made by the gravitational engineers using the Newton Theory of Gravity, and figure out where the ship was on the trackless sea surface.

Amazingly enough, using only Newton's Theory of Gravity, it is possible to design a simple anti-gravity machine that can "nullify" the gravity field of the Earth. As we shall see, although we know how to *design* the machine, it will be some time before our engineering technology is up to the task of actually *building* the machine. To design our Newtonian antigravity machine, we will need to look more closely at the details of the Newton Theory of Gravity.

The basic form of the Newton Theory of Gravity is that masses attract other masses. In a more detailed form, the Newton Theory of Gravity can be expressed as:

"A big mass will attract another mass. The bigger the attracting mass, the stronger the attraction. The closer the two masses, the stronger the attraction. (It goes as the square of the distance between the two masses.)"

How can we use this Newton Theory of Gravity to cancel the gravity field of the Earth?

Well, one way to use the Newton Theory of Gravity to keep the Earth from pulling you down, would be to put another planet, with the same mass as Earth, above your head. The Newtonian antigravity field of the above-Earth will pull you up with the same force as the Newtonian progravity field of the below-Earth is pulling you down. The two forces would cancel each other out and over a broad region between the two "Earths," there would be no gravity. Everyone and everything would be in free fall.

There is no question that from a mathematical point

of view, that this method of nullifying the gravity field of the Earth using the Newton Theory of Gravity would work. But it is also obvious that this not a very practical solution. Even though there is a way to keep two Earth-sized bodies that close to each other without them falling onto each other due to their mutual gravity attraction (read my novel *Rocheworld* to find out how), we do not have another Earth handy to use as the above-Earth. Notice, however, that the Newton Theory of Gravity says that the gravitational attraction gets stronger as the two masses get closer to each other. It turns out there is a way we can use that aspect of the Newton Theory of Gravity to create antigravity.

Let us look at the gravity field of a large knob of rock about 100 meters, a football field, in diameter. (Single rocks of this size are often found in the Sequoia and Yellowstone National Parks in the U.S.A. and many other places around the world.) If it is a very dense rock, it will weigh about four million tons. Although it would admittedly be difficult, we could imagine that we could hire a team of gravitational engineers to lift that rock up on strong pillars and make a small room underneath it. We now have a small asteroid perched on manmade pillars sitting on the roof of our room. In that room, fifty meters from the center of the rock overhead, the gravity field of the Earth would be decreased by the gravity pull of the rock. The amount of gravity decrease would be about ten microgravities (ten millionths of Earth gravity). We have antigravity of a sort, but not very much.

Now, mindful of the admonition of the Newton Theory of Gravity, which says that the amount of attraction varies as the square of the distance between you and the attracting body, suppose we could get closer to the four million ton rock. If we could get ten times closer or about five meters away, then the gravity from the rock would increase to one thousandth of Earth gravity. If we could get a hundred times closer or fifty centimeters away, the attraction would increase to one-tenth of Earth gravity. The rock is now beginning to have a significant effect on the gravity of the Earth. If we could get sixteen centimeters away from a four million ton mass, the gravity attraction would rise to one Earth gravity. The gravity field of the rock is now strong enough to cancel out the gravity field of the Earth, which is a trillion times more massive than the rock.

But how do you get very close to a rock? It doesn't work to dig a hole and crawl inside. You have to make the rock smaller while maintaining its mass so you can get closer to the center while still staying outside. That means we have to find a way to make matter more dense than it normally is.

An atom in normal matter contains a lot of nothing. In the center of the atom is the nucleus, which contains the protons and neutrons that have most of the mass of the atom. Surrounding the nucleus is a tenuous cloud of electrons. An oxygen atom, for example, has a nucleus with eight protons and eight neutrons that is about a trillionth of a centimeter across.

The eight units of positive charge in the nucleus of an oxygen atom are balanced out by eight negatively charged electrons that orbit around the nucleus. It is this outer electron cloud that is the surface that connects the atom to the rest of the atoms in your body (and the outside world). This electron cloud is thousands of times larger than the nucleus of an atom and weighs practically nothing. Thus, an atom is mostly made up of empty space between the nucleus and the outer electron shells.

We know that more dense forms of matter exist. We can see white-dwarf stars in the sky that have the mass of a sun condensed into a ball the size of the Earth. White-dwarf-star densities are about a million times greater than normal densities. We also know that neutron stars exist. Here the mass of a sun has been condensed into a sphere that is only twenty kilometers across! Neutron-star densities are a hundred trillion times greater than normal densities.

Thus, one future magic key to controlling gravity using the Newton Theory of Gravity is to find a method to collapse ordinary matter with its bloated electron orbits into matter with white-dwarf-star densities or greater. We can't do it now, but one of these days we may develop the technology. When we do, we can envision our four million ton rock condensed into a ball thirty-two centimeters or one foot in diameter, with a surface gravitational attraction of one Earth gravity. Even better would be to make it in the shape of a disc that is forty-five centimeters (eighteen inches) in diameter and ten centimeters (four inches) thick. This disc would have the property that the gravitational attraction would be the same on both sides of the disc and would be fairly uniform near the center of the disc. The strength of the gravitational attraction near the center of the disc would be one Earth gravity. If this disc were somehow supported on the surface of the Earth, then on top of the disc there would be a gravity field of two Earth gravities; one gravity from the gravitational attraction of the dense mass in the disc, plus one gravity due to the Earth. On the bottom of the disc, near the center, the one-gravity attraction the disc would cancel the one-gravity attraction of the Earth. There would be a gravity-free region under the disc where we could carry out free-fall experiments.

But now we come to another problem. How do we hold the four million ton antigravity roof up over our heads? The pressure on the roof supports works out to four million atmospheres! It would take a remarkable material to stand that sort of pressure. The material exists, however, and it *is* remarkable. It is diamond.

The highest pressure ever made in the laboratory to date has been about two million atmospheres. It was achieved by pressing the flat surfaces of two diamond anvils together using a turn-screw. Believe it or not, since the total area under pressure between the two diamonds is so small, the turn-screw is turned by hand! At two million atmospheres, one of the two diamond anvils used in the high pressure machine "flowed." The other diamond, however, being made of sterner stuff, did not.

How strong is a perfect diamond? Strong enough to help make antigravity possible? Dare we envision a future where one of the attractions at a Disney park is a Freefall Pavilion, rising upwards on massive swooping buttresses of pure diamond, which support a brilliantly reflecting roof of ultradense matter—and under that roof floats a crowd of funseekers, swimming through the warm air with colorful feathered wings attached to their arms, living out the legend of Icarus for the price of admission?

Because of the unfortunate coincidence that the Earth is massive and its surface gravity is strong, while the density of matter that we can make is small, so that its surface gravity is weak, antigravity machines using the Newton Theory of Gravity still involve technologies that are presently indistinguishable from magic. Even though we know how to design such antigravity machines, we cannot yet build them. As we shall see later, this will still hold true for antigravity machines built using the secrets of the Einstein Theory of Gravity. To make any antigravity machine capable of canceling out the gravity field of the Earth will require the use of ultradense matter, and the method of making ultradense matter is still a form of magic practiced only by white-dwarf and neutron stars.

There is a form of gravity cancellation, however, that

can be practiced right now. It uses a combination of Ug antigravity and Newtonian antigravity to create a large volume that is completely free of gravity forces even though the volume is embedded in the gravity field of the Earth and even when the volume has gravity-producing masses in it! This gravity free volume could be built in a few years and profitably used to make exotic materials that cannot be made under the influence of gravity.

Many of the experiments presently carried out on Space Shuttle flights, especially those where the Spacelab is flown as cargo, are called "zero-gravity" materials processing experiments. Some involve forming "perfect" spheres of metal or latex by squeezing out drops of liquid into free-fall. The surface tension forces form the drops into spheres and then the drops solidify into balls. Others involve mixing two metals with greatly differing density, such as lithium and lead (to make a bearing alloy). If you attempted to cast such an alloy on Earth, the bottom of the crucible would contain mostly lead and the top would contain mostly lithium. Another space manufacturing process, called electrophoresis, uses the flow of strong electrical currents through a liquid to collect dilute quantities of precious biological chemicals from blood samples or a watery mass of bacteria and their excretions. The purity of the end product depends strongly on the dominance of the electrochemical currents over the convection currents in the liquid caused by the heated water "rising" in any residual gravity forces.

At the present time, these "zero-gravity" space manufacturing experiments are done using only the Ug form of antigravity. The Space Shuttle "jumps" into space and goes into a free-fall orbit around the Earth. This effectively cancels most of the gravity field of the Earth, but not all of it. The only part of the Space Shuttle that is under absolutely zero net gravity force is the center of mass of the spacecraft. The rest of the Space Shuttle, especially the nose, tail, and wingtips, is experiencing gravity forces due to the tides of the Earth. These residual gravity forces are not large, a few microgravities, and do not cause any large effects in the present crude space manufacturing experiments. But as the manufacturing apparatus goes from the experimental stage on the Space Shuttle to the "making money" manufacturing phase on the Space Station, the apparatus will become larger, the residual gravity tidal forces will become larger, and the tidal forces will begin to affect the quality of the manufactured product.

I have invented a way to reduce these gravity effects by another factor of a million, so that the residual forces are less than a picogravity (a trillionth of Earth gravity). I do this by using various arrangements of massive dense spheres, disks, and rings to nullify the residual gravity effects inside the processing apparatus. (Those interested in the details can read my technical paper in "Recommended Reading" at the end of the chapter.)

Suppose you were floating around in the bay of the Space Shuttle. The Shuttle has all of its control thrusters off and is floating in free-fall, its nose pointing to the ground below. If you were floating at the point in the middle of the bay that is the center of mass of the Shuttle, you would stay at that point, since both you and the Shuttle are in *exactly* the same orbit. If, however, you were up in the nose of the Shuttle, fifteen meters away from the center of mass, you would find that after two minutes of time that you would have drifted some thirty centimeters away from the center of mass of the Shuttle, closer to the nose. Your motion was caused by a residual tidal force of 4.5 microgravities. In two minutes under this intense gravity force you will have reached the tremendous velocity of five millimeters per second and are about to be smashed against the forward bulkhead, where you will be crushed by the intense 4.5 microgravity acceleration. Although you are perfectly capable of surviving this experience, a space manufacturing facility located in the nose of the Space Shuttle would be significantly affected by these residual gravity tidal forces. The "perfect" ball bearings would be elliptical, the "uniform" alloy would have density gradations, and the "pure" biological extract would be contaminated with impurities.

There are two ways to look at how these residual tidal forces occur. One picture uses the concept of orbital motion and the other uses the concept of gravity gradients. The two ways are equivalent as long as the region we are interested in (the inside of a Space Shuttle or a manufacturing facility on the Space Station) is much smaller than the distance to the center of the Earth.

In the orbital picture, the center of mass of the Space Shuttle is in orbit around the Earth, moving at a certain speed appropriate for that orbit. You are in the nose of the Space Shuttle, fifteen meters closer to the Earth. However, at the start of the experiment you have arranged your velocity so that you are not moving with respect to the walls of the Shuttle. You are now moving with the velocity of the Space Shuttle, but you are in a lower orbit which requires a *higher* velocity than the Space Shuttle velocity if it is to be a circular orbit. Since your velocity is too low for your altitude, you are *not* in a circular orbit, but at the peak of an elliptical orbit. As you and the Space Shuttle continue in orbit, the Space Shuttle remains at the same distance above the Earth, while you drop away in your elliptical orbit and soon smash against the front bulkhead. The same picture applies if you start out near the tail of the Space Shuttle, only now in your higher orbit you are going too fast for your altitude and rise up away from the Shuttle orbit.

Now suppose the Space Shuttle were in a perfect equatorial orbit, always following the equator of the Earth, with its wings pointing north and south. If you started your space-float at the end of the north wingtip, you would be at the same altitude as the Space Shuttle, moving at the same speed as the Space Shuttle, but your orbit started out a wingtip's length north of the equator. Your orbit has to cross the equator after a quarter of an orbit, go south until it reaches a wingtip's length after a half orbit, cross back over the equator again and then return to the north after a full revolution. Since your orbit has to cross over the equatorial orbit of the Space Shuttle, you will find that you will float from the wingtip "toward" the center of mass of the Space Shuttle.

A similar effect occurs if the wings of the Space Shuttle are oriented along the equator. Now, however, the line from the wingtips through the center of mass is a straight line, while the Shuttle orbit is curved. If you start out on a wingtip, you are in a higher orbit than the Space Shuttle and going too fast. As you rise in your elliptical orbit, you slow down and the Space Shuttle overtakes you, bringing you closer to its center of mass.

Thus, from the orbital picture, objects inside the Space Shuttle that are not right at the center of mass of the Shuttle move in their own orbits. From the viewpoint of those in the Shuttle, those objects that are above or below the Space Shuttle center of mass move outward, while those objects in a plane tangent to the Earth move inward.

There is an alternate way of looking at the same effect that uses the concept of gravity gradients, or the change of the gravity field of the Earth with distance. Imagine that the Space Shuttle is not in orbit. Instead it is just dropping nose first toward the Earth. If you were floating in the nose of the Space Shuttle, dropping along with it, you would be closer to the center of the Earth than the center of mass of the Shuttle. Since the Newton Theory of Gravity says that the gravity field of the Earth gets weaker with distance, then the gravity field on you is *stronger* than the gravity field on the Space Shuttle and you fall faster than the center of mass of the Space Shuttle, pulling you toward the nose. If you were at the back of the Shuttle bay, you would be in a weaker gravity field, while the Shuttle is in a stronger field and is pulled away from you. Thus, because the gravity field of the Earth changes with vertical distance above the Earth, objects at different altitudes fall at different rates. The farther apart the objects are from each other, the greater the difference in their rates of fall.

This gravity gradient or differential acceleration effect is better known to you as the tidal force. The tides in the oceans of the Earth are caused mostly by the gravity gradient forces of the Moon. The Moon pulls on the oceans of the Earth that are underneath it, and pulls them up away from the center of mass of the Earth, causing the below-Moon tidal bulge. At the same time, the Moon is pulling the Earth away from the ocean water on the far side, causing the opposite-Moon tidal bulge. That is why the tides come about every twelve hours instead of every twenty-four hours.

There is also a horizontal gravity gradient. The reason for the horizontal accelerations is a little harder to understand, but the horizontal gradients are *always* just as important as the vertical gradient. For a spherical attracting mass like the Earth, the horizontal gradients are half the strength of the vertical gradients, but there are two of them. Going back (briefly) to our still-falling Space Shuttle, suppose you were out near one wingtip, falling along with the Shuttle. Both you and the Space Shuttle are falling directly toward the center of the Earth. But since the two trajectories ultimately meet at the center of the Earth, as you fall along your trajectory, your trajectory gets closer to the Space Shuttle trajectory and you observe an inward motion.

If we move our point of view to the center of the mass of the Space Shuttle, we see that the gravity tide pattern from the Earth consists of a tension in the vertical direction that is twice as strong as the uniform compression in the horizontal direction. [See top half of Figure 8.]

To eliminate these residual gravity fields we can use my gravity gradient compensator consisting of six dense masses in a ring around the region to be protected. (A solid ring or any number of masses greater than three can be used instead, but six seems to be optimum.) The plane of the ring of masses is arranged to always be tangent to the surface of the Earth below. The tidal gravity pattern from the six compensator spheres in a ring is almost exactly the same as the tidal gravity pattern from the Earth, except the accelerations are reversed in direction.

This pattern of forces is easily understood if you imagine a small test object in the middle of the ring. If the test object is exactly in the center, the combined gravitational attraction of the six spheres cancels out. If the test object moves above or below the plane, the combined attractions of the spheres will pull it back. If the test object moves toward one of the spheres, the attraction of that sphere increases while the attraction of the sphere on the opposite side of the ring decreases, and the test object is pulled even farther away from the center. By merely adjusting the radius and tilt of the ring of compensator spheres we can "fine tune" the gravity tidal pattern of the compensator to match the tidal pattern of the Earth at any altitude.

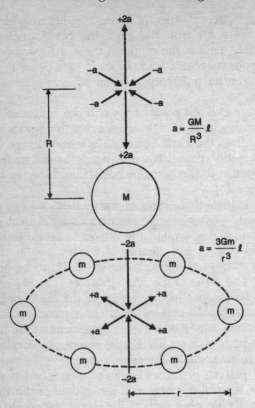

$$a = \frac{GM}{R^3} \ell$$

$$a = \frac{3Gm}{r^3} \ell$$

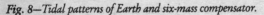

Fig. 8—Tidal patterns of Earth and six-mass compensator.

Since we are not trying to compensate the whole gravity field of the Earth, but only the much weaker tidal forces, we will not need ultradense matter for the compensator spheres, but only normal density materials like lead or tungsten.

If we assume that the six spheres in the compensator are each a 100 kilogram ball of tungsten, then the spheres will be twenty-two centimeters (nine inches) in diameter. The match of the compensating fields to the Earth fields is only perfect at the exact center of the ring. The match is fairly good, however, in a significant region about the central point. Calculations show that if the compensator ring were properly adjusted, the residual gravity forces inside a disk-shaped region about the size of a box of bath powder at the center of the compensator ring would be reduced by a factor of one hundred. At geostationary orbit altitude, the tidal fields to be compensated become smaller and the size of the compensated region becomes larger. The compensator ring can now lower the residual accelerations to less than a picogravity (a trillionth of an Earth gravity) over a disk-shaped volume the size of a large hatbox.

These large volumes of force-free space will certainly be valuable for scientific experiments that require a region free from Earth tides. They also will be useful, up to a point, for space manufacturing. The lower acceleration limit for space processing is set by the self-gravity of the molten metals or liquids being processed. A ball of water and bacteria one meter across will have a self-gravity field at its surface of thirty nanogravities, while a molten ball of steel ten centimeters across has a self-gravity field of twenty nanogravities (greater than the accelerations due to the Earth tides). These self-gravity forces will cause convection currents to flow in the liquid, disturbing the desired equilibrium conditions.

It turns out, however, that with a little bit of Newtonian antigravity magic, we can not only cancel any Earth tides that might affect those materials processing experiments, but we can also cancel the self-gravity field everywhere inside the sample! The shape for a space materials processing experiment sample that gives the most volume with the lowest residual gravity is a thick disk. For a specific example, let us assume a disk of material with the density of water that is thirty centimeters in diameter and ten centimeters thick (about the size of a large double-layer cake). The self-gravity field pattern of this thick disk is quite complicated. It is zero at the center and becomes stronger as you go toward the surface, reaching about three nanogravities at the top and bottom and around the rim.

We first can smooth out the variations in the acceleration due to the "edge effects" by surrounding the sample volume with a "guard ring" consisting of a container in the shape of a ring filled with material that has the same density as the material in the sample chamber. The material in the sample volume and the guard ring need to be kept separated by a thin wall. The material in the guard ring will not be free from accelerations, and convection currents will be set up in it. The thin wall will keep the protected material in the sample volume from being disturbed by these currents.

We then add "guard caps" to the top and bottom of the sample volume plus guard ring. With the guard ring and guard caps in place, we find that the original complicated self-gravity force pattern inside the sample has become very regular and increases linearly with distance from the center. How can we cancel these self-gravity accelerations? Let us take them one at a time.

To compensate for the inward vertical component of the self-gravity of the disk we will use the outward vertical acceleration of the Earth tides. If the Earth tide at the altitude of our manufacturing facility is too strong for the self-gravity of the disk, we cancel a portion of it with our six-sphere tidal compensator. If the Earth tide at that altitude is too weak, we augment the Earth tidal forces using my two-sphere tidal augmentor.

A tidal augmentor consists of two 100 kilogram

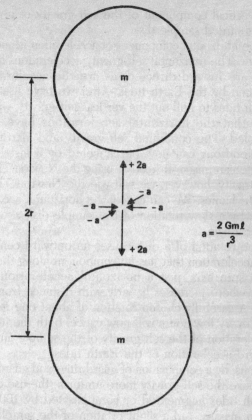

$$a = \frac{2\,Gm\ell}{r^3}$$

Fig. 9—Tidal force augmentor.

spheres placed above and below the sample disk. The gravity tidal pattern the augmentor produces at the point between the two spheres is identical to the tidal pattern of the Earth. [See Figure 9.] Thus, by judicious use of either the compensator or augmentor, depending upon the orbital altitude and the density of the sample of material undergoing processing, we can adjust the Earth tides so they will compensate for the vertical component of the self-gravity of a properly guarded sample disk.

The horizontal component of acceleration is another matter. The horizontal self-gravity accelerations of the disk are inward directed, as are the accelerations induced by the Earth tides. After we have used the Earth tides to null out the vertical self-gravity, we will find that the horizontal accelerations have been doubled. The combined self-gravity and Earth tide accelerations can now be canceled by a last bit of Newtonian magic. Instead of using the Newton Theory of Gravity, however, we will use the Newton Theory of Mechanics. We can cancel the horizontal accelerations by a slow rotation of the sample disk about its vertical axis.

The rotation of a disk causes an outward centrifugal acceleration that has no component along the vertical spin axis, just a horizontal acceleration that everywhere increases linearly with distance from the axis. A carefully chosen rotation of about one revolution every few hours will now cancel both the inward acceleration of the self-gravity of the sample and the inward acceleration of the Earth tides.

Thus, by a combination of guard rings and guard caps to make the self-gravity more uniform, the use of the Earth tides augmented or compensated by 100-kilogram masses, and a slight rotation of the sample volume, it is possible to cancel all the gravity inside a sample volume of material some thirty centimeters in diameter and ten centimeters thick (the size of a birthday cake). The technique can be used at any orbital altitude, but the best results can be obtained in a space manufacturing facility in geostationary orbit. In one example that I calculated, our birthday-cake sized sample disk of water had the gravity fields inside decreased by a factor of a thousand, so that the maximum gravity acceleration anywhere inside the disk was less than a picogravity or a trillionth of an Earth gravity. At this level of acceleration it would take an atom eight seconds to fall its own diameter!

One of these days there will be large space laboratories in orbit, with special isolated rooms where ultra-low gravity experiments can be carried out. There will be no humans near those rooms, for the gravity of even the most petite experimenter would be enough to disturb the delicate experiments floating inside. From some of the laboratories will come exotic alloys, from others ultra-light, ultra-strong foamed metals. From still other laboratories the valuables extracted will not be tangible products like pharmaceuticals and new materials, but that intangible yet infinitely more valuable product of scientific research—knowledge. Perhaps new knowledge about the innermost secrets of gravity.

The Newton Theory of Gravity served the human race well for over 200 years. As the followers of Newton carried out more and more detailed calculations of the motion of the Moon and planets, the better the Newton Theory of Gravity looked. For example, the motion of Mars in its orbit is predominantly due to the gravitational attraction of the Sun, but the mass of nearby Jupiter causes perturbations in that orbit, and the mass of Earth causes perturbations in that perturbed orbit, and the mass of Saturn causes perturbations in that perturbed, perturbed orbit, etc. Finally, perturbation calculations were carried out for the effect of every planet around the Sun on every other planet. All the observations of the planets agreed with the predictions of the amazing Newton Theory of Gravity . . . almost. There was a "slight discrepancy" in the predictions for the orbit of Mercury that wouldn't go away.

The orbit of Mercury is not circular. It is distinctly elliptical. With an orbital period of only 88 days, the astronomers have followed Mercury through hundreds of revolutions around the sun and have been able to measure the parameters of the orbit to high accuracy. The major axis of the orbital ellipse of Mercury shifts a little each revolution, 5599.74±0.41 seconds of arc per century to be exact (about four degrees of total precessional shift since people started measuring a few centuries ago). Calculations using the Newton Theory of Gravity indicate that the perturbations introduced by the other planets in the solar system cause most of this shift, but not all of it. Even after many refinements, the maximum calculated orbital shift due to the planetary perturbations was found to be 5557.18±0.85 seconds of arc per century, leaving a discrepancy of 42.56±0.94 seconds of arc per century between the measurements and predictions of the Newton Theory of Gravity.

Finally, along came Albert Einstein with his new Theory of Gravity. Using his new theory, Einstein calculated the orbit of Mercury and found that in his theory the major axis of the orbital ellipse of Mercury should precess an additional 42.9 seconds of arc per century, in excellent agreement with the measurements. Other competing theories of gravity, when applied to the precession of the orbit of Mercury, give an incorrect value or even the wrong sign.

The Einstein Theory of Gravity is more complex than the two previous theories of gravity. In a simplified form it can be expressed as:

"A mass causes space to curve. Other masses move in that curved space."

In the Einstein view of gravity, mass does not cause gravity. Instead mass curves space and curved space causes gravity. A good analogy is to imagine a rubber sheet stretched over a frame. If you put a heavy ball bearing in the center of the rubber sheet, the weight of the ball would cause a curved depression.

The mass of the heavy ball bearing has "curved" the rubber sheet "space." If you then drop a tiny marble on the curved rubber sheet, the marble would immediately start to roll toward the center as if the large ball were attracting it. But there is no direct attraction between the ball bearing and the marble, the ball bearing is curving the rubber sheet and the marble is responding to the curvature of the rubber (and the gravity of the Earth). If the marble were tossed properly into the curved depression in the rubber sheet, it would go into an "orbit" around the heavy ball bearing at the center.

Because Mercury is close to the sun, the space curvature caused by the Sun has two effects on the motion of Mercury. First, the curved space produced by the Sun causes Mercury to move in an orbit about the sun, just like all the other planets do under the influence of the curved space caused by the Sun. But, in addition, the space near the Sun where Mercury orbits is *so* curved, that some of the space is missing!

A circle drawn around the Sun out near the orbit of Earth has a full 360 degrees of angle in it. But a circle drawn around the Sun in near the orbit of Mercury does not have a full 360 degrees in it; it is missing roughly 0.1 seconds of arc. So every time Mercury orbits the sun, it comes up short by that much. After a century, or some 415 orbits, this missing piece of angle in Mercury's orbit adds up to a noticeable precession of 42 seconds of arc. The prediction and confirmation of the existence of this tiny little amount of missing space by the Einstein Theory of Gravity has led to many other and more dramatic predictions by the theory, such as the big bang, black holes, gravitational waves, space warps, time machines, and even gravity control. Some of the predictions, such as the big bang and black holes, now seem to be verified by observation. The others are still indistinguishable from magic, but we are beginning to envision how they might turn into future reality.

Because the Einstein Theory of Gravity is more complex than the Ug or Newton theories, it can give us more handles by which we can control gravity. There are at least two ways that we can use the Einstein Theory of Gravity to negate the gravity field of the Earth. There are also two ways we can use the Einstein Theory of Gravity to make a mass push instead of pull.

In the scientific studies of electricity, it has been found that electricity and magnetism are related. If you change or move electricity, you make magnetism, and if you change or move magnetism, you make electricity again. This transformation between electricity and magnetism is used to make your automobile run. The electricity in your car battery is only twelve volts, not strong enough to run your spark plugs. This low voltage electricity is used to create magnetism in the spark coil. The magnetism temporarily stored in the coil is then released very rapidly when the points open. This rapidly changing magnetic field then generates the powerful, high-voltage sparks that are used by the spark plugs. By using the magnetic field as an intermediate step, the automotive engineers have found a way to convert weak electric forces into strong electric forces.

The Einstein Theory of Gravity says that gravity behaves the same way as electricity. If you take a mass and the gravity field that surrounds it, and move the mass very rapidly, you can create a new field, the gravitational equivalent of magnetism. It is not magnetism, but a completely new field. If you can then cause that new field to change, then you can create a stronger gravity field than you started with. More importantly, that stronger gravity field can be made to appear at a place where there is no mass, and can be made either attractive or repulsive.

Conceptually, there are a number of ways that such a gravity machine could be made. One idea is to roll up some hollow pipe to form a long coil, like the curly cord on a telephone. [See Figure 10.] We then bend the long coil around until the two ends meet to form a curly closed ring.

If the pipes are filled with massive liquid and the liquid is moved back and forth in the pipes rapidly enough, then an alternating push-pull gravity field will be generated at the center of the ring. If the machine was big enough, and the liquid was dense enough and moving fast enough, then we would have a gravity cata-pult that could launch and retrieve spaceships by its gravity repulsion and attraction.

How big? How dense? How fast? Unfortunately, the machine has to be as big as the distance over which

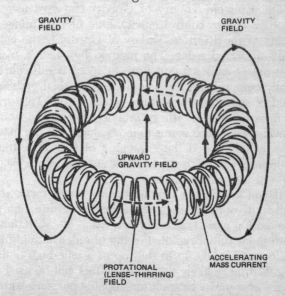

Fig. 10—Design for an antigravity machine that produces a repulsive gravity force.

you want the gravity effects to operate. The liquid has to be as dense or denser than white-dwarf-star material, and the speed of the flow has to be so high that the ultradense liquid will approach the speed of light in a few milliseconds.

I am afraid that it will be some time before we have all that gravitational technology well in hand. But we do have the theory needed to design our gravity catapult, and some time in the long distant future we will have college classes full of bright students taking their first course in Gravitational Engineering, studying the turbulent flow in ultradense matter and producing more and more efficient designs for the gravitational attractor and repulsor beam intensities to minimize passenger discomfort during the launch or retrieval of an interstellar passenger liner.

The Einstein Theory of Gravity can give us yet another way to control gravity. One of the strangest facets of the Einstein Theory of Gravity is the concept of curved space. The method by which a massive object causes a curvature in space is difficult to really comprehend. It is as if the mass had grabbed hold of space and pulled the space into it. This grip of mass on space is still maintained when the mass is moving. The space seems to move along with the mass. This effect, called the "dragging of the space-time coordinate frame," is the basis for another future magic type of antigravity machine.

If you are near a rapidly moving dense mass, you will find yourself "dragged" along in the direction of the moving mass. One could envision a "lift" shaft, lined with pipes full of rapidly flowing ultradense fluid that wafts you rapidly up to the top of a mile-high building. But more likely this "drag" effect will be used in space as a gravity catapult for shipping purposes within the Solar System. This machine would again be in the form of a ring of ultradense matter, but this time the ring would be uniformly whirling from inside-out, like a gigantic smoke-ring.

If a spaceship entered such a toroidal gravity catapult through the hole from one side, it would be expelled out the other side of the hole with a greatly increased velocity. If the spaceship were falling in toward the Sun from the asteroid belt with a high velocity, it would be gently stopped in Earth orbit by threading the torus in the opposite direction. Since the forces on the spaceship during acceleration and deceleration are gravitational forces which act equally on every atom in the ship, all the atoms in the spacecraft are stopped at the same rate and at the same time. So, even though the accelerations and decelerations can be at rates equivalent to hundreds of Earth gravities, the passengers on those spacecraft will not even have to turn in their martini glasses for "landing" in the Earth-Moon system, much less buckle their seatbelts, stow their overhead luggage, raise their seatbacks, and secure their tables.

As unbelievable as these machines for controlling gravity might seem, they at least use a form of matter which we know exists, even if it is presently found only in the interiors of far distant stars. There are speculations that there might exist another type of matter. It has very strange properties. If it ever could be found or made, then a whole new era of gravity control would open up.

All the matter that we know of is the type called regular (positive) matter. Yet both the Newton and the Einstein Theories of Gravity allow the existence of an opposite form of matter, called negative matter. According to the theories of gravity and mechanics, an atom of negative matter would repel all other matter (including other atoms of negative matter).

Now, the first thing you should realize is that negative matter is *not* "antimatter." Antimatter is different from regular matter in its quantum mechanical properties, not its gravitational properties. Although it has yet to be proven experimentally, we are fairly sure that antimatter attracts other forms of matter, just like normal matter. Negative matter, however, would repel other forms of matter.

We do not know how to make negative matter. But when we do, we will discover that it will not cost us any energy to make that negative matter. Because the rest mass energy of a particle is proportional to its mass ($E=mc^2$), the rest mass energy of a negative mass particle is negative! That means that if we always create equal amounts of positive and negative matter at the same time, it will cost us no net energy to do so! One can imagine a future scene in some huge laboratory, where great machines apply intense electric, magnetic, and gravitational forces to some microscopic point in empty space. The energy levels of the fields are raised higher and higher until the "nothing" itself is ripped apart into a ball of regular matter and an equal sized ball of negative matter, the whole process using no net energy except for the losses in the generating machines.

Once we have our negative matter, we can start using it to make antigravity machines. But we must be very careful how we handle the negative matter. Unlike a chunk of regular matter, which responds to your push by moving away, if you push on a chunk of negative matter, it will come *toward* you! (If by mistake, you push on some negative matter, and it starts to move toward you, you must quickly run around behind it and give it a slap on the rear to bring it to a halt!)

Now that we have learned how to control our working material, the simplest antigravity machine that we can make is to form the negative matter into a dense disc and lay it on a good strong floor. If the disc is dense enough and thick enough, then the repulsive gravity field on both sides of the disc will be one Earth gravity. That negative gravity field from the disc would then cancel the gravity field of the Earth. In the region above the disc, the gravity attraction would be zero and you could float there in free fall.

The negative gravitational field of negative matter can also be used for gravity propulsion. If you place a ball of very dense negative matter near a similar dense ball of regular matter (which is incidentally attached to your spaceship), you will find that the negative matter ball will repel the regular matter ball, which in turn will attract the negative matter ball. The two dense balls will start to move off in a straight line at a constantly increasing speed. The acceleration will be the strength of the gravitational attraction of one ball for the other, with the negative matter ball chasing after the positive matter ball and the positive matter ball carrying your spaceship along with it.

You might at first worry that I'm getting something for nothing. First there were two balls of matter, both standing still, with no kinetic energy. Then, after a while they are both moving off together at high speed with no propulsion energy being expended. You might think that would prove that negative matter is impossible, since it looks like the law of conservation of energy is being violated.

But if you look very closely, you will find that negative mass propulsion does not violate any laws of physics. It is true that the ball of regular mass gains speed and increases its kinetic energy $[E=1/2(+m)v^2]$, so it looks like it is getting energy out of nowhere. But while it is doing so, the ball of negative matter is gaining *negative* energy $[E=1/2(-m)v^2]$ and the total energy of the two masses is zero, just as it was when they were standing still. Thus, negative mass propulsion does not violate the law of conservation of energy.

By the same type of argument, you can also show that negative mass propulsion does not violate that other important law of physics, the law of conservation of momentum. For while the momentum of the positive ball of mass is increasing, the momentum of the negative ball of mass is decreasing, resulting in zero net momentum, even though the two balls started out standing still and now are moving off at high speeds.

So far as we know, negative matter doesn't exist. We don't know why it doesn't. After all, both the positive and negative forms of electricity exist, so why not the positive and negative forms of mass? Perhaps there is some yet unknown law of physics that prevents it from forming. But even if we can never obtain this indistinguishable from magic material, we can still devise ways to control gravity with just regular matter, if we just work hard and use enough energy and intelligence.

The Einstein Theory of Gravity is now serving the human race well, and will until a better Theory of Gravity is discovered. We do not know the correct Theory of Gravity yet. The correct Theory of Gravity must include quantum mechanics—the theory of the behavior of atoms and elementary particles. The Einstein Theory of Gravity, despite all its recognized grandeur, ignores quantum mechanics. Because it does not recognize the world of the small, someday it will be replaced. Many brilliant people are now working hard to find a new Quantum Theory of Gravity that will retain all that was good in the Einstein Theory of Gravity and yet will add the new features of gravity effects into the microcosmic world of the atom.

The new Quantum Theory of Gravity will be even more complex than the Einstein Theory of Gravity. The strange Einsteinian concepts of curved space will be mixed up with the even more exotic zoo of "elementary" particles, with their strangeness, beauty, charm, and color. Yet we should not despair that the theories become more complex. For it is their very complexity that will be the tools that the gravitational engineer of the future will use to invent, design, build, test, and make work the machines that will give us control over our common burden, gravity.

Can we really make an antigravity machine? The answer is: Yes. There are many ways to make a machine that will cancel the gravitational attraction of Earth. It is also theoretically possible to make a machine out of massive bodies that will repel a massive object instead of attracting it. The technology required to build such machines is not here right now, but as we gain control over more energy and move into space where we can manipulate large masses without having to contest Earth for their control, we will move into the realm of gravity control technologies that are presently indistinguishable from magic. When that day comes, the children of the human race (or whoever the human race has evolved into by then) will control gravity as easily as our littlest children now control the awesome power of lightning with the flick of a wall switch.

Recommended Reading

Albert Einstein, *The Meaning of Relativity*, p. 102 (Princeton University Press, Princeton, NJ, 1955).

Robert L. Forward, "General Relativity for the Experimentalist," *Proceedings of the Institute of Radio Engineers*, Vol. 49, pp. 892–904 (May 1961).

Robert L. Forward, "Antigravity," *Proceedings of the Institute of Radio Engineers*, Vol. 49, p. 1442 (September 1961).

Robert L. Forward, *Starquake*, Ballantine/Del Rey, NY, 1981. [Science fiction novel that visually describes a number of gravitational machines made with ultradense matter.]

Robert L. Forward, "A New Gravitational Field," *Science Digest*, Vol. 52, #3, pp. 73–76 (September 1962).

Robert L. Forward, "Guidelines to Antigravity," *American Journal of Physics*, Vol. 31, #3, pp. 166–170 (March 1963).

Robert L. Forward, "Far Out Physics," *Analog Science Fiction/ Science Fact*, Vol. 95, pp. 147–166 (August 1975).

Robert L. Forward, "Goodby Gravity," *Omni*, Vol. 1, #4, pp. 88–91 (January 1979).

Robert L. Forward, "Flattening Spacetime Near the Earth," *Physical Review*, Vol. D26, pp. 735–744 (15 August 1982).

Robert L. Forward, *Rocheworld*, Baen Books, NY, 1990. [Science fiction novel that visually describes a zero-gravity region midway between two massive planetoids.]

Robert L. Forward, "Negative Matter Propulsion," *J. Propulsion* Vol. 6, pp. 28–37 (January–February 1990).

Robert L. Forward, *Timemaster*, Tor Books, NY, 1992. [Science fiction novel that describes the many technologies that would arise from the discovery and control of negative matter.]

William J. Kaufmann, III, *Relativity and Cosmology*, Chap. 11 and 12, (Harper and Row, NY, 1973).

✧ THE SINGING DIAMOND

This story was my first attempt at a fiction story. Before that, I had written many science fact articles (many of which sounded like fiction), but this was my first attempt at telling the reader about some interesting science facts in the guise of a story rather than a lecture. It came about during the formative stages of the science-art magazine Omni. *Ben Bova had been named editor of the new magazine and was looking for material. Since I had sold him speculative science fact articles before, when he was editor of* Analog Science Fact/ Science Fiction *magazine, I wrote a draft of a science fact article on antigravity. That article contained many of the ideas for antigravity machines that are discussed in the previous chapter "Antigravity." Since Omni was also interested in science fiction, I took one of the ideas out of the antigravity article and used it as the science background for a science fiction story. I submitted both the technical article and the fiction story at the same time, asking Bova which one he would prefer. To my surprise, he bought both of them. The science speculation article, "Goodbye Gravity," appeared in the January 1979 issue of* Omni, *Volume 1, Number 5, on pages 88-91, while "The Singing Diamond" was published in the February 1979 issue, Volume 1, Number 6, on pages 70-73. Bova mentioned a number of years later that I was the only person who had*

179

published both science fact and science fiction in Omni *magazine. I don't know whether that is still true.*

The physical model for the heroine in the story is the science fiction writer, Joan Vinge. The first time I saw her, it was from a distance at a crowded science fiction convention. She was calmly and slowly making her way through a boisterous crowd of adoring fans, looking very much like an astronaut calmly and slowly making her way through the asteroid belt. I liked the "Red" Vengeance asteroid-belt prospector character well enough to use her again (in slightly different disguises) in the Rocheworld *novels and* Martian Rainbow.

I wrote this story in the first person, since most of the initial action takes place with only one character around. Having observed in action three independent-minded daughters and a contumacious wife, I didn't see anything unusual in having an asteroid belt prospector be a female, and so it didn't occur to me to make that point explicit early in the story. When I sent it to Jerry Pournelle for consideration in a reprint collection of short stories he was putting together, he started out assuming the narrator was male, since the author was male. I heard later he threw the manuscript across the room when he found out otherwise (he didn't buy it either).

My asteroid was singing.

Alone, but safe in my ship, I heard the multitude of voices coming through the rock. They were an angel chorus in a fluid tongue, strange but beautiful.

I followed the source of the sound, stereo headphones connected to a pair of sonarphones buried in the asteroid's crust. The voices were moving slowly through the solid stone. I knew my ears were not playing tricks on me, for I could also see a strange fuzzy ball on the three-dimensional display of the sonar mapper that tracked the singing sound. As the fuzzy ball reached the surface of the asteroid, the singing stopped, cut off in the middle of a tremulous crescendo. I took off the earphones, looked up from the sonar screen, and peered out the port at the black void around me. I could see nothing.

I stopped the pinger that was sending short bursts of sound down into the asteroid I had captured and waited while the last few pulses echoed back from within the body of almost pure metallic ore. This find would bring me a fortune once I surveyed it and got it back to the processing plant.

Most rock-hoppers are content to set up the sonar mapper on a potential claim and let the computer do the job of determining whether there is enough metal in the rock to justify dragging it in. But I always liked to work along with the computer, watching the reflections on the screen and listening to the quality of the echoes. By now, my ears were so well trained I could almost tell the nickel content of an inclusion by the "accent" it put on the returning sound. This time, my ears had heard something coming from the solid rock that had not been put there by the pinger.

I had the computer play back its memory, and again I heard the eerie voices, like a chorus of sirens calling me to leave my ship and penetrate into their dense home. I was sure now that the singing was real and not in my head, since the computer had heard it too. I replayed the data and found that the sound had started on one side of the asteroid, traveled right through the center in a straight line, and then had gone out the other side. I had a hunch, and ninety minutes later was waiting, earphones on, when the singing started again. This time the voices started at a different position on the surface of the asteroid, but as before, they slowly traveled in a straight line, right through the exact center of the rock and out the other side. A quick session with the computer verified my hunch. Whatever was doing the singing was orbiting the asteroid, but instead of circling about it like a moon, the orbit went back and forth right through the dense nickel-iron core! The computer did more work. It determined the orbital parameters, and predicted where the singers would next intersect the surface of my slowly revolving rock. I was outside, waiting at that point, when it came.

For a long time I could see nothing. Then, high above me, I saw a cloud of little sunspecks—falling toward me. The glittering spots in the cloud moved in rapid swirls that were too fast to follow, and the cloud seemed to pulsate, changing in size and shape. Sometimes it collapsed into an intense concentration that was almost too small to see, only to expand later into a glittering ball as big as my helmet. Inexorably, the gravity of the asteroid pulled the swarm of star-midges down toward me. They were getting close. I tried to move back out of their path, but I had allowed myself to float upward in the weak gravity, and my magnetic boots were now useless. Twisting my body around, I tried to dodge, but the cloud of light spots expanded just as it passed me. I screamed and blanked out as my right leg burst into pain. I felt as if I had stepped into a swarm of army ants.

Dazed, I awoke, the emergency beeper shouting in my ear. My leg ached, and my air was low. With a detached glance, I looked down at the agony below my knee to see fine jets of vapor shooting out from hundreds of tiny holes in my boot. Fortunately, most of the holes seemed to be clogged with frozen balls of reddish stuff. My numbed brain refused to recognize the substance.

Using my hands, I dragged myself across the surface of the asteroid to my ship and carefully pulled my suit off. Insult was added to injury as the suit's Sani-Seal extracted a few red hairs as I peeled it off. I looked carefully at my leg. The tiny holes had stopped bleeding, so I was in no immediate danger. I just hurt a lot.

For the next few days I let my leg heal while I listened to the music. I knew that I was imagining it, but the beautiful voices now seemed to have a tinge of menace to them. The computer carefully monitored the motion of the swarm. It returned every 93 minutes, the normal period of a close orbit around an asteroid with such a high density. Once, I had to move the ship to keep it away from the singing swarm as it came up out of the rock underneath.

After I could move around again, I experimented. Tracking the swarm as it went upward away from the surface, I used the mass detector on it at the top of its trajectory. The collection of nearly invisible specks weighed eighty kilos—as much as I did in my space suit!

I put a thin sheet of foil underneath the swarm as it fell, and later examined the myriad tiny holes under a microscope. The aluminum had been penetrated many hundreds of times by each of the specks as they swirled about in the slowly falling cloud. Whatever they were, they were about the size of a speck of dust. I finally counted the midges by tracing the streaks on a print made with my instacamera. There were over ten thousand of them.

I was stumped. What was I going to do? No matter how valuable the asteroid was to me, I could not drag it back to the processing plant with its deadly hornets' nest swirling about it.

I thought about pushing the asteroid out from under the cloud, but my small ship was not going to move a twenty-million-ton chunk of rock at anything like the acceleration needed. I would have to get rid of the stinging swarm in some way, but how do you trap something that travels through solid iron like it isn't here? Besides, it could be that the tiny star specks themselves were worth more than the ball of ore that they orbited. I finally gave up and called for help.

"Belt Traffic Control, this is 'Red' Vengeance in *The Billionaire*. I have a problem. Would you please patch the following message to Belt Science Authority?" I then gave a detailed description of what I had been able to learn about my tiny pests. I signed off and started lunch—it was nearly twenty light-minutes to the Belt Traffic Control station.

In two weeks a few of the small cadre of scientists who lived out in the Belt were there, cluttering up my rock with their instruments. They couldn't learn much more with their gadgets than I had with my camera and aluminum foil. The specks were tiny and very dense. No one could think of any way to trap them.

I was ready to abandon my claim and leave a fortune and its buzzing poltergeist to the scientists when I remembered the Belt Facility for Dangerous Experiments. Their major activity was producing the antimatter that filled the "water torch" rocket engines used in deep space. At each refueling, I would watch apprehensively as electric fields and laser beams carefully shepherded a few grams of frozen antimatter into my engine room. There, each grain annihilated would heat many tons of water into a blazing exhaust.

Antimatter has other uses, however, and nearby a group made exotic materials by explosive-forming. I went to them with my problem. Soon I had a bemused entourage of high-powered brains trying to think of ways to stop my irresistible objects. We were relaxing with drink squeezers in the facetiously named BOOM! room, which overlooked the distant explosive-forming test site. I dressed for the occasion in an emerald-green bodysuit that I had chosen to match my eyes, and a diaphanous skirt that required dexterity to keep it looking properly arranged in free fall. I wore my one luxury, an uncirculated solid-gold Spanish doubloon.

While the discussions were going on, news arrived from the contingent still observing my find. The specks were still moving too fast to take close-up pictures with the cameras available, but at least the size and density of the specks had been determined. They were dense, but not of nuclear density, only about a million times greater than the density of water.

"Our bodies are a thousand times more dense than air and we can move through that with ease," I said. "So, at a density ratio of a million to one, my leg was like a vacuum to them! No wonder they can go through solid iron like it isn't even there."

"Although the asteroid's iron can't stop the swarm, its gravity does hold them," said one scientist. He pulled out a card computer and started scratching with his fingernail on the pliable input-output surface. We clustered around, holding positions by whatever handhold was available, and watched as his crude scratchings were replaced by a computer-generated picture of a flat disc with curved arrows pointing smoothly in toward its two faces.

"What is it?" I asked.

"Flypaper," he said, looking up at me floating above him. "Or, for your problem, Red—gnat paper."

His thick fingers scratched some more calculations, this time in pure math. I followed them without too much trouble. There were no pictures to give me any clues, but it was obvious from the symbols that he was merely applying Newton's Law of Gravity to a disc instead of to the usual sphere.

"We can make the flypaper with the explosive-forming techniques we have developed," he said, "but to keep it from decomposing, we are going to have to contain it in a pressure capsule."

The process looks deceptively simple when one looks out through the eyes of an auto-robot. You merely take a large rotating asteroid as big as an office building and hit it from all sides with a spray of antimatter. When the shock wave passes, you have a small, rapidly spinning plate of glowing compressed matter that is trying desperately to regain its former bulk. Before it does, you hit it from twelve sides with a carefully arranged set of accurately cut chunks of nickel-iron lined with pure carbon. In the split-nanosecond that the configuration is compressed together into an elastically rebounding supersolid, you coat it heavily with another layer of antimatter and let it cool for a week.

The auto-robots brought it to us—still warm. It was a diamond—with a flaw. Right in the center of the barrel-sized crystal was a thick sheet of highly reflecting metal.

"What's that?" I asked the one who had arranged the fireworks display.

"The original asteroid, Miss Vengeance," he replied. "All four million tons of it. It's been compressed into a thin disc of ultradense matter and surrounded by diamond to keep it from expanding back into normal matter. There's your flypaper; let's go use it."

The disc was a foot across and only a centimeter thick, but it took a large space-tug to heave that ultraheavy pancake griddle with its thick diamond casing into an orbit that would reach my claim and its singing hangers-on. Once it was there, it was delicate work getting the sluggish plate placed in the path of the glittering cloud that still bounced back and forth through my property every 93 minutes. Finally the task was accomplished. Passing slowly through the diamond casing as if it were not there, the scintillating sparks floated upward toward the metal disc—and stuck.

"They've stopped!" I shouted in amazement.

"Of course," said a metallic voice over my suit speaker. "They ran into something that was denser than they are, and its gravitational field is strong enough to hold them on its surface."

"For something that dense, it must be a billion gravities," I said.

"I wish it were," said the voice. "I would have liked to have made the gravity stronger so I could be sure we could hold onto the specks once we had stopped them. With the limited facilities we have at the test site, the most matter we can compress at one time is four million tons. That disc has a gravitational field of only one gravity on each side."

After watching carefully for a while, I finally was reassured that the tiny specks were not going to be able to leave the surface of their flat-world prison. I conquered my fear and let my helmet rest against the outside of the diamond casing that encapsulated the shiny disc and its prisoners.

The diamond was singing.

The voices I remembered were there, but they were different from the wild, free-swirling chorus that still haunted me from our first meeting. The singing now seemed constrained and flat. I laughed at my subconscious double pun and pulled back to let the scientists have their prize. They hauled the crystalline cask away with the space tug, and I returned to the difficult months-long task of getting my asteroid back to the processing plant.

I made a fortune. Even my trained ear had underestimated the nickel content. When payoff time came, I knew that from that time on, every expedition I made out into the belt was for fun and gravy, for all the money I would ever need for a decent retirement nest egg was in solid credits in the Bank of the Outer Belt. With no more financial worries, I began to take an interest in my little beasties—for that is what they were.

The scientists had taken the diamond down to Earth and built a superfast robot to act as a translator. The specks, which used to be plastered to one side of the dense disc, were free once they were on Earth. The one-gravity upward pull of the underside of the disc was exactly canceled by the one-gravity downward pull of the Earth. The specks seemed to be perfectly happy. They could easily leave the gravity-free region under the disc, but they didn't seem to want to. Their cloud stayed a compact sphere just below their antigravity ceiling. They continued with their complex intermingling, swirling behavior, passing easily through the ultrahard diamond that held up their four-million-ton roof.

The scientist's high-speed holocameras had been able to determine that their complex notion was not due to natural laws, but was caused by the deliberate motion of each of the spots with respect to the others. A few frames had even shown some of the tiny specks in the process of emitting a little jet of gamma-ray exhaust in order to change their course to meet with another speck for a fraction of a microsecond. Then, many revolutions and many milliseconds later, each of the two specks that had previously met would release another tiny speck, which joined the great swarm in its seemingly random motion.

The most significant frame from the high-speed holocameras, however, is the one that I have blown up into a holopicture over the head of my bunk. I didn't think that you could create a decent three-dimensional likeness of someone using only ten thousand points of light, but it's me, all right. Everyone recognizes it instantly—aristocratic nose, bobbed hair, helmet, mike, freckles, and all the rest.

But that is all the beasties have ever done in the way of communication. For years, the scientists have tried to get some other response from them, but the specks just ignore their efforts. I guess that when you live a trillion times faster than someone else, even a short dialogue seems to drag on forever and just isn't worth the effort. After years of examination and fruitless attempts to communicate, the scientists finally gave up and put the diamond on display at the San-San Zoo.

When I was a young girl at Space Polytech, I dreamed that when I got rich I would spend my later years reveling in the vacation spots around the world and throughout the solar system, but now I don't want to. Sometimes I can stand it for a whole year—but then I just have to go back and hear my diamond sing.

♦ BLACK HOLES

Another result that has come out of research in the science of gravity has been the prediction and then the discovery of that bizarre enigma, the black hole. It is truly a hole, in that anything dropped into it falls forever. It is truly black, in that nothing comes back out, not even light. Even the identity of what went into the black hole is obliterated by the blackness. The power of the black hole is so awesome that it even swallows space and warps time.

Black holes are forms of matter which are predicted not only by the Einstein Theory of Gravity, but many other theories of gravity. We now have good astronomical evidence that they really exist out in space. In our Milky Way galaxy there are probably millions of black holes containing the mass of a large star, while at the very center of our galaxy there is probably a huge black hole containing the mass of a million stars.

We don't have to worry about falling into these monsters of space-time, however, for they can only pull on us at long range with their gravity field, and they are so far away, their gravity field is many times weaker than the gravity field of the Sun. So, we will stay tied to the Sun, keeping comfortably warm, while the Sun orbits around the black hole at the center of the galaxy. After a nearly uncountable number of years, the orbit of the Sun will decay and the Sun will finally join the big black hole at the galactic core, but that will take place long after the Sun and all the rest of the stars in the galaxy have burned out. We and our robots will have left this worn-out galaxy long before that time and continued life in a new, fresh galaxy which we will have designed to suit our tastes.

The reason that a black hole is black, is that the gravity field of the black hole is so large that the escape velocity of the black hole is greater than the speed of light. The escape velocity of an ordinary massive object, like a planet, is the initial velocity a rocket must have in order to leave the surface of the planet and coast off into space without need for additional propulsion. For the Earth the escape velocity is 11 kilometers per second, at the surface of Jupiter it is 61 kilometers per second, and for the Sun it is 620 kilometers per second (0.2% of the speed of light). As long ago as 1795, it was noticed by the astronomer and mathematician, Pierre Simon, the Marquis de Laplace, that at the surface of a planet with the density of Earth and a radius some 250 times that of the Sun, the escape velocity would be equal to the speed of the corpuscles that light was thought to be made out of at that time. Laplace thus concluded that such a planet would be dark. This was the first speculation on the concept of a black hole.

Black holes became more than a speculation in 1915 when Albert Einstein formulated the equations for his Theory of Gravity, the General Theory of Relativity. Only months later, Karl Schwarzschild found one of the first solutions to those equations. Called the Schwarzschild solution, it describes the motion of a small test particle near a non-rotating massive sphere. The Schwarzschild solution is the relativistic replacement for the Newtonian equations that describe the orbits of the planets about the massive Sun.

The Schwarzschild solution to the Einstein Theory of Gravity gives the same results as the Newton Theory of Gravity for a test particle near a mass when the test particle and mass are far apart. But when the gravitating mass is very dense, so that the test particle can get very close, there are differences between the predictions of the Newton Theory of Gravity and the Einstein Theory of Gravity. One of these differences causes an extra precession in the orbit of the planet Mercury. Another causes light passing by the Sun to be bent inward. Another difference causes light signals passing by the Sun to take longer to travel because time runs slower near the Sun. This has been checked by tracking time signals from spacecraft as they pass in back of the Sun. Another difference is that photons of light "get tired" as they try to climb up a gravitational field. Unlike a stone, which slows its speed as its energy becomes less, photons, which must travel *at* the speed of light, are gravitationally redshifted to a lower frequency. The lower the frequency of a photon, the lower the energy. This gravitational red-shift effect has been measured by sending gamma-ray photons up a tower at Harvard and measuring their decrease in frequency as they climbed up out of Earth gravity.

Because we have measured all these effects, we know that the Schwarzschild solution to the Einstein Theory of Gravity is the best description of the gravity field outside a large mass. That solution, however, predicts some bizarre behavior when the mass is very large or very dense so the test particle can get close to it. One of those bizarre predictions is the black hole.

You will all be relieved to know that our Sun is a little too small to turn into a black hole all by itself. When it uses up all its energy it will turn into a white dwarf star. All of its mass will collapse into an object about half the size of the Earth, with a density that is a million times larger than that of normal matter. It will sit there glowing whitely from the heat of its collapse, slowly turn redder, and then turn dark as it cools off over billions of years. If our Sun had been two or three times more massive, the final collapse would not stop at the white dwarf star stage, but would proceed to the neutron star stage, where the mass of a star is compressed into a sphere some twenty kilometers across with a density of a hundred trillion times that of normal matter. If our Sun were larger than three solar masses, however, then the neutron star stage would not be stable.

In 1939, J. Robert Oppenheimer and his student, H. Snyder, showed that the nuclei in a collapsing star are not strong enough to resist the gravitational crushing forces if the initial mass of the star were large enough. Their paper was little noticed because of other things going on in the world in 1939. Oppenheimer became involved in those other things and it was not until after World War II that scientists came back to look at black holes. They found that there was no way to avoid the conclusion that the end point of the evolution of a star with a mass greater than three solar masses has to be a black hole.

A star turns into a black hole when the escape velocity of the star equals that of light. For a star with a given mass M this occurs when all the mass is concentrated inside a radius R called the "Schwarzschild radius" ($R = 2GM/c^2$). For typical stellar mass black holes, this radius is ten kilometers or so. When the collapsing star becomes this small, the star disappears from view and its place is taken by the "event horizon." The event horizon is a highly warped region of spacetime that separates the outside universe from the miniature universe inside. It is a one-way membrane, in that objects can fall in through the event horizon, but things inside the event horizon cannot get back out. It is also the infinite red shift boundary, since light emitted from an object at that radius is infinitely gravitationally redshifted to zero energy. It is the event horizon that is the black hole, not the star. After the event horizon is formed by a collapsing star, the collapse of the star continues on in the same manner as it did before the event horizon formed. The star gets denser and smaller in radius as it collapses. The event horizon, however, stays constant in size after it has formed, with a radius equal to the Schwarzschild radius. In essence, the event horizon is a black shield that prevents anyone from seeing what is going on inside. (It is interesting to note that "Schwarzschild" means "black shield" in German.)

Theoretically, black holes can come in many different sizes and densities. The typical black hole that one reads about in the Sunday supplements is the very dense black hole that is a few tens of kilometers across and has the mass of a number of suns. It is a large star collapsed into a volume the size of a large mountain. The density is 10^{18} times that of normal matter and even 1,000 times that of nuclear matter. A stellar mass black hole is probably spinning fairly rapidly since the original star from which it was formed was likely to be rotating somewhat. During the collapse of the star to form the black hole, the angular momentum in the original star was conserved, leaving the black hole spinning rapidly. The collapsing star increases its spin speed for the same reason that an ice skater increases her spin speed when she pulls in her outstretched arms during a toe spin.

The solution to the Einstein gravity equations that describes a rotating black hole was found by the mathematician Roy Kerr in 1963, almost fifty years after the solution for the nonrotating black hole. The Kerr solution reduces to the Schwarzschild solution when the rotation of the black hole is zero. Recently, other mathematicians have shown that these two solutions describe the only stable configurations for an uncharged black hole.

The black hole could have lost more electrons than protons during the collapse process, so it could have a modest electric surface charge, and since the black hole is spinning, that rotating electricity would produce a magnetic field. The solution for a charged, rotating black hole ring was found by Newman in 1965 as a solution to the combined Einstein gravity equations and Maxwell electromagnetic equations.

One important characteristic about a black hole is that after it is formed, the only things you can measure about the final configuration are its mass, angular momentum, charge, and magnetic field—nothing else. A black hole made out of a collapsing star looks exactly like a black hole made out of a collapsing antimatter star, or for that matter, a black hole made out of a few solar masses of televisions, moldy cheese, or anything.

One convincing candidate for a black hole is the X-ray source Cygnus X-1. Because it is a source of rapidly varying X-rays it must be a compact star, either a white dwarf, neutron star, or black hole. The X-ray source is in orbit around a companion star that is a typical blue supergiant with a mass of about twenty solar masses. The orbital period of 5.5 days obtained from the X-ray data then gives us an estimate for the mass of the X-ray source of eight solar masses. Since stellar theory puts an upper limit on the mass of a neutron star of three solar masses, and this source is well beyond that limit, it must be a black hole.

What does a black hole look like? As a star turns into a black hole, the time it takes for it to turn black is very rapid. In a few milliseconds it goes from full luminosity to less than a billionth of full luminosity. For a human observer, a collapsing star essentially disappears instantaneously. An observer near a collapsing black hole can be one of two kinds, a static observer who sits at rest in the external field of the black hole supported by a powerful rocket, or a free-fall observer who falls into the black hole along with the stellar matter.

When either observer is far from the black hole and

looks in the direction of the black hole he sees a black disk. Around that black circle he can see the normal star pattern, except near the black hole the star pattern is distorted. The black hole does not cover up the star pattern as it passes in front of it; instead the black hole disk seems to "expel" the points of light from that region of the sky. A star image moves to one side or the other of the black disk and slides up and over. If the star image and the center of the black hole disk exactly coincide, then the star image momentarily breaks up into a bright ring of light around the black disk where the photons from the star in back of the black hole have been bent by gravitational focusing. (There are actually a number of rings, one where the photons circled the black hole once before they flew off toward the observer, one inside that where the photons circled twice before they flew off, etc.)

As the static observer moves closer and closer to the horizon the black hole disk gets larger and larger and completely fills the sky. Then all the infalling radiation from the rest of the Universe is observed as a very tiny, highly blue-shifted, incredibly bright spot in the "up" direction. The reason the light is so bright is that the static observer is "accelerating" toward the light in his rocket ship instead of free-falling along with the light.

For a free-fall observer, the view toward the black hole is also black, and it grows in size as the observer falls toward the black hole. But unlike the static observer, the dark patch in the forward direction of the sky never extends around into the back hemisphere. Half of the free-fall observer's sky (or more in the early stages far from the black hole) is always filled with the external star pattern. Because the Doppler red shift of the free-fall observer moving away from the distant stars more than compensates for the gravitational blue shift, the photons from the distant stars are red shifted everywhere, except in a bright band near the observer's equator where they are blue shifted. The free-fall observer notices nothing unusual when he falls through the event horizon. All the observing stops, of course, when the observer hits the singularity at the center of the black hole.

Not all black holes have high density. The larger a black hole, the smaller the density. We are probably living inside a black hole—the Universe. The Universe is very massive, so it doesn't have to be very dense to form a black hole. In fact, if you calculate the density of a black hole the size of the Universe, you find that the density required is one atom per cubic centimeter, very close to the average density of space in our galaxy. Present estimates by astronomers of the average density of the visible mass in the Universe, however, leave us a factor of ten short. This has led to a search for the so-called "missing matter" that is needed to bind up the Universe into a nice neat package. Many candidates for the missing matter, such as massive neutrinos, brown dwarfs, miniature and supermassive black holes, and massive "axion" particles have been proposed, but whether the Universe is closed or open is still an open question. If the Universe is closed and is therefore a black hole, then one could ask why it isn't collapsing. It is, or at least it is trying to, but for some unknown reason the Universe got started with a big bang that has all the matter flying outward. After a long enough time, the gravitational pull will overcome the initial momentum and the Universe will collapse.

One could have a black hole that is galactic in size. The average galaxy has about 100 billion stars. If you crammed all those stars into a volume with a radius of about 2000 times that of the distance between the Earth and the Sun (an astronomical unit or AU), you would form a black hole. Although this black hole is only about eleven lightdays in radius, the spacing between the stars would still be large enough, almost one AU, that collisions between the stars would be infrequent. If our solar system fell into such a galactic-sized black hole, the tides from the miniuniverse would be strong enough to separate the planets from the Sun, but they would not be strong enough to do damage to the planets or the Sun itself. The difference in gravity across the diameter of the Earth as the Earth approached the "event horizon" of this incipient black hole universe would be insignificant, about forty microgravities. You wouldn't feel a thing as the Earth fell into a black hole of this size. From the viewpoint of an observer inside the miniuniverse, the Earth would pop into view out of nowhere into the middle of space.

What would it be like to live in a miniature closed universe like this? You will only have a few days to look around, since this miniuniverse is eleven lightdays in radius and is collapsing at nearly the speed of light, but let us imagine that you have at your disposal a rocketship with a faster-than-light warp drive. You take off from Earth in your rocketship on a journey into the unknown like a future Magellan to explore this compact universe only 4000 AU in diameter. You would leave going in a straight line away from Earth, always keeping it in sight through a telescope pointed directly behind. After you had traveled about one-third the way across/around your universe, the view through the rear telescope would show a greatly magnified view of Earth because the strong gravity of all the stars between you and the planet would curve the light rays, giving a magnified image. At the half-way point in your journey, the image of Earth through the rear telescope would have expanded to fill practically the whole rear hemisphere of view. At the same time, a lookout peering through a front telescope would see the same magnified view of Earth, but of its other side. As you completed your journey, the view of Earth through the rear telescope would continue to expand and become fainter, while the view through the forward telescope would shrink until it coincided with the view of the real thing through the forward porthole as you return triumphantly back home, having circumnavigated the Universe while always traveling in a straight line.

It is as difficult for us to imagine living in a closed, finite, curved universe as it was for early man to comprehend living on a closed, finite, curved world. Since there were only six continents and seven seas on the Earth, it seemed obvious at the time that when you come to the last continent there *had* to be an edge to the world somewhere. But we now know that there is no edge anywhere on the globe. It is the same in our galactic-sized miniuniverse. Even though there are a lot of stars, there are a finite number. As you go to each one and look around, each star seems to be at the "center" of the universe, with equal numbers of stars in all directions. There is no edge, there is no way out, and alas, the singularity approaches.

Although large black holes have interesting properties and characteristics and are fun to speculate about, it will be a long time, if ever, before we could attempt to make them in order to develop some form of future technology. But black holes can come in many sizes, and the smaller ones involve masses that are small enough for the human race to dream about using in new technologies that are presently indistinguishable from magic.

Small black holes were first discussed in the scientific literature by Stephen Hawking. It had long been known that for a black hole to form spontaneously by gravitational collapse, the amount of mass involved had to be larger than the mass of the Sun. Hawking speculated that miniature black holes much smaller than the Sun could have been formed by the Big Bang at the beginning of the Universe when the pressure of light and other matter was very high. They could be any size, from solar masses down to about ten micrograms.

These small black holes are very dense and very interesting. They have very small diameters, most of them much smaller than an atom, with the smallest, the ten microgram mass version, being only 10^{-35} meters across. The miniature black holes would be attracted by the Earth, the other planets, and by the Sun into orbital trajectories. Most of these orbits would be elliptical orbits out in space around the Sun. Since the miniature black holes are so tiny and so dense, however, they could even be in an orbit that passed right through the Sun or a planetoid.

Although they are small in size, the miniature black holes would have a significant gravity field. In passing through a body made of normal matter, a miniature black hole would produce powerful tidal forces at atomic ranges that would cause drag to take place. After bouncing back and forth through a planetoid a number of times, the miniature black holes would slow down and be captured. There could be swarms of them in the center of the Sun and planets, slowly eating them up. The rate of capture is very low, however, since the miniature black holes are so small they can only swallow one atom at a time.

A few years after Stephen Hawking invented the concept of miniature black holes, he found a way to make them disappear! While going through some detailed calculations about the interaction of the ultra-strong gravity field of these ultradense objects on the space-time vacuum near their surface, he discovered that his newly invented miniature black holes would *not* be black. They would seem to glow instead.

Stephen Hawking has developed a picture one can

use to attempt to understand the reason why black holes look like they are emitting radiation. According to the theory of quantum mechanics, what we call vacuum is not empty, but is full of pairs of "virtual particles" that are created temporarily out of nothing, exist for a while, then merge back into nothing. [See top half of Figure 11.]

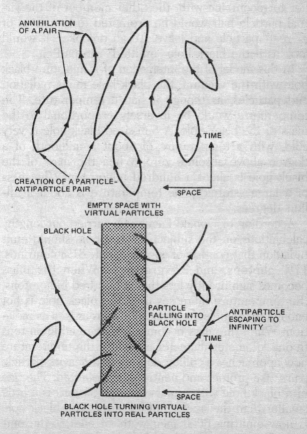

ANNIHILATION OF A PAIR

TIME

SPACE

CREATION OF A PARTICLE-ANTIPARTICLE PAIR

EMPTY SPACE WITH VIRTUAL PARTICLES

BLACK HOLE

PARTICLE FALLING INTO BLACK HOLE

ANTIPARTICLE ESCAPING TO INFINITY

TIME

SPACE

BLACK HOLE TURNING VIRTUAL PARTICLES INTO REAL PARTICLES

Fig. 11—"Empty" space filled with virtual particles, with and without a quantum black hole.

Most of the virtual particles in the vacuum are low energy photons, but even charged particle pairs like electrons and positrons occasionally appear for a short period of time. If a small black hole were placed in this emptiness full of energy, its powerful gravitational field would swallow one of the virtual particles if it got too close. [See bottom half of Figure 11.] With no partner to recombine with, the other member of the virtual particle pair would be promoted to the status of a "real" particle and leave. To an onlooker, it would look as if the black hole "emitted" the particle.

In this model of the interaction of a miniature black hole with the vacuum, the black hole emits radiation and particles, as though it had a temperature. The temperature would be inversely proportional to the mass of the black hole. A Sun-sized black hole is very cold, with a temperature of about a millionth of a degree above absolute zero. When the mass of the black hole is about a hundred billion tons (the mass of a large asteroid), the temperature is about a billion degrees.

According to Donald Page, who carried out lengthy calculations on the subject, such a hole should emit radiation that consists of approximately 81% neutrinos, 17% photons, and 2% gravitons. When the mass becomes significantly less than a hundred billion tons, the temperature increases until the black hole is hot enough to emit electrons and positrons as well as radiation. When the mass becomes less than a billion tons (a one kilometer diameter asteroid), the temperature now approaches a trillion degrees and heavier particle pairs, like protons and neutrons, are emitted. The size of a black hole with a mass of a billion tons is a little smaller than the nucleus of an atom. The black hole is now emitting 6000 megawatts of energy, the output of a large power plant. It is losing mass at such a prodigious rate that its lifetime is very short and it essentially "explodes" in a final burst of radiation and particles.

Thus, those black holes that have a mass significantly greater than a billion tons have a low temperature, are losing mass slowly, and have a lifetime longer than the present fifteen billion year age of the Universe, so they would still be around if they were formed during the Big Bang. Those miniature black holes that are significantly less massive than a billion tons would have evaporated long since.

No one has found any evidence of tiny black holes. If there are any trapped in the Earth or Sun, it would be difficult to prove it. There is, however, one indication that there might be some miniature black holes in the center of the Sun. Most of the fusion reaction burning that takes place in the Sun occurs in a small dense hot region near the center. According to theory, the fusion reactions go through a complicated cycle that converts hydrogen atoms into helium, then burns the helium to produce carbon, oxygen, nitrogen, and the other elements up to iron. The theoretical calculations, backed by atom-atom collision experiments on Earth, are now able to predict the present size, temperature, and burning rate of the Sun quite accurately. They also predict that the fusion reactions at the center of the Sun should produce a large flux of neutrinos. The neutrinos, being able to pass through lightyears of lead without being stopped, immediately leave the center of the Sun, while the heat and light generated in the core of the Sun takes ten million years to get out through the optically opaque outer layers of the Sun.

There are so many neutrinos coming from the Sun that it is possible to detect them on Earth despite their low interaction rate. A number of different detectors for solar neutrinos have been operating for many years now, but the number of detected neutrinos has been one-third that predicted by the otherwise successful solar fusion theory.

One explanation for the low numbers of observed neutrinos is that there are miniature black holes in the center of the Sun helping along the fusion process. That means the normal fusion process doesn't need to be as active and as a result emits fewer neutrinos. There are other explanations for the shortage of solar neutrinos, but most of them are just as speculative as the miniature black hole explanation.

If it turns out that small black holes really do exist, then I propose that we go out to the asteroid belt and mine the asteroids for the black holes that may be trapped in them. If a small black hole was in orbit around the Sun in the asteroid belt region, and it had the mass of an asteroid, it would be about the diameter of an atom. Despite its small size, the gravity field of the miniature black hole would be just as strong as the gravity field of an asteroid and if the miniature black hole came near another asteroid, the two would attract each other. Instead of colliding and fragmenting as asteroids do, however, the miniature black hole would just penetrate the surface of the regular asteroid and pass through to the other side. In the process of passing through, the miniature black hole would absorb a number of rock atoms, increasing its weight and slowing down slightly. An even more drastic slowing mechanism would be the tides from the miniature black hole. They would cause stresses in the rock around the line of penetration and fragment the rock out to a few micrometers away from its path through the asteroid. This would cause further slowing.

After bouncing back and forth through the normal matter asteroid many times, the miniature black hole would finally come to rest at the center of the asteroid. Now that it is not moving so rapidly past them, the miniature black hole could take time to absorb one atom after another into its atom-sized body until it had dug itself a tiny cavity at the center of the asteroid. With no more food available, it would stop eating, and sit there and glow warmly for a few million years. After years of glowing its substance away, it would get smaller. As it got smaller it would get hotter since the temperature rises as the mass decreases. Finally, the miniature black hole would get hot enough to melt the rock around it. Drops of melted rock would be pulled into the miniature black hole, adding to its mass. As the mass of the black hole increased, the temperature would decrease. The black hole would stop radiating, the melted rock inside the cavity would solidify, and the process would repeat itself many centuries later. Thus, although a miniature black hole left to itself has a lifetime that is less than the time since the Big Bang, there could be miniature black holes with the mass of an asteroid, being kept alive in the asteroid belt by a symbiotic interaction with an asteroid made of normal matter.

To find those asteroids that contain miniature black holes, you want to look for asteroids that have anomalously high temperatures, lots of recent fracture zones, and anomalously high density. Those with a suspiciously high average density have something *very* dense inside. To obtain a measure of the density, you need to measure the volume and the mass. It is easy enough to get an estimate of the volume of the host asteroid with three pictures taken from three different directions. It is difficult to measure the mass of an object in free fall. One way is to go up to it with a calibrated rocket engine and push it. Another is to land on it with a sensitive gravity meter. There is, however, a way to measure the mass of an object at a distance without going through the hazard of a rendezvous. To do this, you need to use a mass detector or gravity gradiometer.

This is a device that measures the gradient or the changes in the gravity attraction with distance. These gravity gradient forces are the tidal forces by which the Moon causes tides to rise on the Earth, even though both the Earth and the Moon are in free fall. There are a number of different ways to make a gravity gradiometer. The one that I invented uses two dumbbell

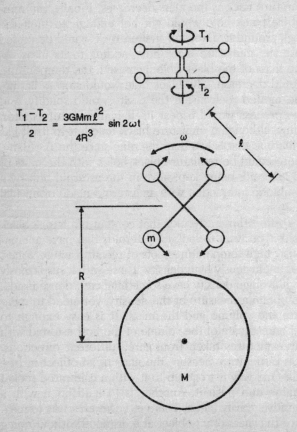

$$\frac{T_1 - T_2}{2} = \frac{3GMm\ell^2}{4R^3} \sin 2\omega t$$

Fig. 12—Method of operation of the Forward Mass Sensor.

shaped masses connected together at the center in the
shape of an X. [See Figure 12].

When a single dumbbell is placed near a gravitating body such as an asteroid, one mass or the other
on the dumbbell will be closer to the asteroid. Since
the gravity field of the asteroid gets stronger with
decreasing distance, the near mass of the dumbbell will
be pulled harder than the far mass, causing the dumbbell to ultimately align itself with the direction to the
asteroid. This natural alignment of a long object in orbit
around a gravitating body is used by many Earth-point-
ing satellites and by the Space Shuttle during resting
periods. By building my gradiometer with two crossed
dumbbells at right angles to each other, one dumbbell is torqued clockwise while the other is torqued
counterclockwise. The amount of differential torque
between the two arms is measured by determining the
change in angle between the two arms. This is a lot
easier than trying to measure the angle of one arm with
respect to some reference direction.

I use one more trick in the operation of the gravity gradiometer instrument that I invented. I deliberately rotate the sensor at fifteen revolutions per second.
In this rotating reference frame, the tiny differential
angles between the two arms turn into tiny differential vibrations, and it is a lot easier to measure vibrations than angles. My gravity gradiometer could detect
the mass of my fist at thirty centimeters (one foot), me
at two meters (I mass over 100 kilograms), and an
asteroid-sized black hole at 1000 kilometers.

Once you have found a suspiciously warm asteroid
that seems awfully massive for its size, then to extract
the miniature black hole, you give the surface of the
asteroid a strong shove and push the asteroid out of
the way. The asteroid will shift to a different orbit,
and where the center of the asteroid used to be, you
will find the miniature black hole. The black hole will

be too small to see, but if you put an acoustic detector on the asteroid you will hear the asteroid complaining as the black hole comes to the surface. Once the black hole has left the surface you can monitor its position and determine its mass with a mass detector.

It is not too dangerous being near a black hole if you are careful. A modest sized one, with a mass equivalent to that of a 250 meter diameter asteroid made of rock, would have a gravity field of about one Earth gravity at a distance of thirty centimeters (a foot). If you approached this miniature black hole by yourself, you would be in danger unless you carefully put yourself in orbit about it ten meters or more away (your orbital period at ten meters distance would be about four minutes). Two people could get right up next to the miniature black hole if they put their hands and knees together to make a space between them. Their combined center of mass is now in the space between them, and if they carefully arrange their approach so that the trajectory of the black hole does not intersect either of them, they can put the black hole between them where they can both take a close look. The gravity forces they would experience would be about the same as if they were crawling on their hands and knees on a floor back on Earth. A black hole the size of an asteroid is smaller than an atom, so you can't see it directly. It will cause bending of light rays passing by it, however, so you could see it by placing a fine illuminated grid in back of it and looking through a microscope at the grid to find a flaw. The flaw will be caused by the bending of the light by the black hole floating in front of the grid.

The next step in corralling the invisible black maverick is to put some electric charge on it. This means bombarding the position of the miniature black hole with a focused beam of ionized particles until the black hole has captured enough of them to have a significant charge to mass ratio. The upper limit will depend upon the energy of the ions. After the first ion is absorbed, the black hole will have a charge and will have a tendency to repel the next ion. Another upper limit to the amount of charge you can place on a black hole is the rate at which the charged black hole pulls opposite charges out of the surrounding space. You can keep these losses low, however, by surrounding the black hole with a metal shield.

Once a black hole is charged, you can apply forces to it with electric fields. If the charged black hole happens to be rotating, you are in luck, for then it will also have a magnetic field and you can also use magnetic fields to apply forces and torques. The coupling of the electric charge to the black hole is very strong—the black hole will not let go. You can now use strong electric or magnetic fields to pull on the black hole and take it anywhere you want to go.

If the black hole were very small, only boulder sized, and you were successful in getting and keeping a lot of charge on it, you could conceivably bring the charged miniature black hole down to Earth and keep it there. The force that can be applied to a maximally charged black hole by a reasonably strong electric field of a few hundred thousand volts is more than enough to levitate a boulder-sized black hole in the gravity field of the Earth. The chances of losing the black hole due to a power failure or other accident would be high enough, however, that it would be better if black holes were left in high orbit.

Once you have charged black holes that you can manipulate at will, you can use them in a number of ways. By putting them in a mixture of deuterium and tritium gas, you can cause fusion reactions to take place without having to have the deuterium-tritium mixture at high temperatures and pressures. The black hole will act as a catalyst for the fusion reaction. The density of the deuterium-tritium gas near the black hole will be greatly increased by the gravity forces of the black hole and the fusion rate in that region will increase dramatically, creating a "hot spot." Most of the reaction products will come out of that region and deposit their energy in the rest of the gas and the usual shielding around the fusion reaction chamber. The resultant heat can then be used to power a thermal power plant. A few deuterium and tritium atoms will be lost to the black hole, but those losses should be small.

Even if miniature black holes are never found and the only black holes we ever have are large stellar and galactic sized collapsed masses, these large black holes may still be very valuable in directing us toward some still unknown form of future technology that is indistinguishable from magic. For by merely observing these objects in detail as they interact with the matter around them, we will be observing phenomena that we cannot replicate on Earth, or even in our solar system. Phenomena involving warped space, distorted time, and contorted ultradense matter that will test our theories as we stretch them to cover these bizarre happenings. We are learning, and will continue to learn, as we attempt to model what we see, and out of that learning will come new, better, theories that are the spells that we will need to invoke new forms of future technology that are presently indistinguishable from magic.

Then, if we can find (or make, by using our new theories) miniature black holes, we will have the magic wand that we will need to bring new forms of future magic into being. Limitless sources of energy, gravitational communication, space warps, time machines, and more, might be ours. Some of these new technologies we may see in the near future, some we may see in the far future, some may never be in any future— all would be indistinguishable from magic to us today.

Recommended Reading

Robert L. Forward, "Gravity Gradient Mapping From the Lunar Polar Orbiter," *The Moon*, Vol. 16, pp. 3 ff (1976).

Stephen Hawking, "Gravitationally Collapsed Objects of Very Low Mass," *Monthly Notices Royal Astronomical Society*, Vol. 152, pp. 75 ff (1971).

Stephen Hawking, "The Quantum Mechanics of Black Holes," *Scientific American*, Vol. 236, #1, pp. 34 ff (January 1977).

J.B. Hutchings, "Observational Evidence for Black Holes," *American Scientist*, Vol. 73, pp. 52 ff (1985).

William J. Kaufmann, III, *The Cosmic Frontiers of General Relativity*, p. 110 (Little, Brown and Co., Boston, 1977).

Kip Thorne, "The Search for Black Holes," *Scientific American*, Vol. 231, #6, pp. 32 ff (December 1974).

✧ ACCELERATION CONSTANT

After "The Singing Diamond" was published, I thought of a sequel, "Acceleration Constant." While "The Singing Diamond" was designed to teach the reader that it is conceptually possible to make an "antigravity" machine that will nullify the gravity field of the Earth over a small region, "Acceleration Constant" was designed to teach the reader that orbit-like trajectories aren't always determined by the laws of gravity and orbital mechanics. It is possible, by using the acceleration capabilities of a spacecraft's propulsion system to add to, or subtract from, the gravitational acceleration of the mass being orbited, to make the orbital radius independent of the orbital speed. In fact, it is possible to put a spacecraft into an orbit around a point where there is no attractive mass at all. I used these massless and non-free-fall orbits again in a later novel, Timemaster.

Such pseudo-orbital trajectories, however, do require a remarkable propulsion system. One which can maintain a constant acceleration over long periods of time. No rocket known can do the job, except perhaps an antimatter rocket. Even the unidirectional neutrino rocket described in the story has flaws, which I quickly gloss over in the story. It is interesting to note, however, that some recent unusual experimental results on neutrinos indicate that they might have imaginary mass.

If that is true, then the neutrinos can have a finite momentum even if they have zero net energy. That, in turn, implies that if a unidirectional neutrino drive engine could be made, it would require no energy to make a neutrino-antineutrino pair, but since the resulting neutrinos have momentum, they would provide thrust to the neutrino drive engine that produced them.

I wasn't able to sell this story to Omni, and because it was a sequel to a story that had originally appeared in Omni, I thought it didn't have a market elsewhere. It sat in my files for a number of years until a new agent read it and realized that it could stand on its own. It was finally published in the March 1986 issue of Analog Science Fiction/Science Fact, Volume 106, Number 3, *on pages 76-88.*

I was embarrassed.

I was living a cliche right out of the old science fiction pulp thrillers—beautiful heroine clad in a scanty plastic spacesuit in the clutches of a Bug-Eyed Monster.

I swallowed my chagrin and puzzled over my predicament. I was in the capture-hold of the Borc's strange conical spaceship. The hold was in vacuum. I had a suit on, but it was a sports model with only a one-hour tank. I looked up at the alien on the other side of the crystal ceiling. Its myriad of lidless buglike eyes stared at me—unblinking.

As the Borc ship kept up its constant acceleration of 2.8 times Earth gravity, I began to worry. At constant acceleration, I was getting farther and farther away from Earth and any possible resupply of oxygen. Would they stop to let me out? I was afraid not—for Borcs never stop.

✧   ✧   ✧

The constant acceleration was the first thing the Belt Traffic Control computer noticed about the ship as it dove in from deep space. By the time the radars had picked up its presence on the distant fringes of the asteroid belt, the speed of the object had exceeded the velocity of any of the planets—yet it continued to accelerate. The computer activated an often-tested but never-before-used alarm.

"ALIEN SHIP DETECTED!" modulated the cool mechanical voice.

I had been visiting the Chief Traffic Controller, John McManus, while my ship was being refueled. John used to be a rock-hopper like me, but had to give up prospecting and take an inside job after his legs got chewed up between a couple of million-ton asteroids.

When the computer alarm sounded, I floated to the back of the control room and watched the professionals go to work. The constant acceleration of the unknown ship made it easy to analyze where it came from. Yet that very consistency was puzzling. No one ever ran a ship at high acceleration. It was too wasteful of power.

The controllers traced the track of the ship back along its course. It had come from Jupiter—in a straight line toward the Sun—never deviating from a constant 2.8 gravities acceleration.

"How fast is it going now?" I asked.

One of the younger controllers replied without taking his eyes off his screen. "Over a hundred kilometers per second, Miss Vengeance." As he spoke, the spot on the screen curved in a broad arc, then continued to plummet inward toward the sun.

John gave a soft whistle. "A J-hook turn—every centimeter of it at constant acceleration. First they go hell-bent-for-leather straight at the Sun, then swoop around in a big arc until their tail is pointed backward. Now they are slowing down by applying acceleration in the opposite direction. I wonder where they're going to stop?"

As John spoke he was punching a keyboard. Soon a blow-up of a section of the asteroid belt was on the screen. There was a flashing X that showed the place where the alien ship was predicted to come to a halt.

There was nothing at that point. However, the pattern of large and small asteroids around the blinking X was familiar to me. The aliens were approaching the region where I did my prospecting. I knew the territory well, for that was where I hopped from rock to rock in my ship, *The Billionaire*, looking for the one rock out of many with enough iron and nickel in it to make it worth dragging back to the Belt Processor.

A year ago I had been lucky, and had found a huge, high-nickel asteroid. Now my ship's name was more of a brag than a wish, but I still kept prospecting. I guess it was in my blood.

Suddenly everything clicked, and I blurted out, "John, that spot is where I made my big strike! You remember—the asteroid that had the cloud of ultradense midges in a bouncing orbit that went back and forth right through the rock."

"The fast-living ones that the scientists think are intelligent, but who won't talk to us?"

"Yes. Perhaps this ship contains more of the midges and they are looking for their friends."

"I doubt it," said John. "If I remember, those gnats couldn't stand one gravity, much less 2.8 gravities." He turned from his screen, and with a thoughtful frown asked, "Say, Red. While we're busy tracking this ship, would you go to a spare console and look up the surface gravity of Jupiter in the library files?"

The computer confirmed John's hunch.

"There's no real surface on Jupiter," I reported back, "but the gravity deep under the cloud layer is 2.8 gravities."

"I thought so," said John. "Whoever those beings are, they like home so much that they even brought their own gravity. I guess they don't like free-fall."

"Maybe it's unhealthful for them," I said, hitting closer to the mark than I realized.

Earth was warned, but there was little that could be done except to alert the various national police forces, who dug out ancient codes and disentombed some nuclear warheads. There was no panic, for one alien ship poking about in the asteroid belt does not make an invasion.

John and his assistants scanned their wide-angle screens, searching for some belter who could get a close glimpse of the alien craft, but none of the prospector or scientific ships was in position. The radars tracked the alien while it approached the empty spot in space where my asteroid used to be.

I thought they would come to a stop and look around, but I forgot their penchant for constant acceleration. The ship approached the rendezvous point and not finding the asteroid, changed course and took off again. This time they went along the asteroid belt instead of across it—still at 2.8 gravities.

"They must be looking around the belt for the asteroid," said John. We continued to watch as their speed increased to higher and higher velocities under the constant acceleration.

"They are well over two hundred kilometers per second now," said the young controller after an hour, "and they are still accelerating. At that speed they are going to go flying off into space!"

"Look at your computer readout," said John. "They have pointed their exhaust just enough to keep them going in a big circular trajectory around the Sun that follows along the asteroid belt, while keeping them at 2.8 gravities."

The refueling of my ship was complete. My original plan had been to go back out into the belt to do more prospecting, but I had received an urgent call from my publisher. My book, *The Singing Diamond*, in which I had described my adventure with the rich asteroid and its buzzing swarm of fast-living creatures, was starting to slip in the best-seller lists. These new aliens, who seemed to be interested in the whereabouts of my midge cloud, were in all the news and the publishers wanted me to come back for some publicity shots. When I left Belt Central the next day, the alien ship was still accelerating, although most of its acceleration was now going into keeping it orbiting in the asteroid belt rather than increasing its speed.

As I poked along toward Earth with my antimatter fueled "water-torch" drive, the alien flashed around the asteroid belt, each orbit taking only nine days instead of an asteroid's five years.

I had a great time on Earth. Although I really don't care for crowds, all those lovely people were making me even richer than I already was, by pushing my book back up to the top of the best-seller lists. I went to autograph parties, had countless interviews, was seen in the best restaurants, and made my second appearance in one year on the *Tomorrow* show.

While I was having fun, the aliens continued to search the belt. A few scientific ships had been able to get close enough to the trajectory of the alien craft to take pictures while it came flashing by at one percent of the speed of light. The intruder ship was a thirty-meter-high cloud-grey cone. The back end— where you would normally expect to see huge rocket nozzles emitting a flaming exhaust—was black. The smoothly rounded surface showed some evidence of a door hatch, but little else. If the scientists had been intrigued before, they were excited now. The aliens didn't use rockets. They had some kind of space drive!

After going around the asteroid belt a few times, the alien ship changed course and came toward the Earth. The Earth authorities started to get worried, but the panic was over before it got started. At 2.8 gravities, it only took the aliens a few hours to switch from an asteroid belt orbit around the Sun to a polar orbit around the Earth. But again, what a strange orbit. They flew at thirty kilometers altitude! Neither airplanes nor space interceptors could keep up with them.

There is not much air at thirty kilometers, but enough for the alien's ship to produce a continuous sonic boom with its sixteen kilometer per second speed. It circled the Earth every 43 minutes, its outward pointing space drive producing an inward acceleration of 2.8 gravities that augmented the Earth's one gravity pull, so they circled the Earth nearly twice as fast as if they had been in a free-fall orbit.

With the aliens in sight (and sound) overhead, the publicity people for my book went into high gear. They arranged a photographic interview with *Anybody Who Is*, the photo/video news magazine that makes and destroys public personalities with the flick of a video editor's erase pen. The photographer assigned to me was a professional, with an expense budget to match. He wanted a shot of me at the San-San zoo, sitting next to my swarm of gnats swirling in free fall inside their diamond cage with its gravity trap.

Instead of the usual "pretty girl in a skimpy dress admiring a large diamond" shot, the photographer decided to have me wear a space suit, for that was what I was wearing when I first encountered the pesky little swarm. True to the code of the photographic journalist, however, my own deep-space work suit would not do. We went to Vacuum Sports, a small specialty store situated in the recently renovated area of old downtown Beverly Hills.

I've got to admit the suit looked good. It was designed for light travel and games in the vacuum tunnels and caverns of the Moon, asteroids, and orbital stations. It had a modest propulsion pack for free-fall games, and an hour's supply of air in a super-pressure tank. It omitted such niceties, however, as food, water, and disposal facilities that are essential in a real work suit. The feature that sold the photographer was the tough, transparent plastic film that stretched from boots to hips and wrist collars to upper torso, with a bare midriff effect between.

We went back to the zoo and the photographer started to arrange the pose. I had my helmet on, and had it pressed against the side of the barrel-sized diamond. In the center of the diamond was a flat plate of ultra-dense matter—four million tons of it. The plate was the gravity trap that our scientists had made to capture the pesky little midges bouncing back and forth through my asteroid. The diamond casing was to keep the ultradense matter in the plate from expanding back into normal matter. The matter was so dense that the gravity field generated by the plate was one gravity on each side. But since the Earth was contributing its own gravity field, there were two gravities on top of the disc, and zero gravity underneath. Below the disc, the one-gravity downward pull of the Earth was canceled by the one-gravity upward pull of the plate, creating a zero-gravity region where the cloud of dense gnats swirled in free-fall. As the dense bodies of the tiny midges moved through the ultra-hard diamond like it wasn't there, the crystal would protest with a singing sound.

We didn't realize it at the time, but while we had been shopping, the sonic booms from the alien ship had stopped. The aliens had left Earth orbit and gone out in a wide arc that would bring them down at high speed directly toward the San-San zoo. As the photographer was setting up his lights, the alien ship was descending toward us—its invisible drive engines slowing it down from its immense speed. I was all posed, mentally saying "cheese" through the fishbowl of the helmet, when the ship came down upon us like a runaway elevator.

I looked up at the sound of rushing air to see the blunt end of the alien craft drop down the last twenty meters. It came to a momentary stop just above my head—then took off again—all at constant acceleration. In that split second while the ship was nearly motionless, a pair of long mechanical arms reached out of an open hatch to grab the barrel-sized diamond. The arms flipped the gem upside down, trapping the swarm of specks on the dense disc encased inside. As the arms swiftly pulled the diamond toward the hatch opening, I was in the way. Together, the diamond and I were scooped through the cavernous doors in the base of the ship.

Through the closing hatch doors, I looked down to see the Earth dropping rapidly away as the ship accelerated upward towards space. I then looked up to see a strange sight above me. Floating in a slightly bluish liquid on the other side of a large glass viewing port were a group of miniature hot-air balloons. Each had a spherical orange gas-bag about a meter across. Where the neck of the balloon would normally be, there were a number of short tentacles encircling a mouth with many sharp-looking triangular teeth. Hanging by six long, violet cords from the topside of each balloon was a smaller, heavier gondola part. These were purple, with four short tendrils hanging down. There were large and small black spots all over the purple bodies.

I pried myself off the diamond and slowly lowered my heavy limbs to the floor. I tried sitting up, but the weight of the backpack was just too much in the 2.8-gravity acceleration. I carefully lay on the floor and turned my head to look more closely at the beings floating above me.

There were four of them. Three were smaller, with yellow-orange gas sacs and a bright violet lower body. They were constantly in motion, moving from one control panel to another, the splayed tips of their lower tendrils flitting over the illuminated buttons on the wall panels. The fourth being was a slightly larger creature, with a dark orange balloon and a gray-violet underbody. It was now hovering right over the viewing port. One of the tendrils carried a small weighted sack, and another tendril was pulling tiny yellow spheres from it. The tendril would reach up into the space between the upper body and the lower body and release the small ball. It would shoot rapidly upward and would immediately be captured by the tiny eating arms hanging beneath the orange globe, to be pierced and devoured by the slashing triangular teeth.

After finishing its snack, the large creature went over to a trapezoidal platform with buttons on the sloping sides. It lowered itself on the flat top of the trapezoid and let its four tendrils hang down around the sides. The fine "fingers" at the end of the tendrils played among the buttons and one of the four large arms in the hold lifted from its fixture and swung toward me. Carefully cradling my body in the high gravity, the arm lifted me up until I was just underneath the crystal ceiling. I was able to move my helmet so it could touch the glass. I could now hear.

There was an overall hum that ran through the ship like an expression of controlled power of enormous magnitude. That must be the invisible drive engines that somehow kept the ship at constant acceleration. I could also hear high pitched chirps and twitters. These seemed to occur when I could see surface vibrations on the violet portions of the creatures. Living in liquid, it was obvious that they must use some type of sonar for communication. The liquid was not water, however, but ammonia, hydrogen, and methane gas under thousands of atmospheres of pressure. I lifted a leaden hand and felt the glass. It was hot to the touch. Although Jupiter is farther from the Sun than Earth and gets less sunlight, the planet itself emits heat from inside. These creatures must live down where the temperature is higher than normal Earth temperatures.

Suddenly, the larger creature released a particularly large bubble from its orange gas-sac and shot over in my direction. As the bubble left its body, I heard a flatulent "Borc!" The being then used finer jets of gas until its double-lobed body was hovering right above me, its myriad of jet-black bug-like eyes staring unblinking at mine—one foot and thousands of atmospheres away. It was then that I recognized the musty old cliche that I was living out.

The being twittered at me. There was no way that I could imitate the nearly inaudible high-pitched sounds that came from its body, so I replied with the only sound that I could vocalize.

"You—Borc!" I said, feeling like a cartoon character.

There was a moment's pause in the twittering. I was afraid that I had committed a breach of Borc etiquette. I then decided that since I could not vocalize its language, I would have to get it to try mine.

"I am 'Red' Vengeance," I said. "I am human. I need to get some air in forty minutes or I'm done for!" I went on, knowing full well the conversation was fruitless. The larger Borc tried some human speech using its gas bag jets, but the best it could do was to get the rhythm.

I was beginning to lose hope that they would understand my predicament in time, when I felt a subtle shift in the gravity forces in the ship. The maneuver was done fairly smoothly, but I could tell that the ship had stopped accelerating in a straight line away from Earth, and was now moving into a circular path. Again, the centrifugal force of the circular path was such that there was always 2.8 gravities toward the base of the ship.

I was not the only thing that felt the slight unbalance in forces as the ship shifted into a circular orbit. The diamond did also. The weighty cargo slid to the other side of the hold. As it moved, the ship swerved wildly as its unseen drive engines attempted to adjust to the shifted load. There were rapid changes in acceleration, and for almost a full second we experienced free fall. I watched as the Borcs above me were tumbled about by the swirling currents in their control room. One of the smaller Borcs was thrown into its gas sac. When the two parts of the body separated again, there was a violet dye staining the bluish liquid from where its lower body had banged into its teeth.

"*Ouch!*" I said in sympathy. "I bet that is the Borc equivalent of falling on your chin and biting your tongue!"

But the injury was more serious than that. The larger Borc stayed at the control panels, bringing the still wavering ship under control, while the other two gathered around their injured comrade. The lower violet body was limp, but the yellow-orange gas sac was still flailing its stubby feeding tentacles. It seemed to be trying to grasp the six tendon-like strands that arched over its top. The two uninjured Borcs pulled thin silver tubes from recesses in the control room wall and aimed them at the writhing yellow-orange balloon. I heard shrill sounds and watched, horrified, as the gas sac portion of the injured Borc's body was torn to shreds by the ultrasonic lances from the tube. The Borcs were careful, and only the yellow-orange portion was subjected to the disintegrating power of the beams. Soon the six violet cords were lying on the floor around the sluggishly moving lower body. I could now see a raw-looking orange-violet stripe near the tip of each cord.

One of the tube-carrying Borcs jetted over to a cage-like compartment in the far wall. In the cage was a cluster of what looked like orange rags. The Borc did something with his tube through the holes in the door, and then opened it quickly to remove a limp, nearly deflated orange balloon. The ring of teeth and the feeding tentacles were motionless. In its deflated state I could see the top of the bag. There were six nozzles there, each emitting tiny bubbles of gas that floated quickly up to the conical ceiling. The nearly empty gas-bag was held on the floor next to the recovering violet body, and the six long thin arms each grasped one of the six gas ports, shutting them off.

The Borc that had been holding the gas-bag down to the floor now allowed it to rise. After a few minutes with its valves shut, the orange bag was floating in its normal position above the violet body, with the six long arms under enough tension to keep them away from the tentacles and teeth of the bag. The revived Borc stayed there, feeding its now awake and ravenous symbiote a supper of baby balloons. Slowly the orange sac expanded, turning a translucent yellow-orange as it did so.

I now began to realize what it was that I had seen. No wonder the Borcs always traveled at 2.8 gravities. They had to—or they would be eaten alive! The Borcs consisted of an intelligent spider-like violet creature that captured and controlled a vicious semi-intelligent orange gas balloon which served as its float. I looked more carefully at the violet body and could discern no evidence of any kind of eating port. The symbiosis must have been going on for a long time, for it looked as though those six long arms reaching up to grasp the orange balloons in a dangerous embrace were not just for control of the gas jets. The raw looking orange-violet stripes on the arms were suckers.

Well—the Borcs had their problems, but I had mine. I had only twenty minutes of air left. I started banging on the glass window to get their attention. They had not forgotten me, however. The hatch below me opened. There was only the clumsy mechanical arm between me and a whirling empty sky. They were going to throw me out!

I'm afraid I screamed a little as I grabbed the arm around its mechanical wrist and held on tightly. The arm reached out the hatch and around to the outside of the ship. It was an amazingly long, articulated structure. (It would have to be, I thought. Any outside repairs would have to be done with these arms, since a Borc would not dare put its two antagonistic halves into the close quarters of the same spacesuit.) Holding me carefully against the gravity forces, the arm carried me up to the pointed nose of the ship and beyond. As we traveled upwards, the gravity forces became less and less. Finally, about three meters past the nose of the ship, the arm gave a little toss, and I found myself floating in free fall.

Around and around me at about forty meters distance, the Borc spacecraft was whirling in a close orbit, with me at the center. It took about six seconds for the ship to make one complete orbit. It was like watching a giant toy on the end of a string that I whirled about my head, but there was no string. The invisible drive engines in the spacecraft supplied the force that the missing string could not.

I squinted outward through the glare of the Sun and saw the welcome sight of one of Earth's geosynchronous orbit communication stations a few hundred meters away. With a whistle of relief, I moved my left hand to the jet-pack controls on my chest and did a fancy barrel-roll toward the welcome space-suited figure exiting an open port on the station.

"Greetings!" I boomed through my suit-mike, as I skidded to a full-jet stop not one meter from my new-found friend. "Got any spare air?"

"Miss Vengeance!" exclaimed the nearly invisible visage behind the well-tinted visor. "Get in here quickly! Those sport suits were not made for deep space work; you'll get sun-burned!"

I'll never forgive that photographer for making me switch from my regular work suit to the sports model. I was burned everywhere the suit was clear, and that suit had a lot of clear area. Having a redhead's complexion didn't help any either. By the time I recovered, even my freckles had freckles.

After staying long enough to make sure that I was rescued, the Borcs broke from their 2.8-gravity circle and headed in a 2.8 gravity straight line for the asteroid belt. By the time a few scientists and I got out to the belt with our dolphin translator computers and sonar generators, the gnats were once again in a small cloud about ten centimeters across, their dust-speck sized ultradense bodies bouncing back and forth through the iron and rock of an asteroid as if it were a vacuum. Circling the asteroid and its buzzing cloud, the Borcs waited for us in one of the constant acceleration orbits.

We came out prepared to spend as long as necessary learning how to communicate with the Borcs. However, the Borcs had their own translator—the mites. They had had plenty of time in the zoo to observe the human race and learn its language. (Although they had never let on.)

As we approached, we saw the bottom of the Borc ship open again, and one of the mechanical arms threw out a flat sheet of metal. As we exited our port to examine the floating plate, we saw the swarm of flashing specks rising up out of the surface of the asteroid in front of us.

"Stay away from those bees!" I warned. "They won't go out of their way to get you, but they sure sting if you are stupid enough to stand in their path!"

We watched as the swarm passed through the metal plate. It seemed to me that their activity increased as they did so. Our chief scientist and linguist, Abdul Battu, retrieved the plate. He looked at it, smiled broadly, then passed it to me.

"It's for you," he said.

I looked down at the plate. It was covered with tiny little holes. The first batches formed large block letters, which got progressively smaller and smaller until the rest of the plate could only be read through a microscope.

"**WELCOME! MISS VENGEANCE**," it said, "WE ARE GLAD you were not hurt . . ."

"Well—having an ultra-fast translator is going to make things easy," I said. "I wonder why the bugs talk to the Borcs, when they never would talk to us?"

"I suspect that somehow they belong to the Borcs," said Abdul. "Let's get that plate inside to a microscope and see what it says."

Well—it turns out that the Borcs are a very, very old race. They have fully developed some areas of science, but were limited in many others because their planet has no solid crust and their strange physical makeup limits their space travel to constant acceleration missions.

Their space drive is a marvel of elementary particle physics. The Borcs have completely unraveled the mystery of how one elementary particle turns into another. They use antimatter to power their engines just like we do, but instead of their antimatter turning into pions and gamma-rays as it does in our "water-torch" engines, they somehow control the reaction so that the annihilation of the anti-hydrogen and the normal hydrogen always produces two identical high-energy neutrinos, with no energy lost as heat or gamma rays. Their control is so complete that the two neutrinos both shoot off in the aft direction, while kicking the ship in the forward direction. Since neutrinos, once formed, can pass right thorough almost anything, the unstoppable neutrinos just shoot right out through the base of their ship!

After a few days, my first-hand knowledge of the Borcs became less useful to the scientists. I now spent my time in the lounge, poring over some new gravity and thermal survey maps covering my claim in the asteroid belt. I was planning my next prospecting trip, while waiting for the shuttle back to Earth and my ship.

Abdul was going through the fifteenth information plate when he finally learned why the Borcs had the swarm of midges. He told me about it one evening while we were relaxing in the lounge. He looked great in a white silk jump suit and turban, his piercing black eyes peering out from his jovial bearded face. I had on my electric-blue feather-dress, and was having a hard time keeping the artificial feathers out of my face in free fall.

"It's amazing, Red," he said. "It turns out that the bugs are a computer. An intelligent computer made of manufactured—but living—ultra-dense beings that live a trillion times faster than either humans or Borcs."

"I guess you need a computer like that if you are going to design neutrino drives," I said, sipping slowly at a Borc Bombshell floating in front of me. I eyed the two squeeze-bulbs that had been strung together with threads, and switched the straw from the violet-colored bulb to the orange one. The whole idea was to down both of the equally potent drinks without letting the two bulbs drift together through room currents or your mishandling of the straw.

"Well," said Abdul with some hesitation. "The problem the older Borc had given the bugs was one that takes a lot of computer time to solve, but it really wasn't very important."

"What!" I exclaimed. "The Borcs went to all that trouble just to play games?"

"I'm afraid so, Red," he said. "The Borcs have a game that is very much like our 3-D chess. Now—it has long been known that any game like chess, which has no random factors, should allow the person who makes the first move either to win or force a tie—if you only knew the right moves to make. Yet to date, no human-made computer has been fast enough or smart enough to figure out the moves even for our 2-D chess. A good thing too—for it would spoil the game of chess forever."

He paused, took a careful sip from his squeezer of hot mint tea, and continued, "The older Borc was a runner-up in a 3-D chess tourney on Jupiter. He was annoyed, and being rich and powerful, he made a computer and set it to work on the problem of how never to lose. According to our estimates, he started them working 6,550 years ago. He would come out to check on their progress every fifty years or so. This time, when he arrived, he found that you had trapped his bugs and stolen his asteroid."

"You mean the larger Borc is over 6,000 years old!" I exclaimed.

"More like 15,000 years," Abdul replied.

"Fortunately he has his bugs back, so they can continue to work on his problem," I said.

Abdul laughed. "It turns out the bugs had solved the problem not too many years before you trapped them. They were waiting for the elder Borc to return so they could give their final report. He has it now."

"I bet he's anxious to get back to Jupiter so he can win in the next 3-D chess tourney," I said.

"No, I'm afraid not," said Abdul, with a rare frown. "As I said before, once the answer is known, there is no more challenge to the game. I don't know how a distraught Borc looks, but I bet he's about ready to let his gas sac eat him from the tone I am getting from our correspondence. He doesn't even want to go back to Jupiter. He liked the game so much—and has ruined it so completely for himself—that he's afraid that he will unwittingly reveal the strategy that the bugs worked out for him. Once he does, the game will be ruined for everyone else. He's afraid of what will happen to their culture, even their civilization, with such a fundamental element gone."

"But he can't stay here forever," I said. "Even with their super-efficient neutrino drive, he's going to run out of fuel sometime."

"He can stay here and get the 2.8 gravities he needs to survive by splitting his spacecraft into two parts and rotating them on ends of a tether," Abdul said. "But sooner or later he will run out of either food or energy and have to go back to Jupiter."

Suddenly I had a brainstorm. "I know a way," I said. "It will take a lot of time and effort, but I think we can make a comfortable home away from home for our Borc friend—right on Earth."

It did take time—two years in fact. We found a field of granite boulders in the Australian outback with nobody around for hundreds of kilometers. Capsules containing laser-beam suspended antimatter were brought in from the production facility out in the belt. The antimatter was used to compress explosively hunks of granite and carbon into ten centimeter hexagonal tiles of ultra-dense matter encapsulated in diamond. The half-million ton slabs were laid in a compact pattern on the flattened top of a large granite knob until nearly one thousand of them had tiled an area three meters across. The thickness of the ultra-dense matter had been adjusted until the gravity field just above the plates was 1.8 times Earth gravity. When the Earth's gravity pull was added, the resulting 2.8 gravities would keep any Borc from "biting his tongue."

I was in the welcoming contingent that stood in the hot December sunshine of "Down Under," awaiting the Borc elevator. The conical ship came screaming out of the sky—right on schedule. My old friends, the mechanical arms, reached out the open hatch. Three arms struggled with a large, clear, cylindrical pressure capsule filled with blue liquid, a lot of machinery, and a violet and orange Borc. The other carried a much smaller cask of diamond with its cargo of gnats.

"He brought his translator," I said.

Just as quickly as it came, the space ship elevator left again, pulling gravities straight for Jupiter. We have a lot to learn from this willing exile and his talking super-computer. If he can only hold out as long in Australia as he did on Jupiter, it shouldn't be too many millennia before we humans can take our neutrino drive ships down into Jupiter itself and then—comfortably ensconced in our gravity-controlled cabins—return the visit.

✧ SPACE WARPS AND TIME MACHINES

In the previous chapters on "Antigravity" and "Black Holes," I discussed the physical meaning of some of the solutions to the equations of the Einstein Theory of Gravity, the General Theory of Relativity. In this chapter, I discuss how these and other solutions to the Einstein equations produce some bizarre predictions for the behavior of certain of these structures, including behavior that emulates such science fiction concepts as space warps and time machines.

There are two basic ways to get from "Here" to "There" in a hurry. One way is to find some future technology that allows movement through the space between Here and There faster than the speed of light. The other way is to obey the cosmic speed law, but find some method of getting from Here to There without having to go through all that empty space in between. To do that, what is needed is that good old science fiction plot-speeder-upper, the space warp.

It turns out that there are a number of possibilities for space warps based on the Einstein Theory of Gravity. These space warps are "bridges" or "tunnels" that shortcut through higher dimensions from one point in our space to another. All of these space warp concepts have some theoretical problems, yet those problems might not be insurmountable for a sufficiently advanced technological civilization. Of the many types of space warps produced to date using the Einstein Theory of Gravity, the one that Hollywood likes best is the black hole.

As I discussed in the chapter "Black Holes," shortly after Einstein published his Theory of Gravity, Schwarzschild found an exact solution to the equations for a nonrotating spherical mass. The solution correctly predicts the precession of the axis of Mercury's orbit about the sun. It also predicts that a sufficiently dense star will create an optically black "event horizon" in the space around itself, a black shield in space and time that forever prevents anything from getting out. This is the infamous "black hole." The full mathematical solution found by Schwarzschild not only describes the shape of space and time in this universe, right down to the center of the black hole, but it also includes a mirror image solution that exists in the "other universe" on the "other side" of the center. In essence, the Schwarzschild solution to the Einstein Theory of Gravity describes a "Wormhole" through space from one universe to another.

There are some significant problems with this Schwarzschild Wormhole Space Warp much loved by Hollywood. First, there is the event horizon that forms the black hole shield around the mouth of the wormhole in this universe. It only allows one-way travel. You can enter the Wormhole, but you can never come out. Second, even if you enter the Wormhole by falling through the event horizon, you will find that the Wormhole is not a true "hole" since the collapsing star that formed the black hole is blocking the throat and preventing your passage to the universe on the other side. There is no way to "avoid" or "tunnel through" the collapsing star, since both you and it are inexorably falling toward the center where a singularity in space and time is forming that will crush both you and the star.

The fact that a user of a Wormhole *must* hit the singularity at the center of the black hole is strongly emphasized by the mathematically oriented physicists who study black holes. They point out that although Einstein showed us that space is equivalent to time, there is a major difference between a space-like dimension and a time-like dimension. If you get far away from everything and don't do anything, then you can stand still in space—but you can't stand still in time. You can slow down time by flying off into space in an ultrafast rocketship or by setting up housekeeping on a very massive planet, but you can't stop time. You must keep on moving inexorably through time (t), in one direction only $(+t)$, until you come to the end of time $(t=\text{infinity})$.

In the Schwarzschild solution describing the Wormhole Space Warp, there are three space dimensions and one time dimension. But at the event horizon, the radial space dimension takes on the behavior of a time dimension, while the time dimension takes on the behavior of a space dimension. [See the left side of Figure 13.] This means, that, once inside the event horizon, despite all the rockets, all the forces, all the future magic you can command, you must keep on moving inexorably through space in the radial direction (r), in one direction only $(-r)$, until you come to the end of space at the singularity $(r=0)$. From this mathematical point of view, you can no more increase your radial distance from the Schwarzschild singularity at the center than you can turn back the hands of time. Thus, the Schwarzschild Wormhole, despite its popularity with Hollywood, is not a very useful space warp. Fortunately, there are a number of ways to modify the Wormhole to make it more user friendly.

If the collapsing star is electrically charged, then the Schwarzschild solution converts into the Reissner-Nordstrøm solution. This solution, found shortly after the Schwarzschild solution in 1918, describes the structure of spacetime outside a massive object that also contains an excess of charge. There are now two event horizons, an outer event horizon which is slightly inside of where the event horizon would be if the collapsing mass were not charged, while outside the singularity is an inner event horizon. [See the right side of Figure 13.] The greater the charge, the greater the radius of this inner event horizon.

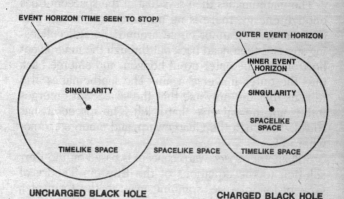

Fig. 13—Schwarzschild Wormhole Space Warp and Reissner-Nordstrøm Chargewarp.

To use this charged black hole space warp, or "Chargewarp," a spaceship would follow the collapsing charged star and pass through the outer event horizon. Once inside the first event horizon, the radial space dimension will have taken on time-like qualities, in that the spaceship must inexorably continue moving inward to constantly decreasing radial dimensions, following the collapsing charged star down toward the singularity. As the collapsing star becomes smaller and smaller, a second event horizon would form. Once inside the inner event horizon, the matter in the collapsing star would continue falling inward toward the center under its self-gravitation, where it would form the singularity. The spacecraft would also have to pass through this inner event horizon. Inside the inner event horizon, however, time and space have once again reversed roles and it is now possible for the spacecraft to turn on its rockets, halt its motion in the radial direction, and go into orbit about the singularity.

The mathematics then says that, if the spacecraft has enough energy, there is no mathematical reason why the spacecraft cannot circle around the still collapsing star and then head back out through the inner event horizon and the outer event horizon, and emerge back into the outer universe again. The mathematics also tells us that the universe that the spacecraft emerges into is not the universe that it left. The spacecraft has traveled through the Chargewarp, and emerged somewhere else.

Still another space warp concept is based on the Kerr solution to the equations of the Einstein Theory of Gravity for a dense, spinning mass in the form of a rotating ring. Since all stars have some rotation, when a star reaches the end of its life and collapses, one would expect it to turn into a dense spinning mass. Left to itself, however, a collapsing star will find ways to shed its angular momentum, usually by throwing material off from its rapidly spinning equator. With the excess angular momentum gone, the star will finally form into a rotating pancake shape, not a rotating ring.

However, it is possible (and given the human race's proclivity for fooling around with nature, probable), that this pancake shaped collapse could be induced to form a ring-shaped collapse, with all the dense mass out in a rotating ring. This Kerr solution to the Einstein Theory of Gravity then describes a space warp—a

Ringwarp. The gravity tides are strong near the surface of the ring and it is dangerous to approach too closely to the ring. There is no mass in the center of the ring, however, so there are no gravity tides there. If you go through the center of this rotating ring you do not come out the other side. [See Figure 14]. Instead, as you pass through the ring in either direction, you will enter a hyperuniverse. In this hyperuniverse the spacetime has different properties than the normal spacetime of this Universe. Mass in the hyperuniverse is negative and repels instead of attracts. To get out of the hyperuniverse back into our Universe, merely traverse the Ringwarp again. Either direction is okay.

There is a problem with the Kerr Ringwarp, in that in order to open up the Ringwarp enough to allow two-way travel, it is necessary that the mass in the rotating ring be moving at the speed of light. If, however, the rotating massive ring source for the Ringwarp also carries an electrical charge, then the charge and angular momentum augment each other. The requirement for rotation is lessened and the event horizons can be eliminated at a rotation rate that produces a peripheral velocity of the ring slightly less than the speed of light.

Thus, according to our present understanding of this solution of the Einstein field equations, a highly charged, rapidly rotating, ultradense ring, warps space enough to form Ringwarps that can be used without leaving this Universe. We do not know if the hyperuniverse opened up by a Ringwarp is the same for all such Ringwarps. If it is, then by making and opening Ringwarps in orbit around distant stars we can travel from one star system to another by merely popping into the Ringwarp in our solar system and popping out again in another Ringwarp around some distant star system. We do not yet know whether the theory for

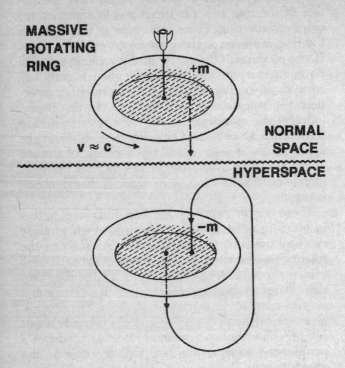

Fig. 14—The Kerr Ringwarp.

interconnection of Ringwarp hyperuniverses will allow the distance between the Ringwarps in the hyperuniverse to be made less than the distance between the Ringwarps in this Universe. If it can be made significantly less, then we have a new method of space travel that allows us to travel faster than the speed of light.

Any of the space warp concepts that involve

singularities in spacetime will always have problems. The mathematically oriented physicists who study the exotic behavior of black holes can easily show that even minor perturbations, such as those caused by a spacecraft trying to use a space warp, should cause the space warp to distort or collapse. Although one could argue that a technological civilization that is sufficiently advanced to create a stellar-sized space warp should be able to control any potential instabilities in the space warp, the mathematicians are probably correct. Fortunately, there is a space warp concept that is an exact solution to the equations of the Einstein Theory of Gravity, and yet does not involve singularities, or even stellar masses. This is the Morris-Thorne Field-Supported Space Tunnel. [See Figure 15.] These are tunnels through space that are kept from collapsing to a singularity by threading the throat of the tunnel with special fields.

The fields holding up the Space Tunnel have to be exotic fields that have a tension greater than their energy density (electric and magnetic fields have a tension that is *equal* to the energy density). Such fields are known to exist in high energy density matter such as is found in neutron stars. Other versions of these fields have been made in the laboratory at low energy densities.

The best example of an exotic field that has the proper properties are the vacuum fluctuation fields between two closely spaced metal plates. According to quantum mechanics, the vacuum is not empty. It is full of random fluctuations of the electromagnetic field. [See the top half of Figure 11 in the Chapter "Black Holes."] When two conducting metal plates are brought very close together, the vacuum between the plates is limited in the number of fluctuations it can support, and thus becomes "emptier" than the vacuum outside the plates. This energy difference forces the two plates

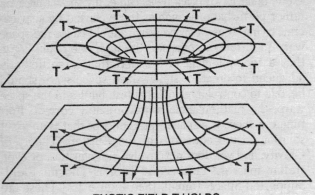

EXOTIC FIELD T HOLDS
MORRIS-THORNE SPACE TUNNEL OPEN

Fig. 15—Morris-Thorne Field-Supported Space Tunnel.

together, creating a force that is large enough to be measured in the laboratory. Since the energy of the vacuum is defined as zero, this means that the space between the plates has negative energy density. Being negative, the energy density is automatically less than the tension, and the field between the plates has the desired exotic properties needed to hold a Morris-Thorne field-supported Space Tunnel open.

Thorne and his students have "designed" a space warp that consists of two perfectly conducting spheres completely covering the spherical holes in spacetime that form the "mouths" of the Space Tunnel. (This is hard to visualize unless you are used to thinking in four dimensions.) Although the two spheres are quite large, and have a comparatively small door in them to let a spacecraft pass through, their inner surfaces are only a microscopic distance apart, since the distance as measured through the Space Tunnel is very small, while the distance between the mouths in our outside Universe can be lightyears apart.

The two spheres have a large amount of identical electric charge on them. This has two effects. First, the identical charges on each sphere cause them to electrically repel each other. This electrical repulsion force is sufficient to exactly counterbalance the vacuum fluctuation forces that are trying to pull the two closely spaced conducting spheres together. Second, the strong electric fields on the outside of the spheres act to keep the Space Tunnel throat open in the region from the outside surface of the sphere off into flat space at infinity. These electric fields are what keep the Space Tunnel open.

Electric fields are not quite exotic enough, however, to hold the Space Tunnel open at its throat. Right at the throat, in the microscopic region between the interiors of the two spheres, an exotic field with a tension greater than its energy density is needed. That exotic field is supplied by the vacuum fluctuation forces between the two spheres. The equations obtained show that the smaller the spacing between the spheres through the Space Tunnel, the smaller the spheres need to be to keep the Space Tunnel throat from collapsing, and the easier the space warp will be to build.

If you assume that the minimum spacing between the two conducting spheres will be determined by the fact that the conducting spheres have to be made of atoms, then with a spacing between the spheres of one percent of the radius of an atom, the diameter of the spheres required is one astronomical unit (the distance from the Sun to the Earth). To get the size of the Space Tunnel down closer to the size of a spacecraft would require much smaller spacing between the spheres, and they would have to be made of some form of collapsed matter that wasn't made of atoms, just the nuclei of atoms.

Although still nearly impossible to build from a technological point of view, the Morris-Thorne Field-Supported Space Tunnel design has many nice features: mathematical singularities are not involved in the construction, the amount of mass needed is less than a stellar mass, the throat of the space warp is large enough to pass a spacecraft, there are no tidal effects to damage the ship or crew, there are no infinite blue shift horizons to fry the crew with radiation, and the distance through the Space Tunnel can be made much shorter than the separation of the Space Tunnel mouths, allowing for faster-than-light transport from one part of space to another. For a description of how one might build a Space Tunnel and use it for travel through space and time, and a discussion of how the resulting causality paradoxes will be resolved, read my novel *Timemaster*, which in turn is based on the more mathematical papers by Morris, Thorne, Friedman, Novikov, Echeverria, Visser, Garfinkle and myself in the Recommended Reading list at the end of the chapter.

It is an axiom of relativity, where time and space are treated on an equal footing, that a faster-than-light space warp is operationally equivalent to a time machine. If one observer sees you using a space warp to move from one place to another faster than the speed of light—say, entering the space warp at Sol and arriving at Alpha Centauri one hour later—a different observer, who just happened to be passing by in a spacecraft moving in the right direction at a fast enough speed, would swear that you arrived at Alpha Centauri *before* you left Sol. Thus, if space warps are theoretically possible, then time machines should be too.

One of the technologies I see in our future that is presently indistinguishable from magic is the ability to travel in time. If a present-day scientist were confronted with a real time machine, he would certainly say that the machine had to be run by the rules of magic. His argument would go like this: Science is based on logic. Anything that produces logical paradoxes is not science. Time machines produce logical paradoxes. Therefore, if time machines exist, they must use magic, not science.

Yet, two of the most respected and tested theories of physics, both the Einstein Special Theory of Relativity and the Einstein General Theory of Relativity, allow time to be manipulated. Although we are presently far from being able to control the energies and masses that will be required to make a time machine suitable for human use, these theories give us the physical principles behind time travel.

How do we make a time machine?

What most people don't realize is that one type of time machine already exists. Various versions of these machines can be found in university and government laboratories. They are used every day by the scientists there, but they do have some limitations. They are only good for one-way time travel, and they can only handle a few atoms at a time. These present-day time machines are based on Einstein's Special Theory of Relativity. To understand how they work we need to know a little bit more about this remarkable theory that is now almost a law of nature.

Einstein's Special Theory of Relativity should really be called the Einstein Theory of Mechanics at High Velocities. The Einstein Theory of Mechanics replaced the old Newton Theory of Mechanics. The Newton theory described how matter moves through space and time. The matter gains and loses heat energy and kinetic energy as various forces act upon it, but nothing else happens to the matter. The Newton theory worked very well for objects moving at ordinary speeds, but it was not adequate when the velocities of the masses began to approach that of the speed of light. The newer Einstein theory correctly predicts the behavior of matter and energy, while Newton's old theory fails when the amount of energy in a particle becomes large and the particle is moving near the speed of light.

The Einstein Theory of Mechanics is called a theory of relativity because that is the way that Einstein stumbled onto the correct theory. In his usual insightful manner, Einstein didn't try to think about planets in orbit, or falling spheres, or billiard balls, or the other mechanical things that occupied the thoughts of Newton and other theorists thinking about mechanics. Instead, he asked a more personal question: "What do people see and sense when they are moving?"

Einstein knew that experiments had shown that there was no way for a person to tell that they were in motion, as long as it was constant motion. For example, suppose we had two observers: Jill in a rocket ship and Jack floating lazily in space. Jill turns on her engines for a while and accelerates up to a high velocity toward Jack, then turns the engines off. She is left floating in free-fall just as Jack is. She looks out her cockpit window to see Jack flashing past. It is obvious to both Jack and Jill that they are in motion relative to each other, but since both are floating in free-fall neither can prove which is moving and which is standing still. They can both see the stars, and perhaps Jill would be moving with respect to the stars and Jack wouldn't. Jack might argue that he was the one that was standing still because he sees the stars stationary. To Einstein, however, each observer is just as important as the other. It doesn't matter that all the stars in the universe would have to be moving to make Jill stationary.

To the genius mind of Einstein, an observer like Jill was just as important as the rest of the universe. This was no time for a democratic vote as to who was moving and who was not. The only thing that counts is a physical measurement, and since there was no method of measuring absolute velocity, both Jack and Jill's points of view were equally valid. Jill in the rocketship could be moving and the universe sitting still, or Jill could be standing still and the rest of the universe in motion. All points of view and all frames of reference are equally valid. Everything is relative—and that's where the name "relativity theory" came from.

At first glance, the Einstein Theory of Mechanics doesn't seem to follow common sense. Of course Jill's rocketship is moving and the rest of the universe is standing still. But Einstein just continued on in his methodical way, saying, "But suppose it *is* true that we can't tell the difference between a spaceship moving one way and the whole universe moving the other way?"

In his usual technique of thinking unthinkable thoughts, Einstein then asked himself, "What would I see if I could travel at the speed of light and were to look at a light wave traveling alongside of me?" If Einstein used the Newton picture of the way things worked, the answer would be that he would see the electric and magnetic fields in the light standing motionless—not vibrating. Yet it was the vibration of the fields that gave the light beam its frequency . . . its energy . . . its very existence. According to the laws of electromagnetism, unless a light beam vibrates, it cannot exist. Newton's law led to a paradox.

Einstein thought other unthinkable thoughts. "Suppose I were traveling at nearly the speed of light and I sent out a beam of light ahead of me. Being light, it would seem to me to be moving at the speed of light, but since I am sending it off from a moving platform, would not some other observer see the light beam moving *faster* than the speed of light?" Yet the velocity of light coming from fast-moving stars had been measured by astronomers and was always the same, no matter what the velocity of the star was— another paradox.

To Einstein, the only consistent answer to any of these questions was: "No. No matter how fast or slow I am going, the result of any experiment (especially a measurement of the speed of light) must be the same for all observers whose frames of reference are moving at a constant velocity, no matter what that velocity is."

Now according to any reasonable extrapolation of Newton's laws, this was impossible. Different observers should measure different velocities of light, depending upon whether the motion of their frame of reference added or subtracted from the motion of whatever was being observed. Yet—Einstein accepted his own "impossible" answer and proceeded to produce a set of mathematical equations describing space, time, matter, and energy that would produce the desired result of a constant velocity for light no matter what speed the frames of reference of the observers were moving at.

The equations that Einstein came up with were awkward. They even involved square roots. Ignoring their strange looks, Einstein proceeded to examine the implications of those equations. The results predicted by those strange set of equations are astounding in their abandonment of common sense, yet, all of the predicted results have been proven to be true time and time again.

They are: Space can be converted into time—and vice versa. Mass can be converted into energy—and vice versa. As you travel near the speed of light, space shrinks, time expands, and mass increases. If you travel at the speed of light, space shrinks to nothing, time increases to eternity, and your mass (if you had any to start with) increases to infinity.

The impossibility of the last means that it is impossible for any material object (like Einstein himself) to attain the speed of light because it would take an infinite amount of energy to accelerate an infinite mass. Light, being a form of pure energy, has no rest-mass per se, and so can (and to exist—must) travel at the speed of light. Yet what a queer universe the photon lives in. Since its space has shrunk to zero and its time has expanded to eternity, the photon exists everywhere along its trajectory at all times!

The most amazing result from the Einstein Theory of Mechanics that is hardest for people to accept is the slowing down of time at high velocities. This is best illustrated by the famous twin paradox: There are two astronauts, Jack and Jill. They are twins. One astronaut, Jill, travels off on an interstellar spacecraft and spends a long time traveling at nearly the speed of light, while her twin, Jack, stays at home. Upon the return of the traveler, Einstein's equations say that while the stay-at-home Jack has aged considerably, Jill is still young since she has been traveling in her time-machine, the relativistic spacecraft.

Thus—one way to make a time machine is to find a way to move at velocities close to that of light. Unfortunately, this special-relativity time machine only works one way. It can allow you to go into the future at a slower rate than normal, but you cannot go back in time. Still, this kind of time machine would have its uses. If you were sick and there was no cure for your disease, a short sojourn in a relativistic rocket ship could keep you from dying until the medical researchers could find the cure for what was ailing you. If you had a rich and very healthy aunt, then a few days spent at 99.99998% the speed of light could insure that you would be able to enjoy your aunt's inheritance while you were still youthful.

These special-relativistic time machines are being used today. In many of the laboratories studying the properties of the atomic nucleus, there are large machines called "atom smashers" that use electric, magnetic, and radio fields to accelerate tiny charged particles to very high velocities. These particle beams are then shot into metal foil targets. Most of the high speed particles pass right through the foil, but occasionally one of the particles plows head-on into the nucleus of one of the metal atoms, smashing the nuclei into bits.

Some of the "bits" are very interesting, since they are particles that exist inside the nucleus, but we normally don't see them because they have a very short lifetime. Some of the particle lifetimes are so short, a trillionth of a second, that the particles would travel less than a millimeter before they decayed if it were not for the time machine that kept them alive. For the atom smasher is also the time machine.

The energy that the atom smasher puts into its beam is so high that the bits of smashed nuclei that come out of the miniature explosion are moving at nearly the speed of light. Since the bits are moving so fast, their lifetimes are increased 10,000 times or more, and instead of living only a trillionth of a second, they now live a few hundred millionths of a second and can travel tens of meters from the highly radioactive target chamber out through the steering magnets and into carefully designed instruments that measure the mass, charge, spin, and other exotic properties of that short-lived bit of nuclear stuff.

When the time machine properties of the Einstein Theory of Mechanics were first discussed, many people refused to believe that such a thing could happen. How could one twin stay young while the other grew old? If such a thing could be done, it wouldn't be done by scientists, but by magicians using some magical youth potion. But the true magical elixir of eternal youth was brewed by a scientist, Einstein, who gave us a new picture of the basic fabric of the universe, the space and time we live in.

The reason that the paradox of the twins is hard for us to believe comes from our limited experiences with high velocities. Our supersonic jets and rockets may go fast enough for most of us, but even our fastest rockets, boosted to their highest speeds by close encounters with the rapidly moving planets of Jupiter and Saturn, still travel at only one-ten-thousandth of the speed of light. Unfortunately, the unusual effects predicted by Einstein's Special Theory of Relativity only become significant when you are traveling at speeds greater than half the speed of light. Because of this limited experience with high velocities we have developed a "common sense" that says that time is some absolute quantity that ticks the same way for all things.

This strong, but erroneous belief in "common sense" is often backed up by people trying to use the principle of "relativity" to prove their point. "If everything is relative . . ." they would say, " . . . and all points of view are equally good, then the idea of the traveling twin Jill living longer than the stay-at-home twin Jack leads to a logical paradox."

Their argument goes like this: "Jill takes a ride on a relativistic rocketship, while her lazy twin Jack stays curled up in front of his fireplace on Earth reading *War and Peace*. Jill returns some decades later just as Jack is reading the last page. (Jack is a slow reader.)

"According to Einstein, Jill will be young and perky, having aged but a few years, while Jack looks and feels like Rip Van Winkle.

"Well, if everything is relative, and Jack's point of view is just as good as Jill's point of view, then according to 'relativity' it would be equally good to say that while

Jack was reading in front of the fireplace, the Earth was taking *him* on a relativistic ride, while Jill sat cooped up in her motionless rocket. The situation would be even more symmetric if we imagined Jack and Jill meeting out in empty space in two identical rocket-ships, then flipping coins to see who travels and who waits. Since the 'all points of view are equally good' relativity principle says that we can either assume that Jack is moving while Jill is standing still, or that Jill is moving while Jack is standing still, then the Einstein "time dilation" effect leads to the paradox that: depend-ing upon which point of view you choose, Jack ages slower than Jill, or Jill ages slower than Jack. These results are mutually contradictory, thus, there is a logical paradox generated. Since the Einstein idea of "time dilation" is what caused the paradox, it must be wrong, and the time that a person lives does *not* depend upon their velocity."

To resolve the Twin Paradox problem, let us set up a carefully designed experiment. Jack climbs into his rocketship "FRAME 1" (short for Frame of Ref-erence 1), and goes out into space and turns off his rocket so he is no longer accelerating and is moving at a constant velocity. Once he has stopped the engines, the name of his rocketship now means some-thing real—the unique frame of reference in which Jack resides. Jill also takes off in her rocketship "FRAME 2" and after getting up speed relative to Jack, she aims her vehicle carefully at Jack's space-craft so that their side portholes will pass facing each other. She then turns off her engines, leaving her floating in space. They both go to the side portholes in their vehicles. They set up their cameras and clocks (digital quartz chronometers with microsecond accu-racies and large numbers on the readout). Fortunately Jill is a good pilot and the ships pass each other with a relative velocity of 99.9% of the speed of light and with their portholes within a few centimeters of each other. There are simultaneous clicks of their two cameras and each sees that the readouts on both clocks indicate the same time.

Jill now continues off into space, and within a few hours is in the outer regions of the solar system on her way to the stars. They compare clock ticks by radio signals, but they both know that you can't tell anything definite by that technique, for both think that the other's clock is slow.

The resolution of the paradox comes at the turn-around point. Up until that point, special relativity says that the aging question is ambiguous. In order to compare the relative times of the two clocks (or the ages of the two twins), they must both be at the same place. Now instead of having Jill turn on the rocket engine in "FRAME 2" and destroying the validity of her rocketship's name, let's have her hitchhike back. For the purposes of the experiment, we have sent David out earlier in his rocketship "FRAME 3." David went out a few light years, then turned around and headed back into the solar system at 99.9% light speed, right next to the track Jill would be coming out on. Jill contacts David and arranges for a ride back in on "FRAME 3." As they pass, Jill hops off "FRAME 2" and onto "FRAME 3," carrying her clock with her. "FRAME 2" continues on its way out into the starry sky, keeping true to its name.

(One might think it would be difficult for Jill to make the transfer from a frame of reference moving at +99.9% of the speed of light to a frame of reference moving at -99.9% of the speed of light carrying a heavy quartz chronometer, but Jill, like Jack, is quite nimble.)

Jill rides back in with David in "FRAME 3," and when David zips by Jack, Jill is down at the side porthole, her youthful face grinning in exuberance as she snaps a picture of her gray-haired twin Jack and his aging quartz chronometer with a time indicated on it that is many years later than the time on Jill's clock.

We know that Jill will be the younger twin because she is the one that violated the "principle of equivalence of reference frames" by jumping off "FRAME 2" and coming back on "FRAME 3." By abandoning her original coordinate system that she started with, Jill can no longer claim "everything is relative." The stay-at-home twin Jack is still with his original coordinate system "FRAME 1" and thus has not moved, paying a price for this stodginess by aging at a precipitous rate compared to the traveling twin.

Suppose David had gone the other way, and had arranged to pass by Jack at 99.9999% of the speed of light, and Jack and his chronometer had left "FRAME 1" and jumped on "FRAME 3." Then sometime later when "FRAME 3" had caught up with and passed Jill in "FRAME 2," it would have been Jack who was younger. (At 99.9999% of the speed of light, Jack is aging slower than Jill moving at 99.9% of the speed of light).

Except for a few who still cherish the idea of an inviolable, unchangeable time, the human race has absorbed this unusual behavior of nature at high velocities, and has learned not only to live with this "one-way" time machine, but to use it.

There is yet another type of "one-way" time machine. You are living on it—the Earth! This type of time machine uses one of the magical properties of gravity predicted by the Einstein Theory of Gravity, the General Theory of Relativity. According to the Einstein Theory of Gravity, a high gravity field causes time to run slower, just as high velocities do. The amount of time slowing in the field of the Earth is not very much, although it is measurable if you have an accurate enough clock. A clock in the basement of a building will run slightly slower than one on the top floor of the building. To get a significant amount of slowing, the gravitational field has to be very strong.

One way to obtain a strong gravitational field is to find a neutron star or a black hole and send your spacecraft into a close orbit around the mass. You are now down in the gravitational potential well of the star and are living slower than those further away. Since you are in a free-fall orbit, the strong gravitational forces pulling on you are canceled by the centrifugal force of your orbital rotation. The problem is that when you are in orbit about a dense star, the only place where the gravity and centrifugal forces exactly cancel is at the center of mass of the spacecraft (or you!). The other points are not quite in free-fall and are subject to the tidal forces due to the change in the gravity field of the star with distance and angle. For an orbit around a neutron star or black hole, these tidal forces can reach hundreds of Earth gravities per meter. These tidal forces are strong enough to literally tear you limb from limb. If you go even closer, the tides will be strong enough to straighten out the helical twist in your DNA!

In the very distant future, however, it may be that our future magicians will be able to make a one-way gravitational time machine that won't kill you with its crushing tidal forces if you try to use it. This time machine would be a hollow ball of ultradense material. The gravitational potential inside such a hollow ball is uniform. The gravitational potential can be quite high, giving a strong time slowing effect, yet, because there are no variations in it, there are no gravitational forces, since it is the variations in the gravitational potential that cause the accelerations.

Many people think that the slow-down of time in gravitational fields and for fast moving objects has only been confirmed for high-speed elementary particles. In one of the better justified boondoggles in the annals of science, however, nothing can beat parlaying a test of Einstein's theories of relativity into a trip around the world. In 1971, American physicists Hafele and Keating borrowed two identical, highly accurate portable clocks from the U.S. Naval Observatory, and obtained a grant from the Office of Naval Research to pay for three around-the-world tickets (one seat for each of them and a seat for one of the clocks). The twin clocks were set to the same time in Washington, DC. One clock-twin stayed in Washington where it was only subjected to the slow-down in time due to its position in the gravity field of the Earth. The other clock-twin took off at a speed of 1000 kilometers per hour (600 mph) and went on a round-trip journey around the Earth at an average height of ten kilometers (six miles) above the Earth's surface.

The time as measured by the moving clock twin was slowed down by the fact that it was moving at a velocity close to that of light (well . . . it was closer to the speed of light than the stay-at-home twin). The time as measured by the stay-at-home twin was slowed by the fact that it was subjected to a much greater gravitational field than the elevated twin (well . . . it was 1.0016 times greater). However, the velocity effect was larger than the gravitational effect, so upon return to Washington, the moving clock was found to be slower by exactly the amount predicted by the two theories of relativity. Just to check, the scientists and the world-traveling clock went back around the Earth the other way, where the rotational speed of the Earth subtracted from the airplane's speed rather than adding to it. Again the scientists got the correct result. (This was probably the cheapest test of relativity ever made; it only cost $8000, of which $7600 was spent on air fares.)

Scientists have already built a magic time machine that stretches the life-times of tiny particles by 10,000 times. When will we be able to build a time machine big enough to keep large particles (like us) forever youthful? We have already built and are using the first model of that magic time machine. It's called the Space Shuttle.

The Space Shuttle is a great space-travel machine, but as a time-travel machine this first version leaves something to be desired. The orbital velocity of the Shuttle is nearly eight kilometers per second (26 millionths of the speed of light). If you stayed in an orbiting space shuttle for a year, you would age more slowly than your twin on the ground, but only by about one-hundredth of a second. To make real time machines out of our space-traveling rocket ships, we need to make them go at nearly the speed of light. It will be difficult, but we can see the technology to build these magical time machines coming in our future. They are discussed in more detail in the chapter, "Starships."

The Einstein Theories of Mechanics and Gravity have given us one-way time machines that allow us to slow our rapid progression into the future. What about a time machine that will allow us to go into the past as well as the future? The Einstein Theory of Gravity allows many shapes for such a time machine. In fact, it seems that any rotating object that is dense enough to produce a region with a twisted ultra-gravity field can produce time-confusing regions. There are some shapes, however, that can produce time-travel regions that might be usable by humans.

One gravitational mass configuration that can act as a time machine is a large, rapidly rotating, dense object that is collapsing to a black hole just as its spin speed is rising to that of the speed of light. This is the Kerr Ringwarp. [See Figure 14.] The Ringwarp is not only a space warp, but a time machine. The mathematics of the Kerr solution indicate that as you come down from overhead and start to approach the plane of the ring, the strong gravity field of the ring starts to change your space and time compared to that of an observer far away. Your space becomes smaller and your time becomes longer. The spinning of the dense ring causes even stranger things to happen. The twist that the rotation puts into your spacetime converts part of what you would call space into what the outside observer would call time, and converts part of what you would call time into what he would call space. The Kerr solution then says that as you pass through the plane defined by the dense ring, the spacetime conversion becomes complete. Your forward space dimension has been turned into a time dimension while your time dimension has turned into a space dimension.

What is more amazing, is that when you go through the hole in the ultra-dense ring, you don't come out on the other side! Instead you find you have entered a strange type of hyperspace. In this hyperspace you feel perfectly normal, even though one of your three space directions has been interchanged with time. If you go in the hyperspace up near the rotating ring and move in the direction against the rotation of the ring for a number of rotations, you will observe nothing unusual happening to you. In your travels near the rotating ring, however, you will have traveled backward in space (the forward direction being determined by the direction of rotation of the ring). If you then return back through the hole in the ring, your time and space dimensions will be restored to normal. But don't forget that while in hyperspace you went backwards in space and what used to be space is now time. Although you have returned back to your original position in space, you will find that your position in time has moved backwards a number of years!

This magical result obtained from the Kerr solution to the Einstein equations can be found in a highly mathematical paper published by Brandon Carter in the Physical Review, the most prestigious scientific journal in the field of physics. In that paper Carter concludes: "To sum up . . . the central region has the properties of a time machine. It is possible, starting from any point in the outer regions of the space, to travel into the interior, move backwards in time . . . and then return to the original position."

Now, there are many mathematical theorists who insist that such a special shape for a rotating mass will not happen. It may be true that nature will not naturally form a ring-like time machine from a collapsing star, but with a little guidance and some presently indistinguishable from magic technology applied by our far-future ancestors, perhaps a star bigger than our sun can be made into a ring-shaped time machine one hundred kilometers (sixty miles) in diameter—and maintained despite the fact that it would not be stable if left alone. At a size of one hundred kilometers, the gravitational tides from the dense mass of the ring are weak enough that they will not cause damage to people and well-built spacecraft passing through the center of the ring. A time machine of this size would be big enough and safe enough to send an entire rocket ship back in time.

The Kerr time machine does have the problem that in order to get the time-travel effect, the mass in the spinning ring has to move at a speed equal to that of light, and that can never be attained, just approached. There are other solutions to the Einstein field equations, however, that improve upon the Kerr solution. A rapidly spinning dense ring with a large electric charge on it will form a time machine even when the speed of the mass in the ring is below the speed of light. Since the original star has enough rotational energy to reach near-light speeds after collapsing from a diameter of ten million kilometers to a diameter of one hundred kilometers, all our far-future magicians have to do is make sure that the star stays highly charged as it collapses and it will form a time machine.

Even if it turns out that a ring-shaped time machine can't be built, it isn't all that important. A spinning ring is not the only shape for a time machine. Another configuration for a time machine is a spinning cylinder. [See Figure 16.] First described by Frank Tipler, the theoretical model for this time machine uses a mathematical approximation, so it is not as rigorous as the Kerr model. The approximation used is to assume that the long spinning cylinder is infinitely long. It is equivalent to saying that you are concerned only about the gravitational fields near the middle of the cylinder and the ends of the cylinder are so far away that the slight differences in the gravity field due to the fact that the cylinder is finite are not large enough to worry about.

Tipler's time machine is a long cylinder of ultra-dense mass with a spin speed at its surface that is one-half that of light. The time-mixing region is near the midpoint of the cylinder, but *outside* the mass of the cylinder. The important feature of the Tipler Time Machine is that it allows travel both backward and forward in time (depending upon whether you circle with or against the spin of the cylinder), and neither the time traveler or the time machine has to move at velocities close to that of light. In his paper, Tipler concludes: "In short, general relativity suggests that if we construct a sufficiently large rotating cylinder, we create a time machine."

The Morris-Thorne Field-Supported Space Tunnel can also be converted into a time machine. If the two mouths of the tunnel are generated side-by-side, they are like twins born at the same time. If you enter one mouth of the tunnel, you instantly exit the other mouth. Now, if one of the tunnel mouths is taken on a relativistic journey by a space tug, then, on its return, it will be "younger" than the stay-at-home tunnel mouth. If you enter the older mouth you will exit the younger mouth some time in the past, and if you enter the younger mouth, you will exit the older mouth sometime in the future. If the younger mouth is still there upon your exit from the older mouth, the process can then be repeated and you can continue to make time jumps into the future. The amount of time you jump over on each traverse is the difference in age of the two mouths.

Notice that this time machine, like all the other time machines that are allowed by the Einstein Theory of Gravity, can only take you backward in time to the

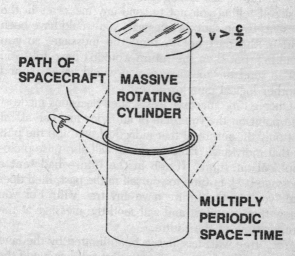

Fig. 16—The Tipler Two-Way Time Machine.

moment that the machine is turned on, and forward in time to the moment that the machine is turned off. Einstein's laws do not allow a future time-machine maker to go back into time to tell himself how to make the machine. Thus, at least one of the possible time-machine paradoxes is avoided.

Once we have a time machine that allows us to go both forward and backward in time, however, then other paradoxes arise that are even more confounding than the twin paradox. Exhuming an old cliche: "What is to prevent you from going back in time and killing your grandfather before he has any children?"

It doesn't take time travelers to cause trouble. Even messages sent back and forth in time can produce logical paradoxes. For instance, you could send a message to your future self asking it to send a message to your past self telling you not to send any messages in the present. If you sent the message, you would have been told in the past not to send the message, so you wouldn't, but then the future wouldn't have told you not to send the message so you would have . . . and another logical paradox arises.

Once a time machine exists, then decisions made at one point on the time-line of an individual can affect not only the future of that individual, but also the past of that individual. Time machines will also raise philosophical questions. If you in the future had sent a message back in time to yourself in the past, then does the "you" in the future have any free will? For you know that you must and will send the message at the proper time in the future.

Yet, "free will" has always been limited by the laws of nature. For instance, if your past self has made the decision to jump off a bridge, your future self is bound by that decision. When time machines exist, your future decisions, in the same way, can bind your past self to the consequences of that "yet-to-be-made" decision.

There are other paradoxes brought about by the assumption of the existence of a two-way time machine, but they all boil down to the violation of a strict time-ordered cause-and-effect relationship. There are those who would argue that this alone is enough. The very fact that causality would be violated means that time travel is impossible. Nothing more needs to be said. ("I'm sorry, young man, I can't buy your story that you came from the future to warn us about an asteroid about to strike the ocean off the East Coast. You are logically impossible. Go away!")

Amazingly enough, there are presently a series of papers appearing in the scientific literature that discuss in great mathematical detail the problem of paradoxes created by time machines. The first of these papers are those by Friedman et al., Echeverria et al., and Novikov to be found in Recommended Reading at the end of this chapter. To everyone's amazement (including the amazement of the scientists writing the papers), they find that instead of their mathematics showing that the existence of logical paradoxes proves that time machines cannot exist, their mathematics indicates that the logical paradoxes cannot exist! For every paradox that they can dream up (for example, someone deciding to go back into time to shoot himself), a detailed mathematical analysis of the way that nature will behave according to the known laws of physics shows that nature will automatically adjust itself so that the paradox will not occur!

These results are now embodied in the Novikov Principle of Self Consistency, which states that: "The only solutions to the laws of physics that can occur locally in the real universe are those which are globally self consistent."

In the example of the person deciding to got back into time and shoot himself, either he changes his mind, or the gun doesn't work, or the bullet misses, or he kills someone who looks just like him, or something else happens to prevent the paradox. Admittedly, the event that prevents the paradox may have a low probability of happening, but once a time machine exists, then possible physical events around that time machine are constrained so that the Principle of Self Consistency is observed, and low probability events become high probability events.

Once you have made a decision to jump off a bridge, nature will severely limit your possible future courses of action. In the same way, once you have made a decision to turn on a time machine, nature will severely limit your future courses of action to prevent you from creating any paradoxes.

The scientists involved in these publications are continuing their research, trying to come up with a paradox that has no escape routes, like the gun not firing. So far, they have been unable to find any. Those of you that think you can come up with an unbeatable paradox are encouraged to read the technical papers. You will find out there how nature will conspire against you to prevent the paradox from occurring.

Suppose there *was* a time machine. Suppose it were something as simple as a time-phone, a telephone that allowed messages to be sent into the past. The time-phone would only be used after the occurrence of some disaster, such as an asteroid hitting the Earth. After the disaster had occurred, a message would be sent into the past to warn the people of the impending problem so that they could evacuate the affected area and at least save lives. In the future, the evacuation has already taken place, the asteroid struck, and the people have come back to rebuild. One of their first jobs would be to send the evacuation message back in time, for if it is not sent, then they would all be dead. Although there might be some thoughts about testing the paradox by *not* sending the message, I'm sure in this case it would be sent, for the consequences of not doing so would be too great. Besides, the Principle of Self Consistency will ensure that the message gets sent.

A time-phone will also give us a broader perspective of events before any major political or social decision is made. As a result of the existence of a time-phone, we will have an "awareness" that extends further into the future than the merest instant that you and I are presently limited to. By using the time-phone, we can be made aware of future events and avoid their consequences. Just as modern airplanes use long-distance radar to search the space ahead of them for storms, and change their routes to avoid them, so time machines will allow the pilots of the nations to search the time ahead of them for disasters and avoid their consequences.

It may be tens of thousands of years before the human race has turned what is now future magic into future technology. It will be a long time before our engineering technology can control collapsing stars in order to make a time machine big enough for a vehicle loaded with human time travelers. Long before that time, however, our gravitational engineers may be able to make miniature time machines with the dimension of an atomic nucleus that will allow messages encoded on gamma rays to be sent backward and forward in time.

To make a time-phone we would need to make a superheavy nucleus and strip all the electrons off it to be able to get at the dense, highly charged nucleus inside. Then, using whirling electric and magnetic fields, we would spin up the supernucleus like the rotor of a motor. The rapidly spinning, highly charged supernucleus would then create a north and south magnetic pole at its spin poles. A super-strong magnetic field could then pull or push on the magnetic poles until the nucleus is stretched out into a long spinning cylinder or spread out into the shape of a rapidly rotating ring. [See Figure 17.] These high density, highly charged, rapidly rotating objects would be time machines for nuclear-sized time travelers, extremely short pulses of gamma rays with wavelengths smaller than the time-transfer region.

HIGHLY EXCITED HEAVY NUCLEI

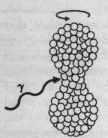
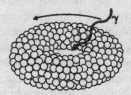

PROLATE WITH NARROW WAIST

OBLATE WITH THIN CENTER

Fig. 17—Miniature space warps and time machines for gamma ray signals using dense, highly charged, rapidly rotating superheavy nuclei.

A message would consist of a small number of gamma rays, each at a slightly different frequency corresponding to its "code word" in the message. At these high energies, gamma ray detectors are quite efficient, and the decoding of the cluster of photons that emerged a few weeks in the past or future would be relatively easy.

In the far future when our present technology evolves and makes possible what we now consider magic, our gravitational and time engineers will construct time-phones and time-craft as easily as we now construct space-phones and space-craft. One of these days, instead of being a slave to the ever-ticking clock, we will be able to send our time-craft on a journey through sixty minutes of time into the past or future as easily as we now send our space-craft through the sixty light-minutes of space to Jupiter.

Recommended Reading

Brandon Carter, "Complete Analytic Extension of the Symmetry Axis of Kerr's Solution of Einstein's Equations," *Physical Review*, Vol. 141, #4, pp. 1242–1247 (January 1966).

Brandon Carter, "Global Structure of the Kerr Family of Gravitational Fields," *Physical Review*, Vol. 174, #5, pp. 1559–1571 (25 October 1968).

Fernando Echeverria, Gunnar Klinkhammer, and Kip S. Thorne, "Billiard Balls in Wormhole Spacetimes with Closed Timelike Curves—Classical Theory," *Physical Review*, D44, #4, pp. 1077–1099 (15 August 1991).

Robert L. Forward, "How to Build a Time Machine," *Omni*, Vol. 2, #8, pp. 92–94, 122–123 (May 1980).

Robert L. Forward, "Space Warps: A Review of One Form of Propulsionless Transport," *Journal of the British Interplanetary Society*, Vol. 42, pp. 533–542 (November 1989).

Robert L. Forward, *Timemaster* (Tor Books, NY, 1992). Contains a detailed description of the construction of a Morris-Thorne Field-Supported Space Tunnel using frames of negative matter—following the prescriptions of the papers by Morris and Thorne, Garfinkle and Strominger, and Visser; its conversion into a time machine following the prescription of the paper by Morris, Thorne, and Yurtsever; and a resolution of the time machine paradoxes that result using the arguments of the papers by Friedman et al. and Novikov. During my research prior to writing the novel, I invented a defensive "weapon" based on a time machine, called the "Timetrap." When I sent my notes to Thorne for comment, he realized that

I had found a new set of solutions to a problem that he and his students were working on at the time. He incorporated my notes into their scientific paper, "Billiard Balls . . ." by Echeverria, Klinkhammer, and Thorne, and referenced my science fiction novel as the source.

John Friedman, Michael S. Morris, Igor D. Novikov, Fernando Echeverria, Gunnar Klinkhammer, Kip S. Thorne, and Ulvi Yurtsever, "Cauchy Problem in Spacetimes with Closed Timelike Curves," *Physical Review*, Vol. D42, pp. 1915 ff (1990).

David Garfinkle and Andrew Strominger, "Semiclassical Wheeler Wormhole Production," *Physics Letters*, Vol. B256, #2, pp. 146 ff (7 March 1991).

William J. Kaufmann, III, *The Cosmic Frontiers of General Relativity*, p. 238 (Little, Brown and Co., Boston, 1977).

Michael S. Morris and Kip S. Thorne, "Wormholes in Spacetime and Their Use for Interstellar Travel," *American Journal of Physics*, Vol. 56, #5, pp. 395–412 (May 1988).

Michael S. Morris, Kip S. Thorne, and Ulvi Yurtsever, "Wormholes, Time Machines, and the Weak Energy Condition," *Physical Review Letters*, Vol. 61, #13, pp. 1446–1449 (26 September 1988).

I. D. Novikov, "An Analysis of the Operation of a Time Machine" (English translation), *Soviet Physics JETP*, Vol. 68, #3, pp. 439–443 (March 1989).

Frank J. Tipler, "Rotating Cylinders and the Possibility of Global Causality Violation," *Physical Review D*, Vol. 9, #8, pp. 2203–2206 (1974).

Matt Visser, "Traversable Wormholes: Some Simple Examples," *Physical Review*, Vol. D39, #10, pp. 3182–3184 (15 May 1989).

✧ TWIN PARADOX

In the previous Chapter, "Space Warps and Time Machines," I pointed out that the human race already has access to time machines large enough for people to travel in. These time travel machines are our rocketships that take us not only long distances through space, but short distances through time. Even though rockets are very limited time machines, they still present us with logical paradoxes that are difficult for the average person to accept, such as the "twin paradox." If one twin takes a round trip journey in a high-speed rocket, while the other twin stays at home, upon return, the traveling twin will have aged less than the stay-at-home twin.

Being, by nature, one who questions authority, even such an authority as Einstein, I once mused on how I might arrange things so that the stay-at-home twin would stay younger than the traveling twin. I couldn't find a way to do it using physics, so I resorted to biology. The following story is the result.

What you will read here is the original version written in May 1982. A substantially cut version was published in the August 1983 issue of Analog Science Fiction/Science Fact magazine, Volume 103, pages 78-86. I liked these twin characters enough to use them again (with slightly different first names) in my novel Martian Rainbow, and the robotic doctor appears again

*in the final scene of the long Baen paperback version
of my novel* Rocheworld.

———

"Marcia! Stop that crying! You know I don't like to
hear women carrying on like that." Alan Armstrong bent
his well-muscled arm, and with a firm forefinger lifted
the tear-streaked face of the beautiful brunette out of
the curly golden fleece on his bare chest.

"But you're going away for so long," she sobbed, "that
by the time you come back I'll be old and wrinkled.
I want to go with you."

"Now don't be silly, beautiful," Alan said. "*Bright Star*
may be the largest spacecraft made by man, but nearly
all of it is fuel and the cockpit can only hold one man.
As much fun as it would be to take you along, I'm afraid
you'll have to stay here."

He raised his finger further, and leaned back to look
at her tilted face. "I have to go to a press conference
in a few hours, so I'll give you a last kiss now," he said.
"While I'm gone, you'd better pack and leave. I've sold
the condo and furniture and have the money invested.
I was able to get eleven percent interest. When I get
back in seventy-six years, my half-million will be worth
more than one billion dollars." He tilted her head even
further back, dazzled her with a boyish smile and gave
her a lingering kiss she would remember forever. With
a soul-rending sigh, he climbed from the bed and
headed for the closet, leaving Marcia sobbing in the
pillow. By the time Alan had finished dressing, Marcia
had calmed down.

"You'd better take the Liberian Sword," she said. "I'll
need the Nissan Continental to carry all my stuff.
Fortunately Mom still keeps my old room as a guest
room."

Alan kept looking at himself in the mirror as he

replied. "I sold the Continental too. You'll have to take a taxi."

Ten years earlier, radio astronomers around the world were astounded as the frequency spectrum around the hydrogen line was suddenly saturated with hundreds of narrow-band signals. They came from the direction of Arcturus, a giant red star some thirty-six lightyears away. Someone then remembered that the first commercial television programs had started seventy-two years ago in the early 1940s. The Arcturians must have picked them up and replied.

The signal exactly on the hydrogen line contained a primer that started with numbers in a base-twelve system, and proceeded from simple arithmetic through boolean logic into a formalized language, liberally aided by pictures. As soon as the language lessons had progressed to the point where simple messages could be understood, the primer beam told the scientists what information was on the other beams and how to decode them. One channel contained copies of the television programs that the aliens had intercepted. Shortly, *Howdy Doody*, *Milton Berle*, and *I Love Lucy* were reruns again, with a time lag of seventy-two years. Other channels contained specialized knowledge on various different branches of mathematics, physics, engineering, chemistry, biology, and astronomy. They didn't go too far into the subjects, though, as if the Arcturians were trying to prevent culture shock. All the channels repeated after a few months.

The main message was a simple one. By pictures and the logical language that was taught on the primer channel, Earth was told that, if it could develop the technology to send a single human being to Arcturus, then the Earth could join the galactic civilization. The human ambassador would be brought back in one of their spaceships that would also carry the Arcturian representative to the Earth. The Arcturian had the title of "Bringer of Enlightenment," and seemed to be a combination of ambassador and teacher.

After some initial squabbling, including the covert destruction of some radio telescopes in a vain attempt to keep secret the knowledge in the beams, the political entities on the planet finally patched over their differences. They joined together to build *Bright Star*, the first interstellar spacecraft. The human race was in a hurry to cross those thirty-six lightyears to Arcturus, so the starship would accelerate at one Earth gravity until it reached its coast velocity of more than ninety-nine percent of the speed of light. *Bright Star* used a fuel made of ninety percent hydrogen and ten percent antihydrogen. To make the antimatter, massive solar-powered antimatter factories were built on the surface of Mercury where there was plenty of sunlight and vacuum for the banks of high-current particle beam machines. Slowly the cryogenically cooled superconducting magnetic bottles filled with the antihydrogen fuel. After a well-publicized worldwide search, the best example of a human being was chosen, and the U.S. astronaut Alan Armstrong became the world's first ambassador to an alien species. After ten years of work, the antimatter tanks on *Bright Star* were finally full, and it was time for Alan to go.

Alan strode onto the brightly lit platform in the NASA press room and sat calmly in one of the two swivel chairs there. Most of the world's ten trillion people were watching him over the global television hookup. Alan was introduced by the Director of the *Bright Star* Project and the questions from the invisible cloud of newstapers on the other side of the stage lights started. Some questions were thoughtful ("Will you converse with the aliens in the logical language used in the radio messages, or will you expect them to have learned English from our television broad-casts?"). Some questions were trite ("Will you miss your girlfriends?"), and some were stupid ("Aren't you afraid the Arcturians will make slaves of us?"). But Alan adroitly fielded them all using a combination of his ready wit and dazzling smile.

The questions finally died down and it was time for the part of the press interview that Alan was dread-ing. He knew it was necessary, for it would never do for the press to think that he would go off on a sev-enty-six year long journey without at least saying goodby to his brother. Besides, there was that ideal human interest gimmick built into the interview; a real-life example of the Einstein Twin Paradox. For his brother, Able Armstrong, was his twin—an identical twin—or at least, he used to be.

A door to one side of the room opened and Able limped in. Alan flinched inwardly as he stared at the mutilated caricature of the handsomely symmetric image that greeted him in the mirror each morning. Able hobbled his way onto the platform and stuck out his right hand at Alan, while supporting himself with a cane held in his good left hand. Alan rose and bravely shook his brother's mutilated paw, its only appendages being a stump of a thumb and a reconstructed little finger. Alan assisted Able into the video-swivel chair next to his and sat down again.

Able spoke first.

"I hear you've got the hottest rocket this planet can make. Be sure you check the seams on the casing before you light the fuse," he joked, the grin under-neath the eye patch twisting his face into a distorted grimace.

Alan felt light-headed, and the room of bright lights faded. The face of his twin wavered and grew bloody as Alan's mind recreated that terrible day back when they were kids. They had made a crude rocket from a piece of pipe and some gunpowder stolen from their father's gun closet. They had lit the fuse, but nothing had happened. Alan, being the oldest by a few minutes, told Able to go take a look. As Able picked up the homemade rocket, it blew up, taking his right hand, right eye, and most of his left kneecap.

Alan had gone on to fulfill the promise of their joint genetic inheritance. He had become an astronaut and now was designated as the first human ambassador to another civilization, while Able had to be content with an engineering degree, building the rockets that he would never fly. Alan's vision faded, and after a pause that had the newstapers curious, he replied.

"With you building 'em, Able, I don't have to worry."

"What do you two think about the Einstein Theory?" piped up the shrill voice of a newstaper. "Do you really think that Alan will age slower than Able?"

Alan started to answer, but Able waved his claw and replied.

"Certainly he will," Able said. "Alan will be traveling most of the thirty-six lightyear distance to Arcturus at over ninety-nine percent of the speed of light. At that speed he will be aging only one year for each eight years on Earth. Counting the nearly three years he will need to accelerate up to speed and slow down again at the end of the journey, it will take him nearly thirty-eight years to get there. The aliens don't have faster-than-light space drives, so it will take them about the same time to come back. Alan will have been gone some seventy-six years, but will have aged only fourteen years.

"But that doesn't make sense," blurted an annoyed newstaper.

"How can one person age slower than another?"

"I assure you it's true," said Able. "I use this time-stretching feature of high-speed travel every day when I'm analyzing the life-times of the short-lived particles generated by the matter-antimatter reaction in the *Bright Star* engines. Believe me, the time stretching effect really happens. Einstein was right."

"Don't you wish it were the other way?" said another anonymous questioner hidden in the glare of the lights. "As it is, you'll probably be dead before your brother gets back."

Able frowned a little at the question, the eye-patch adding a menacing touch. He started to reply, but Alan interrupted him.

"There are almost ten trillion people around the world watching right now," said Alan in a superior tone. "When I return, even the youngest baby now living will be a doddering old wreck, ready for the grave. Despite what the calendar will say, I will have the body of a healthy forty-four year old man. Unless I get myself killed in an accident, I will be the last man now living in the world to die of old age."

Next for Alan were weeks of parades through the major cities of the world. Every street was drab, but the crowds were ecstatically happy, for the crushing world-wide fifty percent surtax that had been imposed to build *Bright Star* had been lifted. When Alan left the solar system, he would not only take the wishes of the world with him, but also half of the Gross World Product for the past ten years. The people of Earth could then return to their normal lives, hoping that the investment that they made at such great sacrifice would be returned with interest to their great-grandchildren some seventy-six years later.

Far out on the outskirts of the solar system, Alan pressed the igniter button and pushed the throttle forward. Deep within the bowels of the gigantic ship, laser beams and electric fields gingerly teased tiny pellets of antihydrogen ice from their magnetic containers and shepherded them through superconducting channels to the engine. The antimatter pellets sparkled slightly as they interacted with the random air molecules in the highly evacuated tubes.

The engine of *Bright Star* was invisible. It was made of magnetic fields in the form of a spherical thrust chamber connected to a bell-like rocket nozzle. The antimatter ice pellets were injected at high speed into the thrust chamber where they met a stream of liquid hydrogen and annihilated, turning the excess hydrogen to a blazing plasma that streaked out through the magnetic nozzle, pushing *Bright Star* forward.

The shielding for the superconducting rings grew red as Alan increased the thrust level, and the large radiators that gave *Bright Star* a dart-like shape took up the glow as they radiated the waste heat from the engine away into empty space. It was three hours after Alan had pushed the ignition button that the light from the blazing exhaust finally reached the weeping, cheering crowds on Earth as a bright star blossomed in the sky.

Communication with Earth rapidly went from bad to worse. Even before Alan had started, the six hour round-trip communication time from Earth to the parking orbit of *Bright Star* had made real conversation impossible. After eight months under acceleration, *Bright Star* was a quarter of a lightyear away from Earth and had reached sixty percent of the speed of light. It now took three months for a message from Alan to reach Earth and longer than that for the reply to catch up to the accelerating vehicle that was racing away at nearly the same speed as the laser beam message. Alan was now living, thinking, and speaking slower than the controllers on Earth. Even with the computer applying corrections, communications became essentially impossible. As the last messages came through, Alan noticed that the controllers for his mission had been replaced with a bunch of youngsters. They were probably trainees, since there was little for them to "control" on this mission. They seemed to know their stuff, though. He also got a sign-off message from his brother, but it was sound-only; Able had been assigned somewhere off in the boondocks where the communications link weren't up to video.

After not quite three years Earth time and less than eighteen months Alan time, *Bright Star* had reached its planned ninety-nine point two percent of light speed, and the engines were turned off while the spacecraft coasted on its way to its destination. For four years Alan tended the ship, watched the programs in his video library, and played games with "James," the semi-intelligent computer that ran *Bright Star*. Bored, Alan started growing a moustache and soon was the proud possessor of a ten-centimeter-long yellow handlebar. Three years out from Arcturus, Alan and James carried out a survey of the Arcturian planetary system. It was quite similar to the solar system. Arcturus III was obviously the home of the aliens, since it had large oceans, a deep atmosphere, and was a strong source of radio emissions of all kinds, including the beams still being sent toward Earth. Alan and James checked a few of the frequencies. The messages hadn't changed, and were repeated every few months. There was no new knowledge being sent. That would come only when Alan demonstrated the Earth's right to the knowledge by arriving under his own power.

What was unusual about the planetary system was the large number of moons about Arcturus III. The telescope on *Bright Star* was not capable of resolving them at two lightyears distance, but it could measure their size. They ranged from one hundred to one thousand kilometers in diameter, and there were over two dozen of them.

The survey done, it was time to stop. Alan turned

Bright Star around so that its invisible magnetic nozzle was pointing at Arcturus. He sagged in his chair as he started the three years of one-gravity deceleration. He was a tenth of a lightyear out from Arcturus and still decelerating when James spotted the first alien ship and alerted Alan. Alan was appalled when the spaceship turned out to be one of the "moons" that had been in orbit around Arcturus III. It was moving away from the planet and heading in their direction at high acceleration.

"The reception committee," said Alan to himself. "I'd better get out my credentials and my uniform."

For a day, the object grew in size, but instead of stopping, it continued to accelerate. It shot by him at thirty-five percent of light speed, then shrank in size again as the reddish arc of Arcturian sunlight on it grew wider to expose more and more of the spacecraft, revealing to Alan's awed eyes a complex of unfathomable structures embedded at seemingly random intervals over the eight hundred kilometer diameter artificial sphere. Alan sat in shock in front of the video screen as the unbelievable image of the star-liner accelerated off into the black void of space.

The scene was repeated again in the following month, then there was a period when he saw three spacecraft arrive and two others leave their orbits about Arcturus III. None of them were smaller than a hundred kilometers in size. Most were spheres, but there were other shapes with distinctly different markings that indicated that there was more than one alien race involved in trading at this interstellar hub of commerce.

Still under constant deceleration, the speed of *Bright Star* slowed to sub-relativistic velocities and Alan entered the outskirts of the Arcturian planetary system. There was still no sign of a reception committee, in fact, there was no sign that they had even seen him coming. He was certain that the highly luminous plasma of his antimatter exhaust would have been detected, for it would have been brighter than any star in the heavens. They were just ignoring him—as if he were too small to bother with.

He put away his dress uniform.

Feeling like a stone-age Indian paddling into New York harbor, Alan made his way across the planetary system to Arcturus III. The planet was large and had a surface gravity and pressure much higher than Earth. As he matched orbits with the planet and started to catch up with it, he noticed a small object streaking straight for him at high acceleration.

"A defensive missile!" he cried. Rotating his spacecraft, he rammed the throttle forward and tried to escape by jetting to one side of the missile trajectory. The ten kilometer long windowless cylinder matched his every move, drew alongside, then grabbed his tiny ship with a tractor field. Alan turned off his engines and waited.

The tug accelerated at exactly one Earth gravity, the acceleration he had used upon arrival, and then decelerated to bring *Bright Star* to a halt in the belly of a gigantic orbital space station. Around the equator of the station was painted a band of alternating red and black triangles. A robotic voice spoke over his ship radio, talking to him in a weird conglomeration of the television languages used in the ancient forties through eighties.

"Hey there, man. You can come out, but keep your spacesuit on, okay man? Like it's dangerous. The Bringer of Enlightenment, Third Class will show up soon to rap with you. He goes by the moniker of Teacher-of-the-Whiskered. You treat him with respect, see! If you do, then everything will be A-OK. But you try any funny stuff and you'll be ventilated. Understan', man?"

Alan replied using the logical language taught by the

language radio channel. Hearing this, the robotic voice switched languages.

"You will turn off all power and self-protection devices on your ship. You will put on your environmental maintenance suit. You will exit your ship. You will wait for Teacher-of-the-Whiskered."

Alan put on his spacesuit and cycled through the airlock. His suit pressure rose to counteract the two atmospheres of pressure in the alien space station. He took a look at the sensor readouts in his collar. The air was mostly nitrogen and the amount of oxygen was too little to allow him to breathe unaided. In addition, the large amounts of water vapor, methane, and hydrogen sulphide not only made the atmosphere humid and smelly, but downright dangerous.

As soon as he had taken a few steps away from the airlock, the huge bulk of *Bright Star* was lifted from the deck and hoisted on invisible tractor beams to the far side of the multi-kilometer diameter hold. Alan watched in panic and apprehension as giant machines tore *Bright Star* into pieces, like a vicious kid pulling a butterfly apart. The living quarters up front were detached with surgical precision from the main body. The radiator wings went next. They were crumpled and shoved into what looked like a gigantic pulverizer. Alan worried about the antimatter that remained in the storage tanks. There wasn't much left, but if the superconducting containers were breached, even a space station this large could end up with a big hole in it. A small, remora-like missile attached itself to the remains of *Bright Star* and hauled the trash off to some distant dump.

Alan soon lost sight of the tiny living quarters that had been his home for seven years as it was taken off into the distance. He turned to look around him. Most of the mobile things near him were obviously robots, built like thick-legged centipedes with pincers on the front for carrying things. There were a number of aliens, however. They looked like a six-legged tiger-centaur. They had a head, eight limbs, and a short tail. The front two limbs were raised off the ground, while the other six remained as legs for walking in the high gravity. The hands on the fore-limbs had evolved from six-toed paws into a star-shaped hand with six identical finger-thumbs. Each one of the digits could oppose any of the others on the almost symmetric hand. The fur was black around the crocodile-length muzzle, which shaded off into a silvery pelt, and turned white at the paws and the tips of the pointed ears and tail. The only items of clothing were saddlebag-like pouches hanging along their sides.

The aliens were curious enough to glance at him as they went slowly by, but they didn't stop and stare. They all looked basically the same, although there were slight differences in size, shape of the muzzle, subtle markings on the pelt, and the transitions from black to silver on the muzzle, and silver to white at the extremities. Alan couldn't tell if they had different sexes or even if they had sexes. He did notice, however, that most of the aliens had two dozen or so long white whiskers that curved out from the black muzzle, while a few of them had no whiskers, although it was obvious from the cavities in the black muzzle fur that the skin underneath had made provision for the missing whiskers.

"Those un-whiskered ones are probably the females," Alan guessed, but he couldn't see any other differences.

Alan then noticed an alien off in the distance that was actually hurrying. It looked like all the others, but around its neck it wore a large medallion in the shape of a six-pointed star. The points of the star were long and wavy like the blade of a Turkish dagger. The starburst pattern was repeated on its side-packs. The alien fixed its attention on him and came to a halt not a meter away. It had no whiskers.

"I am called Teacher-of-the-Whiskered," it said. "I am a Bringer of Enlightenment, Third Class. It is my duty to instruct you and the rest of the creatures on your planet in the way of enlightenment." The alien stopped and peered forward to stare through Alan's visor with its silvery eyes.

"What is that object under your breathing orifice?" it asked.

"A moustache," replied Alan. "It is very similar to the whiskers that some of your people have."

The nostrils of the alien dilated as if it were smelling something strong but not palatable.

"It seems I have a lot of teaching to do," said the alien. Its demeanor changed as it continued. "But I am proud that I have been chosen to bring Enlightenment to such bewhiskered and rumpless ones as you are. May the Great Light of the Supernova Incarnate fall on me as I carry out its mission of bringing Enlightenment to the Universe." It was obvious that the alien was pleased with itself by the way it licked its chops, but Alan was appalled when the meter-long rasped tongue flicked out from between rows of shark-like teeth to lick first the top and then the bottom of the black fur covering the long crocodile snout.

Another alien with whiskers ambled slowly over. Its side-packs had the same red and black pattern that was painted around the belt of the orbital space station. The pattern was on all the robots and most of the aliens Alan had seen, except for the alien that had greeted him. The whiskered alien pulled a rectangular panel from a side-pack and consulted it.

"Identification?" the station official asked the other alien.

"Teacher-of-the-Whiskered, Bringer of Enlightenment, Third Class," replied the whiskerless one eagerly.

The official nodded, then scratched with one of its fingers at the panel. Alan noticed that although the front paws of the aliens had evolved into a weak-looking hand, each of the six fingers still retained a needle-sharp retractable claw.

The official finally looked at Alan. It came over and peered into his helmet.

"You traveled here using only your own technology?" it asked.

"Yes!" he replied.

"Do you accept Teacher-of-the-Whiskered . . ." here the official glanced down at his illuminated panel. ". . . Bringer of Enlightenment, Third Class, as your sponsor-and-mentor and trustee-owner of your planetary system until you qualify for recognition?"

Alan hesitated, trying to think of a polite way to ask if he and the human race had any other choice than to be owned by a missionary, third class, but the official didn't even bother to wait for his reply. He curled around and clanked his panel against the one held by Teacher. The pattern of script was transferred and the official slowly waddled off.

"It is time for me to return you to your home world," said Teacher. "I'm sure you must miss it. Please follow my android."

Teacher motioned to a robot standing to the rear which was built along the lines of the aliens. Its side-packs had the same starburst pattern that Teacher wore. Teacher then climbed aboard one of the many low-slung open-sided wheeled vehicles around, and zoomed off into the distant stretches of the cavernous hangar.

"Follow me," said the android and started off in the direction Teacher had taken. As Alan walked, he noticed a circular region on the floor that followed along with him. At the edges of the circle there were little dust eddies. Alan soon figured out that the circle indicated where the gravity changed from the Arcturian value of about three gravities to Alan's one-gravity field.

Alan tried talking with the android as they walked. He found the robot was very intelligent and quite willing to answer questions. It seemed that its owner had nothing to do with either the Arcturian or Galactic governments and was merely a novice missionary sponsored by a religious sect. Most of the races in the galactic civilization had no use for religion and even less use for sub-standard cultures such as the human race. As a result, the galactic bureaucrats had worked out an arrangement that kept one unwanted group busy keeping the other unwanted group under control.

The sect that supported Teacher had as their symbol and God a supernova explosion that occurred 200,000 years ago, only a few lightyears away from the "Homeland." The people of "Homeland" were forced to develop interstellar flight in a hurry to escape the sub-relativistic plasma cloud from the supernova. Although the supernova killed most of their race, it did act as a Bringer of Enlightenment to the remainder, and those hard-driving, dedicated individuals continued to proselytize as they spread through the galaxy. Shape, reproduction method, or social structure didn't matter. In fact, Teacher, the tiger-centaur, was a fifth-culture convert, and had never even seen a member of the frog-like race that had founded the sect.

The sect was small, but vigorous. Members pledged a dozenth of their income, which was used to maintain large radio arrays to detect the first signs of an emerging technological civilization. The civil authorities didn't want the missionaries bothering those cultures that were too savage, so they put limits on the amount of information that could be sent during the contact phase. They also limited the personal visits of the missionaries to only those planets where the cultures demonstrated their technological capabilities by sending a representative to the nearest galactic base.

"Why the emphasis on whiskers?" asked Alan.

"Every individual joining the sect has to make a physical sacrifice," said the android. "The sacrifice is different for each race, and is meant to be ornamentally significant but physically minor. For the original race of frog-like beings, it meant having the tip of your tongue forked. For Teacher's race, it was the removal of the largely ornamental whiskers. I see the human race has whiskers too. Do they serve a useful purpose?"

"No," admitted Alan.

"Good," said the android. "That should make it easier for your race to be accepted by the Arcturian sect. It was of some concern that your dental structure indicates that you are omnivorous instead of being purely carnivorous. It would be difficult for the Arcturians to associate with someone that eats plants for food like an animal. But whiskers are an indication that you are more than an animal, you are a person, and their removal means that you can transcend being a person, to become a mini-god, just a step below God-Head itself—the Supernova."

The effusiveness of the android's speech made Alan realize that he was not talking to an intelligent being, but a computer program, written by a highly intelligent person, but that person also believed fervently in a certain religious message. He had been walking behind the android for nearly ten kilometers and although he was not tired, portions of his anatomy were beginning to chafe and itch inside his spacesuit.

"How much longer do we have to walk?" asked Alan as they passed through a corridor with airlocks at both ends, and entered another large room. "Is Teacher's ship visible from beyond this building?"

"This building *is* Teacher's ship," said the android. Teacher's ship was a small one, only ten kilometers in diameter. They walked another kilometer and entered the cavernous door leading to what looked like a cargo bay. In the far end of the cargo bay, Alan saw with relief the life-support section that had been torn from *Bright Star*. After bidding goodby to the android, Alan cycled through the airlock, shucked his suit, and took care of urgent business. He was relieved to find that all the life support equipment was receiving power and was operational. There was, however, a new piece of equipment in the middle of the control room in place of his chair. It looked like a tall oriental screen, and was folded around in a half-circle. The panels of the screen were not decorated, but instead glistened with millions of tiny colored lights in seemingly random patterns. As Alan approached the screen, he saw Teacher standing inside the encircling panels.

"Welcome, Student Alan," said Teacher. "I believe you know what a hologram is?"

"Yes, Teacher," said Alan. "But I have never seen one in full color with this amount of resolution."

"It is very useful when it is not possible for beings to share the same atmosphere without environmental maintenance suits." There was the sound of a buzzer. Teacher looked off to one side and nodded.

"What was that?" asked Alan.

"We are under acceleration," said Teacher.

"I don't feel anything," said Alan.

"The gravity generators in the cargo hold have adjusted to cancel the acceleration of the spacecraft and leave it at the gravity level you are accustomed to."

"How fast are we going?" asked Alan.

"We are accelerating at 112 times the gravity on your planet Earth," said Teacher. "We should be up to speed soon. But all this talk about the motion of the ship is more properly the concern of the ship and its robots. We have more important things to talk about, such as the revelation of the God-Star, the Bringing of Enlightenment, and the number of stars throughout the Universe that are now being blessed by the God-Star's light. You are to watch the scenes that the screen will show you. I will return later to ask questions to determine whether you have paid attention."

The holographic image of Teacher was replaced by a swirling cloud of stars. The dry voice of a narrator began . . . "In the days before the Enlightenment, the peoples of the galaxy were without hope, for the God-Star . . ." Alan watched attentively, but sighed. The six-legged Arcturians didn't use chairs, and it looked like he was fated to spend the next four years attending church school standing up.

At first, Alan tried hard to please Teacher and parroted the answers that had been presented in the holovideos. Later he tried asking some questions about some of the logical flaws he saw in the presentations, such as the fact that supernova explosions are fairly common, and what had made the explosion of the God-Star any different from the rest.

The question provoked a tirade. "Until you have been Enlightened, you are nothing but an animal, you ungrateful plant-chewer. If you persist with these blasphemous questions, I shall turn around and return to Arcturus. You will be thrown out into space, for you smell too bad to eat."

Alan soon realized that the people of Earth were going to have to embrace the religion of this third-class missionary if they were going to obtain access to the technological knowledge that Teacher controlled. Fortunately, sun worship was old hat to the human race, so supernova worship should be easy.

Alan played along with Teacher-of-the-Whiskered, and after a year of lessons and preaching, he finally agreed to be proselytized into the worship of the God-Star. Teacher was delighted when Alan announced his decision, and Alan was again treated to the awesome display of the huge rasped tongue reaching out from the cavernous mouth to lick the upper and lower muzzle in a display of pleasure. When the time came for the initiation ceremony, Alan almost backed out when he found that it wasn't sufficient to just cut off his moustache. The whiskers would still be there under the skin, and a stub of a whisker was just as impious as a long sweeping hair. Alan's handlebar moustache had to be pulled out—one hair at a time.

As the spaceship carrying Alan and the Arcturian missionary drew close to the solar system, Alan had ingratiated himself enough with Teacher that the alien allowed him to talk directly with Earth. By inference and innuendo, Alan got his message across, and when they came to a halt in Earth orbit, the people designated as Earth's official contacts with Teacher were Matthew Kamehameha, Mark Nkrumah, Luke Gollagong, and John Redwing, all from cultures who were well aware of both the positive and negative effects of the visit of a missionary from a technologically advanced civilization.

Alan was pleased with himself for getting the message across to the Earth authorities, but he was a little puzzled that such youngsters had been sent. None seemed to be over twenty-five. Of course, he was no spring chicken himself. Technically he was 106 years old, and financially well off, for his investments had done well in the last seventy-six years. Physically, he felt even younger than the forty-four years Einstein had given to him.

Teacher remained in orbit in his comfortable three-times-Earth-gravity, two-times-Earth-pressure environment, while a mobile version of the holoscreen was sent in the alien's place. Teacher was soon busy and happy conducting worship services every twelfth day, and supervising the dewhiskering of an apprehensive but brave crowd of scientists and engineers, who once permanently shorn, were allowed access to the knowledge in the ship's computers. Women were not discriminated against, for there are just as many hair follicles on the upper lip of a maiden as on the most burly, bewhiskered he-man; it just took a smaller pair of tweezers to pull them all out.

When things had finally stabilized so that Alan was no longer needed on Teacher's ship as an intermediary, he was allowed to return to Earth. The pilots on the shuttle that brought him down were young and taciturn, and although there was a sizable crowd there for his landing, Alan was quickly whisked off to a nearby building. There he was met by a young man and a human looking robot. The robot was made of shiny black plastic with a caduceus on its chest.

"I'm Dr. Prasdner," said the young man. "We'd like to give you a quick checkup, then you can have your holovideo conference with the press." Alan looked around for equipment, but could see none. Instead, the plasticoid approached him and said politely, "If you will just unseal your shirt, the exam will be over in a few seconds."

Alan opened his shirt front, and noticed as he did so, that a number of tiny lights built into the front of the robot scanned his face and chest.

"May I touch your neck?" asked the plasticoid, reaching toward him. Alan noticed that the fingertips contained dozens of tiny sensors.

"Sure," said Alan. One hand of the robot touched the side of his neck, the thumb on the carotid artery, while the other hand touched his head on the other side.

"Nice bedside manner," thought Alan to himself as he noticed that the fingers were warm. He felt tiny sonic pulses passing through him as the robot moved its hands over his body.

"He is in excellent physical shape," said the plasticoid. "He can take it."

"Take what?" asked Alan, puzzled.

"Sit down," said Dr. Prasdner, motioning to a chair. "Why?"

"Sit down," said the doctor. Alan sat down apprehensively. The plasticoid moved behind him and placed one hand on Alan's shoulder, where its sensitive fingertips could monitor Alan's vital signs.

The door of the room opened and a young couple walked in. The man looked just like Alan, except he was only twenty-five years old. The look-alike had a twenty-five-year-old version of Marcia on his arm.

"Hello, Alan," said himself.

"What's going on!!" said Alan, his heart pounding. He turned to the doctor. "Have you cloned me?"

"No," said the copy. "I'm Able."

Alan looked back at him, then looked at the girl. ". . . and she?"

"Is Marcia," said Able.

"But . . ."

"Within one year after you left, the scientists studying the Arcturian biology channel stumbled onto the secret of the mechanism that the aliens use to prevent themselves from dying. Think about it. Only a civilization in which everyone lived forever could operate an interstellar commerce system based on spacecraft limited to speeds less than the speed of light."

"But your hand and leg and eye! And that can't be Marcia, she was over thirty when I left."

Able looked over at Dr. Prasdner. Prasdner sighed and said, "Old age is caused by a set of genes that 'turn off' the body repair mechanisms. This 'death-wish' gene is hard on the individual, but better for the species, since it allows room for new variations to arise. The longevity secret is basically a means to prevent the body-repair mechanisms from being turned off. Once the 'death-wish' genes are shut down, not only do you stop aging, but you body begins to repair any damage that might have been done. In Able's case, even his missing eye and hand were regenerated. You can't even find a scar now."

"Wow!" said Alan. "You mean that I can get back twenty years and my moustache at the same time! Great! Give me the shot, Doc. Then watch out, Marcia. I've been away from girls for a long time. You'll sure look good decorating my billionaire's pad."

There was a strained silence in the room. Alan looked around at the faces.

It was the robot medic that finally spoke.

"To achieve longevity involves taking a culture of synthetic viruses that enter each cell and modify the genes to turn off the 'death-wish' gene," said the robot. "But the treatment has to be administered before you are thirty-five years old, otherwise it is not effective."

"That's why we didn't tell you on the way out," said Able. "It was already too late."

Alan slumped in his chair. The doctor looked concerned and glanced up at the robot, its hand still monitoring Alan's vital signs. The plasticoid remained silent. After a few moments, Alan sat up and gave a harsh laugh.

"Well," he said. "The joke's on me. I went away expecting to come back younger than my twin, but Einstein was outfoxed by the medics. Still . . ." He forced a grin. "I've got a billion dollars and a lot of years to spend them in. How about it Marcia? Shall we take up where we left off? That is if you don't mind shacking up with an old man of forty-four."

Marcia held Able's arm even tighter, swallowed and finally lifted her eyes to meet Alan's.

"I've been married to Able for seventy-five years," she said. "And we've just renewed the marriage contract for a thousand more."

"Alan needs rest," the plasticoid said.

❖   ❖   ❖

The doctors did their best, and Alan stayed alive and healthy for another eighty-four years. He died as he had hoped, of a cerebral aneurysm in the arms of a nubile-looking centenarian that was jaded with making love to youngsters. Alan's age was 190 calendar and 128 Einstein-adjusted when he died.

The Earth stopped its business for one day to watch the funeral of its first interstellar ambassador. There was more than one now, as the Earth slowly made its way into the lower echelons of galactic society. It was tough being the lowest culture on the totem pole, but that didn't stop the Earth from investing ten percent of its gross world product on research to find a faster-than-light drive. The drive was theoretically impossible, but the human race had never forgotten how to dream, even if it still had to dewhisker its youth.

Able and Marcia still visit Alan's tomb at the spaceport in Brasilia every hundred years. There, on the long spire reaching up to the sky, are the words that Alan himself had chosen for his tombstone. The words were typical Alan.

"Here lies Alan Armstrong. He was the first man in the world to visit another star, and the last man in the world to die of old age."

✧ FUTURE SPECULATIONS

Scientists are only human. Although they have been trained to always try and think objectively about the world around them, there are limits. There are some topics that many scientists will refuse to even discuss. The taboo topics vary somewhat with the scientist. For instance, there are still some scientists who refuse to accept the strong theoretical and observational evidence for black holes. Other scientists, for good reason, have a difficult time believing that Nature will ever allow us antigravity, space warps, time machines, or faster-than-light communication. They admit that certain mathematical solutions to the Einstein equations allow these anomalies under certain drastic assumptions, but they firmly believe that some version of "cosmic censorship" will ultimately prevail and Nature will prevent us from ever exercising those solutions.

There are other scientists who have a hard time believing in the feasibility of the extreme versions of spaceflight such as interstellar travel, or Skyhooks, Space Fountains, and Rotavators. Usually, however, they are at least willing to admit their doubts are based on economic or engineering feasibility, not physical feasibility. I, personally, have been told in loud and no uncertain terms by a Nobel Laureate, that *any* attempt to even *discuss* the possible practical use of antimatter was "crazy."

I too have my doubts about the reality or attainability of many concepts, but I try to maintain an open mind.

In my opinion, if science is to be any good to us at all in describing the behavior of the universe, then *everything* must ultimately be describable in scientific terms. To give an extreme example, either God exists or He does not. In my view of science and the way scientists should operate, if God does not exist, then it is the job of science to attempt to prove that he does not exist. If God does exist, then He must come under the purview of science and it is the job of the scientist first to prove He exists, and then to build up a body of experimental, observational, and theoretical knowledge that will ultimately enable the human race (or whatever the human race has evolved to by then) to understand Him.

God is an extreme example of a taboo topic that most scientists will refuse to discuss in an objective, scientific manner. There are many others, such as UFOs, ESP, and astrology. The reason why most scientists refuse to get involved in a serious discussion of these taboo topics is that the very phrases that describe those topics are ill-defined and laden with decades, if not centuries, of emotion-riddled, crackpot-oriented, yellow-journalistic baggage. They do not want their names or reputations associated in any way with the phrase.

They also have a legitimate scientific reason for avoiding discussion. The taboo topics have been dreamed up by naive human minds, and just because someone can think of a concept and give it a name does not make it real. These skeptical scientists do not see any "handles" by which they could grapple with these ill-formed concepts in order to understand them from a logical scientific point of view. Without that understanding, it is impossible to prove or disprove the reality of the concept.

I believe I have found some ideas that may give us a handhold on some of these slippery concepts *if they are true*. It is important that you realize that, in my opinion, all of the following topics are wishful thinking and are *not* scientifically valid concepts. But, if they are real, perhaps these speculations will help us to bring these concepts under the umbrella of scientifically acceptable topics that are open for discussion. Then, if the scientific method can be applied successfully, perhaps these presently taboo topics can graduate from wishful thinking into future reality. The taboo topics I will attempt to shed light on are: Free energy, reactionless drives, extra-sensory perception (ESP), and life after death.

Free Energy

One of the goals of every backyard inventor is to invent a source of free energy, a battery or perpetual motion machine that produces energy and does useful work, but never runs down. It is probably too much to hope that some future technology will allow us to get "something for nothing," but it may be possible to use the theory of quantum electrodynamics to do something almost equivalent to that—extracting energy from the vacuum.

The Theory of Quantum Electrodynamics is the theory for describing the microscopic behavior of electricity and magnetism. It is one of the more successful physical theories, since it has been checked experimentally many times and found to be accurate. In quantum electrodynamics a region of space is divided up into a large (infinite) number of modes of potential oscillation for the electromagnetic field. The state of the electromagnetic field is defined by counting the number of photons in each mode. The "vacuum" state is defined as that state where there are no photons in any of the modes. Yet, according to quantum electrodynamics, each mode of oscillation, even when the space is at absolute zero, has in it a zero-point oscillation with an energy equal to "half" a photon.

This residual electromagnetic field produces fluctuating electromagnetic forces that have observable consequences.

One place where the effects of the electromagnetic fluctuations show up is in the calculation of the energy states in a hydrogen atom. The electric fields of the quantum fluctuations cause perturbations to the orbit of the electron around the proton. Even though the perturbations average out over the orbit, the electron moves in a slightly shifted orbit compared to that calculated from the electric field of the proton alone. This produces most of the shift in the energy levels of the hydrogen atom that was experimentally observed in 1947 by Willis Lamb and Robert Retherford.

Since, according to quantum electrodynamics, each mode has on the average a zero-point energy of half a photon, and since there are an infinite number of modes, this means that empty space has an infinite amount of energy. Richard Feynman, examining this paradox, tried to put a bound on this infinity by assuming some physically reasonable cutoff for the shortest wavelength mode, such as the Compton wavelength of a proton (2×10^{-16} meter). Even this cutoff gives an energy density of 10^{15} times that of water for the vacuum. This density is comparable to the density of the proton itself! The paradox remains. Feynman and others found a way around the infinities by a mathematical technique called renormalization, but no one has a good explanation why the extremely high predicted energy densities don't have a large gravitational effect. In summary, theory says there is a nearly infinite source of energy in the electromagnetic fluctuations of the vacuum, and it is possible to interact with the electromagnetic fluctuations and obtain energy. One technique involves the use of small black holes.

In the Theory of Quantum Electrodynamics, not only is the vacuum full of electromagnetic energy, it is also full of "virtual" particles that are created out of nothing, exist for a while, then merge back into nothing. [See the top half of Figure 11 in the Chapter "Black Holes."] Stephen Hawking showed that if a small black hole were placed in this emptiness full of energy, its powerful gravitational field would swallow the virtual particles if they got too close. With no partner to recombine with, the other member of the virtual particle pair would be promoted to the status of a "real" particle and leave. To an onlooker, it would look as if the black hole had "emitted" the particle. Thus, it would seem that the black hole has extracted energy from the vacuum.

In the details of Hawking's theory, however, it is shown that a virtual particle that is swallowed by the black hole has "negative" energy, so the total energy-mass content of the black hole is *decreased* by the addition of the virtual particle. So, although it looks like the black hole allows us to get something out of the nothing called the "vacuum," in reality the energy came out of the mass of the black hole rather than the vacuum.

Since there is yet no theory that proves it is impossible to extract energy out of the vacuum, and the example of the "hot" black hole seems to show that it might be possible, there has been a lot of speculation on space drives that somehow use the energy of the vacuum for propulsion. So far, the best description of a possible vacuum fluctuation "drive" is in Charles Sheffield's science fiction novel *The McAndrew Chronicles*.

I have found a way to extract a small amount of energy from the electromagnetic fluctuations of the vacuum. It is a vacuum fluctuation "battery" and it is based on the Casimir effect. In addition to the well-known Lamb-Retherford shift in the hydrogen atom, there is another, lesser known, effect of the electromagnetic vacuum fluctuations called the Casimir force.

The Casimir force is a short range attraction between any two objects caused by the presence of the electromagnetic fluctuations in the vacuum. A calculation by Casimir of the force between two conducting plates showed that the conducting plates restrict the number of normal modes that can exist in the vacuum between them. Although there are an infinite number of modes between the two plates, that infinity is smaller than the infinite number of modes that would be allowed if the plates weren't there. In a straightforward calculation of the number of normal modes and the zero-point energy in those modes, Casimir predicted that the electromagnetic vacuum fluctuations between the plates would have a negative energy density that was proportional to the third power of the spacing between the plates. There thus would be an attractive force between the plates that was proportional to the fourth power of the spacing. The force was independent of the material in the conductors.

Later, the analysis was broadened by Lifshitz to include dielectrics. It was found that any two plates, whether conductor or dielectrics, would experience a fourth power force law, but one that was also proportional to the dielectric constant of the plates. The Casimir result for conducting plates is obtained when the dielectric constant of the plates is allowed to go to infinity. The equations describing the Casimir effect are only valid down to a separation distance proportional to the minimum wavelength at which the plates are still a good conductor or the dielectric constant is not unity. For distances closer than that, a different equation takes over. The attractive force will still increase with decreasing distance, but at a rate proportional to the third power of the separation distance. Both Casimir and Lifshitz were aware that these forces due to the fluctuations of the vacuum were known previously as "surface tension," "surface energy," and "van der Waals" forces that occur between uncharged atoms and objects.

Since the Casimir force produces very high force levels at close spacings, and according to Lifshitz, those force levels vary according to the dielectric or conducting state of the plates, it is conceivable that one day the Casimir force could be a significant factor in the operation of microcircuits with sub-micrometer dimensions.

The experimental measurement of the Casimir force has been carried out a number of times with varying degrees of success. Usually the experiment is carried out between a curved dielectric lens and a flat dielectric plate. The first successful measurements were carried out in the 1950s by some Russian scientists on quartz, with separation distances down to 1000 angstroms (about 300 atoms). Later, other dielectric plate experiments were carried out with slowly improving precision. The closest separation distance obtained was fourteen angstroms (about five atoms) with two crossed cylinders of mica. At fourteen angstroms, the measured force between the two mica cylinders was over ten tons per square meter!

The Casimir force has some of the properties of the gravity force since it is purely attractive, is independent of the material in the plates, and is a function of the inverse power of the separation distance, although the variation with separation distance goes as a higher power than the gravity force. Although there is no rigorous proof known that the vacuum fluctuation field is a conservative field like the gravity field, it is highly probable that it is. Even if the vacuum fluctuation field is a conservative field, that does not mean we cannot use it to obtain energy. The gravity field of the Earth is a conservative force field and yet hydroelectric dams extract energy from the gravity field by using water coming from a region of high gravitational potential. In reality, of course, the energy extracted from a hydroelectric dam came originally from the Sun, which evaporated the water from the oceans at a low gravitational potential and placed it in lakes at a high gravitational potential. The hydroelectric dam is then seen as a mechanism that uses the gravitational force of the Earth as a "catalyst" to convert the gravitational potential energy of the water into kinetic energy that can in turn be converted into electricity by the turbines. Hydroelectric dams are also used for energy storage. During times of low electrical demand, electricity can be used to pump water back up to a lake at high gravitational potential.

In the same manner, I have shown that we can prepare a conductor in a foliated state which is in a "high" vacuum fluctuation potential energy state due to its large surface energy, and then use the Casimir force as a means to convert the potential energy into kinetic energy as the foliated conductors cohere into a solid block of conductor that is in a "low" vacuum fluctuation potential energy state. The part of the hydroelectric turbines can be played by any mechanism that can convert kinetic energy into electricity, but I use the electrostatic repulsion force between two conducting plates with the same polarity of charge.

The general concept for the construction of an aluminum foil "vacuum fluctuation battery" is to take a large number of leaves of ultrathin aluminum foil that are arranged in a stack with the leaves separated by a few micrometers. Each leaf is connected electrically to an active bidirectional power supply and the shape and position of the leaf is monitored by sensors. The power supply gives each leaf a small amount of positive charge. The positive charge will create an electrostatic repulsion between the plates that will keep the plates separated despite the attempt of the Casimir force to pull them together. This electrostatic suspension system is unstable, of course, so the position of each leaf will have to be electronically stabilized by feedback from the position sensors through the active power supply. Stability may also be enhanced by partial mechanical support of the leaves using frames of insulating material such as aluminum oxide or by unique geometries.

The voltages applied to the end leaf and the next-to-the-end leaf are then adjusted so that the electrostatic repulsion between these two leaves is lowered until the electrostatic force is slightly less than the Casimir force at that distance. The Casimir force will draw the two leaves together, doing work against the repulsive electric field between the plates. By adjusting the electric field to always be slightly less than the Casimir force, the active bidirectional power supply can extract electrical energy out of the kinetic energy of the motion of the plates as they move from large separation distances where the vacuum fluctuation potential energy is near zero, to the minimum separation distance where the vacuum fluctuation potential energy is large and negative. The process is repeated by the next leaf from the end until the foliated conductor is condensed into a solid block. Alternatively, all the leaves could be brought together at the same time, like compressing an accordion. Thus, by cohering the multitude of aluminum leaves in a foliated conductor into a single block of aluminum under the careful control of an electronic servo system, it is possible to extract electrical energy from the vacuum.

If the collapse process is halted before the aluminum films cohere, then the vacuum fluctuation battery can be "recharged" by making the applied electrostatic force slightly larger than the Casimir force. The leaves will be pushed apart at the cost of supplying energy from the bidirectional power supply.

Another version of the vacuum fluctuation battery that might be easier to fabricate and have more stability would be a wide flat spiral of foil built along the lines of a Slinky toy. Here there is only one conductor to make contact with and each turn of the spiral acts against the neighboring turns. The spiral configuration allows a substantial compaction of the foil from large spacings to small spacings while maintaining uniform spacing.

Unfortunately for those looking for large amounts of free energy, the numbers indicate that this vacuum fluctuation battery would require significant advances in precision manufacture and control of extremely thin structures before it would even begin to approach the watts per pound capability of even an ordinary chemical battery.

The important aspect of the vacuum fluctuation battery is that it shows that there is at least one way of getting energy out of the quantum fluctuations in the vacuum. And if there is one way, there may be other ways that are more efficient. We are probably not getting something for nothing, however, and the vacuum does not seem to be a source of continuous "free" energy. The vacuum fluctuation field is probably a conservative field, but there is no known proof of that in the literature. Since the vacuum fluctuation field seems to be the source of what "holds matter together," it is probably limited in energy density to chemical energy levels. Still, it is important that I have identified a non-thermodynamic method of extracting that chemical energy, as well as a method for getting chemical energy out of what are normally considered non-reactive chemicals (aluminum foil).

Reactionless Drives

Another dream of the backyard inventor is to invent a reactionless space drive—some collection of gizmos in a box, that when energized, will make the box rise into the air and speed off to the stars. Usually the gizmos are gyroscopes, for nearly everyone at one time or another has held a gyroscope in their hand and watched it perform its magic feat of levitation. With one end sitting on your finger, the rest of the gyroscope balances out horizontally, its center of gravity far away from its single support point—yet it does not fall!

In their early years, before book learning finally convinced them it was impossible, practically every space enthusiast, Robert Goddard and Wehrner Von Braun among them, has felt that there *must* be some way to remove that last support, yet still have the gyro continue to levitate, or perhaps drift slowly upwards to the stars. Yet, as each struggled with the concept of a reactionless drive based on gyroscopes, all were forced sooner or later to realize that it would not work. They were beaten by nature's conservation laws.

The law of conservation of energy is not the problem, for a rapidly spinning gyroscope certainly has enough energy to lift itself a considerable distance in the Earth's gravity field. No, it is one of the other conservation laws: the law of conservation of linear momentum.

If you start with a gyroscope sitting on the surface of the Earth, and you end up with a gyroscope moving upwards in the sky with a finite velocity, then by the law of conservation of linear momentum, some other mass must be moving in the opposite direction. The upward moving gyroscope must have had something to push against, like your finger.

The wheel of a gyroscope is spinning furiously. Certainly there must be a way to use that circular motion of the wheel to produce an upward motion of the whole gyroscope. Yet, as many a frustrated inventor has found, when model after model refuses to budge from the floor, there is yet another conservation law standing in the way of progress—the law of conservation of angular momentum—spin. But suppose that the conservation laws of linear and angular momentum were not true laws, just approximations.

Many years ago B.E. (Before Einstein), the world was dominated by four conservation laws: Conservation of mass, conservation of energy, conservation of linear momentum, and conservation of spin. The physics textbooks of that time insisted that each was always separately conserved despite some unresolved anomalies. For instance, there was that perpetually glowing pitchblende in Madam Curie's laboratory that seemed to indicate that energy was coming from nowhere. Also, calculations of the only known heat source for the Sun, gravitational contraction, seemed to give a lifetime for the Sun that was less than the age of the Earth, indicating that there might be some other energy source keeping the Sun hot.

Suppose you had shown a scientist of that time three one-kilogram bricks on a table, one of frozen hydrogen, one of red-hot iron, and one of room-temperature uranium. If you then asked the scientist which brick had the most energy, the scientist would have first noticed that since all the bricks were at the same height in the Earth's gravitational field, and they all weighed a kilogram, that their gravitational potential energies were the same. If the scientist then measured the temperature of the bricks, he would have said that the hot brick of iron would have more heat energy than the others, and he could even calculate how far that heat energy could lift the iron brick against the Earth's gravity given an efficient way to convert the heat energy into kinetic energy. Obviously the red-hot kilogram of iron had more energy than the room temperature kilogram of uranium, and the frozen kilogram of hydrogen ice had the least energy of all.

Then Einstein developed the Special Theory of Relativity to explain what happens to objects traveling near the speed of light. One of the magical but logical consequences of this theory was that the conservation laws for mass and energy were not strictly true! The theory predicted that mass could be changed into energy and vice versa.

The concept must have been mind-boggling at first. Mass is measured in kilograms and energy is measured in joules. They don't even have the same units. How can you convert one into the other? It would be like turning a sow's ear into a silk purse! The magical conversion of mass into energy does take place, however, and the conversion factor is a phenomenally large one, the speed of light—squared! From Einstein's Special Theory of Relativity there comes that famous equation: $E = mc^2$. This equation predicts that if some way could be found to carry out the conversion, a tiny amount of mass will produce an amazing amount of energy—ninety megajoules per microgram!

The scientists could now understand what was going on in Madame Curie's laboratory. The nuclei in the atoms of pitchblende were changing from one element to another, and giving off energy in the process. The new element weighed slightly less than the old element and the difference in mass showed up as gamma ray or particle energy. The scientists then knew that nature was able to violate the conservation laws for mass and energy, but search as they might, there didn't seem to be any device by which humans could control the conversion.

Albert Einstein told us in 1905 that mass could be converted into energy and he even gave us the conversion equation. But it took 37 years before Enrico Fermi found the method by which the energy stored in the excess mass of the uranium nucleus could be released. The process ultimately proved to be amazingly simple. You just put two or more large blocks of uranium or plutonium near each other and a chain reaction starts, automatically producing heat (or an explosion).

When Fermi and the other scientists finished their experiments and measurements on all the elements and their isotopes, they found that the very heavy elements, like uranium and plutonium, had an excess of mass per neutron or proton compared to carbon, while elements like iron had a deficiency of mass per nucleon. At the other end of the periodic table, the very light elements like hydrogen and lithium also had a mass excess. If the uranium and plutonium could be fissioned into iron-like elements, the difference in mass would be released as energy. In the same way, if the lighter elements could be sequentially fused together to build up iron-like elements, then again there would be an excess of mass that would be converted to energy.

If you were to ask a modern-day scientist which contains more energy: frozen hydrogen, red-hot iron, or room-temperature uranium, you will get a different answer. For the modern scientist can see energy sources in those bricks that could not be seen before. The frozen hydrogen, if fused to iron, will release more energy than the fissioning of uranium to iron, and the red-hot iron, which used to be thought the better in the energy sweepstakes, is now seen to be comparatively devoid of energy, despite its high temperature.

Thus, the advent of special relativity produced a new energy source and reduced the number of conservation laws. We now have only three: conservation of mass-energy, conservation of linear momentum, and conservation of angular momentum. The physics textbooks firmly insist that each is always separately conserved despite some unresolved anomalies. For instance, the high speed jets that are coming from rapidly spinning black-hole quasars seem to indicate that an object which should be sucking matter in, is instead propelling it out. Also, the number of neutrinos being emitted by the fusion reactions in the Sun is only one third of what it should be, indicating that there is still some other yet unknown source of energy keeping the Sun hot.

Einstein did not stop with his Special Theory of Relativity. He next went on to develop his theory of gravity, called the General Theory of Relativity. The Einstein Theory of Gravity is an extension of the Newton Theory of Gravity. In the Newton theory, gravity is a force field generated by a mass. The gravity field generated by a mass is the same whether or not the mass is hot, moving, or spinning. In the Einstein theory, however, gravity is not caused solely by mass, but it is also produced by energy, *and* linear momentum, *and* spin!

In the Einstein theory the mass of a gravitating body produces the usual Newtonian gravitational attraction that we are familiar with. The heat, stress, and other sources of energy in the gravitating body not only add to the Newtonian attraction, but also produce gravitational stress patterns in the nearby space. The linear motion of the gravitating body also produces a gravitational field, but it is different than the Newtonian gravity. The linear momentum gravity forces tend to "drag" a nearby test body in the same direction the gravitating body is moving. Similarly, according to the Einstein theory, the angular momentum in a spinning body causes nearby objects to move in curved paths.

If mass, energy, linear momentum, and angular momentum all produce gravity, doesn't that indicate that they are all just different aspects of some more fundamental entity? We scientists studying the Einstein Theory of Gravity have given this entity a name—the mass-energy-momentum tensor, but just naming something does not mean that we really understand it.

This multi-aspect appearance of the "thing" that causes gravity in the Einstein General Theory of

Relativity is reminiscent of the fable about the blind men and the elephant. One of the blind men felt the trunk and said that an "elephant" was like a snake, another felt the tail and said that an "elephant" was like a rope, another felt a leg and said that an "elephant" was like a tree trunk, while a fourth felt the ear and said that an "elephant" was like a leaf. They were all partially correct, but none could comprehend the "elephant" as a whole. Scientists today are in the same predicament. We see aspects of the "mass-energy-momentum tensor," but we still cannot comprehend it as a whole.

Could it be, that in some future day, just as we can now interconvert two of those gravity-producing components of the mass-energy-momentum tensor—mass and energy, that we could interconvert mass, energy, and the two types of momentum?

How could that be? They are different things. Yet, with Einstein giving us the equations and the conversion constants, and Fermi giving us the experimental techniques, we found that a room-temperature brick of uranium could give us more energy than a glowing brick of iron. Could there be other sources of energy hidden in ordinary things that we could extract by conversion of linear momentum and angular momentum to energy? What we need are the right conversion equations and the right experimental techniques.

Suppose we wanted to convert linear momentum to energy. What type of conversion constant do we need? Well—energy is in joules, or kilograms times velocity squared, while linear momentum is kilograms times velocity. To convert linear momentum to energy, we need a conversion constant with the units of velocity. The natural choice is the velocity of light, giving us the conversion equation between energy E and momentum p of $E = pc$.

Since the numerical value of the speed of light is

so high, this equation predicts some remarkable results. A one kilogram mass moving at one meter per second velocity has only one joule of kinetic energy in its motion. Yet, if the speed of light is the correct conversion constant, the linear momentum in that motion, *if* we could find the method to convert it completely into energy, would produce an additional 300 million joules! (Just stopping the mass will not do. That only transfers the linear momentum to your hand, and thence to the ground. The linear momentum must somehow be destroyed, not just transferred to the Earth.)

But let's go on. To convert angular momentum to linear momentum we need a unit of length. There is a fundamental unit of length, called the Planck length. The Planck length is very tiny, $\Lambda = 1.6 \times 10^{-35}$ meters. This is a trillion, trillion times smaller than the nucleus of an atom. To convert angular momentum a to linear momentum p, we divide the angular momentum by this very tiny number, $p = a/\Lambda$. That means a very small amount of angular momentum will make a very large amount of linear momentum . . . or mass . . . or energy. The equation for the interconversion would be:

$$E = m c^2 = p c = a c / \Lambda$$

The smallest amount of angular momentum that you can have is one unit of atomic spin—an electron orbiting a nucleus. If we could find a mechanism to convert that single unit of atomic angular momentum, then the angular momentum destroyed would reappear as either 6.5 kilogram meters per second of linear momentum (a brick flying through the air), 22 micrograms of mass, or 2000 megajoules of energy, the energy of a half a ton of TNT!

It may be that some day gyroscopes will take us to the stars. But instead of massive whirling disks of brass or steel, the gyroscopes will be the nebulous whirling particles in the atom. Once we have the proper future technology, we will be able to convert some of those spinning bundles of angular momentum into the energy and momentum that we will need to push a spaceship close to the speed of light.

But we need to find the magic trick that will make the conversion. You don't destroy angular momentum by grabbing a spinning object and bringing it to a stop. When you do that, the angular momentum is merely transferred through your body, to add to or subtract from the spin of the Earth. Unfortunately, we no longer have Fermi around to show us how to convert momentum to energy, as he once showed us how to convert mass to energy.

What we need is a scientific magician, who can convert what is now indistinguishable from magic into a working technology. Who is the person that will finally be able to "see" this mass-energy-momentum "elephant" that we grope around like blind men? Who will give us a Spin Drive to the stars?

Extra-Sensory Perception

My father-in-law, Edwin Dodson, used to be Plant Supervisor of Construction of the C&P Telephone Company of Maryland. One day after dinner he told me about watching one of his maintenance crews while they were looking for an underground cable. The approved company procedure was to get out the low frequency electrical tone generator and pickup designed by the scientists at AT&T Bell Labs, use the generator to insert a strong electrical signal into one end of the cable, then use the ultrasensitive pickup loop to scan along the surface of the ground above the path of the buried cable. Instead of taking out the scientifically and managerially approved AT&T kit, however, the crew made some dowsing rods out of two pieces of pipe and two bent copper wires and proceeded to use ESP to search for the cable. What impressed me about the story was: Those same men had to *dig* the hole!

The phrase ESP means different things to different people, including mind reading, foretelling the future, psychokinetics, and dowsing. All of them involve the mind being able to obtain information through extra sensory channels other than the known sensory channels of seeing, hearing, feeling, smelling, and tasting.

Since the people on the repair crew were the ones that had to dig the hole, it must mean *something* that they chose ESP over known technology. I don't believe in ESP, but I am aware that others do. I am constantly looking for some new physical law of nature, or some new way of using a known law of nature to duplicate some of the purported effects of ESP. I think I have found one, a little known quantum-mechanical phenomenon called the Aharanov-Bohm effect.

In the realm of the small, the accepted theory is called Quantum Mechanics. In the Theory of Quantum Mechanics objects like electrons and photons have both particle properties and wave properties. If you take two beams of laser light and shine them on a screen at an angle they will interfere with each other to produce a fringe pattern on the screen. Where the light waves are in phase they augment each other and where the light waves are of opposite phase they cancel each other out. It was a triumphant confirmation of Quantum Mechanics when Davisson and Germer repeated the experiment with two beams of low energy electrons, proving that the electron had a wavelength inversely proportional to its energy.

It was then pointed out by Aharanov and Bohm that the phase of the electron wave was a direct function of the electric or magnetic potential and thus these potentials could be measured directly by merely observing the position of the fringe pattern in a two electron beam interference experiment. This announcement and its subsequent experimental confirmation for both the electric and magnetic potentials caused a considerable flap among conservative scientists. From a classical point of view the potential is merely a convenient mathematical fiction since it can have any value it wants and the physical results are the same. In classical mechanics, the only observable is the difference between two potentials, not their absolute value. This is why an electrical worker can handle a power line charged up to an electrical potential of 100,000 volts as long as he doesn't let any part of his body touch something at a different electrical potential.

In these interference experiments, however, the potential was found to be directly measurable. The experiments have been done in a number of ways. In one experiment a beam of very low energy electrons was split into two equal beams by a negatively charged wire. The two beams then went off in their separate ways until they were separated by a number of micrometers. There they were deflected back in the other direction by a pair of charged plates. The two beams met again and formed a round bright spot on an electron-sensitive screen. Overlaid on the circular spot was a pattern of interference lines.

In the open area between the two beams was a long, thin, tiny electromagnet. A tiny current was passed through the electromagnet causing a tiny magnetic field to exist *inside* the electromagnet. The electromagnet was so long and so far away from the two electron beams that there was essentially no magnetic force on the electron beams due to the electromagnet. This was proven since the circular spot did not shift in position. When the electromagnet was activated, however, the fringe pattern inside the circular spot did shift—and by just the amount predicted by Aharanov and Bohm.

The two electron beam system had detected the presence of the magnetic field at a distance. Even when the electromagnet and the electron beams are completely shielded from each other by a perfect superconducting magnetic shield, the electron beams can still sense the presence of the magnetic field at a distance. It is this ability of the Aharanov-Bohm effect to obtain information from inside shielded enclosures that makes it an interesting candidate as a possible channel for extra sensory perception.

Different underground bodies have slightly different electric and magnetic potentials. This depends upon the materials they are composed of, their temperature and water content, and their interaction with the Earth's magnetic field and the underground galvanic currents. If the brain has a sensor that can use the Aharanov-Bohm effect to detect the strength and extent of those potentials, even through a shield, then this might be the mechanism for the dowsing aspect of ESP. It is difficult, however, to see how the Aharanov-Bohm effect could be used for the other aspects of ESP.

In all the experiments done to date the size of the experimental apparatus has been very tiny, micrometers in dimension. Also, all of the experiments have made the assumption that the quantum phase had to be measured around a closed loop. This limits the usefulness of the technique as a sensing mechanism, since it requires that the measurement path encircle the field to be measured, even through the sensing beams do not have to pass through the field to sense it.

A later publication by Aharanov has hinted that if a reference phase were available that was not affected by the potential, the beam that was affected could be compared with this reference phase without the necessity of the measuring apparatus encircling the field to be measured. One method of carrying out this measurement would be to use two particle states that can interfere but that are acted on differently by the potential fields. The existence of such states is an open question since two states which are acted upon differently by a potential are, in principle, distinguishable from each other and therefore will not interfere.

On the other hand, there is no doubt that something can be learned from the gravitational analog of the Aharanov-Bohm effect. This is the Schiff orbiting gyro experiment. The axis of a gyro in orbit around the Earth will precess due to the warpage of space caused by the mass of the Earth. The change of the direction of the gyro axis can be measured by using an optical stellar inertial reference frame which is negligibly affected by the local space curvature.

If we could somehow find a way to measure potentials directly in a simple manner, then this could lead to completely new sensing technologies for prospecting, communication, and military applications. Then if we can develop sensors that can detect potential, perhaps we can find similar sensors in our brain. These would finally give us a scientific understanding of extrasensory phenomena and remove ESP from the pages of the tabloids and place it onto the pages of scientific journals.

Life After Death

One of the most magical concepts invented by the human mind is the concept of the human spirit—a spark of something, which is our intellect, and which is supposed to live on after our body dies. Of all the many types of future science that might some day come true, one that would be completely unexpected would be a scientific understanding of the spirit.

I believe that in our present, very limited understanding of the Universe and the way it works, there exists a clue, an inkling, of one possible version of what a spirit might be. It would have all the magical properties that we envision for the spirit and yet does not violate the laws of nature as we now think they are.

First, I am going to define what I mean by "the spirit": The spirit is an entity which is the animating principle of individual life, especially of individual life in thinking or highly organized beings. The spirit grows and develops as the body grows and develops. However, the spirit is separable from the body at death and is immortal.

Is there any scientific evidence for this definition? To start with, let us see what present day science has to say about separating the intellect or spirit from the human body. Later, we can discuss how our intellect could exist separate from all matter as an independent, immaterial, and immortal entity. Science is already fairly sure that your intellect is relatively independent of the specific matter in which it resides. When you were born as a baby, your brain had built into it a number of instinctive reaction mechanisms that kept the body alive. But except for those animal-like mechanisms, your brain was a blank slate upon which your environment, parents, siblings, pets, and teachers started placing experiences. You learned and grew. You developed response patterns and intelligence. Finally you developed a personality. When this process was completed, your memories, your habits, and your personality were in your brain in the form of coded molecules, coded synapse levels, and coded pathway patterns set up in and among the nerve cells in your brain.

The important thing to recognize is that the information content that presently makes up your intellect is in the *patterns*: patterns in molecules and patterns in the intercellular nerve interconnections. The nerve cells are the same nerve cells that were in the baby, but now they are arranged into patterns. It is the *patterns*, not the cells, that form your intellect. The patterns would be the same if all the cells and atoms had been replaced by other equivalent cells or atoms.

So far, the only patterns that are complex enough to demonstrate intelligence have been formed in the living nerve cell tissue of flesh-and-blood bodies. Over the years, however, there have been a number of research projects on artificial intelligence, in which attempts have been made to develop intellect patterns in electronic systems rather than in living tissue. Unlike regular computers, which have highly structured designs and make mistakes if they are wired wrong, these neural analog artificial brains, or "neural nets," are deliberately formed as unorganized structures of "nerve cells." Care is taken so that the wires from the television camera "eyes" are connected to the "cells" in the "brain" instead of to each other, but at the start it doesn't matter to what part of the brain the wires are connected. The lights that indicate a response are connected to the brain cells instead of to each other or to the television camera, but again, that is all the logic that is built into the device. When the machine is finished, it is a completely imbecilic, randomly wired mess of electronic components that can do nothing.

The researchers, then, acting as teachers, proceed to show things to the television eye, such as pictures of people or the alphabet, and observe the response patterns of the lights connected to the "brain." If the researchers like the response pattern, they push a "Reward" button, which sends a signal down the pathways that are being used and increases the likelihood of those pathways being used the next time. If they don't like the response, or they wish to change it, they push the "Punish" button, until the machine changes the response to the liking of the "Teacher." In this manner, the researchers train the machine, and form patterns of preferred pathways between the electronic nerve cells. These neural net machines have learned, in an elementary and crude way, many things—like running a maze, learning the alphabet, or driving a car. We thus have the first beginnings of an experimental approach to the understanding of intelligence in machines. Right now, the machines only have the IQ of a worm, and there are many problems ahead, but as we gain an understanding of how these machines learn, we will gain an understanding of how *we* learn.

Perhaps some day there will be an electronic brain impressed with the patterns copied from a protoplasmic brain. We will then have an intellect in two forms, protoplasmic and electronic. What we will learn then is almost beyond future speculation. Is pride intellectual? Or emotional? Can a machine envy? hate? love? Or are those reactions found only in human intellects burdened with hormone-driven flesh-and-blood bodies inherited from their animal forebears?

Thus . . . one part of our question seems to be answered. Science seems to see a future where in a limited way an intellect can one day be independent of the human body. But can the intellect be a spirit—free of all forms of matter? Can it be immortal and exist without any type of body, protoplasmic or electronic, to impress its patterns on? I would like to give one possible way that this could be. It is very speculative (and probably not true), but at least it gives us some clues as to where we might find some form of future science that is presently indistinguishable from magic.

As science learns more about the Universe and the space and time in which we live and move, we are beginning to realize that space and time are not simple things that just exist and are unaffected by the rest of the Universe. Experiments have shown that space seems to have a structure and characteristics of its own. To give one example: in high energy experiments on

parity non-conservation, in which right-hand spinning
and left-hand spinning particles should have been
emitted in equal numbers, there was found a strong
preference for left-handed particles. The explanation
that the mathematics gives is that space is not uniform,
but has a "left-handed twist" in this part of the Universe. There is also strong evidence that the structure
of space is determined by matter itself. There are theories of cosmology that indicate that with no matter or
energy there would also be no space and no time. If
you create a small amount of matter, then this matter forms a weak, tenuous space near itself and it begins
to take time to do things.

If we have a large chunk of matter and form it into
a hollow shell, then inside this miniature Universe there
forms a relatively strong space and time, and a small
particle of matter inside the shell begins to have inertia
or mass. You have to give the mass a push to get it
moving through the space defined by the large shell
of matter, and it takes time to move from one part to
another. As the mass of the outer shell is increased,
the space gets stiffer and you have to push the little
piece of matter harder to get it moving, and it takes
longer for it to travel.

Here we see a glimmer of how mass and energy,
which are solid, physical things like our body, can
influence the structure of space and time, which are
ethereal, immaterial things like our concept of the
spirit. This effect of matter on space and time is
closely related to gravity. In the Einstein Theory of
Gravity, space, time, and gravity are all mixed up and
are considered different aspects of the same thing.
This is why one sometimes hears that according to
the Einstein Theory of Gravity, the Sun does not make
a gravity field, but instead the mass of the Sun curves
the space near it. The planets then move in this
curved space-time in force-free "straight" lines, which

look to us like curved orbits. We attribute this to a force, the gravity force, pulling the planets around in their orbits.

Thus, according to the Einstein Theory of Gravity, physical things like matter affect ethereal things like space and time, and the space and time in turn affect the motion of the matter. If the matter has patterns in it, these patterns will in turn be impressed on the space and time. If the space and time have patterns, then other matter will react to those patterns. We know that this is true for large bodies like the stars and planets. Is it equally true for small bodies like atoms?

Let us speculate. Could it be that as the atoms and molecules in our brain form into the pattern containing our intellect, these atoms and molecules impress their pattern into the space-time matrix? If so, then we would now have the pattern that is our intellect impressed not only on some material object such as the nerve cells in our brain, but also on an ethereal object such as the space-time in which we live. This ethereal copy of our intellect could be the spirit.

At first glance it might seem that the mass of the atoms and molecules in a human body would be too small to significantly affect space and time. The atoms, however, although small in total mass, have very dense nuclei, and it is *density*, not mass, that counts in curving space. The curvature of space induced by an atomic nucleus near its surface is fifteen trillion times greater than the curvature of space induced by the mass of the entire Earth! All of these tiny curvature fields from all the atomic nuclei in the atoms in the brain would then form a complex pattern in space-time that is a replica of the pattern of the intellect outlined by our brain cells.

How would these localized points of space curvature behave? We don't know, because there is yet no complete theory of quantum gravity or quantum space-time. Since the space-time curvature effects are limited to a very tiny region near the nucleus of an atom, they cannot have a strong coupling at great distances. But the influence, although weak, can reach out to neighboring electrons and atoms, affecting their motion through ethereal space-time effects.

We must be cautious with these speculations, however, since a quick calculation will easily show that the nuclear and electrical forces exerted by an atomic nucleus are many, many times larger than the space-curvature effects. Also, no experiment has yet found any evidence of a space-curvature effect. Yet, the theories indicate it is there, and it just may play some part in the operation of our intellect.

How might our brain interact with its "spirit"? The curvature effects are small, but the brain is a unique organ in its drive to find *patterns* in the many-faceted sensory environment impinging upon it. An excellent example of the brain's desire to find patterns is found in the old belief that there were canals on Mars. Mars is covered with craters arranged in random patterns. However, the brain behind the eyes of the first observers of Mars wanted so much to make some sense out of that random dot pattern, that it forced the dots into linear structures, and led the hand to draw the non-existent Martian canals. This tendency of the brain to pull patterns out of noisy information is one of its strongest attributes. It may be that some day an understanding of this pattern-extraction process will give us a clue to an experiment to demonstrate the existence of an immaterial pattern like the spirit.

We now begin to see how the matter in our body could form a pattern of our intellect in space and time. The ethereal intellect would change and grow as the body changes and grows. In turn, this ethereal pattern in space-time could possibly influence the motion of the electronic and ionic currents in the brain cells. The awareness and influence of the intellect pattern would be strongest in the immediate space-time region where the material particles of the nerve cells exist, but its awareness and influence could extend not only through the space around us, but could also extend into the time around us. Theoretically, this could be all the way to eternity, so that in this magical view, the spirit would be immortal. However, as in the case of space-curvature, I would suspect that as the time interval gets farther and farther away from the period of time where the matter generating the pattern exists, the influence would become weaker and merge into the other patterns in space-time matrix. (Shades of the Force!)

All of this speculation is very far from presently known, hard, scientific fact. But that only indicates our lack of knowledge about the true nature of intelligence and microscopic space-time interactions.

It now looks as if the concept of our spirit as an entity containing our intellect, that is formed by our body, and yet is immaterial and exists after the body is gone, cannot be arbitrarily dismissed as unscientific nonsense. And it may be, that on some future day, rather than denying the existence of the spirit, science will prove that the spirit *does* have a physical reality and that there *is* life after death.

Recommended Reading
Free Energy:
Timothy H. Boyer, "The Classical Vacuum," *Scientific American*, Vol. 253, #2, pp. 70 ff (August 1985).

Daniel C. Cole and Harold E. Puthoff, "Extracting energy and heat from the vacuum," *Physical Review*, Vol. E48, #2, pp. 1562–1565 (August 1993).

Richard P. Feynman and A.R. Hibbs, *Quantum Electrodynamics* (McGraw-Hill, NY, 1965).

Robert L. Forward, "Extracting Electrical Energy From the Vacuum by Cohesion of Charged Foliated Conductors," *Physical Review B*, Vol. 30, pp. 1700–1702 (1984).

E. G. Harris, *A Pedestrian Approach to Quantum Field Theory*, Chap. 10, (Wiley-Interscience, NY, 1972).

Stephen Hawking, "The Quantum Mechanics of Black Holes," *Scientific American*, Vol. 236, #1, pp. 34 ff (January 1977).

J.N. Israelachivili and D. Tabor, "Measurement of van der Waals dispersion forces in the range 1.5 to 130 nm," *Proc. Royal Society of London*, Series A, Vol. 331, pp. 19 ff (1972).

Charles Sheffield, *The McAndrew Chronicles*, pp. 72–112, 234–5, (Tor Books, NY, 1983).

Reactionless Drives:

Robert L. Forward, "Spin Drive to the Stars," *Analog Science Fiction/Science Fact*, Vol. 101, #5, pp. 64–70 (27 April 1981).

Extra-Sensory Perception:

Y. Aharanov and D. Bohm, "Significance of Electromagnetic Potentials in the Quantum Theory," *Physical Review*, Vol. 115, pp. 485 ff (1959).

Dietrick Thomsen, "Gauging the Aharanov-Bohm Effect," *Science News*, Vol. 129, p. 135 (1 March 1986).

Life After Death:

Robert L. Forward, "Speculations on the Spirit," *Galileo*, Vol. 2, #3, pp. 16–18, 94–95 (November 1979).

✧ A MATTER MOST STRANGE

In the previous chapter, "Future Speculations," I discussed a number of possible new sources of energy using future technologies that today would be indistinguishable from magic. In this fiction story, I describe a potential new source of energy that is literally "strange," but it is not magic. The theory of strange matter is highly developed and well accepted by the scientific community. There are even experiments being planned to search for drops of strange matter generated by the high speed collision of heavy nuclei on heavy metal targets. (See "The Search for Strange Matter" by Henry J. Crawford and Carsten H. Greiner, in the January 1994 issue of Scientific American, *Volume 270, Number 1, pages 72-77.)*

In the story, I describe what such a search would entail from the viewpoint of the researchers involved. To put a little drama in the plot by creating a deadline date that put the researchers under pressure, I postulated that the Super-Conducting Supercollider was in imminent danger of being canceled in the year 1998. Little did I realize that my prediction would come true five years before that date.

This story was published in the table-top book Microverse *published by Byron Preiss Books in 1988.*

Matt knew there was trouble ahead.

He had been summoned to the office of the Director of Brookhaven National Laboratory. Director Stevens normally never bothered to talk to the visiting scientists who came to use his facility, except perhaps at parties. Matt stared at the picture on the opposite wall as he waited in the reception room. It showed Leon Lederman, Melvin Schwartz, and Jack Steinberger at Brookhaven in 1961, shortly after they had proved that there were two kinds of neutrinos.

"Those were the days," Matt thought, soothing his anxiety by stroking his neat beard, flecked with strands of prematurely grey hair.

The secretary finally ushered him in, and Calvin Stevens introduced him to Congressman James Deal, the Chairman of the House Science, Space, and Technology Committee, and Secretary of Energy "Billy" Hurley, formerly on the Board of Directors of the Tennessee Valley Authority, and now President Peterson's newly appointed "hatchet man" at the Department of Energy.

"Professor Shaw is Principal Investigator of the 'S-Drop Experiment'," said Director Stevens. "It's an attempt to find evidence for a new state of matter called 'strange' matter."

"'Strange' matter?" queried Billy Hurley, looking at Matt.

Matt started the set speech he used to explain his experiment to lay people. "All massive particles, like the protons and neutrons that make up the atoms in your body, are in turn made up of more basic particles, called quarks. Quarks come in six different types, labeled quixotically, 'up,' 'down,' 'strange,' 'charm,' 'top,' and 'bottom.' A proton can be imagined as a bag containing two 'up' quarks and one 'down' quark, while a neutron is one 'up' and two 'down' quarks. All known particles can be represented by some combination of two or three quarks.

Quarks have never been seen individually. They always seem to come in 'bags' of two or three.

"If you get enough quarks together at one time, however," continued Matt. "Say, fifty or more, *and* some of them are strange quarks ... then you can form large bags, or drops, of a new type of matter, called strange matter. The purpose of our experiment is to slam the heaviest ions Brookhaven can accelerate into a heavy metal target, and search the resulting debris for S-drops—drops of strange matter."

"What are the chances of success?" asked Billy, critically.

"It's hard to say," Matt replied. "Although the theory suggests that large drops of strange matter should be stable, the smaller drops we can produce at Brookhaven may only be marginally stable. Then, there is the problem of identifying the few S-drops produced from all the other particles coming from the target."

"What is the probability of success?" persisted Billy. "Give me a number."

Matt couldn't force himself to lie. "Less than one percent," he finally admitted.

Billy leaned back. He didn't like this job Peterson had asked him to do—but at least he wouldn't feel bad about canceling this marginal experiment. He turned to the Director of Brookhaven. "Tell him the bad news, Cal," he said.

Calvin Stevens squirmed. "By the direction of President Peterson, Brookhaven National Laboratory is to be closed down at the end of this fiscal year," he said.

"What!" Matt exclaimed in disbelief.

"Can you get your experiment completed by September thirtieth?" continued the Director. "If not, you might as well shut it down right now."

"Every cent saved means that much more for the

scientists trying to complete the Superconducting Super-Collider," said Congressman Deal.

"Peterson's new budget for 1998 has zero dollars in it for the SSC," explained Secretary Hurley. "He is determined to balance the budget—and he isn't going to do it by stripping the ragged shirts off the backs of the poor. I've consulted with the chief scientist types at the Department. They all agree that real breakthroughs in high energy physics come only from those machines at the highest energy—and in the USA, that machine is the SSC. To save the SSC, the rest of the machines have to go."

"But there is good science going on at those smaller machines," protested Matt.

"'Gap filler' science," said Chairman Deal, almost sneering. "We've got poor who need our help to make it through these belt tightening times. We can't afford a welfare program for second rate scientists."

Matt winced internally, but held his temper. "It's not me or the other scientists I'm worried about," he said. "The people who'll get hurt will be the graduate students. I've got two who are counting on my experiment to get their Ph.D. degrees."

"They had better change their majors to something more practical," said Billy. "By next year, the only place that will need particle physicists will be the SSC. Unless, of course, they go to work for the Department of Defense. The Air Force will be turning most of the particle accelerators into antimatter factories as soon as you scientists leave."

Calvin brought the discussion back. "Can you get your experiment done in time?" he persisted.

"We were planning on three months of beam time to produce conclusive results," replied Matt. "But we can make do with one month if we have to." He thought for a while. "If we work twenty-four hour days, we can get the experiment ready a month before the end of the fiscal year." He got up abruptly. "You give me no other choice, so I'd better get busy," he said, and left without shaking hands.

Working day and night, Matt and his two graduate students, Yong-Shi Wu and Patti Morrison, struggled to get their experiment operational. Yong-Shi was the computer and software whiz, while Patti was the electronics and hardware expert.

One evening, Matt dropped in unexpectedly at the experimental building after midnight. The downstairs control room was empty. He went upstairs—no one in the offices or the lounge. Then he heard voices and the noise of a powerful electric motor echoing back through the long corridor that led from the control building to the experiment floor proper. He checked the indicators above the door to the corridor. The beam was off and the radiation monitors were green. He made his way through the narrow walkway until he was on top of the wall of concrete blocks that shielded the control room from the experimental area. The gate on top of the meter-thick wall was open, and someone had taken the safety key with them down into the experimental area. The voices were clearer now. He descended the circular staircase that spiraled down the other side of the six meter high wall, and walked through the zig-zag portal into the experimental area. He looked up in shock.

"Patti!!! What the *hell* are you doing!" Matt roared. His voice echoed back from the twenty meter high ceiling of the gigantic metal shed that covered the experimental area. Yong-Shi Wu, and some people that Matt recognized as Patti's friends, were trying to look inconspicuous in the far corner.

High above, hanging from the overhead crane, was a forty ton block of dense concrete. Standing on top of the block, one hand casually holding the steel suspension cable and the other hand holding the crane controls, was a thin young woman with long, bushy red-brown hair pulled back into a ponytail. She was dressed in faded blue jeans, scruffy fluorescent-red jogging shoes, and a bulky white sweatshirt that said, "North Pole University."

"Oh! Hi, Professor Shaw," said Patti down from above. "I was hoping to have this done before morning."

"When I *usually* show up," said Matt, disapprovingly.

Patti's eyes dropped, her shoulders hunched forward, and she seemed to shrink, as she went into her "mooching" pose.

"What are you up to?" Matt asked again, sternly.

"Well . . ." started Patti. "The other experiments in the hall had to stop because they couldn't be finished before the shutdown. So, instead of having our experiment crowded into the small area we were originally allocated, I was just rearranging things to take advantage of the extra room."

"There's *got* to be more to it than that," replied Matt, still frowning. "All we need for the first phase of the experiment is the target for the heavy ion beam to collide with, the bending magnet to separate out the S-drops from the rest of the particles, and the time-of-flight detector that shows the particle is really an S-drop. They fit into our area just fine."

"But since there is more room," said Patti. "We can bring in our equipment for the second phase—where we capture the S-drops."

"*If* the S-drops exist," reminded Matt. "Remember . . . First we have to prove they exist. Second, we try to capture them and grow them large enough that they are stable."

"But we have only one month of beam time," said Patti. "I was just trying to make the most of it."

"Well . . ." hesitated Matt.

"It's our last chance!" persisted Patti.

"Let's see what you have in mind," said Matt, giving in.

"I'll meet you on top of the right shield wall," said Patti, perking up. She pushed buttons and started to lower herself down. Matt found a ladder and climbed to the top of the thick wall that shielded one experiment from another.

"The block I was lifting came from the wall at the end of our area, right behind the beam dump that absorbs everything that comes through the S-drop detector," said Patti, pointing as they walked along. "Instead of throwing the S-drops away in the beam dump, I was planning to take them through a hole in the wall into the next area. There I was going to set up the decelerator, the holding ring, and the storage bottle."

"There is certainly room for them there," admitted Matt, stroking his grey-flecked beard.

"And the equipment is just waiting for us in the storage annex," said Patti, eagerly.

The crane was soon busy. The remaining blocks in the wall were removed, opening up a hole. Yong-Shi set up a laser beam that passed through the center of the S-drop detector and simulated the path that the S-drops would take. The red beam went through the break in the wall, six feet above the floor, and passed down the length of the adjoining area.

Soon Patti was flying back again. This time she was balanced on a ten meter long segment of the S-drop decelerator. It was a particle accelerator that had been redesigned to run backwards. As Patti slowly lowered the thick cylinder with its banks of rf generators hanging off the sides, Matt, Yong-Shi, and the others pushed and pulled on the ends until the laser beam threaded through the five centimeter bore of the long tube. The support feet were lowered to the floor, and Patti went flying off to get the next section, while final adjustments were made on the feet until the laser beam was exactly centered in the bore. Soon all three segments were in place and the thirty meter long decelerator was ready for vacuum checkout.

Next came the holding ring. The major component was an old magnet salvaged from the Brookhaven "junk" yard. It was ten meters in diameter and a meter thick. There was a ten centimeter gap between the top coil and the bottom coil where the magnetic field was strong and constant.

Between the poles of the magnet was a new vacuum chamber, especially designed for holding and growing S-drops. The magnetic field passing through the chamber kept the S-drops moving in a circle. Once every revolution they would pass through a container of liquid deuterium—hydrogen atoms with an extra neutron in their nucleus. The rapidly moving S-drops would absorb the neutrons and grow heavier.

The remainder of the chamber contained an S-drop accelerator that made up for the speed lost by the S-drop as it passed through the liquid deuterium. The whole thing was designed to keep the S-drops circulating through the liquid deuterium again and again, growing heavier and larger with each passage. Around the ring was a cluster of gamma ray detectors, for as the S-drops grew, they gave off energy in the form of soft gamma rays.

Finally, there was the storage bottle. An electronic switch in the ring could divert an S-drop from its circular path and send it off into the storage bottle. There it would be suspended in the center of a vacuum chamber by a combination of electric and magnetic fields. Associated with the bottle was an accelerator that could shoot deuterium atoms at the stored S-drop, and more gamma ray detectors to monitor the energy given off as each deuterium atom was swallowed by the S-drop and converted from normal matter into strange matter.

As Patti had planned, they were through before morning came. There was a lot of work to do, however, baking out the vacuum systems, aligning the various pieces of equipment with charged particle beams instead of laser beams, and making the software play with the hardware, but finally they were ready— just forty days before the end of the fiscal year.

There was great excitement when the high energy beam of heavy gold ions was first switched into their experimental area. Everyone was gathered around the control console, watching the indicators intensely.

"All we need is just *one* S-drop," muttered Patti. "That would show that Tennessee hill-'Billy' he was wrong!"

Hour after hour, massive nuclei of pure gold slammed into the tungsten target and created a profusion of particles. Some of the particles made it through the bending magnet and passed through the detector, but none of them had the right mass, speed, and charge to be an S-drop.

The hours passed into days—the days passed into weeks—but no "strangers" dropped in for a visit. Finally, they all had to admit that their experiment was going to be just one more experiment that had looked for something new—and had failed. Still they pressed on, working around the clock, hoping against hope that the next golden nucleus would produce the long-sought drop of strange matter . . .

It was late on September 30 when Matt pulled off the William Floyd Parkway and drove for the last time onto the grounds of Brookhaven. He saw a familiar car ahead of him, driving slowly along the side of the road. It was a chauffeur-driven stretched Cadillac, with a microsatellite dish in addition to the carphone antenna. In the headlights of the slowly moving car was Patti, long thin legs encased in peacock blue spandex, feet in fluorescent-red running shoes, and her upper body protected from the light Long Island fog by a sweatshirt with a picture of Einstein on the back, sticking out his tongue. Her long red-brown ponytail brushed across Einstein's tongue with every other step.

Patti was on her way to her shift—escorted by her boyfriend, Charles Harris, a wealthy Wall Street stockbroker. Matt beeped his horn as he passed and continued on to the parking area outside the experimental building.

Yong-Shi Wu looked up from the control console as Matt entered the room. The almond eyes in the pudgy face were blinking and red from lack of sleep.

"Any luck?" asked Matt, with little hope that the answer would be different this time.

"Nothing unusual from the detectors, Prof. Shaw," replied Yong-Shi.

"When does your plane leave for Beijing?" asked Matt.

"Eight in the morning from Kennedy," replied Yong-Shi.

"Then you'd better get some sleep," said Matt. "Add today's data to your thesis tape and get on your way."

"Shall I shut down the experiment, Prof. Shaw?" Yong-Shi asked.

"No," said Matt. "I saw Patti coming in to take over her shift. We might as well keep collecting data until the beam goes down at midnight."

"I will wait until midnight, then," said Yong-Shi, putting his data tape back.

"No!" said Matt, gruffly. "Another four hours of null data won't make any difference to your thesis results. Get your data and get out of here. I don't want you missing your flight."

Yong-Shi put the tape on the drive and was busy at the control console when Patti mooched in. Shoulders hunched over, hands stuffed in the pockets of her sweatshirt, she went around the control room looking at all the dials.

"Everything okay, Yong-Shi?" Patti asked. She took a pair of bluejeans off the wall and pulled them over her spandex tights.

The tape drive started whirling. Yong-Shi leaned back in the comfortable console chair, rubbed his eyes, and yawned. "Number eight gamma ray detector is intermittent," he reported.

"Must be that damn connector, again," said Patti. "But I'll check in here first." She walked behind some cabinets and started wiggling the wiring.

The outside door opened and a young business executive dressed in a black Homburg, shiny black shoes, grey silk scarf, and expensive grey wool topcoat timidly entered the control room.

"I just wanted to ask Patti when I should pick her up," explained Charles.

Patti came out from behind the cabinet. "The 'Final Count-Down' party starts at eleven thirty in Beam Operations," said Patti, brushing the dust off her hands. "Pick me up ten minutes before then and we can drive over. You coming, Yong-Shi?"

"I think I had better pack and hit the sheets," said Yong-Shi.

"He's leaving for Beijing in the morning," explained Matt. Yong-Shi took the tape off the drive, crammed it into his back-pack, and started for the door.

"You're leaving!?!" exclaimed Patti. "I didn't realize it would be so *soon*." She grabbed Yong-Shi and gave him a hug. She was slightly taller than the chubby Chinese and he squirmed in embarrassment.

"I'm going to miss all those long nights we spent working together to make this kludge operational," she said, looking down at him.

Matt noticed a perturbed frown on Charles's face. Patti saw it too, frowned back at Charles, and deliberately planted a kiss on Yong-Shi's forehead. She gave him another hug and let him go. As Yong-Shi went through the door, she waved goodbye and called out, "Give my regards to Sui-May and let me know when you get married."

Patti turned back to the apparatus. "The problem isn't in the cabinets," she said. "So it must be in that connector." Ignoring the ladder propped in the far corner, Patti slipped off her blue jeans and Einstein sweatshirt, leaving her clad only in her peacock blue spandex body suit and fluorescent-red running shoes. Matt noticed that she was getting fat. That was very unlike Patti, who had always been skinny—but the pressure she had been under these past months was enough to make anyone fall off their diet.

Patti walked over to the chalk board, ran her fingers down the rail until they were white with chalk, and started to free climb the huge concrete blocks between the control room and the experimental area.

"Patti!" exclaimed Charles, moving under her. "Don't take chances!"

Patti halted in mid-climb, sides of her shoes jammed into a thin seam four meters off the floor and a finger through a lifting ring. "I've done this dozens of times, Charles," said Patti. "Stop worrying."

Finding a clear place between the bundles of cables going over the six meter high wall, Patti hoisted herself until she had a firm grip on the top edge. A few more moves and she was facing outward. A quick flip, and she was lying flat on the top of the wall, dark-brown eyes glowing with accomplishment. Matt and Charles stopped holding their breath.

"Be back in a few minutes," she said. Matt and Charles watched as the blue spandex-covered fanny moved off—following the cables in the narrow crawlway.

"An amazing young woman," said Matt, quietly.

"That's why I've been in love with her ever since high school," said Charles. "She is lightyears ahead of me in intelligence and talent. All I can do is make money."

"That takes talent, too," said Matt.

"All it takes is a pleasant personality and a convincing line to sell stock," said Charles. "I hope my line has been convincing enough for Patti." He looked at his watch. "The Tokyo exchange has just opened," he said. "I'd better keep on top of the first few hours to protect my clients. Tell Patti I'll be back before eleven-thirty." He went out the door.

Matt went to the control console. The main screen had slowly growing bars showing the amount of data collected. The "S-drops" column was blank. Up in the right corner was an engineering display monitoring the high voltage supplies to the gamma ray counters. The indicator for counter eight was erratically shifting from a green OK to a yellow LOW. Suddenly it changed to a steady green OK.

"Did that work?" echoed Patti's voice from the crawlway.

"Yes!" yelled Matt. Patti reappeared and soon was back down on the floor. She shivered slightly as she put on her faded jeans and Einstein sweatshirt.

Patti took over the control console while Matt went upstairs to his little "Professor's Office" to plow through his grant paperwork. A little after eleven, he came back down. Patti was sitting back in the chair, bare feet up on the console, looking at a small object.

"Any 'strangers' show up?" Matt asked.

"Afraid not," said Patti. She tapped a key with a big toe and the screen changed. She put the object on her finger, and Matt realized it was a ring, a huge diamond solitaire.

"That's some rock you have there," said Matt, admiringly.

"Charlie gave it to me last night," said Patti. "And asked me to marry him—again." She patted her rounded tummy. "I guess he wants to make me an honest woman."

"Oh!" said Matt, flustered. "I thought you were gaining . . ."

"Weight?" said Patti, giggling. "You might say that. Except that I expect to lose it all in five months." She suddenly turned pensive. "I'm normally very careful. But I got careless during that depressing period right after the bottom fell out of particle physics. I sometimes wonder if it was really carelessness or just Mother Nature playing tricks on me with my own hormones. I thought seriously about having an abortion—you can't be a post-doc and raise kids at the same time—but I kept putting it off." She looked at the clock display on the screen. "Almost time for Charlie to come." She tapped her big toe on the keyboard again and the tape drive across the room started to rewind. She bent over, slipped on her shoes, and stood up.

Matt went to the tape drive and removed the reel of tape. He walked over to Patti.

"Here's your Ph.D. thesis," he said, handing it to her.

Patti took the reel that symbolized ten years of her life. Four grinding years getting her B.S. in Physics at CCNY, another four grinding years getting her Masters and passing the Ph.D. qualifying exams at SUNY-Stony Brook, and two years with Matt Shaw, designing, building, and operating this experiment. But the grind wasn't over. It would take the good part of another year to turn the null data on that tape into an acceptable thesis. And when she was done and had received her doctorate, it would have been for nothing. She had sent out literally hundreds of job applications all over the world, and had received not one positive response. No one wanted another average female particle physicist when there were hundreds of men and women, some better than she was, clamoring for the few post-doc positions left open in the field.

She shrugged, tossed the reel of tape into a nearby trash can, mooched over to her work desk, and started stuffing her back-pack with her personal belongings.

"Patti!" exclaimed Matt.

"I'm tired," said Patti in a discouraged tone. "I quit."

Matt fished the reel of tape from the trash and took it over to her. "You can't quit now," he said. "You've almost got your Ph.D.! Think of your future. Think of your career!"

The door opened and Charles walked in. Patti perked up and greeted him with a big kiss. Supporting herself by holding onto his arm, she turned to face her Professor.

"My future is with Charlie," she said. She patted her tummy. "I'm going to make a career of being a wife and a mommy . . ." A defiant look came on her face, "A damn *good* wife and mommy," she added. "With Charlie I'll be happy and wanted and loved. Which is more than I can expect from a life as a scientist." She grabbed her backpack. "Goodbye, Professor Shaw." They left, leaving Matt still holding the reel of tape.

Dejected, Matt returned to the console and collapsed in the chair. He looked at the screen clock. "2327 TUE 30 SEP 1997," it said.

"Only thirty-three minutes left, then the beam goes off . . . forever," said Matt to himself. He leaned back in the large comfortable chair and let his tired eyes close.

The early morning sun sent a bright shaft of light through a window and woke Matt up. It was six a.m. He had fallen asleep and the beam had been off for six hours. There was a voice coming from upstairs— it had an urgent tone—but whatever was being said was being repeated in an automatic manner. Puzzled, he made his way up the stairs. There, on a shelf, was a small television monitor sitting on top of a video recorder. It was repeating a scene from *Star Trek*, Yong-Shi's favorite television program. The picture showed Mr. Spock speaking over the intercom.

"Intruder Alert! Intruder Alert! We have a 'stranger' on the lower deck."

Matt went quickly down the corridor, let himself through the safety gate, and taking a portable radiation monitor with him, clambered quickly down the circular staircase. Slowly he entered the experimental area, radiation monitor held out in front of him.

The first experimental area was quiet. As he moved through the broach in the shield wall into the second experimental area and started to walk down the long length of the decelerator tube, the ticks from the radiation monitor became more active. The needle was still in the green area, however, so he continued on. As he approached the holding ring, the needle on the monitor dial began to creep into the yellow area. The radiation was especially intense near the segment of the chamber that contained the liquid deuterium.

Matt activated the auxiliary control console in one corner. The bars on the screen indicated no data had been lost while he was asleep—but most importantly, the column labeled "S-drops" was no longer empty. Sometime in the last few minutes of beam operation, a drop of strange matter had been formed. For the last six hours it had been circulating around in the holding ring, feeding on the liquid deuterium and growing fatter and heavier.

"I'd better get it out of there before it gets too heavy and flies out of the holding ring!" said Matt. Holding his breath, he activated the switching circuit. If everything had worked correctly, the heavy drop of strange matter should have been transferred from the holding ring into the storage bottle. Grabbing the radiation monitor, Matt ran back. The gamma radiation from the holding ring was gone. He went over to the storage bottle and waved the monitor around it . . . Nothing. Had he lost it?

Then he remembered that S-drops only gave off radiation when they were being fed. He ran back to the auxiliary console and turned on the gun that shot deuterium atoms across the center of the storage bottle. Instantly, the four gamma ray detectors surrounding the bottle started to indicate cascades of low energy gamma rays as the neutrons in the deuterium penetrated through the electron clouds around the drop of strange matter and became one with it. He called up a computer routine that calculated the total amount of energy being emitted in gamma rays for every neutron swallowed.

"Over three percent!" exclaimed Matt. "Three percent of the mass of the neutron is being converted into energy! That's better than fusion energy! And 'Billy' Hurley thought that new physics only came from the highest energy machines."

He turned off the deuterium gun and the drop of strange matter stopped emitting gamma rays. "Best of all, there is no residual radioactivity when you turn it off," he gloated. "And when it gets too big, you just hit it hard with a large, high-speed nucleus, and you can break it into *two* S-drops and start up another power plant."

"How big *did* it grow during those six hours, anyway?" he asked himself. He pulled down another routine that used the electromagnetic fields in the storage bottle as a "spring" to weigh the S-drop.

"It's over a trillion times heavier than a uranium nucleus!" he exclaimed. "It's almost big enough to see!" He remembered they had a borehole telescope for inspecting the inside of beam lines. He found it and took it to the storage bottle. It took a long time to arrange the floodlights and the telescope just right. Then, a final twist of the focus knob brought a tiny speck of silver into view.

"There it is," whispered Matt to himself—a thrill running through his body. "A Nobel Prize for me . . . Instant Ph.D.'s for Patti and Yong-Shi . . . And perhaps salvation for Brookhaven, its researchers, and all the other 'second-rate' facilities in the country . . . But best of all, it's a new source of radiation-free nuclear power for the world. . . ."

Suddenly he became concerned. Nuclear fusion had once promised to be free of residual radioactivity, but secondary reactions had made fusion reactors almost as dangerously radioactive as fission reactors. Would there be something about strange matter energy conversion that would negate its advantages?

Then, from the back of his mind came the memory of an article he had read on "strange stars." According to the article, if a *single* drop of strange matter fell into a neutron star, the whole star would turn into an ultradense ball of strange matter. Yet, according to the same theorists, nothing like that should happen with normal matter. Since a drop of strange matter has a cloud of electrons around it, it would interact with normal matter in much the same way as a normal atom, which also has a cloud of electrons around it. The electron clouds would act as barriers to keep the strange matter from getting to the protons and the neutrons in the nuclei of the normal matter.

"But suppose . . ." muttered Matt to himself. "That the strange matter drop were allowed to get too large—like almost happened to me—and it got too heavy to hold and fell down into the Earth. Would the S-drop go all the way to the center of the Earth? And are the pressures at the center of the Earth high enough to crush the clouds of electrons shielding the strange matter and allow it to eat up the Earth?"

He didn't know the answer. And even after the theorists had repeated their calculations and showed that even large drops of strange matter would not eat up the Earth—could you be *sure* their calculations were correct?

"I am the only one that knows we were successful," Matt said to himself softly, right hand stroking his beard as he pondered. "I could break up this S-drop into smaller ones that would evaporate away into harmless alpha particles and no one would be the wiser. Yong-Shi would still get his Ph.D., Patti would get what she wants, and no one else would bother to try the same experiment if I reported a failure."

He paused to sigh deeply—his mind churning over the positive and negative options.

"Is the world ready for this?" he asked himself.

"What shall I do?"

✧ FASTER-THAN-LIGHT

All scientists know, deep down in their souls, that they will never be allowed to break the ultimate speed limit—the speed of light. Yet, time and again, they are given clues by Nature that perhaps—just perhaps—there might be a way to achieve faster-than-light (FTL) travel. The clues are many and varied, and any one of them just might be the chink in the armor of causality that will allow real scientists, not just those found in science-fiction stories, to not only travel faster than light, but also travel through time.

For it is one of the truisms of physics, that the existence of any sort of FTL phenomenon usually implies the existence of an analogous time travel phenomenon. In Einstein's Special Relativity Theory, an observer moving at high speeds will see a faster-than-light spacecraft arrive at its destination before it left its starting point, in effect, traveling backward in time. In addition, many "wormhole" space warp concepts can be converted into a time machine by taking one of the mouths of the wormhole on a round-trip journey at high velocities to "younger" it compared to its stationary-mouth twin. Thus, a study of FTL phenomena must *necessarily* address the issue of the causality paradoxes caused by the existence of time machines.

To this date, FTL travel and time machines do not seem to be *forbidden* by the known laws of physics. (This, however, does *not* mean they are allowed.) There are many scientific publications which have looked into this question in considerable detail, and have been unable to find any violation of any conservation law or any other accepted laws of physics by FTL travel except the causality principle, which is not a physical law but a philosophical assumption. Even scientific studies of the problem of the violation of the causality principle by time machines seems to have resulted in reasonable-sounding solutions, in both the classical and quantum domain, to the inevitable paradoxes that time machines raise.

To date, there is no strong experimental evidence for either FTL phenomena or time-travel phenomena—just hints. But in the process of trying to understand the observed possible FTL phenomena, we will probably learn more about the physical laws of the universe, since the present laws seem to allow FTL and time machines.

FTL Phenomena in Theories

When it comes to predicting FTL and time-travel phenomena, our theories are not cooperating. Normally, one expects theories to be constricting—putting limits on what is possible. The experimentalists then come along and find some new phenomena that can't be explained by the existing theory, which requires the generation of a newer theory with broader boundaries that allow the existence of the newly-found phenomena. In the case of FTL and time travel, the tendency is the other way. There are many theories that seem to point to, or allow, the existence of FTL and time-travel phenomena, while the experimental evidence is lacking. The problem theories are not maverick ones, but include such well-respected and tested theories as the Einstein Theory of Mechanics at High Velocities (Special Theory of Relativity), the Einstein Theory of Gravity (General Theory of Relativity), Quantum Mechanics, and Quantum Electrodynamics.

Special Relativity: The very theory that gives us our ultimate speed law, the Einstein Special Relativity Theory, also gives us a way to break that speed limit. The equations of the theory allow the existence of three types of particles:

• Bradyons—particles which have positive rest mass, which are created moving at less than the speed of light, and which increase their speed as they gain energy. They cannot, however, increase their speed enough to reach the speed of light.

• Luxons—particles which have zero rest mass, which are created moving at the speed of light, and which always move at the speed of light no matter what their energy.

• Tachyons—particles which have imaginary rest mass, which are created moving faster than the speed of light, and which decrease their speed as they gain energy. They cannot, however, slow down enough to reach the speed of light. Although the rest mass of tachyons is imaginary (we have no good idea what imaginary mass means), that causes no problems to the theory, since the tachyons are never at rest anyway, while the energy and momentum of the moving tachyons are calculated to be normal and positive, so the tachyons obey all the usual conservation laws of physics.

The Special Relativity Theory, being *the* correct theory for the description of mechanics at high velocities, is also embedded in other theories. There it leads to other theoretical predictions of FTL phenomena. The Maxwell equations for the propagation of electromagnetic waves, and the Schrödinger equations for the propagation of quantum probability waves, contain two solutions for the direction of propagation of the waves. One is the standard retarded wave solution which describe waves which travel from the past to the future. The theories, however, also allow an advanced wave solution, which describe waves which travel from the future into the past. These advanced waves could conceivably be used to send messages into the past. To no one's surprise, the advanced waves have not been experimentally observed. Since they have not been seen, their existence in the theory is conveniently ignored by both experimentalists and theorists, who use only the retarded wave solutions. Yet . . . why does the theory allow their existence if experimentally they do not exist? Certainly there is new physics to be found if we can understand the reason why the theory of fallible humans allows advanced waves while the reality of almighty Nature forbids them. Attempts have been made to come up with models of reality that explain the non-observance of advanced waves. A number of theorists, including Wheeler and Feynman, and John Cramer, have proposed models involving combined and coordinated advanced and retarded waves to explain why advanced waves are not seen. Some of these models, if true, could conceivably be used to provide FTL communication.

General Relativity: The Einstein gravity equations are replete with outrageous solutions describing machines that allow not only FTL travel through wormholes in spacetime and tunnels through space, via hyperdimensions and other universes; but also time travel using all those machines plus others. These are discussed in more detail in the Chapter "Space Warps and Time Machines".

• Black Holes: Black holes by themselves (despite the claims of Hollywood) will not do as space warps. Although the black hole equations describe a wormhole in spacetime that leads to a "white hole" exit "somewhere else," and you can pass through the event horizon of a black hole without damage if the black hole is large enough (galactic in mass), the mass that formed the black hole is clogging up the throat of the wormhole and the mathematical equations describing the space inside the event horizon show that even the most powerful spacecraft imaginable cannot avoid hitting the mass.

• Reissner-Nordstrøm Chargewarp: Adding charge to a black hole allows a powerful enough spacecraft entering through the event horizon of the Chargewarp to maneuver around the charged mass at the center to get to the "white hole" exit. The exit universe, however, is not the one the spacecraft left. To use a Chargewarp for FTL and time travel, you would need to find another Chargewarp in the new universe that connects back to our universe.

• Kerr Ringwarp: To make a Ringwarp requires manipulating a rapidly rotating mass (typically 100 times solar mass) while it is trying to collapse into a black hole. Instead of allowing the star to contract into a spinning oblate sphere, you force it to collapse into a dense rotating ring, empty in the center. The mathematical equations for this mass configuration describe two infinite regions, connected through the hole in the ring. One region is this universe and the other is a hyperuniverse where matter is negative and time is spacelike. The Ringwarp can be used as both a space warp and a time machine. Two-way use, however, requires that the ring rotate with a peripheral velocity of the speed of light, which is not possible. (Don't worry, the answer to that problem is in the next section.) The Ringwarp also has other "engineering" problems that would require a highly advanced technology to overcome, such as: the means for forcing the formation of the ring shape, the stability of the ring during the passage of a spacecraft, and the generation of radiation from instabilities in the fluctuations of the vacuum induced by the Ringwarp.

• Kerr-Newman Charged Ringwarp: Adding charge to a rotating massive ring allows the formation of a two-way space warp and time machine while requiring a peripheral velocity slightly less than the speed of light. The machine still has the other "engineering" problems of the Kerr Ringwarp.

• Morris-Thorne Field-Supported Wormhole: This is a "tunnel" through space from one point in space to another. Its construction does not require dealing with black holes. It exhibits no strong tidal effects or other nasty properties like instability and radiation. The construction of the machine does require that the wormhole be held open by an "exotic" field, a field that has an energy density less than its tensile strength. Normal electric and magnetic fields have an energy density that is exactly equal to the tensile strength of the field. Superstrong electric fields can be used to hold up most of the tunnel, but right at the throat, an exotic field must be used. Such exotic fields exist. The "Casimir vacuum" between two metal plates is one such field, and Thorne and his students have "designed" a wormhole that uses the Casimir vacuum as the required exotic field. The smaller the throat, the higher the negative mass density needed in the field to hold open the throat. For a 10-meter throat, the density is minus 10^{22} g/cc. For a 20-kilometer throat, the density is minus 10^{14} g/cc—neutron star density. To get down to the density of negative water, the throat would have to be millions of lightyears across. The method of "growing" the wormhole from a microscopic primordial quantum-foam wormhole is not obvious.

The wormhole can easily be turned into a time machine by just taking one mouth of the wormhole on a short round-trip relativistic journey to make it younger (say by one week) than the stay-at-home mouth. (See Thorne, 1994 for a technical discussion, and Forward, 1992 for a fictional description.) Once the two mouths are brought back and placed side-by-side, then to travel to the future, you enter the younger mouth and you exit the older mouth one week later than the time you entered. To travel to the past, you enter the older mouth and you exit the other mouth one week earlier than the time you entered. You can then repeat the process, going back in time in weekly jumps, until you reach the time at which the time machine was first formed.

Quantum Mechanics: The Theory of Quantum Mechanics contains many unusual concepts, such as particle creation and annihilation, quantum tunneling, quantum jumps, instantaneous collapse of the wave function of a system, and the continuing "quantum connectedness" of distant particles that have interacted in the past. Many present models of quantum connectedness seem to involve an instantaneous-action-at-a-distance phenomena with potential for allowing the FTL transfer of information. There are many different "models" or "interpretations" of what the equations of quantum mechanics mean from a physical point of view. Some examples are the:

• Copenhagen Reality-Created-by-Observation Model: (Example: Schrödinger's cat in a box is neither dead or alive until someone looks.) The process of observation (measurement) collapses the wave function of a system from a variety of probabilities to a certainty. This is the interpretation accepted by most physicists, but there are many variations.

• Bell Instantaneous Quantum Connectedness Model: Schrödinger showed that when two quantum particles, A and B, interact briefly, then move apart a great distance, the mathematical probability waves that represent A and B do not separate cleanly, but remain "phase entangled." When the wave that represents particle A is changed, a corresponding change occurs instantly in the wave that represents B. Bell's Theorem shows this superluminal "Instantaneous-Action-At-A-Distance" connection between two phase-entangled systems is not a mere theoretical artifact, for it produces measurable experimental results that are different than those produced by other models. Experiments to verify Bell's Theorem have produced results that cannot be explained by subluminal connections alone. No one, however, has come up with a workable scheme that can use the instantaneous collapse of a wave function to transmit information (or people) faster than light. In fact, there are strong theoretical arguments that it can't be done. The theory shows that although each random quantum collapse event involves superluminal connections between particle A and B, the superluminal effects become unobservable when attempts are made to nonrandomly affect a pattern of many random events in order to transmit information.

• Everett Many-Worlds Model: This model gets around quantum uncertainty paradoxes by assuming that all possible results take place during the collapse of the wave function of a system, and the universe duplicates itself to accommodate all results. This model solves some of the paradoxes of half-dead cats, but at the expense of creating an infinitely multiplying multitude of universes where *everything* is possible.

• Hidden Variables Model: This model postulates some new force that does *not* act faster than light, is "hidden" from present physics, and which causes things to happen at a distance as if there was a FTL connection. This model is now felt to have been proven wrong by the experiments backing the Bell Instantaneous Quantum Connectedness Model.

• Cramer Transactional Model: This model by John Cramer postulates that every quantum event involves an exchange of advanced and retarded wave solutions to the Schrödinger equation. Since this model uses advanced waves, it has obvious FTL implications.

I would say that it is a general consensus of physicists that although the presently accepted "Copenhagen" model of quantum mechanics can predict accurately what will happen in the real world, it is poor at giving a physical "picture" of what is going on. We all hope that someone will come up with the "real" model of quantum mechanics that provides not only the correct mathematical answer, but a better physical picture of life in the small. In the meantime, the accepted and experimentally tested models seem to require the existence of FTL connections between particles separated by great distances. Although the theories seem to conspire to prevent us from using those FTL connections to transmit information (or people) faster than light, the fact that those FTL connections exist in the theory is interesting.

Quantum Electrodynamics: The Theory of Quantum Electrodynamics describes the microscopic behavior of electricity and magnetism. It is one of the more successful physical theories, since it has been checked experimentally many times and found to be accurate. In quantum electrodynamics a region of space devoid of matter is divided up into a large (infinite) number of modes of potential oscillation for the electromagnetic field. The state of the electromagnetic field in that space is defined by counting the number of photons in each mode. The "vacuum" state is defined as that state where there are no photons in any of the modes. But the vacuum state is not empty, for according to quantum electrodynamics, each mode of oscillation, even when the space is at absolute zero, has in it a zero-point oscillation with an energy equal to "half" a photon. This residual electromagnetic field produces fluctuating electromagnetic forces that have experimentally observable consequences.

One effect of the electromagnetic vacuum fluctuations is called the Casimir force. The Casimir force is a short range attraction between any two objects caused by the presence of the electromagnetic fluctuations in the vacuum. This effect is also known as "surface tension," "surface energy," and "van der Waals forces" between uncharged atoms and objects. A calculation by Casimir of the force between two conducting plates showed that the conducting plates restrict the number of normal modes that can exist in the vacuum region between the plates. Although there are an infinite number of modes between the two plates, that infinity is smaller than the infinite number of modes that would be allowed if the plates weren't there. In a straightforward calculation of the number of normal modes and the zero-point energy in those modes, Casimir showed that the region of vacuum between the plates would have less energy than the normal vacuum, and would have a negative energy density that was proportional to the third power of the spacing between the plates. There thus would be an attractive force between the plates that was proportional to the fourth power of the spacing. The force was independent of the material in the conductors. Experimental measurements of the Casimir force have been carried out a number of times with varying degrees of success. The closest separation distance obtained without the plates touching was fourteen angstroms (about five atoms) with two crossed cylinders of mica. At fourteen angstroms, the measured force between the two mica cylinders was over ten tons per square meter!

According to the Theory of Quantum Electrodynamics, the speed of light from plate to plate in a Casimir vacuum should be faster than the speed of light in a normal vacuum by a small amount (about 10^{-12}). So we have yet another well-accepted and tested theory that predicts FTL phenomena.

Other Theories: In addition to the more accepted theories, there are other, more speculative theories that also predict FTL phenomena and time machines.

• Penrose Twistor Theory: Penrose has devised an 8-dimensional theory for the structure of spacetime, partially based on the nice mathematical properties of complex numbers. One prediction is that if the space between Earth and Mars is sufficiently "distorted" in 8-D "twistor space," then the 4-D physical space associated with that portion of twistor space "disappears," and Mars is now right next to Earth, just a short rocket jaunt away. This not really FTL travel, since the disappearance of space will probably happen at light speed, but it achieves the same result. Making twistor theory match up with observed experiments has not been notably successful, and not much has been heard about twistor theory from Penrose lately.

• CPT Symmetry Theory: This theory states that there should be a symmetry of behavior in experiments where charge, parity (mirror-image orientation), and time are interchanged. Experiments, however, have found that there exist asymmetries.

The decay of the neutral kaon into two pions is predicted to take place at a different reaction rate with time than the combining of two pions into a neutral kaon, indicating a time-asymmetry bias of spacetime. Could this be a handle on time that could lead to time travel?

Parity symmetry would imply that luxons (photons and neutrinos) could exist in either right-handed or left-handed versions (direction of spin compared to direction of motion). Photons exist in both polarizations. Neutrinos, however, are always generated with left-handed polarization, while antineutrinos are right-handed. Does this indicate that space has a left-handed "twist" in this region of spacetime or that neutrinos exist in a different "space" than photons?

• Superstring Theories: Superstring theories are the latest theoretical hope for finding the "Theory of Everything." In these theories, the elementary particles are supposed to be Planck-length strings instead of points. The different elementary particles are then represented as "modes of vibration" of the string. Nearly all superstring theories predict the existence of FTL modes, which imply the existence of tachyonic particles. This again indicates that FTL phenomena are ubiquitous in physical theories. In the 10-D and 26-D versions of Superstring Theories, the extra dimensions are "rolled up" so that we don't observe them. This leads to speculation about using these dimensions for FTL travel. One could "unroll" a rolled-up dimension, use it to travel in a tachyonic mode, then roll it up. If dimensions in general can be rolled up, then it might be possible to roll up one of our three space dimensions, rapidly move to a new point in the rolled up dimension, then unroll it.

• Cosmic String Theories: These are galaxy-sized linear "discontinuities" in spacetime that are postulated to have formed during the Big Bang. According to some Cosmic String Theories, if these hypothetical cosmological discontinuities in spacetime pass each other fast enough, they can temporarily produce a time machine.

• Point Particles: According to the curved-space mathematics of the Einstein gravity theory, black holes have a finite circumference, but zero radius and zero volume. One could say they are point particles. Electrons, muons, and quarks also seem to be point particles. For example, the radius of the electron must be less than 10^{-20} cm (10^{-10} the size of an atom) to agree with the g-factor measured on trapped individual electrons. How can a particle in 4-D spacetime have zero dimensions? Are point particles quantum black holes? And since these supposed point particles have mass, spin, and charge, they should produce mathematical infinities—charge singularities and angular momentum singularities as well as mass singularities. Mathematical singularities are not allowed in the real world of Nature, so at what size are point particles no longer points?

Many relativists have pointed out that the gyromagnetic ratio of the maximal Kerr-Newman solution to the Einstein General Relativity equations and the electron are the same. Theorists have replaced the proton in a hydrogen atom with an equivalent Kerr-Newman source generated using the General Relativity equations, and calculated the hyperfine structure of the resultant atom. It agrees with experiments on real hydrogen atoms to ten places *with the exception of an exact factor of 2*. Do we need quantum gravity to understand elementary particles? Is Nature trying to tell us something?

• Spin Space: Many elementary particles have a property called spin. Typically the spin of a particle is either 0, 1/2, or 1. Although spin has some of the properties of classical angular momentum, it is not angular momentum. It is something else that leads to bizarre experimental results. Spin 1/2 particles, such as neutrinos, electrons, protons, and neutrons, are called fermions. Spin 1 particles, such as photons and pions, are called bosons. Fermions seem to have a tendency to avoid each other, and obey a different statistical law than bosons, which seem have a tendency to clump together. The statistical laws for fermions and bosons are not only different from each other, but they are also different from the classical statistical laws that govern the toss of a coin or the motion of a ball in a roulette wheel. (A bosonic roulette ball would have an increased tendency to fall into the number 33 slot if it had been in that slot before.) There is something even stranger about spin 1/2 particles, however, that indicate that they live in a different "space" than we do. You have to turn them over twice to turn them over! Ultracold beams of polarized neutrons, which have spin 1/2 and a magnetic moment that allows you to manipulate them with magnetic fields, were split into two beams. One beam was rotated using magnetic fields and then interfered with the other beam. The neutrons had to be rotated 720 degrees through physical space before their spins were realigned in the original direction in order to cause interference. Is there such a thing as spin space? Is Nature trying to tell us something?

Experimental Evidence for FTL Phenomena

There are three areas where there is some experimental evidence that indicates the possible existence of FTL phenomena: the firm proof of the FTL quantum connectedness of widely separated "entangled" particles, the possible observation of tachyons in cosmic ray showers, and the probable measurement of an imaginary rest mass for neutrinos.

FTL Quantum Connectedness: As discussed earlier, when two quantum particles, A and B, interact briefly, then move apart a great distance, the mathematical probability waves that represent A and B do not separate cleanly, but remain "phase entangled." When the wave that represents particle A is changed, a corresponding change occurs instantly in the wave that represents B. The actual experiments to demonstrate this involved generating two photons at the same time, using a process which causes them to both have the same polarization, although the exact state of polarization of the two is unknown until a measurement is made on one of them. These two "entangled" photons are then sent off in opposite directions. At one end of the laboratory, the polarization of one photon is measured, which instantly causes the polarization of the other photon at the opposite end of the laboratory to be "known" rather than "unknown." A photon with a "known" polarization reacts differently to a polarizer at various orientations (either passes through or is reflected) than a photon with an "unknown" polarization. By randomly varying the orientation of polarizers at different ends of the laboratory, measuring the results, and comparing them with Bell's Theory, the experimenters proved that there was a coupling between the two distant photons. The measurements on the two widely separated photons were made in time intervals that were less than the light travel time across the laboratory, showing that whatever the mechanism causing the coupling between the two distant photons, it operated at a speed that was faster than light. These experiments prove that FTL phenomena exist in quantum mechanics. So far, however, no one has found a way to use this FTL coupling to transmit either objects or information faster than light.

Tachyons in Cosmic Ray Showers: In the 1970s and 1980s, some experiments were carried out to detect tachyons produced in an ultrahigh-energy cosmic ray shower. When an incoming cosmic ray particle hits an air molecule in the upper atmosphere, it produces a shower of particles of many different kinds. The idea behind the experiment was that along with the millions of ordinary bradyon particles produced, all of them with so much energy that they are moving at speeds just below the speed of light, a small number of tachyon particles might be produced with so much energy they would be moving just *above* the speed of light, rather than many times the speed of light. These high-energy tachyons would be moving slowly enough to stay in the detector long enough to activate it. Three of the experiments, which collected thousands of shower events over periods ranging from months to years, produced positive results. In a significant number of shower events, the detectors noticed the arrival of particles some 50-70 microseconds before the main shower front arrived. Unfortunately, other similar experiments didn't notice such an effect, so the positive results have not been accepted. The experiments have not been repeated to date.

Imaginary Neutrino Rest Mass: There are three types of neutrinos—the electron neutrino, the muon neutrino, and the tau neutrino. The rest mass of all three has been assumed to be zero. Recent measurements on the electron neutrino and the muon neutrino, however, have been coming up with negative values for the rest mass squared, which implies that these neutrinos might have imaginary rest mass. If they have imaginary rest mass, then they could be tachyons.

Measurements of the electron neutrino rest mass are carried out by measuring the end point of the energy spectrum of the electron emitted in the decay of tritium. (The neutrino, which can pass through lightyears of lead without interacting, is essentially undetectable.) Tritium (a hydrogen atom with one proton and two neutrons in its nucleus), decays into helium-3 (with two protons and one neutron), plus an electron and an electron neutrino. Since the helium-3 nucleus is so much heavier than the other two particles, it hardly moves, and it is the electron and the electron neutrino that share nearly all of the energy released in the reaction. Sometimes the neutrino gets most of the energy, leaving the electron with almost none, and sometimes the electron gets most of the energy. The experimenter plots the spectrum of electron energies that are observed and tries to determine the low-energy end point. If the neutrino has a rest mass, then this end point on the energy spectrum has an abrupt termination instead of tailing off smoothly to zero. For various experimental reasons, the quantity that is calculated from measuring the minimum energy seen in the electron spectrum is not the rest mass of the neutrino, but the *square* of the rest mass. The experiments have been getting more and more precise as time goes on, and instead of the expected value of zero, the square of the electron neutrino rest mass seems to be negative. The reported values are:

   (1986) -158±253 eV²
   (1991) -147±109 eV²

In the 1991 experiment, the "signal level" is 1.35 times the estimated error—interesting, but not convincing. Recent experiments at LANL, however, have produced the same results, but with a signal level that is six standard deviations above the estimated error level or a confidence level of 99.9999+ that the correct value is not zero. This implies an imaginary rest mass of the electron neutrino of about $12 \cdot i$ eV ($1.8 \cdot i \times 10^{-36}$ kg or $2 \cdot i \times 10^{-6}$ times the mass of an electron).

It is interesting to note that if the experimenter at LANL had achieved a result where square of the electron neutrino rest mass was non-zero and *positive*, then he would have trumpeted his results in not only the science journals, but in all the newspapers and magazines, as he would be a shoo-in for the next Nobel Prize. Although the neutrino is supposed to have a zero rest mass, a positive rest mass is acceptable in the existing theories of the neutrino, and would be the answer to many puzzling questions about the interaction of neutrinos with the rest of the universe. An imaginary neutrino with its possible FTL properties, however, is not acceptable to the scientific community, since it dredges up unwanted associations with science fiction concepts such as the Star Trek FTL warp drive and time machine paradoxes. The experimenter is afraid that his experimental setup has some unknown error source that is creating this outrageous result, and he doesn't want to publish it for fear of being later proved wrong.

Similar results seem to be coming from measurements of the muon neutrino rest mass. Muon neutrinos are generated during the decay of a pion particle into a muon particle. By using an elementary-particle track chamber to measure the incoming energy and momentum of a charged pion and the outgoing energy and momentum of the charged muon, it is possible to calculate the energy, momentum, and rest mass of the unseen muon neutrino. Again, the quantity calculated is the square of the muon neutrino rest mass. The results to date are:

(1973) -0.29 ± 0.90 MeV^2
(1980) $+0.102 \pm 0.119$ MeV^2
(1982) -0.14 ± 0.20 MeV^2/c^4
(1984) -0.163 ± 0.080 MeV^2/c^4

The latest measurement is two standard deviations above the estimated error level, which gives a confidence level of 95% that the correct value is not zero. This implies a muon neutrino imaginary rest mass of about $0.4i$ MeV/c^2 ($7 \cdot i \times 10^{-31}$ kg = $0.8 \cdot i$ electron mass).

There is definitely something interesting going on, but whatever it is, it is being swept under the rug by most physicists who regard these experimental results as an embarrassing anomaly rather than an opportunity. This leads one to wonder what other experiments could be done to measure the mass of the various neutrinos—experiments with different experimental conditions that might not have the same hidden error sources that are causing the assumed anomalous results.

There is strong evidence that the number of neutrinos being emitted by the Sun is one-third that predicted by theory. Could it be that the tachyonic neutrinos are moving too fast for the detectors? An alternate explanation for the lack of solar neutrinos is that the neutrinos "oscillate" from being one type of neutrino to another with time. The neutrino oscillation theories require non-zero rest mass for the neutrino. What do neutrino oscillations mean if the rest mass of the neutrino is imaginary?

But before we accept the idea that neutrinos might

be tachyons, we must be careful and think through all the implications of a tachyonic neutrino. There are other effects of neutrinos on the details of the structure of the sun, the galaxy, and the big bang, that require rethinking if the neutrino mass is not zero. In addition, there probably should be other things happening if the neutrino has an imaginary rest mass. Only if those things are also observed can we say that the neutrino is a tachyon.

Possible Experiments That Could Be Done

In addition to repeating and refining the experiments mentioned in the previous section, there are other experiments that could be done.

Casimir Vacuum Experiments: It was pointed out previously that according to the Theory of Quantum Electrodynamics, the speed of light from plate to plate in a Casimir experiment setup should be faster than the speed of light in vacuum by a small amount. This is a very difficult experiment, considering that the distance over which the measurement must be made is in the direction between the plates, which is typically measured in nanometers. This potential FTL phenomenon may be measurable, however, if the experiment were designed so that the speed measurement was turned into a frequency measurement.

If the speed of light between Casimir plates is greater than c, then, since rest mass is $m=E/c^2$, does this mean that the rest mass of a particle in a Casimir vacuum is less than its rest mass in normal vacuum? Since the velocity of light between Casimir plates is anisotropic (greater than c normal to the plates but c parallel to the plates) does this also mean that the rest mass is anisotropic to parts in 10^{24}? Prior null experiments on the anisotropy of inertial mass were accurate to parts in 10^{23}. Could those techniques be applied to this setup?

Black Hole Observables: If a nearby black hole is found, and it is determined to be a copious source of neutrinos, then this would prove neutrinos are tachyons, since only a faster-than-light tachyon can escape a black hole. This may also explain why we have not seen the expected gamma-ray explosions of microscopic-sized, asteroidal-mass primordial black holes undergoing their final stages of Hawking radiation evaporation.

Wormhole Observables: Even though it may not be possible for us to build a Morris-Thorne wormhole with present technology, they may have been formed during an early phase of the Big Bang when a Planck-sized quantum fluctuation wormhole was threaded with an exotic field. If the wormhole participated in the general inflation of the universe, then it would be larger in size and mass now, perhaps even large enough to observe. Three possible observables of such an object would be the appearance or disappearance of an object through one of the mouths of the wormhole, the strange effects on nearby masses of the repulsive gravity field of the negative energy density exotic field holding the wormhole open, and the gravitational lensing of background starlight by the negative gravity field of a wormhole mouth.

There are presently three ongoing (and successful) searches for gravitational lensing effects on distant stars, as dark massive bodies in the halo of our Milky Way Galaxy move between the Earth and the distant star (typically a star on the other side of the Galaxy or in the Large Magellanic Cloud). These postulated dark bodies are called MAssive Compact Halo Objects or MACHOs. The bending of the starlight passing near the MACHO causes it to be concentrated behind the MACHO. When the star, MACHO, and Earth are nearly in alignment, then an observer on the Earth will see a smooth increase in the observed brightness of the star by factors of 3-10, over a period of days to months, followed by a smooth decrease with exactly the same shape. The shape and amplitude of the peak will be the same in the blue and the red. These requirements help distinguish a MACHO brightening from other things that could cause a temporary increase in the observed brightness of a star. To date a number of candidate MACHO events have been seen. Since such a search is going on, it would be simple for those doing the search to also look for the lensing effects of Gravitationally Negative Anomalous Compact Halo Objects (GNACHOs) such as large primordial wormhole mouths.

I recently participated in the preparation of a paper suggesting such a search. The paper, "Natural Wormholes as Gravitational Lenses" by John G. Cramer, Robert L. Forward, Michael S. Morris, Matt Visser, Gregory Benford, and Geoffrey A. Landis, was published in *Physical Review Letters* on 15 March 1995.

Interestingly enough, the analysis in the paper shows that the lensing effect of a GNACHO is not that of a diverging lens (as one might first assume). Instead, the gravitational field of the GNACHO acts to push the incoming starlight away in such a manner as to form a paraboloid-shaped "light caustic" something like a "shock front", where the light rays deflected at different distances from the GNACHO pile up along the "front" leaving a paraboloid-shaped shadow. Thus, as the GNACHO passes in front of the star, there is first a rise in the observed intensity, a sharp cutoff to zero intensity as the observer enters the shadow zone, then a sharp rise to another peak as the observer leaves the shadow zone, followed by a more gradual falloff. Thus, the effect of a GNACHO on the observed intensity of the distant star image consists of both magnification (near the edge of the caustic) and demagnification (zero intensity in the shadow zone). The whole process is expected to take many days to months, similar in time scale for the observed MACHOS. The GNACHO signal is distinctly different from the MACHO signal, and for some values of the "impact parameters" the magnification of the star intensity by the GNACHO is actually higher than that of a MACHO of similar mass magnitude.

In summary, our theories give us plenty of encouragement that FTL phenomena and time travel could exist, despite the causality problems this could produce. While our experiments to find usable FTL phenomena have not been conclusive to date, there still are experiments that need to be done, to clarify old results and look for new effects.

So, although we scientists know, deep down in our souls, that we will never be allowed to break the ultimate speed limit, the existence of these theoretical and experimental hair-line cracks in the light barrier encourage us to continue to try. We keep our right foot pressed hard against the floorboard, pushing our scientific apparatus to ever higher speeds, one eye in the rear-view mirror, checking for the speed cop behind each billboard that we pass, hoping against hope that one of these days we will get away with it, and break through the last speed barrier between us and infinity—in both space and time.

Recommended Reading

John C. Cramer, Robert L. Forward, Michael S. Morris, Matt Visser, Gregory Benford, and Geoffrey A. Landis, "Natural Wormholes as Gravitational Lenses," *Physical Review*, Vol. D51, No. 6, pp. 3317–3120 (15 March 1995).

Robert L. Forward, "Far Out Physics," *Analog Science Fiction/ Science Fact*, Vol. 95, No. 8, pp. 147 ff (August 1975).

Robert L. Forward, *Timemaster* (Tor Books, New York, 1992).

Nick Herbert, *Quantum Reality: Beyond the New Physics* (Anchor Press/Doubleday, New York, 1985)

Nick Herbert, *Faster Than Light: Superluminal Loopholes in Physics* (New American Library Penguin, New York, 1988).

William J. Kaufmann, III, *Relativity and Cosmology* (Harper and Row, New York, 1973).

William J. Kaufmann, III, *The Cosmic Frontiers of General Relativity* (Little, Brown and Co., Boston, 1977).

Yakov P. Terletskii, *Paradoxes in the Theory of Relativity* (Plenum Press, New York, 1968).

Kip S. Thorne, *Black Holes and Time Warps: Einstein's Outrageous Legacy* (1994).

✧ SELF-LIMITING

In a previous science speculation chapter, "Future Speculations," I discussed some future concepts for obtaining "free energy" out of things that normally are not considered energy sources, such as linear and angular momentum. I predicted that the conversion of a single unit of atomic angular momentum into energy should produce the energy of a half a ton of TNT—if only some method could be found to accomplish it. This potential source of energy would be even more powerful than the source of energy realized from the fissioning of atomic nuclei in a nuclear bomb. All we need to do is find the technology needed to carry out the conversion.

What has always amazed me, is that the technology needed to obtain energy out of an atomic nucleus by nuclear fission turned out to be very simple—so simple it is almost like magic. No sophisticated high technology machines are needed. You merely bring two large pieces of enriched uranium or plutonium near each other and the nuclear chain reaction starts—like magic! There is even evidence that a few million years ago, a large, particularly rich body of uranium ore in the French Congo spontaneously went critical and started generating heat when it was flooded during the rainy seasons. The ore from that lode is depleted in the isotope of uranium that fissions, compared to *the normal uranium isotopic composition found in other ore bodies.*

For many years after hearing about the natural nuclear reactor in the Congo, I mused about how a similar thing might happen involving life forms who— driven by evolutionary pressures—bring about a nuclear chain reaction. The following short story was soon written in my mind. But, from a fiction point of view, the plot concept seemed limited to short story length, while from a scientific point of view, the evolutionary pressures seemed weak, so I just stored the concept in the back of my mind and let it rest there for a number of decades, where it served as a focus for collecting relevant ideas on similar subjects. In about 1990, I finally thought of a plausible scenario and a plausible alien life-form, where the evolutionary drive for the life-form to develop nuclear power was much more believable. To develop that scenario properly required a novel-length story. The novel is Camelot 30K, *and I won't spoil the plot by telling you what form of nuclear power the aliens develop. Once I had started on the novel and its aliens, however, I finally felt free enough to get this short story out of the back of my mind and put it in print, where it appeared in the May 1992 issue of* Analog Science Fiction/Science Fact, *Volume 112, Number 6, pages 90-92.*

———

There are no millionaires on Xanax.

It is, however, easy to make a living on Xanax. Lord Melcor insures that. When a young xanit leaves the hatchery, he is apprenticed to a tradesman, who shares his dwelling and teaches the apprentice his trade. When the tradesman dies, the young xanit takes over the dwelling and the trade. By applying a little effort, the zorins flow in. Most of the zorins are spent on necessities and taxes, but Lord Melcor is easy on his people, and there are always some zorins left to go into the money pit for use in old age.

As the years pass, the money pit slowly fills with stacks of 100-zorin coins stamped with the likeness of Lord Melcor. The coins are a lustrous silvery-gray, made from a precious metal extracted by magical processes from rare and poisonous ores by Lord Melcor's alchemists.

By middle age, the average xanit has over a thousand 100-zorin coins in his money pit. About that time he is assigned an apprentice. For a few years, the work is harder, since the apprentice must be taught. But soon the apprentice takes over and it is time to retire. It is now the time of life for sitting on eggs, while playing long games of pastil with other retired xanits, and most fun of all, telling stories of the old days to young hatchlings.

Fortunately for xanits, the end comes swiftly. One morning, late in life, a xanit rises from sleep to see that his wrinkled skin has turned from a healthy green to a dull grey. He knows then that he has only one day to live, and will die in his sleep that night. The xanit takes the last of the zorins out of his money pit, gives a generous bonus to his apprentice, and then goes out into the streets to give the rest of his money away.

It is not easy to give money away on Xanax. The average xanit, when asked, will reply that he has enough. But occasionally, there will be some that have suffered an illness or accident, and whose money pit does not have enough zorins. They tell the giver how much they need and he willingly gives it to them, for there is no dishonesty and no greed on Xanax.

Then, one day, something went wrong in the development of an egg, and Queed was hatched. Queed made it through the hatchery and his apprenticeship without incident, but when his mentor turned grey and set to the task of giving away the last of his money, Queed wasn't satisfied with his generous bonus, but lied and said that he needed it all. The mentor believed him, and gave Queed all of his fortune.

The next night, Queed expanded his money pit. A typical money pit would hold about a thousand 100-zorin coins. Queed made his money pit ten times larger. When full, it would hold ten thousand 100-zorin coins— a million zorins worth! Queed's greedy body vibrated in ecstasy at the thought of being a millionaire. He was appalled, however, when he saw that his two bags of money only covered one corner of the deep pit. He would have to find a faster way of making money than working at his trade. Then Queed thought of an idea, an idea so foreign to Xanax that there wasn't even a word for it. Queed would "rob" the zorins from the money pits of his neighbors.

Once Queed had made this breakthrough in dishonesty and greed, the bags of coins in his money pit grew rapidly. Each day he would walk the streets until he saw a middle-aged tradesman leave his dwelling to go on some errand. Since Xanax dwellings do not have locks, Queed would simply walk in and take the zorins from the money pit. He didn't bother with the smaller coins, but only stole the massive silvery-grey 100-zorin coins.

Each night after a robbery, he would go to his money pit and get out his rapidly growing treasure. The coins were warm. He played with them, and stacked them, and counted them. Then, he would put them back into the large bags that held one thousand coins each and return them to his money pit. Soon, there were nine bags arranged around the perimeter of the pit, with a hole in the middle for the last bag. When that hole was filled, Queed would be a millionaire.

The next day, Queed was very lucky. He saw a prosperous middle-aged tradesman and his apprentice both leave a well-appointed dwelling. He quickly went inside and scooped stacks of 100-zorin coins from both money-pits into his bag. As he hurried back to his dwelling with his heavy load, Queed was overjoyed. The bag of silvery-gray coins felt much heavier than the ones at home. He entered his dwelling, and leaning over the money pit, he gloated as he dropped the bag of coins into the hole that was waiting for it. Queed could hardly wait until it was night-time and he could take out all the coins and count them. He was now certainly a millionaire!

As the heavy bag of silvery-grey coins made of pure plutonium 239 dropped into the waiting hole, the money pit went critical and exploded . . .

There are no millionaires on Xanax.

❖ ABOUT THE AUTHOR

Dr. Robert L. Forward is a science consultant, writer, and futurist specializing in studies of exotic physical phenomena and future space exploration with an emphasis on advanced space propulsion concepts. Dr. Forward obtained his B.S. in Physics from the University of Maryland in 1954, his M.S. in Applied Physics from UCLA in 1958, and his Ph.D. in Gravitational Physics from the University of Maryland in 1965. For his doctoral thesis he built and operated the world's first bar antenna for the detection of gravitational radiation. The antenna is now at the Smithsonian museum.

Dr. Forward has 40 years of experience in advanced space propulsion, experimental general relativity, gravitational and inertial sensors, low noise electronics, and space sciences. For 31 years, from 1956 until 1987, Dr. Forward worked at the Hughes Aircraft Company Corporate Research Laboratories in Malibu, California in positions of increasing responsibility, culminating with the position of Senior Scientist on the Director's staff. During that time he built and operated the world's first laser interferometer gravitational radiation detector, invented the rotating gravitational mass sensor, published over 70 technical publications, and was awarded 18 patents. He left Hughes in 1987 in order to spend more time writing and consulting under his own company, Forward Unlimited, P.O. Box 2783, Malibu, CA 90265, 24 hour voice mail box: (805)983-7652.

From 1983 to the present, Dr. Forward has had a series of contracts from the Department of Defense and NASA to explore the forefront of physics and engineering in order to find new energy sources that could produce breakthroughs in space power and propulsion.

In addition to over 100 professional publications and 19 patents, Dr. Forward has written over 60 popular science articles for publications such as *Omni*, *New Scientist*, *Encyclopaedia Britannica Yearbook*, *Focus*, *Science Digest*, *Science 80*, *Analog*, and *Galaxy*. In addition to this book, he has two published science fact books, *Mirror Matter: Pioneering Antimatter Physics* (with Joel Davis) and *Future Magic*, and ten published science fiction novels, *Dragon's Egg* and its sequel *Starquake*; *Rocheworld* and its four sequels, *Return To Rocheworld* (with Julie Forward Fuller), *Marooned on Eden* (with Martha Dodson Forward), *Ocean Under Ice* (with Martha Dodson Forward), and *Rescued From Paradise* (with Julie Forward Fuller); *Martian Rainbow*; *Timemaster*; and *Camelot 30K*. The novels are "hard" science fiction, where the science is as accurate as possible. The preliminary background research for five of the novels produced new scientific or engineering concepts that, upon further study, were found to be technically valid, and were subsequently refined and published in refereed scientific journals.

Dr. Forward is a Fellow of the British Interplanetary Society, Associate Fellow of the American Institute of Aeronautics and Astronautics, a member of the American Physical Society, Sigma Xi, Sigma Pi Sigma, National Space Society, the Science-Fiction and Fantasy Writers of America, and the Authors Guild.

✧ INDEX

ROBERT A. HEINLEIN

"Robert A. Heinlein wears imagination as though it were his private suit of clothes. What makes his work so rich is that he combines his lively, creative sense with an approach that is at once literate, informed, and exciting." —*New York Times*

Eight of Robert A. Heinlein's best-loved titles are now available in superbly packaged Baen editions. Collect them all.

PODKAYNE OF MARS (pb)	87671-6, $5.99	☐
(trade)	72179-8, $10.00	☐
GLORY ROAD (trade)	72167-4, $10.00	☐
FARNHAM'S FREEHOLD	72206-9, $5.99	☐
REVOLT IN 2100	65589-2, $4.99	☐
METHUSELAH'S CHILDREN	65597-3, $3.50	☐
ASSIGNMENT IN ETERNITY	65350-4, $4.99	☐
SIXTH COLUMN	72026-0, $5.99	☐
TAKE BACK YOUR GOVERNMENT (nonfiction)	72157-7, $5.99	☐

If not available at your local bookstore, fill out this coupon and send a check or money order for the cover price(s) to Baen Books, Dept. BA, P.O. Box 1403, Riverdale, NY 10471. Delivery can take up to ten weeks.

NAME: _____

ADDRESS: _____

_____

I have enclosed a check or money order in the amount of $ _____